DEEP ROUGH

A MIAMI JONES CASE

AJ Stewart

Jacaranda Drive Publishing

Los Angeles, California

www.jacarandadrive.com

This book is a work of fiction. Names, characters, places and incidents are either products of the author's imagination or are used fictitiously, and any resemblance to actual persons, living or dead, business establishments or locales is entirely coincidental.

Cover artwork by Streetlight Graphics

ISBN-10: 1-945741-01-5

ISBN-13: 978-1-945741-01-2

Copyright © 2016 by A.J. Stewart

No part of this book may be reproduced, scanned or distributed in any printed or electronic form without permission from the author.

Books by AJ Stewart

Stiff Arm Steal
Offside Trap
High Lie
Dead Fast
Crash Tack
Deep Rough

For Evan. Who comes up with the best names for everything.

And Heather, always.

CHAPTER ONE

The wedding ceremony started exactly as such ceremonies do. There was music—a string quartet playing Pachelbel's Canon in D. There was a gang in classic tuxedos waiting at the front. The groom and six—count them—six groomsmen. They looked like an a cappella group. They each stood with their hands clasped before them, surely the idea of a wedding planner, and looked down the aisle between the two sets of white folding chairs. The aisle was a blue carpet laid over a wooden platform that itself had been erected over immaculately grown grass. Six young women in coral dresses, the color and design of which suggested that their maiden voyage would also be their last, swayed down the aisle. The bride's team moved to the opposite side to the groomsmen, backed by a large hospitality tent.

The string quartet broke out of Canon and into Wagner's Bridal Chorus with practiced efficiency. The change in tune caused the congregation to turn their heads as one toward the doors of the clubhouse, and the bride stepped out past where Danielle and I were standing at the back. The bride was in a white dress rather than anything my mother would have called a gown. It was slimming and tight and pushed her breasts toward the sky. She wore a wide smile. The man on her arm, the father of the bride, wore a smile that suggested he was happy but not at all comfortable with two hundred pairs of eyes on him.

The bride and her father marched past us, in time with Wagner, a military precision that felt out of place. Danielle wiped a tear from her eye, even though she had never met the bride before. Perhaps it was a woman thing. Danielle had gone with an unusual choice of attire—brown pressed trousers with a white blouse and tan vest. It was very Annie Hall, and I wondered as I watched the bride pass by if Danielle had dressed in such a fashion as to ensure she didn't look better than the bride, which I had heard was very bad karma. I don't think the same rule applied to the groom, but it was moot anyway, because he definitely looked better than me in his tux, despite the late afternoon sun. I looked like a newsreader from Los Angeles, my blond mess of hair a counterpoint to the suit that I used for weddings and funerals.

The bride was handed off by her father and the groom linked her fingers in his. I wasn't sure if the fellow standing before them was a priest, a pastor or a civil celebrant, but the couple turned away from us, and once they tore their attention from each other they offered it to him. He nodded sagely and gave a smile to the congregation that spoke of the joy of the occasion and of his desire to get things over with so he could remove his heavy frock and get out of the hot spring sun. He cleared his throat and prepared to speak.

That was when I noticed the harbinger of trouble.

Only two of us noticed at first, at least to my eye. Me—from the back of the congregation, looking out beyond the wedding party toward the sprawling expanse of the eighteenth green of

DEEP ROUGH

South Lakes Country Club—and the girl who was standing second in line from the bride. She noticed because the girl beside her, whom I assumed was the maid of honor given her exalted position next to the bride, was the first to go down. Slowly in the beginning, like the first minutes of the Titanic, and then faster and with the inevitability of the aforementioned ship. First her left leg gave out some, in that way that women's legs sometimes do when they are wearing those ridiculous high-heeled shoes and they misstep. But the maid of honor was standing still, and her faulty leg made her wobble more than trip. The girl next to her gave her a look of contempt, perhaps the result of being beaten out for the maid-of-honor honor.

The winner of that honor turned to the girl next to her, and for a second their eyes met over coral frills. Then the maid of honor doubled over, gripping her stomach as if she had been shot, which she had not. She grabbed at the bridesmaid next to her, gripping a puffy sleeve and moaning softly. Softly but loud enough for the sound to travel to my ears at the back, and to draw the attention of the silent congregation.

Then the maid of honor vomited with great intensity into the bridesmaid's chest. It was loud and unpleasant and voluminous. The girl must have hit the wedding eve buffet hard. Her body spasmed like an Abrams tank spewing forth artillery shells. Boom, boom, boom. I thought for a moment she might suffocate, and gave passing consideration to who of the well-dressed and well-heeled in attendance would offer mouth-to-mouth resuscitation. But then the bombardment stopped, and the maid of honor sucked in a great chunky breath of air. And then the bombardment began again.

Nausea is like yawning. It's contagious. I once offered a yawn to the governor of Florida while he was giving a stump speech and he actually broke into a gaping yawn himself. He didn't thank me for it, but the result was thanks enough. There were no yawns at the South Lakes Country Club. There was the collected sound of gulping and of breath being held, and hands over mouths.

Then the mother of the groom lost her lunch. Right onto the deck platform. The father of the groom spun in his seat like he had been electrocuted, but to his credit he went straight to the aid of his ailing wife. Someone in the first row of the bride's side of the congregation stood, did something that resembled a dance move that would look unbecoming on anyone over the age of eighteen—one hand on her stomach, one hand on her buttocks, bend over and twerk it all about. Then she deposited her insides on the gentleman next to her.

And then it got bad.

First, the bridesmaid who had worn the initial barrage began wiping her dress. Once she realized she was collecting vomitus by the bucketload on her hands she started waving her arms frantically, raining the front rows in what looked suspiciously like carrots and peas, as if they were sitting in the wet zone seats at Sea World. Then she stopped suddenly, her eyes bulging, and she launched her cookies out past the maid of honor.

And right into the bride. I'm no expert on the subject but I was pretty confident that those stains were never coming out of a white wedding dress. The bride stood mouth agape, looked down at her vomit-splattered pearls and then back at the bridesmaid who had deposited on her. Then she took off.

I didn't blame her. It was runaway bride stuff, but it was all warranted. Things were not going well. I bet myself dollars to donuts that the wedding planner had a contingency for a South Florida rain squall bursting across the golf course, but I was equally certain that current events had not come up at online wedding planner school. The bride broke for the aisle, kicking her shoes off deftly as she went. She was fast for someone in such a tight dress, and she made it halfway down the aisle toward Danielle and me before her bare feet came to a great screeching halt.

She bent over a touch, like an honorific in a Japanese restaurant, and then she looked right at me. I didn't know her. She didn't know me. Danielle and I were there simply because Ron and I had solved a case for her father, and he had asked us along as thanks. To be fair Ron had done all the work, and he and the Lady Cassandra were sitting in the middle of the congregation as a result. I was only invited to the reception. But Danielle had considered it bad form to turn up just for the beers and canapés without attending the ceremony, so we came early and stood at the back. I would most certainly hold Danielle responsible for having to witness what we had seen as a result.

The idea of the Titanic came to me again. It wasn't the most original train of thought, but I am a former baseball player cum private detective, not Lord Alfred Tennyson. This time I saw the movie in my head, the version with Leo and Kate, the one that Celine Dion aptly sang went on and on and on. The big ship is going down. The stern is pointing at the moon and the massive propeller is spinning in midair. And in my mind I see a man gripping a railing by one hand, hanging high above the churning ocean below. The railing is too wide and his hand cannot hold on, and in that second the man's face conveyed the certainty that his grip would fail and he would fall to his death. I don't know who the actor was, or if I even remembered it right, but that guy deserved an Oscar. That was acting. That was a face of pure terror.

The bride gave me that same face. Only she wasn't acting. She stood motionless in the middle of the aisle, her eyes searing into me. Confusion and terror. Confusion: What on earth is happening, and why is it happening on this day of all days? And then terror: It doesn't matter what or why. It's just happening and it's happening right now.

It was a reminder to never wear white. I had done so a few times during my baseball career and it was almost always a guarantee that I'd end up in the dirt. I'd overbalance during a pitch, or a drive would get smacked straight at the mound, or I'd have to field an infield dribble and flick it to first base, and I'd end up face down on the clay, my uniform fully soiled. Never seemed to happen when I was wearing gray or green. Always white.

The bride would no doubt remember the lesson too. She grimaced hard, and then every orifice in her body opened simultaneously. It was, short of seeing the final seconds of a human life, the most unpleasant thing I had ever witnessed. Grotesque to be sure, but what I felt more was sorrow. Granted people put too much stock in weddings. They were way overdone, production numbers filled with stress and angst that was never fully compensated for. But for those who did put their stock in the event, they seemed to mean so much. And the bride was clearly one of those people. I could see that from her dress, now stained colors that never appeared on any rainbow, and from the size of the congregation and the location of the ceremony. And at that moment I just felt sorry that it was going to stick in her mind until the day she died, for all the wrong reasons.

As I watched the bride expel and then collapse onto the deck, Danielle turned and ran. Away from the mess and the chaos, into the clubhouse. As a sheriff's deputy she had seen all the worst that the human condition could offer, and I found it hard to believe she was squeamish. I was right. As quickly as she left she returned, pulling on a pair of latex food service gloves. She didn't break stride. She left the bride on her hands and knees in the aisle and called across the growing commotion. Seats were being cast aside as people retreated from the turmoil and others joined in.

"People, please move slowly away from the deck. If you feel ill, please move this way." She pointed at the adjacent fairway with two hands, like one of those guys directing traffic at the airport.

"If you do not feel symptoms please move this way." She pointed the other way, toward the large practice green that sat under the window of the clubhouse bar.

I moved to offer help to the bride and Danielle caught my eye and shook her head.

"Might be contagious," she said quietly.

She took out her cell phone and made a call to the Palm Beach County Sheriff's Office. Calling in backup. I heard her tell whoever was on the line to call the paramedics and the health department. Then she ended the call and repeated the directions for people to move away.

Her directions were partially heeded. Those who had not succumbed to events moved quickly away, gathering by, but not on, the practice green. Even in the commotion this was a crowd that knew that trampling a putting green was bad form. But those who felt symptoms did not move in the other direction. For the most part they stayed were they were, or fell to their knees.

Danielle moved away and left them where they lay. She pushed me back to the door of the clubhouse.

"What the hell?" It was all I could think to say.

"Might be food poisoning. Might be viral. If it's the latter, it might be airborne."

Danielle pushed the allegedly healthy group further back down onto the first tee, away from the strewn chairs and crushed flowers. She told them she was a sheriff's deputy and that no one was to leave until the paramedics arrived. Then she marched back up to the clubhouse and told a woman who wore a name badge to tell the valets to not allow any cars to leave and that they would deal with the sheriff if they did. Then she returned to me. At my count there were sixteen bodies down, and we ran our eyes over them to ensure no one was in mortal danger of choking. Danielle said we had to wait for the medics, who would be properly equipped.

So we stood there, like photographers in Vietnam, watching the horror but not getting involved.

CHAPTER TWO

The paramedics arrived first. Two trucks, four medics. They must have been shocked at what they saw but they didn't show it. They were pros, and like Danielle, they had seen folks at their worst. They donned gloves and masks and waded in. They wandered through the mess of bodies, performing triage, looking for those worse off. I don't know how they could tell one from the other. Some folks had it coming from all exits, and some just orally. That didn't seem to be the determining factor for them, and they split up. One attended the bride first, which felt right in the circumstances.

The paramedics called for more ambulances and announced a contagion protocol, which didn't mean anything at first but became apparent as gurneys were wheeled out covered in plastic. Several sheriff's deputies arrived before the extra ambulances and Danielle directed them to the crowd on the first tee. Uniforms always worked better at crowd control than someone who simply proclaimed themselves a deputy. There were some unhappy folks in that bunch, and several men demanded that they be allowed to leave, but the deputies offered them the option of vomiting their guts up in a cell on

Gun Club Road, and as one they choked back their complaints and stood down.

It was the health department team that put the fear of God into everyone. These guys turned up in hazmat gear, as if a nuke had accidentally exploded in West Palm Beach. They had the full helmets and everything. Astronauts wear less equipment. They cordoned off the area around the decking and began taking samples from the fallen. A couple of them went over to the group on the first tee and conducted interviews to ascertain how everyone was feeling. They took a handful of people away—I assumed it was because they said they weren't feeling so fresh.

My rule of thumb when dealing with government officials of any kind is to keep mum. I could have the cold sweats and I'd say I'm feeling like a bunch of roses. It probably wasn't protocol, but I preferred to never be led away by a guy wearing a hazmat suit. I've seen E.T.—Spielberg doesn't lie.

Over the course of the next hour the sick were taken away to the hospital, the name of which we were not told, which only reinforced my E.T. theory. More health department folks arrived in hazmat suits, and then a unit from the Florida National Guard arrived in a truck. A team of eight carried a bundle to about the fifty-yard mark of the first fairway, and then dropped their bundle. They proceeded to erect a tent in record time. It was a geodesic thing, large enough to house the truck it had arrived in. Two more soldiers wheeled an air-conditioning unit out to the rear of the tent and fired it up, and the tent puffed out like a balloon.

A dude in a hazmat suit asked the gathering on the first tee to enter the tent. He should have yelled fire, because it would have been more effective. No way a crowd of movers and shakers from both sides of the Flagler Memorial Bridge was entering an alien-looking tent at the direction of a guy dressed for the apocalypse. He almost started a riot, albeit of the Palm Beach variety. There were frowns and stern words under breath. Then a woman who wore no more protection than a pair of rubber gloves and a paper mask took control and informed the group that there was a possible viral outbreak and that the group was unlikely to have been infected but state procedure demanded for their own safety that they be screened.

The gathering stood around looking at each other. The woman who had taken charge came over to Danielle and me.

"Deputy Castle?" she asked Danielle.

"Yes, ma'am."

"Connie Persil, Florida Department of Health. Thanks for your call. And for keeping things in order."

"That's my job. What's the situation?"

"Some kind of contamination. We'll need to test everyone and the environment to be sure."

I asked, "Isn't it odd that so many got sick at the same time but the rest of us didn't?"

"You are?"

Danielle said, "Connie, this is Miami Jones."

Connie nodded. "Not that odd. I'd say some of the group were connected in some way, and the others were not."

"So what happens now?"

"We send samples from the affected to the lab. And the folks who are not showing symptoms, we have a protocol to follow."

"Protocol?" I asked.

"So people know what to look for in the coming days. And so we can keep track of everyone."

"What do you need from me?" asked Danielle.

Connie looked toward the tent. "I need someone to be first in."

We wandered over to the tent, and a guy in a hazmat suit handed us paper face masks to put over our mouths. It felt like he was handing out aspirin to combat a bout of radiation poisoning.

Danielle stopped by the nervous crowd.

"Ladies and gentlemen, there is nothing to be concerned about," she said. "They simply want to check on us and let us know what to look for in the coming days, in the unlikely event any of us gets sick, too."

"Is this life-threatening?"

Danielle looked at Connie Persil.

"Sir, if it is what we believe it to be, then the most likely symptoms are diarrhea and nausea. Unless a patient has an underlying sickness, that is usually all. But this is why we want to give you a checkup and a fact sheet on what to look for. Then you should be able to go home."

Danielle nodded and I took the lead because someone had to. I stepped to the front of the tent where a captain from the Army National Guard unit stood waiting, mask in place.

"Nice tent," I said.

"It's a drash. It's a marvel."

"What's a drash?" I asked. "Sounds painful."

"Deployable rapid assembly shelter," he replied. "Basically a pop-up tent. But better."

He held open the flap and gestured for me to step inside, so I did. He was right. It was better than any tent I'd ever camped in. For a start, the air-conditioning worked. Cool air was gushing in from the far end, making it much more comfortable inside than outside on the fairway. The tent had a floor made out of some kind of polyester or nylon. It was cavernous. I kept walking and Danielle dropped in beside. She was looking at the frame overhead. It looked like honeycomb. We moved deep inside the space to allow others to enter and to be closer to the cooler air. Ron and Cassandra followed us in. Ron's silver mane had lost some of its usual bounce and his face was pink. Cassandra looked resplendent in an understated gown. She hadn't broken a sweat.

"My, what a novel venue for a wedding reception," she said with a smile. I smiled back. I liked her. She was old-school Palm Beach, loaded to the gills, but she was a real keep calm and carry on sort of person.

"I hope there's an open bar," Ron said with a wink. He was trying hard but he wasn't quite as unflappable as his lady. Once the group had assembled inside the tent Connie spoke again. She stayed by the door and didn't remove her mask.

"Thank you, ladies and gentlemen. I hope you are more comfortable in here. We will keep you as short a time as possible. Our medics will give you an examination to check for possible symptoms. Then we will provide transport home."

"You'll provide transport?" asked a guy in a charcoal suit.

"Yes, sir. It is unlikely, but anyone who is infected may transmit contagions via surfaces in your vehicle. Until we know what we have it is better we take you home and you stay there."

"How long?"

"Until we learn what this is. Our initial tests should come through tomorrow."

Another squat man who was sweating like a fountain said, "I'm not leaving my car here. It's not secure."

A tall man stepped forward. He had thinning gray hair and a matching mustache. "Ladies and gentlemen, for those of you who don't know me, my name is Keith Hamilton. I am the president here at South Lakes Country Club. I assure you that I will personally arrange for twenty-four-hour security in the parking lot until this matter is resolved."

"You'll look after our cars?" said the squat man. "Your damned club made everyone sick."

"Sir, there is no evidence that these people got ill at the club." Hamilton looked at Connie Persil for support. She gave it.

"Sir," she said to the squat guy, "the fact that people got ill today doesn't imply any link to this club. The incubation period could be days to weeks, depending on what they have contracted."

The squat man harrumphed and crossed his arms.

A medical team came in, set up and proceeded to give everyone the once-over. It was like my annual physical, without the get intimate and cough routine. They gave us photocopies outlining potential symptoms that were general enough to encompass everything from a case of the sniffles to the bubonic plague.

I took the lead again and then moved back to the rear of the shelter near the air-conditioner to wait. Danielle joined me and then Ron and Cassandra followed. Ron introduced me to Keith, the club president. Ron was a member of the West Palm club despite now living on the island at Cassandra's ocean front apartment.

"This is bad news, bad news indeed," said Keith in a hushed voice.

"They'll sort it out," said Ron.

"But the timing couldn't be worse. What with the tournament next week."

"Tournament?" I asked.

Keith eyed me like a pirate looks on a landlubber. "The Aqueta Open. It's a major PGA Tour event. And we are hosting it next week."

That explained all the hospitality tents around the place. "That is poor timing."
"Poor? It's more than poor. It's devastating. And downright suspicious."
"We'll figure a way through," said Ron.
"I don't know, Ron. This feels like the last straw. What with everything that's been happening."
"Don't worry, Keith. It's a storm in a teacup."
Keith shook his head. He looked beaten.
Once everyone had been checked, Connie Persil directed the group out to the parking lot where a bus waited. It was gray in color but the shape and size of a school bus, and wore the words Florida Department of Corrections on the side.
"You are kidding, aren't you?" said the squat guy from the tent.
"No, sir," said Connie. "It was the first available and we didn't want you to wait any longer."
"I'll charter a damned coach," he said.
"A company can't legally charter to quarantined people."
"Quarantined?"
Connie nodded. "Yes, sir. This will get you home ASAP."
I took the lead one more time. "Come on, let's get home." I stepped up onto the bus. It brought back memories. Of school, not prison. But the interior was essentially the same. The big difference was that in my childhood memories it was freezing cold Connecticut, but this was broiling hot Florida. And it was hot. The bus was a prison vehicle and it had no air-conditioning. Even for inmates that seemed cruel and unusual. I made for the back seats, where the bad boys sit, and tried to ignore the fraying tempers. Danielle joined me, as did Ron and Cassandra. Keith Hamilton sat down with a sullen flop. We tried opening the windows but got no dice. It felt like a slow cooker inside. Tempers were fraying and I tried to imagine how

a bus ride like this adjusted the attitude of men destined for time on the inside. It didn't feel humane, even for criminals. For Palm Beach elite it was unbearable.

Never had a department of corrections bus done such a tour of one of the wealthiest parts of the entire country. It was like an early release program for a Ponzi scheme. We wound past some of the finest homes and apartment complexes in Palm Beach. Those who disembarked would have been horribly embarrassed if the emotion hadn't been sucked from them by a combination of the day's events and being parcooked in the bus. We reached Cassandra and Ron's apartment on Ocean Boulevard. Ron tapped Keith Hamilton on the shoulder.

"Get some sleep," said Ron. "I'll call you."

"I'll see you at the club tomorrow," he said.

Danielle said, "I'm not sure you should go out tomorrow, Keith."

"Sorry, deputy, but I have a tournament to run." He turned back to the window and looked out toward the ocean, the cool water like a mirage from our hot seats.

We ventured back onto the mainland and did a tour of the less salubrious part of the area, aka West Palm Beach. These were still gorgeous homes, but incomes were denoted in the hundreds of thousands rather than the millions or even billions on the island. Then the bus puttered north and then east and by the time we reached Singer Island the sun had checked out for the day. We passed all the nice rebuilt minimansions, and stopped outside of the seventies rancher that Danielle and I called home.

We dragged ourselves off the bus and walked like zombies through the front door, over the shag carpet in the living room and out onto the back patio. There were two loungers waiting there, overlooking the evening lights reflecting off the

Intracoastal Waterway. We each flopped down, exhausted, and sat in silence for a time.

"Remind me never to get married on a golf course," Danielle said.

"Where would you like to get married?"

"Why do you ask?"

"Enquiring minds want to know."

"Do they? I'm not sure. What about you, where would you get married?"

I closed my eyes. I felt a headache coming on despite not having had a single drop to drink. Maybe that was why.

"I wouldn't care where," I said. "The only thing that matters is the who."

Danielle may have said something more, but I couldn't say for sure, because I fell asleep before I could hear it.

CHAPTER THREE

The phone woke me. Danielle and I had dragged ourselves to bed at some point, but I had woken during the night, thirsty and with a headache. I got some ibuprofen and water and sat on the sofa in the living room, which was where I was when the phone rang. I flopped my feet into the thick carpet and padded to the kitchen to answer the call.

"Miami Jones."

"Miami, it's Ron. I just got a call from Keith."

"Keith?"

"Hamilton. The president of the country club."

"Right."

"He's at the club."

"Okay."

"Did you hit the beers last night?"

"Huh? No, I'm still waking up."

"Well, you remember yesterday?"

The images came cascading into my mind like an avalanche. It woke me up better than smelling salts.

I said, "Why is he at the club? We were supposed to stay home in case we got sick."

"Do you feel sick?"

"I feel fine." The ibuprofen and the water had done their trick. A decent smoothie for breakfast and I'd practically be Jack LaLanne.

"Me too. And Keith too, evidently. He's at the club. He says it looks like a disaster movie."

"It can't be any worse than yesterday."

"That's certainly true. But he says the health department is on the warpath. He says they're trying to shut down the tournament."

"After what I saw yesterday, that might not be the worst thing in the world."

"Keith's convinced it's sabotage. If the tournament were canceled because of the club, it would be the end of South Lakes. Keith has asked me to come and check it out."

"And you want some help?"

"I need some help."

"I'll meet you there in an hour."

I took a sixty-second shower, tossed on a palm tree print shirt and a pair of cargo shorts and then went back to the kitchen for breakfast. The cooler weather of winter was giving way to spring warmth, but it was early for pineapple. Regardless, it was still good so I took the fruit from the fridge and sliced a chunk off and tossed it in the blender. I like to keep my pineapples intact in the fridge and just slice off a piece each time, rather than cut them up ahead of time. The spiky top takes up a lot of space in there, but I don't have a family of eight. There's still plenty of room for the beers.

I tossed in some berries and oranges and a banana with a little water and ice and blended up breakfast. I took one to Danielle, who was in bed, and I told her about the call from Ron. She said she felt fine and we should check it out.

The early morning air was brisk, but we left the top down on the Porsche Boxster as we drove out to the South Lakes Country Club. The club sat west of Lake Worth, on a slice of land that had once been the back of beyond in Palm Beach but was now surrounded by suburbia. It was a large course, twenty-seven championship holes that could be configured in a variety of ways, but outside of tournament play was usually set up as an eighteen-hole par seventy-two and a shorter nine-hole executive course. The executive course was favored by older members who found a full round a physical challenge, and golfers braving the summer heat, for whom a full round could be a death sentence.

I pulled the Boxster into the lot. A security guard asked what our purpose was and I told him we were there to see Keith Hamilton. I assumed Keith had been good to his word and put the guard there to protect all the fancy cars left behind after the previous day's shenanigans. I parked the Boxster between a Mercedes S-class and a BMW M series. My Boxster looked the part in the lot, and I wasn't going to tell anyone I had picked it up well-used with the insurance money from a previous vehicle damaged in the line of duty.

The line of high-end vehicles was counterbalanced by the range of vans and trucks that had arrived courtesy of the Florida Department of Health. Danielle and I walked in the front entrance of the clubhouse, a low-slung building in the old Florida style. The front door was surrounded by royal palms and huge agave plants that looked like dinosaur fodder. The double doors were solid wood in a craftsman style, and I pushed them open and found a woman at the reception desk. She gave us a surprised look, perhaps because we weren't wearing any hazmat stuff.

"I'm sorry, the club is closed today for tournament preparation." She offered me a Florida smile. It was part of her job to be courteous—this wasn't a French restaurant after all—but a Florida smile is something more. It tells a story of someone, of winters in far-off places that now get visited only for Thanksgiving, and a story of taking a leap of faith into an unknown that turned out to be that person's version of nirvana. It's a smile you see a lot in South Florida. A simple facial expression that says I am here because I love it, and don't you love it, too?

I gave her the smile back. I don't always use it, but it's usually there, just below the surface. I came from far away Connecticut, and I lived the cold winters and leafless trees and the people making a sport of avoiding eye contact. I got lucky and got the chance to go to college in Miami. And afterwards when I played baseball in California, I thought I was on the road to some other kind of nirvana. Until circumstances tossed me on my head and I ended up back in Florida, playing for the Mets' minor league team in Port St. Lucie, and I found out that my version of nirvana was here all along.

"We're here to see Mr. Hamilton," I said. I'm not a surname kind of guy. My dad was Mr. Jones and I left all that behind in New England. But even in Florida, golf clubs like to hold onto those old traditions, so I went with the flow.

The woman gave me a nod and another smile and directed us to a conference room. It was a small room, or more accurately it was a large room made small by the use of old concertina walls. There were five men in the room, all wearing frowns. I recognized Keith Hamilton. He was in a blazer and pressed trousers despite the predicted temperature expected to be close to ninety. It was going to be a scorcher. But Keith looked like a Boston banker on his day off. Perhaps he had been. He didn't have the accent, but some folks escaped New England without sounding like the offspring of an Irish father and Australian mother.

Ron sat next to Keith. He was in trousers and a button-up shirt, the sleeves rolled like he'd been burning the midnight oil. Ron nodded to me and offered two seats. They were in a rough circle with no table. It was like my vision of an AA meeting. Ron spoke as I sat down.

"Gentlemen, this is Miami Jones, my boss, and Deputy Danielle Castle, of the Palm Beach Sheriff's Office." I bristled at the boss thing. Our firm had been left to me after the passing of my mentor and friend, Lenny Cox. It was his firm. Then and now. But he had passed the reins to me rather than Ron for reasons that both he and Ron seemed to understand but flew right over my head. It was my signature on the checks by Ron's preference. In every other way we were partners.

Ron pointed at a guy who wore an open-necked Oxford shirt and suit pants. His suit jacket was over the back of his chair. He wore slicked-back black hair and a smirk. He looked like a mob lawyer.

"This is Martin Costas. Martin is vice president of the club." Martin nodded and offered his hand to Danielle first and then me. I couldn't figure whether that was sexist or chivalrous. I really can't keep up with that stuff.

"This is Barry Yarmouth," Ron said, gesturing to the next guy. He was younger than the rest, maybe my age. He wore expensive eyeglasses and a haircut like Beaver Cleaver. He looked like he might have been from Wisconsin. He had that kind of alabaster skin that looks like it will blister after five minutes of sun. I worry about people like that in Florida. I shook his hand and noted he was wearing a Tiger Woods polo shirt and Nike trousers. Perhaps he had arrived for a round, only to find the apocalypse.

"Barry is the club treasurer," Ron added.

"Pleasure," Barry said to me.

The third unknown face wasn't unknown at all. Not once I saw him from the front. He was Dig Maddox, a minor local celebrity. Dig owned a chain of retail garden supply outlets up and down the coast, inspiringly called Dig's. He did his own ad spot on local TV. But he really specialized in growing and selling wholesale sod. I remembered seeing the signs. His company was called Sod It All, which told me all I needed to know about the marketing genius of the man. He had miles and miles of fields out on the wrong side of the turnpike, out near Wellington. Grass as far as the eye could see. South Florida gets plenty of sunshine, but we also get plenty of tropical rain, and most of the lower half of the state was built on a primordial swamp, so it's a great place to grow grass.

Ron said, "This is Rick Maddox."

Maddox offered his hand. "Dig," he said. I wasn't sure if it was a correction on his name or a command, but I shook his meaty paw and sat back.

Keith Hamilton took the baton from Ron. "Miami and Danielle, we make up the board of South Lakes Country Club. Please let me start by offering our thanks to you, Deputy, for taking charge of events yesterday. Things might have gotten out of hand if not for you."

"That's what we do, Mr. Hamilton." Danielle didn't concur with my surname/first name thinking, but then few law enforcement people did. They liked surnames. They were simultaneously personal and impersonal, and with a firm voice sent even the hardest criminal's mind back in time to their childhood and being told off by their mother.

"It's Keith, please, but no, we owe our thanks. Now to matters at hand. The health department is conducting tests to ascertain the nature of yesterday's, um . . ."

"Eruption?" I added helpfully.

"Quite. Now we need to offer them all assistance necessary. Because I don't think I need stress the importance of getting them out of here as soon as is humanly possible."

The other members of the board shook their heads gravely.

"I have asked Ron to take the lead on keeping on top of things. We can't afford for this to interrupt preparations for the tournament."

"How long will they be here?" asked Barry Yarmouth.

"That's the thing," said Keith. "They're saying they might be here weeks."

"That's crazy," said Dig. "So some folks lost their lunch."

Martin Costas said, "Is there any evidence that suggests the club is even the source?"

"Of course not," said Keith.

Ron put his hand up. "That's actually unknown at this point. That's why they are testing. As Keith said, we need to offer every assistance to get that job done so they can get out. In the meantime, we need to look at our options."

"What options?" said Barry.

"Alternative scenarios. If they are still here for next weekend. Or if they close us down."

"Close us down?" said Keith. He looked like he'd choked on a piece of hot dog. "They can't do that."

"Technically they could. I haven't had much chance to ask around yet, but they seem to be concerned about the kitchen. They might be looking for a food-borne virus. In which case, it is possible they could shut the kitchen down. Maybe even the clubhouse."

"Preposterous," said Keith.

Danielle said "That would be protocol if a food-borne virus were found in a restaurant. I don't see the club being different."

"We can't allow that," said Keith.

"Might not be our choice," said Martin. "So Ron's right. We need to consider alternatives."

"Like what?"

"Like additional hospitality tents. Mobile kitchens."

"If the health department allows those things on the grounds," said Danielle. She got a roomful of furrowed brows.

"Then there's also the ultimate contingency," said Martin. "Moving or canceling the tournament."

"That's not possible," said Keith.

"It might be necessary," said Barry.

"All I'm saying is hope for the best but plan for the worst," said Martin. "It's Sunday. We don't have the luxury of time."

"Which is why the timing is so suspicious," said Keith.

"Not the conspiracy theories again," said Barry. "This is not the time, Keith."

"They are not theories, Barry. There are too many to ignore. How do you explain this happening the weekend before the tournament?"

Barry shrugged.

Martin spoke. "The big hospitality tent was only here because the tournament is on next week. That's why the O'Neil family used it for the wedding. Otherwise they might have gone elsewhere, and this wouldn't be happening. It's not really that big a coincidence, Keith."

"I don't buy it."

"Can I say something?" asked Dig Maddox. It wasn't so much of a question as a warning that he was entering the conversation.

"Of course, Dig," said Keith.

"Not to be rude, but this is all board business. Why are they here?" He looked at me.

"I asked Ron to take lead," said Keith. "Investigating things is what he does. He suggested his boss could help."

"Help with what?"

Ron said, "Miami is more removed from the situation than I am. He won't be seen as an insider by the health department people."

"So what?" said Dig. It was a good point. I didn't see why I was there either. The health department would do what they would do, and they would tell the club the results once they were in.

"We need someone to look after our interests," said Keith. "And Ron thinks it would be best if it were someone outside the club. He trusts Miami, so I do too."

"How much is this going to cost?" asked Barry. He was the treasurer of the club and he seemed like the right man for the job.

"That depends on what we need to do," said Ron.

"That sounds like a blank check," said Dig.

I decided to enter the fray. I was bored, and I didn't see the point of being present. But Ron wanted me there for a reason, so I'd back him up.

"If you want, I'll speak with some people this morning. See if we can't get a read on the direction of the wind." I looked at Ron to confirm my yachting metaphor was on the money and he nodded. Score one, Jones.

"I'll let you know what I find out and you can all decide how to proceed. This morning's labors will be on the house."

"You're asking questions, not mining for coal," said Dig.

"Or I could go home and enjoy my Sunday."

"No," said Keith. "No, we appreciate your efforts. We'll let you get on with that . . ." His mouth turned down. ". . . while we discuss these contingencies."

I took that as my cue to leave. Danielle and I stood and offered nods and made to walk out. As we reached the door Keith Hamilton spoke.

"Oh, and for future reference Mr. Jones, the club dress code requires knee-high socks and dress shorts. Or trousers."

I gave him a look like he was an exhibit in a zoo and walked out.

The club was quiet for a Sunday. I imagined the security guy in the parking lot was turning people away. Or maybe the members got a newsletter that told them the course was closed for tournament prep. We wandered through the lobby. The reception girl wasn't there, so we passed through into a large lounge area. There were chairs and coffee tables. The floor was carpet. Then it became hardwood and morphed into a dining room. White linen tablecloths but no cutlery or napkins or condiments. The room was dark despite the sunshine streaming through the large picture windows overlooking the golf course. We moved to look at the view.

There was nothing to see. There were no people around. I wondered who had arrived in the vans and trucks out front. The window looked out over the practice putting green. It was the size of two tennis courts and held eighteen knee-high flags, denoting eighteen holes. To the right was the first fairway, where the healthier attendees of the wedding had been checked out the day before. The pop-up drash shelter was gone. To the left of the practice green the folding chairs from the ceremony still sat in a haphazard mess. There was a trellised arch behind where the happy couple had stood for their nuptials, back when they were still happy. I hadn't seen it the day before, when it had blended into the background of the course. Now the flowers on it were flagging badly, and the platform beneath was strewn with petals. Farther on, the large hospitality tent sat waiting for the tournament to begin. I had grave doubts that was going to happen. There was some kind of tape across the entrance to the tent, and I was trying to focus through the opening to see what was inside when my attention was drawn back closer to home. Two people came out of the door that Danielle and I had stood next to during the brief ceremony. The lead person was all in white, the second all in black. They moved at pace until the one in white stopped, spun around and yelled in a gravel voice.

"I'll kill 'em, I swear I'll kill 'em all."

CHAPTER FOUR

Danielle and I slipped out of the dining room and through the door to the outside. The person in white was a man. He wore a five o'clock shadow like he had been born with it. The stubble was heavier on his jaw than it was on his head. He was clearly agitated. And he was clearly a cook. The white getup was a uniform, and the name of the country club was embroidered on his chest. He was gesticulating at a slim woman in a black shirt and black trousers. She had her palms out like she was trying to tame a lion.
"Calm down, Lex," she said.
"Don't tell me to calm the hell down!" he screamed. He sounded like a two-pack-a-day man. It figured. I'd met my fair share of cooks and kitchen hands. We often kept similar hours. And I knew that as a group they tended to smoke more than the population in general. I never really got it. I always figured they needed their tastebuds working to do their jobs properly. Maybe that explained why they used all that salt.
"Is there a problem?" asked Danielle in her preschool teacher voice. She stepped past me. I let her go. It's amazing how often a fired-up guy will calm down at the direction of a strong woman's voice. Maybe it was a mother thing. It didn't hurt that

Danielle was athletic and lean and pretty damned gorgeous. I may have been biased, but I didn't think so. I'd seen the looks she got.

I followed behind. Danielle could handle herself just fine, if the calming voice didn't work and the guy did something stupid. But it was always good to have a plan B, and I wasn't above giving the guy a fist in the kisser if he got too feisty.

He didn't. He frowned, and gave Danielle an up-and-down look that was more obvious than a construction worker, but he remained mute.

The woman in black spoke. "We're okay. Chef Lex is just blowing off some steam."

I realized belatedly that it was the woman from the front desk, the one with the Florida smile. She had her dark hair in a ponytail.

"I am a sheriff's deputy," said Danielle. "I heard some threats being made."

"He didn't mean anything by it."

"Was he threatening you, ma'am?"

The woman shook her head and her ponytail flopped about.

"I was threatening those pencil-necks in my kitchen," said the gravel-voiced cook.

"Who?" asked Danielle.

"The health department," said woman. "They're testing the kitchen for cleanliness."

"My kitchen is spotless," yelled the cook. "Don't they know what bleach does? Every damned day."

"Sir, I don't think they are inferring you don't look after your environment," said Danielle. "But they must be thorough. There were some very sick people here yesterday."

"You think I don't know that? I was here, damn it. But it all happened before the reception. They hadn't eaten anything yet. Whatever it was didn't come from my kitchen, you get it?"

"I do get it, sir. But they are still required to be thorough."

"Thorough, my eye. They're looking to blame someone. That's what they're doing."

"Sir, why don't you just take a moment to relax and I will go and find out what the situation is. Okay?"

The cook said nothing but the woman said, "Come on, Lex. Let's go upstairs to the bar and get a drink."

"They've probably closed the bar, too."

"It'll be fine," she said. She had the preschool teacher voice down pretty well, too. She patted the guy on the shoulder and he sulked away. I gave Danielle the furrowed brow expression. It was a beauty. I had lines on my forehead fit for industrial farming. Twenty summers of baseball will do that to a guy. We moved back into the dim light of the clubhouse. On the opposite side of the hallway from the dining room was a kitchen. I could tell by the double doors with little portholes in them. We didn't go in because Connie Persil from the health department came out. She was still wearing her face mask. I nearly ran into her and we took a moment to regard each other before recognition kicked in. She glanced from me to Danielle.

"Deputy, Mr. Jones. I didn't expect to see you."

"Mr. Jones was my dad. I'm just Miami. And we were in the neighborhood," I said.

"You should be at home. You might be contagious."

"I feel fine."

"Still, it would be better."

"Have you figured out what this is yet?"

She hesitated and looked at Danielle again. Then she directed us back outside and we stood by the practice green. Once in the open air she removed her mask.

"We've interviewed most of the victims. There's a consistent infection point."

"Infection point?" I asked.

"The common point where current victims were infected."

"Who is it?"

"We don't know the who, yet. That would be patient zero. That's why I say infection point. In this case, everyone who had shown symptoms attended a pre-wedding dinner the evening before last."

"So the dining venue was the source, not the club?"

"The dining venue was the club, Mr. Jones."

"Really?"

"Yes. It seems the large hospitality tent over there was used for the dinner, and the catering was handled by the kitchen here."

"So you're giving the kitchen the once-over."

"Exactly. We took initial environmental samples yesterday, from the kitchen and out here, the seating, the tent, et cetera. But the infection point conclusion means we're doubling our efforts in the kitchen. It's not unusual."

"Do you know what it is?" Danielle asked.

"Not for sure. We should have some results later today. But given the infection point and the incubation period, my guess is norovirus."

"What is that?" I asked. "Is it serious?"

"Serious, but not deadly. Not usually. In layman's terms, it's gastroenteritis. Victims usually suffer from diarrhea and/or nausea. The greatest risk is dehydration. It can be hard to keep even water down. And if the victim has some underlying illness it could get serious, but that's rare."

"And you don't think we have it?"

"What makes you say that?"

"You took your mask off."

She looked at the mask in her hand and shrugged. "You weren't at the dinner. We have a full guest list. And the incubation period suggests you'd be starting to show symptoms by now. You are not."

"So if it is the kitchen, what happens to the club?"

"We close it."

"But the tournament?"

"A game of golf is not my concern, Mr. Jones. Public safety is my concern."

"Could they proceed if the infection is localized to the kitchen and they don't use it?"

"That would be dependent on the environmental samples. It would very easy for the virus to have spread to other areas of the clubhouse."

"How does it spread?" asked Danielle.

"Mostly through human feces and vomitus."

I squirmed and thanked my lucky bat that I never studied medicine. The internal mechanisms of our bodies were a marvel, but decidedly unpleasant.

Connie continued. "Then it can transmit via human contact with carriers, touching infected surfaces. It's possible for it to be airborne briefly—a cough from someone who has recently vomited, for example. If it is what I think it is, then we're talking about a nasty little bug that does just fine outside the body. It can remain on surfaces for days or weeks. There have been documented examples of months or years of survival in contaminated water."

"How do we avoid it?"

Connie held up her hands. She wore latex gloves. "Don't touch anything, don't touch anyone. Short of that, wash your hands often, with lots of soap. Sing the national anthem twice while you're doing it. That's about long enough. Look, I need to get back to it."

"You'll let us know about the results?" Danielle asked.

"You'll know when I stick a closed notice on the door," she said.

Danielle and I stayed outside in the fresh air and watched her walk away.

"What do you think?" she said.

"Looks like the kitchen messed up."

"Or it came in on contaminated food."

"Wouldn't the cook be sick then?"

She shrugged. "Maybe he wore gloves?"

The contour of land ran down from the front of the clubhouse to the rear where the course lay, so the back half of the building was two stories. I looked up at the wall of windows on the second level.

"Nothing better to do," I said. "Let's go chat with the cook."

CHAPTER FIVE

The cook simmered. The line popped into my head and I couldn't wedge it out, and I wondered if I had a future as a screenwriter. But it was a fair assessment. He was a solid guy, thick in the forearms and the chest. He didn't exactly look like a merchant sailor but he could have played one on television. He was sitting with the woman in the black at a high table in the upstairs bar. This part of the club felt newer than the entrance. Maybe it had been renovated. The colors were light and breezy, sea foam greens and turquoise blues. There were pictures of golfers holding trophies around the room. Tournament winners was my guess.

Danielle asked the woman in black if we could join them and she said yes with a nod. They were opposite each other so Danielle and I sat opposite each other as well. We were all set up for a game of canasta.

"Tough day," I said.

The woman nodded. "You could say."

"How do you think this happened?"

"I don't know. It doesn't make sense."

"Health department thinks either the kitchen or the food."

"Health department can kiss my grits," said the cook.

"You saying it isn't remotely possible it came out of the kitchen?"

"That's what I'm sayin'."

"That sounds like denial, my friend."

"I ain't your friend, snowbird."

I winced at the snowbird comment. "You might want to check the attitude, pal. I'm the only one here who's even remotely interested in your side of the story."

"That so? Who the hell are you, anyway?"

"Miami Jones."

"Like the arc of the covenant?"

"No, not like the arc of the covenant."

"There used to be a ball player with that name."

"You're looking at him."

The cook regarded me a moment and rubbed his stubble—the stuff on his chin, not his head.

"So what are you now, some kind of private eye?"

"Yes."

He smiled. His teeth were nicotine yellow. "What, they didn't have any bars you could open?"

"I already have a bar I enjoy, and someone already owns it. And I can go there tonight and spend the money I get paid today. You, on the other hand, are looking at being unemployed." I looked at the woman in black. She had lost her Florida smile. "I didn't get your name earlier."

"Natalie Morris. I'm the catering manager."

"So you were in charge of the wedding food."

She nodded.

"Then you're both on the hook. So help me out here. Tell me why it couldn't happen the way the health department is telling it."

Natalie looked at the cook and he grunted.

"My kitchen is spotless. It's fully stainless steel. We follow a two-step cleaning protocol for all dishware and cutlery. I'm not some truck stop short-order cook. I know what I'm doing."
It was a funny way to put it, because I thought he looked exactly like a truck stop short-order cook. I could see him yelling the orders through the little window in the kitchen while thin waitresses in pink dresses warmed up truckers' coffees. But that was no reason to assume the kitchen was a pigsty. Some of the best food in the country was served in no-name diners clinging to the periphery of the interstate system. On the flip side, so was some of the worst.
So I asked, "Where'd you learn to cook?"
"CIA," he said.
I had to give that my impressed lip curl. I knew he wasn't talking about the staff canteen in Langley, Virginia, where the spies ate their lunch. The Culinary Institute of America was as fine a cooking school as there was on the planet.
"Which campus?"
"Cali."
"What's the building called?"
"Greystone."
"What's the building made of?"
"I'm no architect. It's some kind of stone, all right. But it ain't gray. More like sand color."
I nodded. He knew the place. He either studied there for real or he really did his research on the con he was running. I'd been there, for a function way back when I played ball in Modesto. Some teammates and I had stayed the weekend and played a bit of golf, done a few wineries. It was nice country, but way above my pay grade.
"What's the closest winery to the campus there?"

The cook shrugged. "Can't say for sure. I never paced them out. Beringer is close. But so is Morley, and William Cole. Charles Krug is across the train tracks."

He sat back in his chair and folded his arms and practically dared me to test him more. But this wasn't Wheel of Fortune and I wasn't Pat Sajak.

"So what did the CIA teach you about keeping bugs out of your kitchen?"

"Everything. It's critical. You can be a three-star Michelin guy, top of the world. On the cover of magazines. But you know full well what happens if the health department shuts you down for violations—let alone the bad press from a food poisoning outbreak. It's career-ending stuff. That's what they taught us. Because that's what it is. So don't kid yourself that I don't know what this means. I'll be done, not just here, but pretty much anywhere in the South. I'll have to move back to the Northeast and be some clown's sous chef." He shook his head and curled his lip.

"So you keep a clean environment. But you can't see a food-borne virus, can you?"

"Of course not, but we sanitize every night after service. Every surface, even the floor. The walk-in fridge gets the treatment weekly. I use a bleach solution. It's like napalm on viruses. So they can point the finger, but there's more chance that a virus came in on you than there is that it started in my kitchen."

He certainly talked a good game, but he was fighting for his livelihood so I expected that as a minimum. Then again I'd been in enough South Florida eateries where the kitchen staff wouldn't know bleach from peach schnapps. Those kinds of kitchens were usually the ones that got notices stuck on their front doors, and it didn't take a genius to see why.

"What about the food?" I asked. "Maybe it came from your suppliers?"
The cook looked at Natalie, the catering manager, and she shrugged.
"It's possible. But like I said, it doesn't make sense."
"Why?"
"How many health department people are here right now?"
"All of them?"
"That's what I thought. A lot of folks for one possible outbreak. Now I know there were some pretty powerful people got sick yesterday, so the health department is probably motivated. But here's the thing. If a virus came in from a supplier, what are odds that ours was the only delivery that was contaminated? I mean, if it was on the lettuce, for example. Wouldn't it be on all the lettuce? And if it was, wouldn't there be other venues having the exact same issue? I mean this happened on Saturday night. Every restaurant in the state is open on a Saturday night. There should be outbreaks everywhere. But the health department doesn't seem stretched to me. Like you say, they all seem to be here."
I nodded and looked at Danielle, who raised her eyebrows at me. It was a fair analysis and a good argument. Unfortunately it put the focus right back on the kitchen. Bleach or no bleach, sometimes people got sloppy. Sometimes they got lazy. Sometimes the bleach ran out and they just wiped down the counters with water. Anything was possible. I focused back on the cook.
"Do you use gloves in your kitchen?"
"No."
"Isn't that unsanitary?"
"No."
"Why not?"

"Gloves are stupid. It's the kind of thing politicians put in the health regs to be seen to be doing something rather than actually doing something. Look, if you've got dirty hands and you put on gloves, what happens? You have to touch the damn gloves to put them on. Defeats the purpose. Plus gloves are usually latex, and some people are allergic, so that's a new problem you've created. And no restaurant owner wants to pay for latex-free gloves. They cost a fortune and you'd have to change them constantly or they'd be just as likely to get contaminated as bare hands. The real solution is simple. Wash your hands. Wash 'em good. Wash 'em frequently. We're not home cooks. We're not sticking our finger in the soup. I use a utensil and discard the utensil each time. I've got a collection of teaspoons you wouldn't believe. I go through plenty during a service. Start clean, stay clean. That's the only way."

The guy looked like he belonged on an oil rig but he spoke the right lines, and I was starting to think there was something to what he was saying. But there didn't seem to be an alternative theory, and mistakes could get made. Even NASCAR car drivers crashed occasionally. It felt inevitable to me that Connie Persil would find what she was looking for and close the place down, at least temporarily. And temporarily was going to be long enough to kill the tournament. I'd done what I'd said I would do, and the results were in. Just because the club board members didn't like the answer didn't change it. And it was better they dealt with things early rather than late. I didn't know whether the tournament could be salvaged. That wasn't my area, and to be honest it wasn't my concern.

I was happy to help Ron out. The country club had been a bit of a lifeline for him a few years prior. The woman who was the love of his life had passed away, and he had spiraled downhill. He got remarried hastily, to a woman who enjoyed the finer

DEEP ROUGH

things in life that Ron had access to. But those things—the cars, the clubs, the fancy apartment—were a mirage. They all came about because of Ron's employer. So when he realized that his work was the major source of his melancholy, he decided to give it up. And when the work went, so did the employer-supplied cars and club memberships. He had to downgrade his apartment. And his wife didn't stick around for the lower-rent party. But Ron's a sociable guy. He's like one of those apes that go all funny in the head when they get shunned by the other apes. Solitude doesn't suit him. Me, I could sail away on a solo voyage and be as happy as a clam. At least if Danielle came. That would be better. But I didn't need more than that. Ron did. So Keith Hamilton had done Ron a favor and waived the initiation fee to join South Lakes, and Ron had found a new family in West Palm. The country club and the yacht club on the Intracoastal gave him a new group of apes to hang with. And gave us an excellent source of clients to boot. So I was more than happy to help out. But these were not poor people. They weren't Palm Beach rich, but they did just fine. So if they wanted more than a morning out of me they'd have to pony up. But I just didn't see the point.

We left Lex the cook and Natalie at their table in the empty bar. They said they were hanging around because they had nothing better to do. We wished them good luck and went downstairs to find the board and break the news that they there were basically up a tributary without a canoe. We ran into Keith Hamilton as we wandered back through the dining room. He wore the mood of a Wall Street banker during the depression.

"It's a conspiracy, I tell you," he spluttered as if he couldn't get the words out fast enough.

"We need to talk."

He kept moving. "Come with me."
Danielle and I turned around and followed him back outside. He marched past the practice putting green, out near the first tee. A golf cart was sitting there waiting for us. A stocky Latino guy was behind the wheel. It was a double bench seat cart. Keith dropped in beside the driver and Danielle and I sat facing backward, our feet in little slots where golf bags could sit.
The driver hit the gas, or whatever the appropriate phrase was for accelerating away in an electric cart, and we silently whizzed down the first fairway. I hung on for dear life. We couldn't have been going more than fifteen but it felt like Daytona. We zoomed down the side of the fairway, scooting around a large sand trap that was as white as a beach, and then up a slight slope to the green. The driver stopped suddenly just before the green and Danielle and I were pressed back into our seats.
I heard Keith leap out and let out a groan, the kind of noise you might expect from a teenage boy awoken with the words time for school. I stepped off the cart and offered a hand to Danielle. She took it with a smile that made me feel like a million bucks. She was like that. Perfectly capable of getting off a damned golf cart by herself, but perfectly happy to take the hand of a gentleman when offered. We stepped around the cart and up to the edge of the green. The Latino guy removed his cap and scratched his head as if what he saw defied explanation. Keith Hamilton just stood in silence. I looked at the green.
A large portion of the smooth cut grass was dead. I'm no horticulturist, but I do know some things about lawn care. I know, for example, that green grass is good, and yellow grass is not good. And much of the so-called green I was looking at was not green at all. It was the color of wheat. It was crusty

and dry and dead. And it wasn't from lack of watering. It wasn't some freak natural occurrence. Mother nature did all kinds of crazy stuff, but she rarely wrote things out using the roman alphabet. And this dead grass was in the form of three large letters, writ across the width of the green. Three capital letters.
GUR.

CHAPTER SIX

"What's gur?" asked Danielle.

"Not gur, G-U-R. It's a golf term," I said. "It means ground under repair. Right?" I looked at Keith but he didn't look at me and he didn't respond. The Latino guy nodded at me and pulled his cap back on.

"It doesn't look under repair," Danielle said.

"It's not, at least in this case. Ground under repair usually refers to a section of the golf course that is being fixed up. It could be some tree plantings, or it could be a section of new green, or even part of the fairway that has been churned up and needs resodding. The thing is, it's grass. It doesn't just happen in five minutes. Things need to be given a chance to grow, to take root. So the greenskeepers rope off the area in question and put a sign on it. Ground under repair, or GUR for short."

"I would have thought the sign was somewhat superfluous."

"Not really, because it relates to the rules of golf. On fairways and such, a player must play the lie he or she has. You can't pick up your ball to get a better lie or clean your ball. If you do, you receive a penalty. But GUR is different. The rules allow a player whose ball lands in an area marked as GUR to remove

DEEP ROUGH

their ball and drop it outside the sectioned area, no closer to the hole, for no penalty."

"This doesn't look like repairing damage," said Danielle. "It looks like someone's causing it."

"Someone is," said Keith. "This is vandalism, Deputy. And I'd like to make an official complaint to the Palm Beach sheriff."

Danielle looked at the president and then at the green. Then she nodded. "All right, Mr. Hamilton. Let's talk."

"Give me a moment," he said, and he turned to his Latino greenskeeper.

"Diego. It's tournament week. What can we do?"

Diego scratched his head through his cap this time, and looked at the green as if he had no earthly idea what do to. But that was just the impression he gave, and it was a misleading one. He clearly wasn't considering the what—he was considering the how.

"We can remove the dead parts. I can get replacement green from the executive course and patch it in."

"We're on national television this week, Diego. We can't have the first green looking like Frankenstein's monster."

"No, señor. With some water and some brushing, I can do it." He waved at the front section of the green that was unharmed. "For the practice rounds we keep the pin at the front here. That will give me five days to make the rest bueno. Before the TV comes. Si?" He looked at Keith and Keith nodded.

"Do your magic, Diego." The greenskeeper strode up onto the green and Keith turned us toward the distant clubhouse.

"You don't mind if we walk back, do you?"

"Not at all," said Danielle. I was okay with it. It was a beautiful morning. The sky was a deep kind of blue. There are three kinds of sky in Florida: blue, which was most common, and spoke of pleasant days and tourists and beaches—the chamber of commerce gang loved the blue days; then there was the white days, when the sun got so hot that the atmosphere lost all its color and the ground oozed moist warmth from below—the chamber gang didn't love white days, and neither did anyone else bar Florida Power and Light; and the third kind of day was grayscale, when the mood swept in from the Bahamas and clouds choked the color from the sky and then everything turned black. The humidity bubbled and sooner or later the heavens opened and pelted the earth with rain that could knock a horse off its feet. The chamber of commerce's position on those days was variable. Rain meant lots of income for restaurants and bars, and indoor places like theaters and the children's museum. Their impression of those days was based more on wind speed than color. Rain squalls happened plenty in Florida. There was no topography to slow the passage of storms. The weather swept across the flat state as if it were nothing but open ocean. So rain came and then went. It didn't hang around. But the warm Gulf Stream waters also brought hurricanes. Tourists could live with a refreshing burst of rain to wash away the humidity, but no one liked to spend their tourist dollars bunkered down against the ravages of a hurricane. The commerce folks were most definitely not keen on hurricanes.

But there was zero chance of rain as we wandered back up the first fairway. Danielle dropped in between Keith and me.

"So what is that all about?"

Keith considered his words before he spoke. "I believe there is a concerted effort to damage the club."

"By whom?"

"I don't know. I have my suspicions, but I have no evidence."

"What do you mean by concerted effort?"

"This is not the first incident. It started with small things. Tires being let down on members' vehicles in the lot. Half of our fleet of golf carts was disabled."
"Disabled?"
"We discovered that the battery terminals had been disconnected."
"Cut wires?" I asked.
"No, the terminals had been physically disconnected. The wires were fine."
"So not a difficult fix."
"No, Mr. Jones, not difficult. But you're missing the point. Members bring guests, often clients and such. When half the carts don't work they get embarrassed."
"I can't imagine. Embarrassment. How awful."
"You may mock, Mr. Jones. But the members pay substantial money to be part of this club. Money they can spend elsewhere. At another club, for example. Membership in this club is an achievement. No, we're not one of the Palm Beach clubs. We don't have hundred-thousand-dollar initiations. But we do pride ourselves on both inclusivity and exclusivity. Anyone may join, but you must have reached a certain station in life to be able to do so."
"Be rich, you mean?"
"Hardly, Mr. Jones. Our members are not the multibillionaires of Palm Beach or Jupiter. We are working people. Our members have earned the privilege, and they don't wish to be embarrassed by it."
I nodded and kept my mouth closed. Nothing good was going to come out of it, so I heeded my mother's words from decades before. I figured Keith's version of working people and my version differed slightly. As an investigator I spent a lot of time with people that Keith Hamilton would hire to get

down on their hands and knees and scrub his tile floors. Not a mile from the manicured grass we stood on was the first of an endless number of trailer parks. Single-wides with potted plants and a carport on the side. Places where people lived because even in paradise a CBS construction house was out of their reach. I knew nurses and teachers and laborers who would never pass through the gates of the likes of South Lakes Country Club.

"Okay, Mr. Hamilton. So someone is embarrassing the members. You think this damage to the green is linked?"

"It's all linked. The sabotage, the poisoning, the vandalism."

"Poisoning?"

"Of course. You saw what happened at the Coligio-O'Neil wedding."

"I did, sir. But there's no evidence that was sabotage. The health department is quite confident it was a food-borne virus."

"Our kitchen is immaculate. It didn't just suddenly become a cesspool."

"No one is suggesting that, sir. It doesn't take a lot for a food-borne illness to spread."

"Look, Deputy. I know what I know. Chef Lex might not be much to look at, but he is a top-notch kitchen manager. He has worked in some of the finest establishments in New York and New Jersey."

I didn't think adding New Jersey to the resume added a whole lot, but I kept that to myself. We reached the tee box and cut up toward the clubhouse. We stopped and looked back toward the damaged green. In the distance we could see Diego the greenskeeper, hard at work.

"Mr. Hamilton," continued Danielle, "I don't see the link and I don't see how anyone would contaminate the kitchen in the way it seems to have been. Why target a wedding?"

"Deputy, Mr. O'Neil is one of our most prominent members. It's just like the golf carts. It is a major embarrassment to him. His family and friends, and clients. His in-laws for goodness sakes—they are a Palm Beach family. I can only imagine what they are saying."

Danielle gave him her concerned but not sold look.

I said, "Keith, let's say for argument's sake this is all true. Let's say someone is trying to embarrass your members. There's a big missing part. Motive. Why would someone do it? I mean, the carts and the tires. That could be a disgruntled employee or even a student prank. But the virus, if that's what it is, that's a whole different ball game. That's not kids. So what's the motive?"

Keith gazed at me. He had a wise, old face, lined with experience. He looked at me for longer than was necessary and it ebbed into uncomfortable territory. Then he spoke, quietly.

"I believe there are people who wish to see our club closed down."

"People? What people?"

"Powerful people."

"But that doesn't answer the question. Motive."

Keith began to smile but didn't. "The greatest motive there is. The whole reason the state of Florida exists at all." He kept looking at me, waiting for me to come up with the answer all by myself. But I was already there. There was only one reason people came to a staggeringly hot, sweating swamp of a place like Florida and turned it into a destination.

"Money."

Keith nodded.

"How?" asked Danielle. "How does your club equal money for someone else?"

"Deputy, there are so many ways. When South Lakes was built it was on the edge of civilization in the Palm Beaches. Now we are in the middle of it. You can drive more than half an hour west before the last housing development. This ground we stand on was once jungle, but now it is very expensive real estate."

"You think someone wants to close the club so they can build more houses?" I asked.

"Why not?"

"Does West Palm really need more houses?"

"Thirty years ago Florida had a population of ten million. Now we are over twenty million, and growing. You tell me."

"All right, Mr. Hamilton," said Danielle. "We'll certainly take a look at the damaged grass. And the carts, did you report that?"

"No."

"Why not?"

"I'm an attorney, Deputy Castle. I know what the sheriff will and will not spend time on. And as I said, the carts were disabled, not damaged. You wouldn't have even opened a file on it. And there was nothing to claim insurance on, so no need of a police report."

She nodded. He was on the money.

"I'll take a look anyway."

"And you, Mr. Jones?"

"I don't think there's anything more for me to offer, Keith. Unless we hear different."

And then we heard different.

CHAPTER SEVEN

Connie Persil strode out of the clubhouse and looked around until her eyes fell on us. She marched over with the stilted action of someone walking fast while simultaneously not wanting to appear to be walking fast.
"Deputy, a word."
She eyed both me and Keith, and then turned and walked back to the other side of the practice green. Danielle followed. Connie spoke. Danielle listened. There were no gestures, no facial expressions to give us an inkling of what they were talking about. Connie appeared to be giving Danielle an update of the facts, just the facts. She was more impassive than Dan Rather. Once she was finished she took a deep breath, as if she didn't like to breathe while talking, and glanced at Keith and me. Danielle said something and Connie gave an uncomfortable shrug, and then the two of them walked back to us.
"Tell them what you told me," said Danielle.
Connie paused, like she was a lawyer who was about to breach client-attorney privilege, and then she spoke like a schoolteacher.
"We just got initial results back from the lab."

We said nothing, waiting for her to continue. But she didn't. It was like a pregnant pause that was going full-term. Eventually Keith cracked.

"And?"

"The contamination does not appear to have originated in the kitchen, or the food."

"So where?" I asked. "Do you know?"

"Not all the environmental swabs have been tested. And we need to complete testing of the patient samples."

"But . . ."

"But it appears to be viral."

"And . . ." I was thinking something about blood from stones.

"And the samples that are testing positive are the chairs."

Keith frowned, which was not a great look on an old guy. "The chairs?"

"Yes. So far environmental swabs from all other locations are proving negative."

"I don't understand," said Keith. "The chairs, you say?"

"Yes."

"What sort of virus is it?" I asked.

"The lab is doing more testing of the patient samples to confirm."

This routine was getting old. "But . . ."

"But as I hypothesized, it appears to be norovirus."

"So gastro?"

"In simple terms, you could say that."

"On the chairs."

"That is what the initial data suggests."

"So it's not our kitchen?" asked Keith.

"We are conducting secondary testing, but no, it does not appear so."

"So you're not closing us down."

"I didn't say that."

"But if it's not the kitchen . . ."

"It's still here in the club. We need to pin this thing down."

"We have golfers starting to arrive tomorrow."

"Not here. Not yet. Look, I need to get back to it. I just wanted to keep Deputy Castle in the loop." She said it in a way that told Keith and me we were ever-so-lucky to have been indulged. It wasn't an attitude that was winning me over.

"One thing, Connie," I said. "How would something like this get on the chairs? Just the chairs?"

"That depends on where the chairs came from."

We all looked at Keith.

"No hire chairs have arrived yet. The wedding chairs were ours. We have a stock, for functions."

I turned back to Connie. "So?"

"So I don't know."

"If you were a betting person?"

"I don't gamble."

I had gotten that far by myself. "If you had to hypothesize?" I would have said guess but I figured Connie didn't guess either. But she was the kind of gal who hypothesized.

"Without the full data I can't be sure. But my hypothesis based on available evidence would be that the environment was contaminated purposefully. Now I must get back. Deputy." She nodded at Danielle and walked back inside. I looked at Keith.

"Contaminated purposefully," I said. "Quite the mouthful."

Keith nodded. "Another person might say sabotage."

"They might."

"Let's not jump to conclusions," Danielle said. "I'm going to call it in to the office." She stepped away as she pulled out her phone.

Keith looked at me. "What say you, Mr. Jones?"

"I'd say the game is afoot."
"Not original, but quite right."
"And the PBSO is on it."
"Yes, and while I have full confidence in the sheriff's office, I do believe they have a certain way of looking at things."
"Meaning?"
"Meaning their agenda, like the department of health, is public safety, so-called. Unfortunately that manifests itself as people who get elected for a living doing things that make them look like they are doing things, rather than actually doing things."
That was certainly my experience, but I had to ask the question. "Your point?"
"Closing down the club temporarily is the political play here, Mr. Jones. But even a temporary closure will be catastrophic to us. Possibly terminal. It means the cancellation of the tournament, or worse, moving to another venue. Either way, we can kiss future PGA Tour visits goodbye. And with it, the finances that sponsors and patrons bring. You see my point?"
"I think I do. If someone is really sabotaging you, closing you down right before the tournament is close to checkmate."
"So I repeat, what say you?"
"There is a potential public safety risk. You have to admit that."
"You heard that woman. It's on the chairs. So surely we can clean them. For heaven's sake, I'll burn them if I have to."
I nodded and looked back down the fairway. Diego, the greenskeeper, appeared to be digging out the dead grass. And for all his bluster, Keith was right about the green. That was no accident.
"All right, Keith. I'm on it. But as of now, I'm on the clock."
"Of course. I assume there is some kind of family and friends rate, given Ron's position with the club."

I looked around the finely cut fairways and raked sand traps. I thought of the European cars in the parking lot.
"Sure, Keith. Anything for Ron."
He offered a canine smile that made me think of a fox. "Thank you, Mr. Jones. Where shall you begin?"
"I'd like to talk to any of the board that are still here."
"They're all still here. I'll summon them."
"Don't bother. I'll find them."
I found Martin Costas first. I wandered around the clubhouse and came in through the front. Martin was in the reception lobby when I pushed the double doors open.
"Leaving?"
He nodded. "Work beckons."
"Can have I have a word?"
"Walk with me."
We wandered back outside into the sun. It was warming up. It was going to be a perfect beach day. Martin Costas looked overdone in his suit. At least he wasn't wearing a tie. Either way he didn't look hot. He had one of those Mediterranean complexions that look designed for the sun and never appeared to overheat. Or sweat.
"Did you hear about the testing?"
"I did. Good news, I suppose."
"You suppose?"
"Sure. Good for the tournament. Improves our chances of it happening. But it still happened, so it's not all sunshine."
"Keith suspects sabotage. What do you think?"
"I think there are some suspicious things going on."
"Like putting viruses on chairs?"
"I don't know about that. How would one even do that?"
"So you don't think it's sabotage?"
"The evidence doesn't suggest it, does it?"

"The evidence? What is it you do for a living, Martin?"
"I'm a lawyer."
"Seems to be a few attorneys in the club."
"No, I don't think so. That's one of the reasons I'm a member. There's Keith, of course. Not sure I know another."
"Why does that make you want to be a member?"
"Miami, I work with a lot of folks from the island. It is good for my business to spend time there. I am a member of a number of organizations in Palm Beach, including the yacht club. But this?" He waved back toward the clubhouse, not the parking lot. "This is a sanctuary. My father was a shopkeeper. We lived above the store. I paid my way through law school."
"Which school?"
"Michigan."
"Good school."
"It is."

It also explained why he was now in South Florida. Those Ann Arbor winters were brutal.

"But I learned a thing or two about people, Miami. I learned not to judge a man by the cut of his suit." He looked me over. "Or indeed whether he was even wearing one. These people are real. Yes, we have a couple of lawyers. And we have real estate developers and politicians. But we also have plumbers and gardeners and storeowners. Real people. I like that. It reminds me that the world in which I work exists inside a bubble. It keeps my feet on the ground."

We reached his car and he opened the door with a fob and slipped his feet off the ground and down into a Maserati. The metaphor clearly only went so far.

"So what does the evidence suggest to you?"

"I think there are two things going on. The first is the damage. The carts, now the greens. That feels like someone with an agenda to me. Maybe a disgruntled former employee."
"You dismissed anyone recently?"
"Not that I know of. But hiring and firing doesn't happen at the board level. You should ask Barry or Natalie Morris about that."
"What about a disgruntled former member?"
"That would come before the board. And it does happen. Some folks don't pay their dues, some need to be reminded of club etiquette, that sort of thing. But honestly, I don't recall a member dismissal for quite some time."
He punched a button on the console and the car roared to life and then settled into a purr like a throaty lion.
I continued before I was lost to the engine noise. "You said there were two things."
"If the virus thing isn't an accident, I don't see how it's connected anyway. It would be a whole different level of action from other events. Like I say, I can't even begin to figure how anyone would do it. How does one get hold of a virus? You see what I mean? That's not a disgruntled employee. That's something bigger."
"Any hypotheses?" I figured a lawyer was also more likely to hypothesize than guess.
"Honestly?" It was a word that he liked to use. I wasn't sure what to make of that. "I'm not sure it has anything to do with the club."
"How do you figure that?"
"I'd be checking out the families. At the wedding. I know the groom's side reasonably well. I didn't get the impression the father of the groom was all that impressed with his son's choice of wife. Or more specifically with the in-laws."

I nodded and stood back as Martin slammed the gear selector, which looked like something from a fighter jet, into whatever position it needed to go, and he pulled out of his slot. He backed around me and I stepped toward the window and he stopped.

"Why would the groom's father infect himself and his family?"

"Who says he did?"

"I saw his wife go down. It wasn't pretty."

"Maybe he doesn't value her as much as you think. Or maybe he does. But think about it. Something like that. He wouldn't do it himself. He'd have people. All these guys have people. Maybe his people aren't that clever." He shrugged like anything was possible. "You need anything else, call my office. Or I'll be around later."

I nodded but he didn't see it. He gunned the car and it took off like a ballistic missile, barely pausing for the security guy at the gate, before launching out onto the road. I could still hear the roar of the engine as I wandered back into the clubhouse.

CHAPTER EIGHT

If you believed what you saw on television, you'd think that private investigations work involved a lot of car chases and sultry women, with a good smattering of gunplay and a fedora or two. I don't own a television but that was the impression I got. I suppose they made it like that because no one would watch the reality. The reality was lower-key. There was a lot more sitting around thinking, or in this case wandering around an empty golf club looking for someone to talk to. Unlike the television guys I didn't carry a gun. I did have one, but it stayed locked away as much as was humanly possible. If I had it in my hand then events had most decidedly taken a turn for the worse. Things had gotten that bad once or twice in the past, and those memories still gave me sleepless nights. I had no desire to add to them any time soon. And I certainly didn't own a fedora.

I wandered through the dining room and saw no one. I knew Connie Persil and her team were in the kitchen and I didn't expect anyone else to be in there, so I looped around and headed for the side of the club where I had met the club board earlier that morning. The function rooms were still set up as they had been, with one of the concertina walls closed and one open, creating a small room and large room. Both empty. I continued down a hall and found a couple more doors. One of them had a silver nameplate on the wall by the door, telling me that the space behind belonged to the club treasurer.

I knocked and opened the door. I generally found it a waste of time to wait for someone to invite me in when I knocked on a door. That had been the way I did it at college, with coaches' offices and such. But since then I found that if you got the affirmative to come in you had just wasted time waiting, and if you weren't going to get the affirmative then you often walked in on some juicy stuff.

Not today. Barry Yarmouth was sitting at an old metal desk that looked like it had been lifted from the local army reserve base, circa 1940. He was looking at the door with his mouth open, halfway to yelling come in, but halted mid-command by the door opening. He was working on some spreadsheets on a computer screen, which almost put me to sleep by association.

"Barry," I said, taking a seat in front of his desk. I looked at him. The office lighting wasn't doing him any favors. Unlike Martin, Barry looked moist in an air-conditioned office.

"Um, Mr. Jones."

"Miami."

"Miami. What can I do for you?"

I got the impression that old Barry hadn't yet been updated on the condition of the first green or the news about the viral chairs, so I went another way than that which I was planning.

"What's doing?"

"Um, working on contingencies. Cash flow. If the tournament has to be canceled or postponed."

"Is that likely? Postponement, I mean. I got the impression that if it was canceled it wouldn't happen at all, or at least not here."

"Keith lives in denial."

"How so?"

Barry leaned back from his keyboard. "What you say is true. If the PGA Tour decides that the event has to be called off, it will be canceled, not postponed. The tour calendar is full. They don't keep a week spare in case a club can't complete their obligations."

"What will happen if you can't hold the tournament?"

"It's not what will happen, it's what won't happen. The PGA Tour will never again cast its wealthy shadow across our fairways."

"So you'll never get another PGA tournament?"

"We won't get another PGA Tour event."

"Isn't that what I said?"

"No. The PGA Tour is a body run for the benefit of professional players. They cover most of the top tournaments, including ours. The PGA of America is a separate association, run by and for all people in the golf profession, including players but also teaching pros, those sorts of guys. The PGA of America runs the annual PGA major, but not PGA Tour events."

"They wouldn't want to keep it simple."

"Of course not."

"So what would it mean for the club?" I asked. "Surely lots of clubs exist without holding tour events."

"Most clubs do. But not clubs as extended as this one."

"What does that mean?"

"It means the club takes on a lot of risk in holding an event. We spend a lot of extra money getting the course right. We spend money on facilities, hospitality tents, that sort of thing. We order extra catering, beverages. If the tournament goes well, we get all that money back. We break even. But if the tournament flops, we could take a large loss."

I asked, "How does a tournament flop?"

"A PGA Tour tournament is reliant on the players playing. But the tour doesn't compel them to do so. A player needs to compete in a minimum of fifteen events to be a full member. Other than that they can pick and choose when and where they play. If you're banking on the world number one making an appearance but you don't end up with anyone inside the top ten, well, you won't get the crowds and your sponsors will be unhappy and the TV networks will be unhappy and that could mean lost revenue for the host club."

"So an event's cancellation would be . . ."

"A catastrophe. The tour wouldn't reimburse any of the costs, the sponsors would withhold sponsorship money. It could likely mean the end of the club as we know it. This isn't Augusta National. We need this money."

"What do you think about the conspiracy theories—that someone is purposefully trying to hurt the club?"

"I don't know. I've not seen any of these things that Keith talks about. I don't know how much is reality and how much is drama."

"You think he's making it up?"

"Making it up? No. But he might be embellishing on things. Some people thrive on drama. Lawyers particularly, in my experience."

"What do you do, Barry?"

"For a living? I'm a real estate agent."

I nodded. I had nothing to say to that. Being a real estate agent in Florida was like being on Mars and calling yourself a

Martian. In the last real estate bubble there were more real estate agents than there were houses. The implosion of the South Florida market culled the herd plenty, but they seemed to be coming back out of the woodwork, which made it a terrible time to buy, in my limited experience.

"What do you make of the damage to the green?"

He glanced at his spreadsheets, and then back at me. "Green?"

"The greenskeeper found damage on the first green this morning."

"That's news to me. What sort of damage?"

I told him about the GUR written on the green. He frowned.

"That's not good for the tournament." He looked at the spreadsheets again. "I think I really need to focus on this. We might need these contingencies after all."

I stood to let him get to work, but stopped by the door. "What would a contingency look like?"

He looked up from his screen. "It would look like the sale of the club so the membership doesn't lose everything they've invested."

I closed the door and walked back down the corridor. The contingency sounded like a poison pill, which itself didn't sound like a barrel of monkeys. I wandered back through the reception and into the dining room, where I found Danielle sitting with Natalie Morris, the catering manager. Danielle caught my eye and nodded me over. I took a seat beside her.

"Natalie was just telling me about the wedding," she said.

"What about the wedding?"

"I was just saying to Deputy Castle that the course was closed the last two weeks. We have to allow time for the PGA Tour people to organize the holes, in conjunction with our greenskeepers. For me it involves a lot of vendors. We've erected a small village of hospitality tents out on the executive course. I've got mobile cool rooms waiting for food and beverage deliveries today and tomorrow. Food trucks will arrive this afternoon. And in between we had to cater a wedding."

"That was unusual?" I asked.

"Not unusual to do a wedding. We do plenty. But to do it this week? It's been crazy. Like we didn't have enough to do."

"Why do it?" asked Danielle.

"I do what I'm told. That's my job."

"But why would the club do an added function during such an important week?"

"Wouldn't be my choice, but I assume money."

"You earn much from weddings?"

"We do okay. But this one more so, I guess. With all the tournament prep, we didn't have to pay for an extra tent. In fact we were stretched thin on our own equipment. We had to drag chairs out of the store. Some looked like they hadn't been out since the eighties."

"Is the club that short of money?" asked Danielle.

"I have no idea. I don't think so. You'd have to ask Barry Yarmouth about that. I know the food and beverage side makes a profit. But he just sees the bottom line. He hasn't been around to do the work. He probably thinks these events put themselves together."

"So tell me about the wedding. You mentioned catering. Was that for the reception?"

"Yes, we did that. Of course we never got to serve it, so most of it got tossed out. We'll take a hit on that."

"What else was there?"

"My main thing was the reception and the rehearsal dinner."

"The pre-wedding dinner?" I asked. "The night before?"

"Yes. That's why the health department are so focused on the kitchen. Food poisoning, right? Roughly twenty hours after they ate the people got sick. I know we're in their sights."
I didn't say anything about Connie Persil having cleared the kitchen of guilt, however halfheartedly. Danielle had clearly decided to keep that information to herself, so I followed her lead.
"Who set up the tables and chairs for that dinner?" Danielle asked.
"The tables and chairs? Our facilities guy, Ernesto."
"Where is he?"
"I don't know. I haven't seen him since yesterday."
"He was here? When the people fell sick?"
"No, earlier. Setting up the chairs for the ceremony. I think he left after that. The reception was going to happen here in the dining room."
"The chairs are still out there," I said. "Who's going to pack them up?"
"That would be Ernesto."
Danielle asked, "Can you contact him?"
"Sure." She held up her cell phone.
"Do that," said Danielle. "Ask him to come in."
Natalie made her call and Danielle and I walked outside. I updated Danielle on my conversations with Martin Costas and Barry Yarmouth. She was interested in the news about the groom's father, and the precarious position of the club's finances with regard to the tournament.
"So the timing is great, from a saboteur's point of view," said Danielle. "If you wanted to hurt the club, maybe end it, now would be the time."
"It would seem. Or it could be unrelated, if Martin Costas is right."

She looked at me. It always made my day, no matter how many times a day she did it. Even when she was looking at me like I was a complete idiot, which happened more often than I liked to admit.

The chairs still sat awaiting a wedding ceremony that was postponed indefinitely. I wondered why they hadn't been removed if they were the source of a virus. Were they no longer contagious?

Natalie Morris came out of the clubhouse, her phone in her hand.

"Ernesto's not answering," she said.

I raised an eyebrow at Danielle.

"I'll need his address," Danielle said.

"I'll have to get that from Barry."

"Please do."

"What does Ernesto drive?"

Natalie thought for moment. "A pickup, I think. An older Tacoma. Red, if I remember."

I thanked her and she marched away. I looked back to Danielle.

"You want to go visit Ernesto?"

"I do."

"You an investigator now?"

She shrugged. "The boss told me if I wanted I should check it out."

"That's good. He sees how you're wasted doing patrol work."

"He knows I'm doing this on my day off and he can save some budget by not sending anyone else out."

"Bet the union doesn't like that."

"That's why he said, if I wanted. It wasn't an order."

"He's clever, that sheriff. Since we're going out, maybe we should visit with the victims. You know where they were taken?"

"No. But Connie Persil does."

Danielle went to get the lowdown from Connie while I got Ernesto's address from Natalie. We met at the car. I had left the top down and the seats were like griddle pans. A convertible sounds like a splendid idea in South Florida, but the truth doesn't quite match the fairytale. The two indisputable realities of Florida weather are baking heat and driving rain. Neither makes a convertible the smart choice. We fried our backsides on the leather seats and headed out to the gate. I stopped by the security guy. He was a young black man, and he was wearing a uniform jacket that made him look like a UPS guy.

"You logging the cars that come in and out?"

"No," he said, sounding like he was from the islands. "No one asked me to do that."

"Fair enough. You see a pickup this morning?"

"A pickup?" He frowned like I must have been going crazy from the heat.

"Lot of fancy cars like yours. Don't recall a pickup."

"No? Early this morning? A red Toyota Tacoma."

The guy gave it some thought. I might have been asking too much. He wasn't being paid minimum wage to recall everything he saw. He was a deterrent insomuch as he had a uniform. I felt his pain. PI work was often boring. Being a security guard was terminally so.

"You know, maybe I did. Early."

"Is it still here?"

"No, man. He came early, he left early."

"You see the guy driving?"

"Latino guy, I think. Can't say much more than that."

"Thanks for the help."

"No problem."

I pulled out and headed east and then south.
"So Ernesto came and went," Danielle said.
"So it would seem."
"Wonder why he would do that."
"Let's go ask him."

CHAPTER NINE

Ernesto's address was a two-level apartment block out near the turnpike. The best that could be said about it was that it wasn't a trailer park. This was no comment on its condition, but rather the likelihood it would still be within the state of Florida after a decent hurricane. Otherwise it was my experience that trailer park residents took better care of their homes. The parking spaces in Ernesto's building were mostly taken by sun-bleached cars that hadn't moved in years. Some had flat tires all around, and others had no tires at all.

It wasn't the kind of place I felt good about parking a Porsche Boxster, and I was again reminded that being an investigator I had a tendency to end up in such places, so said vehicle was probably not the wisest choice. But it wasn't the first time I had made that mistake, and it probably wouldn't be the last.

We cruised down the row of apartments, their blinds closed against the sun. Danielle pointed out Ernesto's digs ahead and I pulled right up to his front door. There was no red Tacoma in the lot. I put the roof up, got out and locked the door. We stood under the shade of the walkway for the apartments above and Danielle knocked on the door while I watched the lot. There was no movement. It was a fine Sunday to be out.

And everyone in the apartment block was either out or in, but they weren't moving between the two.
It felt like we were being watched by a thousand eyes but that might have just been paranoia talking. Danielle knocked again. She knocked hard. Law enforcement folks know how to knock with authority. They probably take a class in it at the academy. But no one answered and we heard no movement inside. We wandered around the side of the building, to the rear of Ernesto's apartment. It was a tight fit between the building and the cinderblock wall, and there was nothing to see but a row of rolling garbage cans and an air-conditioning unit that was tucked into the window sash of his apartment. The AC unit was not turned on. We left Ernesto's pad and headed to where we knew we'd find some people.

The victims of the disastrous wedding ceremony had all been taken to the same hospital, and as it turned out, they had all been contained in two adjacent rooms. This was to minimize the potential for the virus to spread. A nurse in pink pajamas showed us to the rooms but warned us that the occupants might still be contagious. She gave us gloves and masks that covered our mouths and noses. She told us not to touch anything, and not to touch anyone. Then she warned us that the mood in the rooms was something short of festive.
How right she was. The father of the bride had succumbed en route to the hospital with his ailing daughter. Father and daughter were in side-by-side beds. The bride-to-be was watching golf of all things, a tournament in Texas. The sound was down but with golf coverage it's hard to notice the difference. The father of the bride was on an IV drip. The

nurse walked in with us and drew his eye, and his ire, immediately.

"How much longer do we have to stay in this damned place?" he spat.

"You and your daughter are suffering from dehydration, Mr. O'Neil."

"Suffering is exactly the word."

She gave that smile that nurses give, the one where there's minimal facial movement and you're never sure after if they didn't actually snarl at you. Then she checked Mr. O'Neil's drip line. He looked tired rather than sick, but I figure a bout of gastro and a night in a hospital would do that to anyone. I let Danielle start proceedings, since she had a better bedside manner and was a hell of a lot more attractive to a guy like O'Neil.

"Mr. O'Neil, I am Sheriff's Deputy Castle. This is Miami Jones. He has been retained by South Lakes to investigate yesterday's events."

"Tummy bug, that's all. The sooner we get the hell out of here the better."

"Sir, you are a member at the club, is that correct?"

"Of course."

"How long have you been a member?"

"Fifteen years, give or take. Why?"

"No reason. Why did you decide to hold the event at the club?"

"That's what clubs are for, isn't it? It's a fine-looking golf course. Why not?"

"Even though it was the week before the tournament?"

"All the more reason. Hell, the hospitality tents were already there. So were the chairs and tables. And I didn't become successful by throwing money away, you know."

I chimed in. "You're a restaurateur, aren't you, Mr. O'Neil?"
He nodded. There was a good dose of pride in that nod. I was glad I went with restaurateur, because the truth was he owned a bar. But that didn't sound quite as good. Not to anyone's ear. And the fact was he didn't own a bar—he owned lots of them. His premier chain of bars was imaginatively called O'Neil's, and was, unsurprisingly, a chain of Irish pubs. These were the kinds of pubs that you found in the malls at Palm Beach Gardens, with a container's worth of fake Irish memorabilia pinned to the walls. They served cold Guinness and pot pies and fish and chips. There was even one at Downtown Disney in Orlando. He had also more recently started an upscale chain of cigar clubs called Cigarro. He opened the first of the cigar places on the island in Palm Beach. The city of Palm Beach has a long-standing hatred of chain anything except high-end fashion stores. No McDonalds, no Burger King, no O'Neil's pub. So O'Neil put his first Cigarro on the island before it became a chain, and the city had been majorly peeved ever since. Especially since O'Neil didn't come from the island. He was the worst kind of interloper. Not from New York or Los Angeles or, God forbid, Georgia. No, he was from West Palm Beach, and that stung both ways.
"You didn't want the reception at one of your own establishments?" I asked.
He turned his face from his daughter, and I moved down the side of his bed. "Of course. That would have cost me nothing. The whole thing would have been a tax write-off. But Sherri-Ann wanted an outdoor wedding, and the other side were pushing that damn Breakers place."
"The Breakers? Nice place for a wedding," said Danielle before she could stop herself. O'Neil and I both looked her. Me with considered interest that this was the comment that had sprung

involuntarily from her trained lips, and O'Neil like she had just walked raccoon poop across his living room.

"Do you know what those thieves charge? It's outrageous. The other side just wanted it on the damn island, that's all. Wanted to rub it in our faces. But I'm the father of the bride, right? So I get a say."

"So you did it at the golf club," I said.

"The country club, yes."

"So what went down must have been a bit embarrassing."

His jaw clenched hard. "I'll deal with that cook when the time comes."

"You mean Chef Lex?"

O'Neil nodded and pushed his head back against his pillow like a petulant child signaling that he and Lex were not BFFs anymore.

"You might be interested to know that the health department says the contamination didn't come from the kitchen."

"Then how?"

"Somehow it got onto surfaces at the dinner."

He shot forward and spat though clenched teeth. "I knew it. That no good, son of a—" He stopped himself and looked at his daughter, who was engrossed in a birdie putt on the television. "I knew it," he repeated.

"Knew what?"

"He's behind it."

"Who?"

"The other side. Coligio."

I had to believe that there was a fair amount of bad karma hanging over the nuptials even before the ceremony, what with the bride's father referring to his new in-laws as the other side. I couldn't imagine it was all sweetness and light coming from the groom's father either. It was personal. It was the

Montagues and the Capulets all over again. And we know how that all turned out. The horrid events at the ceremony clearly weren't the beginning of the bad blood, but they hadn't united the families in grief either.

"What makes you think the groom's family is behind it?"

"Not the family. The father. Look, the kid's all right. I wouldn't let my princess marry a complete dirtbag. He's an okay kid. Got his father's face, but it's not his fault he got smashed by the ugly stick. And the wife, she's as quiet as a church mouse. But the father . . ." He clenched his jaw again. He was going to lock that thing up and be eating through a straw before the day was out if he kept going like that.

"What's wrong with the father?"

"You don't know Dom Coligio?"

I shook my head. "Not personally." It was true, I didn't know him. But I knew of him. And I knew the type. He was a property developer, that uniquely Floridian species of reptile.

"Well, you should be thankful. He's a snake in the grass. He'd sell his own mother for a nickel, then he'd swap out his mother for your mother and ship her off instead."

I nodded. "What has that got to do with the wedding?"

"He didn't want it at South Lakes. He's all down in the mouth about coming onto the mainland, like the United States isn't good enough for him. He was behind this, I can smell it."

I was there—I did smell it. And it didn't smell good. But I didn't see the link. "But Coligio got sick too."

"Did he? He's not here. Not in this hospital."

I looked at Danielle and she spoke. "He's not in the next room?"

O'Neil shook his head.

"But his wife," I said. "She definitely got sick. I saw that happen."

"Maybe she did. Maybe he doesn't care about that. Maybe she didn't follow orders. Maybe she ate the shrimp."
"The shrimp?"
"It's a figure of speech."
"You think he'd poison his own wife to make you look bad?"
"It's the runs, not the plague. We're all on fluids, not antibiotics for heaven's sakes. And there's more at stake than just making me look bad."
I raised my eyebrows and waited.
"The marriage. He wants to kill the marriage. He thinks my little girl ain't good enough for his fancy boy. I got news for him."
"That's drastic." It was, but I again thought of the houses of Montague and Capulet. Maybe a good dose of the runs wasn't so over the top, considering what the alternatives might be.
The nurse came back in and looked at O'Neil's chart, and we all stood in reverent silence as she did.
"Good news, Mr. O'Neil. You'll be good to go home this afternoon. The doctor will be in later."
"About time. What about my daughter?"
"I think another night," she said matter-of-factly. "Her symptoms were severe and she lost a lot of fluid. We want to make sure there's no kidney damage. And you may still be contagious, so stay at home for another day or two."
"Where's your wife, Mr. O'Neil?" asked Danielle. "Is she okay?"
"She's right there, next to Sherri-Ann."
I glanced past the bride-who-wasn't, at the woman next to her. They could have been sisters. I had figured her for a sick bridesmaid when I came into the room. There was a gaggle of them in there. But the mother of the bride was sleeping, blond

hair falling over a face that couldn't have seen more than twenty-five summers.

Danielle and I looked at each other and then at O'Neil. We said nothing. There were no words. We thanked O'Neil for his time, and wished him well. He said he'd be fine once he got out of this hellhole. It really didn't look like such a bad room to me. We considered chatting to the bride but she was fixated on the golf in a way that suggested catatonia, which might have been the result of medication, or just the natural effect of watching golf on television. Either way we left her to her business.

We stopped outside at the nurses' station and asked about the other room. The nurse told us that the mother of the groom was there, along with a selection of others from the groom's side of the wedding party. The groom's father and the groom himself had been discharged that morning. Both were still ill but not dehydrated, so they were put in quarantine in their own home. She told us we could only talk with the groom's mother briefly as she was still experiencing severe symptoms, which sounded like the kind of thing we wanted to avoid being a party to again, so we begged off. She directed us to a bathroom to discard our gloves and masks and wash our hands. We each took a fresh pair of gloves and a mask before we left. They felt like mandatory equipment where we were going.

CHAPTER TEN

The Coligios, aka family of the groom, lived in one of those estates on Palm Beach where you can drive by the gate but not see the house. The hedges were high and the driveway was long, and the intercom at the gate made it clear it didn't want visitors, but acquiesced when Danielle pulled her sheriff's deputy card.

We drove up and parked as the front door opened. A lean black man in a suit stood waiting for us. He didn't look like a Coligio. He looked like Uncle Ben. In a butler's uniform. It felt very old-school and cliché and wrong in a lot of ways I could explain and some I couldn't.

Danielle and I mounted the steps to the massive front door. The place looked like a Scottish castle, just less drafty. The man at the top of the stairs nodded. He wasn't wearing any kind of mask or gloves.

"Good afternoon, sir, madam. I am afraid that Mr. Coligio is currently incapacitated."

"Is he on the can?" I asked.

"Not literally, sir, no." The guy spoke like a schoolteacher and I wondered what the hell he was doing as a butler. Maybe it paid more than I thought.

"Then we can chat."

I made a show of snapping on my gloves. The box at the hospital I had pilfered them from was labeled non-latex gloves, which meant I had no idea what they were made of. Rubber didn't feel like the right word, but they snapped like rubber. I slipped the paper mask over my mouth and raised my eyebrows. The butler's face gave nothing away. He might have thought I was a wise fellow for taking precautions, or he might have thought me the greatest fool he'd seen outside of a circus tent. I had no idea. He gave nothing away. I made a mental note not to play poker with the guy.

He led us inside to a living room the size of a tennis court that looked out through French doors to a massive patio and a sparkling blue pool. There was no water view, but I would bet the Brooklyn Bridge that the view from upstairs was something to behold. The butler asked us to wait and then moved away, his footsteps making no sound on the Italian marble floor.

We stood looking out the window at the pool for a few minutes. I noted that the house was not open concept. This was not a design flaw. Open concept houses were for people who wanted to see the living area from the kitchen while they prepared dinner for guests, or mac and cheese for the kids. That suggested a lot of time spent in the kitchen. Folks who owned Palm Beach mansions had people to work in the kitchen, and they didn't care to look at them while they did it.

"Can I help you?"

We turned from the pool to find the groom himself standing in the room. He had also approached silently, and I wondered what kinds of shoes these people wore, and whether they might be useful in my line of work. The groom wore dark rings around his eyes, but otherwise he looked fit and vital. He wasn't as well dressed as he had been the day before, but he still looked smart in pressed chinos and a crisp polo.

"Nicholas Coligio?" asked Danielle, knowing full well who she was talking to.

"Yes. Look, I know this is about yesterday, but I'm not sure we're quite up for the third degree just yet."

"I understand," Danielle said in her comforting voice. It made me feel good, and I was feeling pretty decent to begin with. "Is your father home?"

"He's recuperating."

I was pretty keen to see this recuperating. The father of the bride had piqued my interest in the notion that Coligio senior had somehow escaped the bug that had swept through the wedding party.

"How are you?" asked Danielle.

"How do you think I am? My wedding ceremony was a disaster, and everyone in my family and in my fiancée's family is ill. I am supposed to be married and in Aruba right now."

I always wondered where Florida people went for vacations or things like honeymoons. Lots of people from other places come to Florida. Makes sense, with the weather and the beaches and the drinks with little umbrellas in them. But when you live in paradise, where do you go to get away? Danielle and I had recently been to Jamaica, and although I liked the people a lot, it didn't feel a lot different. The palm trees were the same, and the sun was the same and the water was the same. The accents and the smell of jerk chicken were different, but I could find those down in Lauderhill if I wanted them. Perhaps I needed to take up snow skiing or something.

"I'm sorry for that," she said. "We're just investigating the events. You know, to get to the bottom of it."

"That damned golf club was the bottom of it," growled a voice from a darkened hallway. Dom Coligio stepped gingerly into the light. He was as Mr. O'Neil had said, an older version of his son. They both had thick black hair and eyebrows to match. And they were both in good condition. I had no doubt the younger version could bench-press more, but the old guy looked like he could do plenty. He was dressed similarly, chinos pressed right down each leg, but his shirt was a short-sleeve button-up. Plain blue, not palm prints like my beauty.

"Mr. Coligio, how are you feeling?" Danielle was really laying on the voice thing. She sounded like Kathleen Turner, back when Kathleen Turner sounded like Kathleen Turner.

"I feel like I've taken a year's worth of dumps in a day." He had a classy house and he dressed classy, but you know what they say about taking the boy from the farm. The metaphor wasn't watertight, because he didn't sound like he was from a farm, unless there were still farms hidden somewhere in the Bronx. He ambled to the sofa, took a long look at it and turned away in favor of a wing-backed lounge chair that didn't look as comfortable but would be easier to get out of in an ablutionary emergency.

He sat heavily and I noted he didn't look so good. It made me revise Mr. O'Neil's theory. You can fake a yawn, but you really can't fake physical exhaustion. It shows in your skin. Coligio senior looked pale in the cheeks and dark in the eyes. Unlike his son, he had bags either side of his nose. The butler guy swept in with a tall glass of water, which Coligio gulped half down.

"Mr. Coligio, we are investigating yesterday's events," Danielle repeated.

"Good. Shut the damn place down. Bulldoze the whole lot, and build something useful, like some homes. Hell, build a

Home Depot. It'd be more use to the world than that dump of a place."

"You blame the club for what happened?"

"I blame the club, and I blame that knucklehead O'Neil for insisting we do it there."

"Dad," said Coligio the younger.

"I know, son, I know. I'm trying. But I should have put my foot down. This never would have happened if we had done things out here."

I felt like saying, because no one ever gets sick in Palm Beach. But then I thought of how many old people live there, and I decided to keep the comment to myself. Score one, Jones.

"You might be interested to know that the health department doesn't think the pathogen originated from the kitchen."

"Well, it sure as hell came from there somewhere."

"It may have been on surfaces touched by the wedding party. We're investigating the possibility that it was put there intentionally."

"Intentionally?" said young Coligio. "You mean someone wanted to ruin my wedding?"

"We have nothing to confirm that," said Danielle. "These are preliminary inquiries."

"Who did this?" said Coligio senior. "Someone at the club?"

"We don't know. Did you get along with the bride's family?"

Senior gave junior a glance and then looked back to Danielle. He didn't avoid eye contact when he spoke to someone. He was laser-focused.

"My son was the one getting married, not me."

"Am getting married, Dad."

"Right, that's what I said. Officer, look around."

"It's Deputy."

"Right. Look around. You can't tell me that we are the same class as that bartender. You just can't. And a father worries about such things. But my son is a grown man, and he makes his own choices. I don't have to play golf with O'Neil. Hell, he couldn't even afford the green fees out here."

"So you didn't want to see the ceremony happen yesterday?"

"In an ideal world . . . hold on, what are you suggesting? That I stopped it by making everyone sick?"

"I'm not suggesting anything, sir."

"Hell you're not. So let me tell you, missy. I know the sheriff. I paid a lot of money to see him elected. So you'll want to be damned careful about spreading that kind of crap—"

Coligio stopped midsentence and frowned.

"Sir, are you all right?" asked Danielle.

He nodded, but it wasn't convincing.

"Dad?" said junior.

Coligio senior let out a prayer to his savior and launched himself out of the chair. He chose his seat well, because the solid arms helped get him up and out quickly, and he dashed away stiff-legged, down the hall.

We all watched him go, and then the younger man turned to Danielle. "My dad had nothing to do with what happened. Look at him. He's as sick as anyone."

"I can assure you, there was no implication in my question," said Danielle.

"Except there was. You implied that someone intended to disrupt my wedding ceremony."

"That was just lucky timing," I said. "Or unlucky, as the case may be."

"Why?"

"The evidence suggests that the contamination took place at the rehearsal dinner. Everything happening the way it did, that was just bad luck. The virus might have incubated shorter, or it might have incubated longer. It was just unlucky it happened when it did." I was talking but I was also thinking. Perhaps what I said should have remained internal dialogue, because I knew next to nothing about the incubation period other than what Connie Persil had told us.

"But you think someone made it happen. You don't think it was an accident?"

"We don't know yet," said Danielle. "The health department is still working on the source, and how it might have gotten there. But there is a remote possibility it wasn't an accident. And your families didn't seem to get along so great..."

"Forget the families. Every set of in-laws has issues. No father thinks a guy is good enough for his daughter. I get that. But it's my job to prove Mr. O'Neil wrong. And he and Dad are both successful guys. They're used to getting what they want. So there was a little head butting. Just guy stuff. Neither of them would do such a thing. Remember, Mr. O'Neil's daughter, my soon-to-be-wife, and my mother are both still in the hospital. No, the families had nothing to do with this."

It was a fair argument, well made. The kid was smart and had the benefit of a good education behind him. There were a lot of dumb rich kids around, but he wasn't one of them. He was smarter than the average bear.

"You have an idea," I said.

He looked at me, maybe sizing me up, maybe trying to figure if I could be trusted. Maybe he was working up the courage to ask where I got my palm tree print shirts.

He said, "I'm not feeling so good myself."

"We'll get out of your hair." I stepped around the big sofa that looked out to the pool, and we walked to the atrium foyer. Then I stopped.

"You think someone did cause it. Don't you?"

"I just want to put it behind us."

It was a poor choice of words, but I let it slide.

"But can you? Tell me what you're thinking."

"There's no proof."

"There's never any proof, until there is. Right now everything's a theory. What's yours?"

"My dad is successful."

"I know. I've seen the billboards."

"You don't become big in real estate development without upsetting a few people."

"Who did he upset?"

"Have you heard of the Bonita Mar Club?"

"Sure."

"You know who owns it?"

"Sure. Nathaniel Donaldson."

"Right. Well, he's a rival of my dad's. And he's got a chip on his shoulder. About a lot of things, but mostly about some deal he tried to do years ago that my dad sealed before him. Some resort thing. He bought Bonita Mar to spite my dad. Dad was putting together a consortium to redevelop the old place, and Donaldson swept in and paid over the odds for it, just so Dad couldn't get it."

"Okay, so boys and their tantrums. It's a big stretch to your wedding."

"Not really. It's always been tit for tat. They're like college kids, playing million-dollar pranks. And spoiling my wedding, that would be a doozy."

I took it in and thanked him for the info, and wished him well in his recovery. The butler was nowhere to be seen, so the kid opened the door. I stopped on the breach.

"What will you do about your wedding ceremony?"

He shrugged. "Eloping in Vegas sounds like a good idea right now."

I nodded. It wasn't very classy but it would get the job done with a minimum of fuss. I thanked him again for his time and stepped down to the car. Danielle was already sitting in the sunshine. I stood for a moment looking over the grounds. They were palatial, but I kind of preferred my little rancher with a water view. That was my story and I was sticking to it. I smiled at Danielle.

"What now?" I asked.

"All that talk about viruses and such has made me hungry. Let's get some lunch."

You've got to love law enforcement types. Nothing puts them off their chow. I slipped into the Porsche and pulled down the long driveway, heading for the best fish sandwich in town.

CHAPTER ELEVEN

I ate my grouper sandwich under the palapa at the outdoor bar at Longboard Kelly's. The place was hopping, with Sunday sun streaming down onto the courtyard and the regulars enjoying a few jars of amber brew in the company of a Jimmy Buffett soundtrack. The stools at the bar were vacant when we arrived so I assumed word of my imminent arrival had preceded me and my favorite spot had been vacated accordingly. Danielle's theory was that most folks wanted to enjoy the sun in the courtyard, not the shade under the palapa. I countered that they were mostly sitting under beer-labeled umbrellas, not in the sun. Danielle's final comment on the subject was that they were regulars like me, and they had their own favorite seats. Then she gave me the look that said the matter was closed, so it was closed.

Either way Muriel stood behind the bar in her tank top, bursting at the seams around her chest. I often wondered if every garment Muriel owned was a size or two too small, but I never thought of a way to ask her where I didn't end up getting a slap in the kisser. Muriel poured me a beer and Danielle a vodka tonic, and we both ordered a late lunch. Talk of gastrointestinal issues had not dampened Danielle's desire for one of Mick's famous fish sandwiches. They were excellent as ever, and worthy of the fame that in truth they didn't have. Mick owned Longboard's, and he liked it low-key. Unusually for a bar owner he actively dissuaded patrons from leaving reviews on those websites that everyone seemed to use to find a bite to eat or somewhere to drink, and inevitably turned great local spots into tourist traps full of pale Yankees taking selfies with their grouper.

I polished off my sandwich and my beer before I realized Ron was not in situ. I asked Muriel if she had seen him, and she said she hadn't in three days, and was fearful for his well-being. I ordered a second beer and as Muriel poured it I called Ron.

"Where are you?" I asked when he answered.

"South Lakes."

"Still?"

"Yeah, where are you?"

"Guess."

"Longboard's," he said. "You're making me sad."

"What's happening?"

"Apparently the virus was tracked down to the chairs in the hospitality tent."

"Knew that."

"Well, the health department folks didn't find anything else anywhere, but they wanted to quarantine the hospitality tent. Keith called the mayor and the mayor called Tallahassee, and someone from the governor's office called the health department folks and asked if we took the chairs away and then decontaminated the tent could we all move on, and they seem to see the logic in listening to the governor's office."

"So it's all settled?"

"Some guys are in the tent steam cleaning it or something. And some new chairs are coming first thing tomorrow. What did you find out?"

I told him about the disappearance or at least lack of appearance of Ernesto the facilities guy, and our chats with the fathers of the bride and groom.

"I think for now Keith will be keen to focus on the tournament and leave the whole sorry thing behind. You should drop an invoice by tomorrow for your time today."

"As you wish. But I'm pretty sure the sheriff's office is going to want to follow up on Ernesto."

"The club's not paying for that."

"I'm happy to forget the invoice."

"No, these guys can afford it."

"Will we see you later? Muriel's worried about you."

"Tell her I'm being held hostage. With all that's gone on, it's going to be all hands on deck here this week."

I left Ron to his mixed metaphor and took my beer and saluted Danielle. She smiled.

"You get all that?"

"I did."

"You guys going to follow up on Ernesto?"

"Not unless someone files a missing persons. Remember this wasn't on the clock. I don't think the boss is going to approve anything tomorrow."

"You're not curious?" I asked.

"I'm a little curious. But I'm a little curious about a lot of things."

She raised an eyebrow and that sent my mind off on a whole other track that wouldn't get shown on television before 10 p.m. I was of a mind to finish my drink, go for a run on city beach, and then have a long, sweaty shower, preferably not alone. I didn't get my wish. Danielle's phone rang and she answered it and frowned. She mouthed the word Connie, and then she listened. Then she told Connie we were at Longboard Kelly's, and gave her the address, and said we'd be here.

She ended the call and said, "She wants to talk."

I said nothing. I saw my long shower running off the canvas of my mind like a washed-out watercolor. We waited twenty minutes and Connie Persil walked in from the rear parking lot into the courtyard. She wasn't in hazmat gear, for which I was thankful. I suspect she knew the power of a health department official walking through an establishment in full uniform. She saw us at the bar and came over.

I offered her a drink and she looked into the bar suspiciously. I wondered what her kitchen must look like. She glanced at Muriel, who offered a broad smile, and said she'd have a diet cola. It wouldn't surprise me if a virus couldn't live in that stuff.

"So what's your news?" asked Danielle as Connie took a sip through a straw.

"The lab completed their PCR assays."

I frowned. "The what now?"

"Their tests. Real-time reverse transcriptase-polymerase chain reaction assay. In essence it detects the RNA of the virus, which is sort of like the virus's DNA. It tells us what the sample is, the genogroup, et cetera."

I got the et cetera. The rest went over me like a fly ball to the outfield. "What does all that mean?"

"It means three things. One, the only positive environmental samples came from the banquet chairs. Literally on the backs of the chairs. We took environmental samples from all over the club, including food and water samples, and we took stool samples from every victim."

"I don't need the play-by-play, just the result."

"It means it didn't come from the kitchen, or the food. And all the people who were at the rehearsal dinner became ill, ranging from slight abdominal upset to full-blown nausea and diarrhea."

I recalled the vision of the bride stopping in the middle of the aisle at her wedding and exploding at the seams. I hated that Connie Persil made me recall that. I never wanted to see that image in my mind ever again.

"The only place we found the virus, other than the patients, was on the chairs."

"How did it get there?"

"That's point two. The assays give us an idea of viral load—that's how much virus is in a sample. The chair backs were covered in it. The seats and legs had none. The tables had none. The food and beverage had none."

She sipped her drink and looked at us over the straw. I figured she didn't usually get such a captive audience for her stories, because she was milking it for all it was worth.

"So how did it get there?"

"Let me put it this way. It wasn't an accident."

I looked at Danielle and she at me.

Danielle said, "Are you saying it was put there deliberately?"

"I am."

"How?"

"I don't really know. The viral load is like the chairs were dipped in a contaminated solution. But that isn't practical, given their location."

"Just to be clear," I said, "you're saying that someone put a highly contagious virus on the chairs that were to be used for a pre-wedding dinner."

"Yes."

DEEP ROUGH

"How long could the virus have been there?"

"Hours, days, weeks maybe. But we could expect to see some other cases if that were so. Other people would surely have come in contact. And we have good reason to believe that didn't happen."

"How do you know?"

"That's the third point. The genogroup of our samples are GII. That's not unexpected. It's the most common norovirus genogroup to affect humans. But it's the genotype, like the subset of the genogroup, that's interesting. It's new. The Centers for Disease Control has no known cases in the United States."

We sat for a while without much further discussion and then Danielle asked if she could call Connie with any questions. Connie said sure. She thanked us for the drink and left.

I didn't finish my drink. I had a bad feeling. Not norovirus. Miami virus. It's when I have a beer in front of me and don't have the stomach to drink it. I wouldn't tell Ron. It would make him cry. I still felt the need for a shower, but this was more of the high-pressure hose variety than my earlier version. I felt unclean, in a lot of ways.

"You think the sheriff will get involved now?"

Danielle looked at the lime in the bottom of her glass. "He won't be happy about it. But I think I've got a plan."

CHAPTER TWELVE

That night I dreamed I was lying naked in the desert, covered in ants. I had no idea what that meant, but the upshot was I didn't sleep well. I woke grumpy so I kept my mouth shut. Danielle made eggs on English muffins and I ate in silence. Then she got on the phone while I had my second shower in twelve hours. Neither of them were as fun as I hoped they'd be, but my mood was a touch better when I came out to find Danielle dressed in her green sheriff's uniform.

"Off to the office?" I asked, somewhat rhetorically.

"Nope." She smiled. Even with my grump on, getting a smile from a beautiful woman in uniform is like rainbows and unicorns to me.

"What did you do?"

"I told you I had a plan. The sponsors of the tournament have to pay for extra law enforcement at the event. So it doesn't hit the sheriff's budget. I told him what Connie had said, and I suggested that if I were on general patrol at the event this week I could take a look around as well. Kill both birds with one stone."

"You are clever, you know that."
"Of course I am. I got you didn't I?"
"Not your clearest thinking, but good for me."
She looked at my shorts. "Go put some big boy pants on. This is the PGA, you know."

When we arrived at the course the world had turned on its head. Miami Jones was wearing trousers and a polo, and looked like a PGA pro, or at least a caddy on his day off, and the club had transformed into a billboard. It was like one big branding exercise, and lime green and tangerine were the colors of choice. The name of the tournament sponsor, Aqueta, was everywhere, and wherever it wasn't, their logo was there in its stead. The logo looked something like the planet Saturn, if it had been run over by a dump truck. I had no clue what business they were in. It could have been financial services, or consulting, or health insurance. It sounded wet, that's all I knew.

We were in a Porsche, so we got directed to the lot where the nice cars get parked. From Thursday on the junkers wouldn't even get in the gate. There was a temporary lot at a college a mile away with free shuttle services for the vehicles that wouldn't show well on the television cut-aways. Danielle attracted a few looks, which I credited to the uniform. Denial is a river in Egypt, and I swim in it regularly.

The dining room was buzzing. Natalie Morris was directing traffic. I asked her if she knew where Keith was, and she didn't, but she used a little walkie-talkie on her hip to find out. She said to try the corporate area, which resulted in a frown from me and directions to the executive course from her.

The executive course had been co-opted for the duration and turned into a small village of hospitality tents and beer gardens. A fake putting green had been erected over one of the fairways by one of the hospitality providers. There was more branding for the sponsor, and signage for other companies that had obviously not ponied up quite as much dough.

We found Keith glad-handing some guys dressed just like him, golf trousers and polos. They were what my late friend and mentor Lenny Cox would have called Midwest types. They had sensible haircuts and sensible shoes and wore sunscreen. They drove nice yet sensible cars and worked in blue-chip companies that had been around since Tom Sawyer was a boy, all solid and true, and they earned excellent money and had the good sense to live in the Midwest, where six bedrooms and four thousand square feet cost you the equivalent of a one-bed junior suite in Los Angeles or New York.

Keith gave us the palm, telling us to wait back where we were, lest the uniform scare the visitors. He laughed at something that clearly didn't warrant it, and shook hands all around again, and then came over to us.

"Marvelous, isn't it?"

It looked like a high-end refugee camp, but I thought better of telling him so.

"Keith, we need to talk."

He smiled. "Walk with me."

Danielle and I dropped in on either side of him and I told him that someone had deliberately put the norovirus on the chairs at the rehearsal dinner. Our walk and talk stopped pretty quickly.

"Are you serious?"

"Very."

"What is the health department going to do?"

"Nothing. The outbreak has been contained."

"That's good."

"So now it's just potentially a criminal matter."

He jerked his head around to look at Danielle so fast I thought he was going to faint. "Not now. Not this week."

"Don't have a turkey, Keith. The sheriff isn't going to come in all guns blazing. Danielle knows how to handle this sensitively." She nodded. "Just some quiet questions. Your sponsors won't even know."

"They won't know?"

"They weren't here. They're not of interest."

Keith pondered this for a moment and then nodded. "All right," he said, as if Danielle required his permission and he was now giving it. Then he turned to me. "Can I have a private word?"

I shrugged and we stepped away toward a tent sponsored by a beer company, which was already looking pretty good to me. Keith put his hand on my shoulder and whispered like I was Paul Revere.

"You and Deputy Castle, you're, um, a thing. Is that right?"

"A thing?"

"Your living situation."

"Cohabitation out of wedlock, is that what you're asking?"

"Not the legal status, but you are an item."

An item. It was starting to sound like Mayberry.

"Yes, Keith. We are an item."

"That isn't going to be a problem for you, professionally, is it?"

I frowned. It hadn't so far. Since I'd known Danielle I'd shot one man dead and let another move on to the next world without offering any assistance whatsoever. Danielle had been shot because of my work, but had never been shot because of hers. But we were still an item. Which stopped me in my tracks. We weren't items, plural. An item. Just one.

"I have no professional involvement here, Keith. Remember? That finished yesterday."

"That was yesterday. This is today. And today the sheriff has people investigating something that could be very embarrassing for the club in a week where we can't afford such a thing. I want to rehire you. Your deputy will investigate and the sheriff will do what he thinks is right for the city. I want you to look after the club's interests. Look at the investigation from our perspective."

"I won't run interference for you, Keith. I don't care if it was you who put the virus on those chairs. Whoever it was will go down."

"No, goodness no. I'm not suggesting you pervert the course of justice. Let me make that absolutely clear. Nothing of the sort. I'm simply asking you to investigate in parallel. Keep me up to speed. Allow for damage control, should we need it. I want whomever did this apprehended even more than the sheriff does. I told you someone was trying to hurt this club. Now it's proven. All I'm saying is, let's find the culprit without fanfare."

"All right, Keith. I can do that. But you are warned. I won't mess with Danielle's investigation. Not one little bit. But we'll find out what's going on, and who did what. And we'll do it as quietly as we can."

"That's all I ask. And if the case weren't to be solved until next Monday, after the tournament, that wouldn't hurt at all."

I shook my head and slapped him on the back and walked back to Danielle.

She didn't speak. She didn't have to.

"He's just hired me back on."

"To mess with me?"

"No. I made it clear that wouldn't happen, and he was pretty keen to be clear he wasn't asking for that. He just wants an eye on things from the club's perspective, and I get to spend the week with you and get paid for it."

"Well, when you put it like that. What's first?"

"I have an itch to scratch. Let's chat with the greenskeeper."

CHAPTER THIRTEEN

We left the executive course and all its hospitality tents and signage, and crossed over to the championship course. We walked down the first fairway across pristine grass. The course was open and lush, dotted with gently swaying palm trees and large but inviting water hazards. Unlike the courses I recalled from my childhood in Connecticut, there wasn't a lot of rough either side of the fairway. The playing surface looked slightly shorter and a touch lighter than the rough, which still looked like the ball would sit up nice and high if players drove their tee shots wayward. The biggest danger I could see, from a playing perspective, was the water and the sand. There was plenty of it. Just like the rest of Florida.

We saw Diego the greenskeeper from the tee box and he was down on his hands and knees when we reached the green. I stood on the edge of the green and looked it over. Just the previous morning there had been large dead letters across the area. Now I couldn't tell there had ever been a problem. The green looked like it had been primed for months. It was short and deep green and it looked pretty fast. The hole was placed at the front of green, on the lower of two levels. Most of the damage had been done on the upper level, and it was there that Diego was down on the grass.

"Morning," I said.

Diego looked up and squinted, and then nodded. "Good morning."

"The green looks fantastic."

"Gracias."

"How did you do that so fast? It really looks brand-new."

He sat back on his haunches and stretched his back out. "We take it from another green. One not on the tournament course. Same process we use to replace the cup when we move it each day. We dig the grass out of the other green and transplant it."

"What are you doing down there?" asked Danielle.

"Brushing the grain." He looked around the green. "It might look good to your eye, but the television cameras are ultra-high-definition. If you have a good TV you can see the individual blades of grass on the fairways. It shows every little flaw. So we must transplant the grass so it matches the grain of this green, and then I brush it to make sure all the blades fall that same way. Makes for better putting, too."

I never knew grass was so technical. I didn't even mow mine. It was longer and fatter and thicker than anything on the South Lakes course, and I had a guy who came in every week to give it a haircut.

"What sort of grass is that?" I asked.

Diego stood, brushed his knees off and walked over to us. I suspected I had hit on his favorite topic. He waved his hands across the view, indicating the golf course as a whole.

"The fairways are Bermuda grass, overseeded with rye grass." He glanced at the green. "The greens are creeping bent grass."

"Easy to maintain?"

"No."

"Really?" asked Danielle. "It's just grass, isn't it?" It sounded like such a dullard of a question, and I was grateful she had asked it before I had. To his credit Diego didn't roll his eyes or anything. He just shook his head.

"No, it's not just grass. It's specific turf. Bred to do the job. Take Bermuda. It's grows beautifully, so much so it can take over native grasses. It's a battle to even keep it from taking over the greens."

"So why use different grass on the greens?"

He shrugged. "Bent grass doesn't tend to thatch, and it provides a smoother, more consistent surface. And of course because of Augusta."

"What about Augusta?" asked Danielle.

"It's where they hold the Masters tournament." I said. "Augusta, Georgia. It's kind of like the holy grail of golf tournaments."

"Yeah, I know the Masters," she said. "But what does that have to do with grass in South Florida?" She looked at me like I was going to answer that one too, but I was all out of Augusta knowledge.

Diego wasn't though. "It's the grass they use on the greens at Augusta. When this course was developed I guess they wanted to copy Augusta. Bermuda grass fairways and bent grass greens."

"Is that unusual?" I asked. "To have more than one grass?"

"No, not unusual. But there are better grasses now, at least for use in Florida. If I were doing it now, I would keep the fairways as they are but change the greens to a different Bermuda hybrid like TifEagle."

"So why not do it?"

He smiled. "Very expensive. And we would have to close the course for six months."

"Doesn't one of the board members grow grass for a living?"

"Dig Maddox?"

"Yeah. Surely he'd do the club a deal."

He shook his head. "Dig could do the fairways, sure. He's got acres of regular Bermuda. But not creeping bent or the hybrids. It doesn't have much use outside of golf courses, at least down here. It's better for up north, cooler temps. Makes those New England lawns look like England. At least that's the theory."

I knew the lawns of Yale University pretty well. My dad had worked there. They definitely liked that old-school English look. But I didn't care about the grass in New Haven, so I changed tack.

"Do you know what caused the dead grass on this green?"

He frowned like I'd just messed up my one-times tables. "A person?"

"I mean, what did they use?"

"Oh. Roundup."

"Weed killer?"

"Si."

"You sure?"

"Pretty sure. I can see the damage to the roots system, and the dead blades are so localized."

"So it kills grass, not just weeds?" Like I say, I have a guy. Gardening was not my area of expertise.

"Si. Unless your grass is Roundup-ready."

"Roundup-ready?"

"They have developed a creeping bent grass that is resistant to Roundup. So you just spray the greens and the weeds die but the grass does not."

"That's pretty handy."

"Si. But we don't have that."

"Why not?"

"Same reason. Would have to replace the greens. Expensive. Plus it's hard on the grass when it's cut this short."

"So whoever did the vandalism to your green could have gotten the weed killer at any garden store?"

"That's right."

"Do you use Roundup here at all?"

"No. Because we overseed, our grass is never completely dormant."

"What does that mean, overseed?"

"Bermuda grass goes dormant in the winter. In places further north it can look dead. Here it just goes a tan color. But in Florida we get most of our golfers in the winter. The snowbirds, you know?"

"Yeah, I know the snowbirds." Those hardy souls who bailed on winters in the Midwest and Northeast and even Canada, locked their houses up after Thanksgiving and headed south for the winter like migratory birds, and then turned around and went back when the snow thawed in March or April.

"But people don't like to play on brown grass," continued Diego. "They don't care if it is natural. They want green, even in winter. So we overseed with a rye grass perennial in the fall. It means we add rye grass seed to the fairways to make them look green when the Bermuda goes dormant."

"Who knew?" I said.

Diego shrugged.

"Where did you learn all this?" Danielle asked.

"Texas A&M. Best turf program in the world."

Based on the brief lesson he'd given us I couldn't argue with that. When it comes to growing stuff those Aggies really knew their wheat from their chaff.

"So we're saying that anyone could have damaged the green."

"Si," he said, looking back to where the letters GUR had been. "Except..."

"Except what?"

"It's nothing, I think."

"Nothing is nothing. You got an idea, I want to hear it. You know more about this stuff than anyone."

"The letters that were in the grass? They were uniform."

"Uniform? Meaning?"

"You know the Roundup you buy at the store? It has a little wand on it so you can spray the weeds."

I nodded. I had no idea. I'd never bought weed killer in my life.

"So it's small, and it sprays a small area. But the letters on the green were big, right?"

"They were."

"So it would take a lot of back and forth to cover that much area. And with a small wand, you would expect the edges of the letters to be inconsistent. Not straight."

"But they were?" I had seen it, but I was focused on what the letters meant rather than the art behind them.

"They were. Perfectly straight. Which suggests they were made with only one or two sweeps for each part of the letter."

"Which means?"

"They didn't use a household wand attachment. When we spray herbicides on course we use either a tank and sprayer attached to a maintenance vehicle, or an industrial wand with a tank that is carried on a man's back."

"So you're saying this was done with industrial equipment?"

"Si. Almost certainly."

"So that narrows the field some."

"Some, but not a lot. Every gardening company in South Florida would probably have one."

I nodded. There were a lot of gardeners in South Florida. With the warm weather and tropical rain, the foliage in Florida was only ever a month or two away from taking back the concrete jungles we had created. If we all spent the summer up with the snowbirds we might not be able to find the roads to get home in the fall.

Danielle said, "We'll let you get back to it. I'm sure you're busy."

"Yeah, I got the PGA Tour guys coming down. They like to point out the problems."

"Thanks for your help."

"De nada."

Diego nodded and wandered back onto the green and I smiled. He looked as Latino as Cheech Marin but had no accent at all, yet he liked to pepper his speech with Spanish phrases. Spanglish was practically our local dialect in South Florida.

It didn't feel like we were getting very far, but in my experience in order to catch fish you first had to cast your net wide, before you pulled it back in. So far we had a viral outbreak that was looking suspicious and green vandalism that definitely was. We had a president who saw saboteurs around every corner, a board member who thought it might have been a disagreement between in-laws, in-laws who blamed each other, a groom who suggested it was a business competitor, a cook with a temper and a facilities guy who had gone AWOL. And we hadn't even gotten back to the first tee.

We reached the tee and wandered up past the practice putting green where we ran into Natalie Morris, directing a burly guy with a dolly full of stacked chairs. She smiled and then frowned at me. I frowned back and I'm better at it.

"You need a pass," she said.

"A what?"

"An access pass." She held up a plastic card that was hanging around her neck from a lime-colored lanyard with the sponsor's name on it. Apparently I needed to be branded. "It'll get you anywhere on course you need to go. Otherwise you're going to get stopped a lot."

"Okay."

She told us to hold fast, and I wondered if she was a sailor. She ran inside and we waited. I looked up at the upper floor of the clubhouse where the bar was. I wasn't all that surprised to see Ron standing behind the window, waving like he was leaving on a cruise ship. Natalie dashed back out and draped a lanyard around my neck like I had won the Congressional Medal of Honor.

She smiled again. "There you go. All official."

"You need to slow down, it's only Monday."

"Keeps me trim." She doubled up on the smile. She really had the whole Florida thing down.

"So it does," I said.

I felt a nudge against my hip and glanced at Danielle.

"Doesn't the deputy need one of these?" I said, fumbling with the access pass.

Natalie shook her head. "Deputy Castle is wearing her access pass." She gave Danielle the smile and then turned and sped away, arms out and ready to point at something that needed doing. I looked Danielle up and down and had to agree that her sheriff's uniform would open most doors at a golf tournament.

"You done?" she said.

"Done what?"

"Flirting with the help."

"This is Florida. That's just being friendly."

"You're not as Florida as you think, Mr. Connecticut."

"You jealous?" I couldn't help but grin. That wasn't my first mistake, but it was a goodie.

Danielle leaned her weight onto one leg and put her hands on her hips so that her right hand rested on the holster clip of her sheriff's issue sidearm.

"When I'm jealous, you'll know."

I dropped the grin. It felt like the smart thing to do. But I was amused. I couldn't imagine why a beautiful, intelligent woman with a sidearm would ever feel jealous about a scruffy ballplayer like me. It should have been the other way around. But I had to concede that knowing which pasta sauce a woman preferred was not the same thing as knowing how she thought. The former was mere observation, the latter was as likely as counting to infinity.

I said, "Ron's upstairs. I think we need a word with him."

"Nice segue."

CHAPTER FOURTEEN

The view from the bar was a panorama of Bermuda grass green and Aqueta lime and tangerine. Ron stood by the window like a king surveying his kingdom. He was in his usual getup of chinos and a button-up shirt. His silver hair sparkled in the sunlight breaking through the UV barrier in the wall-to-ceiling windows. He was lined and tanned and wore the marks of where the skin cancers had been removed, but he had the smile of a raconteur. It was still morning but I was surprised he didn't have a beer in his hand.
"It's coming together," he said as we arrived.
"It's quite the production," I said.
"Isn't it? Like a traveling circus, only more money and fewer elephants."
Danielle said, "They still do elephants in the circus?"
Ron shrugged.
"I spoke with Barry, your treasurer, yesterday."
"Aha."
"He more or less suggested that the club was in financial trouble. Especially if the tournament had been canceled."

"The club bears a fair bit of the risk, that is true. But I wouldn't say there's any financial trouble. The club's financials are solid."

"But if you take all the risk, you must get a good payday out of it."

"You'd like to think so, wouldn't you?"

"So you don't?"

"Not really no."

"So who's making money here?" I asked. "Because there seems to be plenty of it."

"The players, mostly. A tournament purse needs to be well north of six or seven million dollars to attract a decent field."

"Not bad."

"Not at all, for a game they'd all pay to play."

"Is there any profit after that?"

"No. PGA Tour tournaments are essentially run as charity events. The naming sponsor covers most if not all of the purse, and the other sponsors cover the rest. The money made from tickets sales and merchandise goes to cover hosting costs, and anything left is donated to a nominated charity or charities."

"That seems pretty good," said Danielle.

"You'd think so, wouldn't you?"

We both looked at Ron. He didn't take his eyes off the view, but he clearly had more to say.

"The PGA Tour is a tax-exempt organization, like the NFL. Billions of dollars flow through them, but they don't pay taxes on most of it. And many of the tournaments themselves are run by charitable foundations."

"But you say charities get the bulk of the profits?"

"Depends on your definition of the word bulk, I suppose. We did a lot of charitable giving back when I was working in insurance. It's good karma, good PR. The charitable watchdogs suggest as a minimum that a charity or foundation should be using at least sixty-five percent of their revenues to directly impact the beneficiaries of their charity. With tightly run charities it can be as high as eighty or ninety percent. PGA Tour tournaments average around sixteen percent. Some are as low as three percent."

"How is that possible? How do they get away with that?"

"Well, like you say, there's a lot of money around the tour. Even sixteen percent of that money is a heck of a lot. Are you better off getting sixty-five percent of a little or sixteen percent of a whole lot?"

"Seems like the players come out the best," Danielle said.

"Sure, they probably do. But then again, without them there is no tour, there is no tournament, there is no charitable giving."

"So what does the club get from it?"

"We get exposure. People want to play here because it's a tour stop. The tournament also covers a lot of the costs of improving the course to championship standard. So the membership gets a better course as a result. The city and the county and the state all get economic benefit. Some tournaments claim big economic benefits that in reality probably just cannibalize the local economy. But here, we know people come from other states and countries for this tournament. Florida offers a whole package deal, not just a golf tournament."

"But wouldn't those people come anyway?"

"Some would. And that's what makes it hard to quantify."

"So why would Barry say the club is in financial peril?"

"Well, we cover a lot of the expenses up front—take the course improvements, for example. And if the event were canceled because of the club's inability to host, I'm sure the tour's agreement says they don't have to pay us a bean. That's not catastrophic. It costs money to run a country club regardless. But it might mean we don't get the tournament again, and that would almost certainly lead to an increase in membership dues and a loss of prestige for the club. Together those things might hit the finances. But it wouldn't necessarily mean the end of the club. Not unless the membership decided the opportunity cost was too great."

I saw Natalie Morris wander below, pointing for someone to do something. I looked up at Ron before I got looked at myself.

"What do you mean, opportunity cost?"

"Well, the structure of the club is such that we are also a not-for-profit."

"Tax-exempt?"

"Yes. Most private golf clubs are. The idea is that we shouldn't make a profit anyway. If we do, we are overcharging our members in fees. So it's the aim to recover costs. But we are also an equity club. This means that to become a member you must buy a share of the club. Your initiation fee is actually purchasing a share in the club. It's a fair bit of money, but not as much as some."

"How much is a fair bit?"

"About thirty thousand. But other clubs, like Bonita Mar on the island, have fees over a hundred thousand dollars, and then there's also annual membership dues."

Knowing the amount put the favor Keith had extended to Ron in waiving that fee into perspective. My impression of Keith went up a notch.

"Anyway," continued Ron, "If a member wants out they have to sell their share. For clubs like Bonita Mar it's not so hard. It's very exclusive, and there are some very rich people who want in. We're not cheap, but for a lot of professional people we are within reach. But there's a lot more competition. A lot of clubs at the same level. That's where the tournament helps a lot. It makes our membership a prestige item. So if a member needs to sell—let's say they move to California—they can. Plenty of non-members want what they have. But without the tournament, our offering just becomes one of many."

"So it's possible another club is trying to hurt you in order to grab that prestige?"

"That sounds pretty drastic to me."

"How does a bride with all exits open sound to you?"

He frowned at me the way my dad used to when he wasn't pleased with my word choices.

"But there is another consideration," he said. "If we did lose the tournament, and the prestige, and if potential members decided that other clubs were a better choice, then any members of ours who did want out might not be able to sell."

"The memberships could lose value?"

"Sure. It's like owning a stock in a company. Value is what someone else is prepared to pay."

"What would that mean?"

"Well, this is just theory. It's a lot of maybes. But if a majority of the members felt that their investment in the club was going to go bad, they might vote to dissolve the club."

"But then they'd never get their money back."

"Not necessarily. If the club was dissolved the assets would be sold."

It took me a minute, and I looked at Danielle when I got it. As usual she had arrived well before me.

"The land," I said. "They'd sell the land."

"Right. And prime land in Palm Beach County? That would be quite the windfall. What the members invested and then plenty."

"Would that be tax-free?" asked Danielle.

"No. That would be profit and the IRS would want their share. But even after tax it would be a nice chunk."

"So you're saying that someone outside the club might want to sabotage the event to steal the event, or someone inside the club might be doing it to engineer a sale of the club."

"That's about it."

"Why would anyone want to put up with all that?"

"It's part of the game of being rich. Keeping score."

"Count me out."

Danielle put her hand on my shoulder. "We already did. And that's why we love you."

I glanced at Ron and he winked.

I was tossing up suspects on both sides of that coin when we heard a female voice shrieking, He's here! The three of us wandered down the stairs from the bar into the lobby. The front door hung open despite the air-conditioning. A small crowd had gathered outside. They formed a penumbra around a guy who was climbing out of a black SUV. He looked like a golfer. He wore white trousers and a black polo, and a black cap with the logo for a European car manufacturer on it. I thought he must have been getting out of the back of the SUV because he wasn't old enough to drive, but his chest pushed at his polo in a way that suggested there was a good, strong body underneath. He was pale of skin and dark of hair, and offered the gathered group a winning smile. He waved his hand like he'd just holed a birdie putt, and the driver of the SUV pushed through the crowd and made a hole. The young guy shook hands and gave low fives as he walked in. He stepped up to where we stood. He was a few inches shorter than me, so a couple ticks under six. He shot me a wink as he passed and strode inside.

"Who was that?" said Danielle with a grin that suggested it might have been my turn to be jealous. But for better or worse I didn't do stuff like that. People were with other people for their own reasons, and being jealous of them or of attention they might get didn't change that fact. I might never understand why Danielle was with me. I was flawed like a sitcom character, but that was beside the point. She was with me, and that was her call. Don't get me wrong—I was beyond grateful to the relationship gods that they had made it so. I was lucky beyond words. But there wasn't a damn thing I could do to guarantee it stayed that way. So I shrugged.

Ron said, "That was Heath McAllen."

"Who?" asked Daniclle. "Is he a golfer?"

"Number one in the world."

"I thought golfers wore plus fours and paunches."

"Name another golfer," said Ron.

Danielle thought. "Arnold Palmer."

"Another?"

"Jack Nicklaus."

"Another."

"Was there a Greg somebody? And maybe a Bubba? Or was that baseball?"

Ron smiled. "Welcome to the new PGA Tour."

"I really do have to give this game another look."

And she was. She was looking back into the clubhouse at the empty space where the kid had been. So was everyone else. Except me. I was the only one looking out at the parking lot. So I was the only one who saw the truck pull out of the service road that led down behind the executive course. It moved across the back of the lot and stopped at the gate where the security guard stood with his clipboard.

It was an old red Toyota Tacoma pickup.

CHAPTER FIFTEEN

I jumped down the steps to the sidewalk and ran to my car, which was still parked in the fancy car spots. I didn't tell anyone where I was going, but it wasn't the first time I'd madly dashed away without a word, so I figured Danielle and Ron would work it out. I slipped into the Porsche and screamed out of the space without even putting my seatbelt on. That didn't last long. By the time I reached the gate the car was beeping at me like a nagging mother-in-law. I slipped the belt on with one hand and thought about the mother of the groom at the wedding. I really need to rid myself of visions of that wedding. I skidded to a stop and asked the security guy which way the pickup had gone. He pointed west in the direction of the turnpike, and I took off in pursuit.

I picked the Tacoma up pretty quickly. He wasn't exactly going at light speed. From behind the driver was short and darkhaired, and although I'd never met Ernesto the facilities guy, I bet that would fit his general description. The Tacoma's steering was loose and the pickup wobbled around the lane like a newborn deer.

We headed out toward the turnpike on Southern Boulevard. Ernesto's apartment was south from there, so I waited for the truck to move into the other lane to turn left onto the turnpike. But he didn't. He went straight under the turnpike and kept going west. We drove on, past miles of stuccoed fences hiding gated housing developments that seemed to never end. Eventually the truck pulled off the road and into a small light industrial development. He took a slot in the shadow of a palm, and I pulled in right next to him. He wasn't the most observant character because he didn't even bat an eyelid at me. I stepped fast around the front of the Porsche and met him at the grill of his truck.

"Ernesto," I said.

He glanced at me.

"Ernesto, I need a word."

Ernesto frowned.

"I'm no Ernesto, man."

"Really? We're going with that? You want to show me some ID?"

He stiffened. "Who are you, man?"

"Miami Jones."

"Huh?"

"ID?"

He reached for the pocket in his shirt. Then he ran for it. I had to roll my eyes. It was hot out in the sun, west of the turnpike. I really didn't feel like chasing him. But in the end it wasn't too much of a chore. He was short and thick and had the athleticism of a beer keg. I took five strides and grabbed him by the collar and spun him around into the grill of a parked Dodge Ram. He was sweating.

"What do you want, man?"

"A word, Ernesto. That's all."

"I tole you, man. I ain't no Ernesto."
"Really? What's your name?"
"Paulo."
"That's what you came up with?"
"I don't know no Ernesto."
"So show me your driver's license."
"I forgot it at home."
"That so."

He nodded. His eyes were dark and full of fear. He'd been caught, that was for sure, and he had obviously done something pretty bad. Maybe he thought he had killed one of the wedding party.

"No one's dead, Ernesto. Only sick. So you can make it better by just talking."

"I keep telling you, man. I ain't no Ernesto."

"Okay, Paulo. What were you doing at the golf course just now?"

He frowned. He couldn't come up with a story quick enough.

"The golf course," I repeated.

"Delivery."

"You sell golf balls?"

"Huh? No, man. CO_2. Gas, you know."

"CO_2? For what?"

"For the beer lines, the kegs. At the hospitality tents."

A wee little pang of doubt rang in my ear. Doubt about me, not him.

"Who do you deliver for?"

He didn't speak. He just pointed. I left my hand on his chest but I glanced over my shoulder. There was a sign on the building that told me it was the office of West Palm Beverage and CO_2 Supply. I looked back at Ernesto. Except it wasn't Ernesto.

"Paulo?" I said.

He nodded. "Si."

I straightened his shirt out and stepped back.

"Sorry. My mistake."

"Si."

I nodded and walked backward for a half dozen paces and then turned on my heel and slipped down in the Porsche. Paulo was still against the Dodge Ram, watching me. I gave him another nod and pulled out.

I felt like an idiot. It was only compounded when I saw another old red Toyota Tacoma pickup pull out of a side street and drive away in the opposite direction. The darned things were multiplying like bunnies. I decided since I was out this way, I might as well make some use of my time, so I pulled onto the turnpike.

I got off at Okeechobee Boulevard and pulled into an old strip mall. It was original Florida, faded paint and cracked asphalt in the parking lot. I parked right in front of Sally's Pawn and Check Cashing and walked in. There was a Latina girl behind the Perspex screen where the check cashing was done. She looked at me with hope, like I was going to give her something to do, but my face told her otherwise and she slumped back into her seat and kept on chewing her gum.

Sally was behind the glass counter at the back, taping up a packing box. It didn't seem to be going well. It was war and the packing tape was winning. He had about three feet out of the dispenser, and it was winding around itself like a python. One of his hands was stuck to the tape, the other on the box, and his reading glasses were slipping off the end of his nose.

"Need some help?"

He looked up. "Aach, damned internet."

"Internet?"

"Even the bums that buy in a pawn shop are too lazy to come into the store these days. It's all internet orders. Like I'm the damned UPS man."

I took the tape dispenser from him and ripped it with my teeth and then bit the box end off and rolled the tape into a ball.

"You need to get a kid to do that."

"I got a kid. How do you think I got a damned website?"

"Business slow, Sal?"

"Business is business. The top of the iceberg ain't where the business is."

Sal was into a lot things, and not all of them passed muster. I learned not to ask. I had met him back when I played ball and he watched, and we'd developed an odd but true friendship. He was kind of like the father I never should have had.

"What's news?" he asked, wiping a solitary strand of hair across his head.

"I hear the Jets are going to draft a high school quarterback."

"You'll get yours."

"So that should be an improvement."

"What comes around goes around, Patriot boy."

"I've just come from the golf."

"What golf?"

"South Lakes. The Aqueta tournament."

"The what?"

"Aqueta."

"What is that? Portugee?"

"I have no idea." I told him about the wedding ceremony and the vandalism of the green and the whole box and dice.

"Those rich guys, they got nothing better to do?"

I shrugged. "So someone within or something from outside."

"Narrows the field."

"Tell me about it. What do you know about the father of the groom?"

"Coligio? Yeah, he's a big deal. Property developer. Started in office blocks, built half of White Plains, New York, is what I heard. Then he got into resorts and such."

"His son thinks it might have been payback from a competitor."

"Wouldn't have happened in the old days. People had respect. But these days? Who knows."

"He mentioned a name. Donaldson."

Sally nodded to himself. "Yeah, I can see that."

"What do you know about Donaldson?"

"What do I know? What do you know? He's everywhere."

"Yeah, I know about the TV and magazines and the wives."

"The older he gets the younger they get. I should have such problems."

"Tell me about it."

He frowned, although he had so many wrinkles it was hard to tell. "The hell you talking about? You got the nicest filly I ever seen. Even if she is a cop. No one's perfect. Especially you."

"I know, Sal. It's just a turn of phrase."

"You sure you know? You never seem to be in no hurry to make it right."

"What are you talking about, Sal?"

"You the one talking about weddings."

"You think a wedding is what Danielle's waiting for? She's already done that. It didn't work out so good."

"I once peeled a mango that had a big nasty bruise on the inside."

"Are you going senile, old man?"

"But it didn't stop me buying mangos. The next one I had was the sweetest I ever ate."

"I don't know if you are Rudyard Kipling or Dr. Seuss."

"I'm senile enough to kick you to kingdom come."

"Settle down—I don't want to have to carry you to the hospital."

His shoulders slouched like he was tired. "I just worry about you, kid."

"I know."

"People need to know they count. Don't assume they know."

"Okay."

We stood in silence for moment.

"So, Donaldson."

"Yeah, right. Him and Coligio? Well, they're the same but opposite, you know? Donaldson's all big talk and self-promotion. He likes the limelight. With him it ain't how much he has, but how much you know he has. Coligio's different. Quiet money. Ruthless as a shark, don't get me wrong. But he's confident he could own you—he don't need to prove it."

"And payback?"

"Yeah, I remember something. Back in the day, when Donaldson was starting out. He got a good chunk of change from his daddy, so he didn't start from nothing, right? But I recall a deal. Was a big thing up in Rhode Island, I think. Big development. Word was that Donaldson did all the ground work. Might have done a few things outside the rulebook as such. Payola, threats, assaults, that sort of thing. Par for the course. But then he doesn't have enough cash for the deal. And his daddy's kind of saying I gave you ten million, now go make your way in the world, so someone hooks Donaldson up with Coligio. Coligio's got the cash. Long story short, Coligio screws Donaldson over. When contracts are exchanged Donaldson's name is nowhere. And he can't do a damned thing, because Coligio did nothing unlawful. He didn't take Donaldson's money—he just left him out of the deal."

"And Donaldson never forgot?"

"Those guys never forget stuff like that. It's keeping score, right? So I heard Donaldson went into a couple of deals over the years where he swept in at the last moment to steal the deal from under Coligio, only for the deal to go bad and for Donaldson to lose money."

"Salt in the wounds."

"You got it. So Donaldson's got plenty of beef with Coligio. But I gotta think the way it goes down is in a deal. It's not Donaldson's style, this wedding thing. Like I say, he wouldn't just want to get Coligio, he'd want everyone to know he got him. And he can't claim credit for giving folks the runs. There ain't no cred in that."

"What do you think about the inside sabotage thing? The land must be worth plenty."

"Sure. There's a goldmine there. And if you wanted to develop it, the key isn't just getting the members to want to sell, you'd want them to sell at any cost. You'd want to get as low a price as you could."

"But who?"

"How many holes at this place?"

"Twenty-seven."

"Right, so how do you really make property sell in Florida?"

I shrugged.

"Think, kid. You can't see the ocean out there. So what do you want to see?"

"There's already lakes."

"And?"

"A golf course."

"There you go."

"Golf resort property?"

"You got twenty-seven holes. Room for an eighteen-hole course and plenty left over for building luxury homes for the discerning buyer."

"Discerning meaning rich."

"Poor folks don't know art—they just know what they like."

"I don't know art," I said.

"Me neither."

"But that theory doesn't help tell me who. There's got to be something."

"Think. If you got a plan to buy up a golf course to put houses around it, what do you do to make sure you maximize your investment?"

"Don't let anyone else in?"

"Box them out, right. How?"

"You buy the properties around the course. But Sal, none of those properties are actually on the course. They're just near a golf club, and not a club that people who live in that area can afford to join."

"So they're cheap."

I nodded. It wasn't progress as such, but it was the building blocks of a working theory.

"Thanks, Sal. I don't know what I'd do without you."

"You'd buy a whiteboard and some markers."

Sal liked to make me believe that he was just a sounding board, but the reality was he was a fount of knowledge.

We chatted about sports for a while and then I made to leave.

"Sal, you want to see some golf? I'm sure I can get you a VIP ticket. Free beer."

"If I want to fall asleep with a beer in my hand, I'll take some Xanax."

"Fair enough. You take care, Sal."

"You too, kid. And Miami—remember what I said. Don't let the ground shift under your feet."

I left Sal and the check cashing girl and got in the Porsche. I had a lot on my mind. I didn't like that. I liked clarity. Back when I pitched in the minors, and even in my brief stint throwing batting practice in the majors, I always threw best when I had a clear mind. I took a deep breath, in through my nose and out through my mouth. It worked back then, and it sort of worked now. I resolved that I needed to work down my list and check things off. I resolved I needed to visit the island. I resolved that if I was going to the island, I might as well stop into the office on the way to check a few more things off my list.

CHAPTER SIXTEEN

The office for LCI, or Lenny Cox Investigations, was in a new building in the court precinct in West Palm. The court building itself stood tall over everything in the area, a testament to architectural design and the dark side of humanity. Our place was across the lot from the court, so we were surrounded by lawyers and bail bondsmen. Our building had a bank branch on the retail floor, one attorney, and a bunch of companies with names that seemed to change like the wind.

I strode up the stairs. I always take the stairs. I knew a lot of guys who stopped playing pro sports and went to seed. You go from intense physical activity every day—and the appetite to support it—to sitting behind a desk for hours on end, you tend to put on a few pounds. There was more than one guy had a heart attack in his forties. For me the key was movement. I didn't like gyms, and I hated working out. Weight rooms were my enemy when I played. Then I met a genius of a fitness instructor who showed me that all I really needed was my own bodyweight as resistance, and to keep moving. Walk when you can, he said. Every time you can. It worked, so I kept doing it.

And if the muffin top ever showed its ugly head, Danielle was there to drag my sorry carcass onto the beach for a run.

Our office manager, Lizzy, was sitting at her desk when I came in. She glanced up from her monitor, registered it was me, and kept on typing. She looked pale, but she wasn't ill. That was just Lizzy. Jet black hair, lips painted like a fire engine and the complexion of a ghost.

"You get your hair done?" I said.

She cocked an eyebrow at me.

"Looks good."

I stood there waiting for a response but didn't get one.

"So, when you're done there, you want to come in? I've got something needs doing." I nodded to myself and walked into the office I shared with Ron. There was only one desk, but Ron favored the sofa so it all worked out. I sat behind the desk and drummed my fingers on the top, waiting. Lizzy must have been writing a rebuttal to the Magna Carta because she took forever. I was sure there was something I could be doing, but I couldn't think what that was. So I waited.

Eventually Lizzy came in. She had a notepad and pen. She sat in the visitor's chair.

I said, "So you know South Lakes Country Club, where Ron's a member?"

"I do."

"We're doing a job for them."

"A paid job?"

"Yes, a paid job."

She nodded.

"So I need to find out about the properties around the club. Houses, offices, whatever. Who owns them, and have any changed hands lately."

"Okay."

I nodded. And waited. Then I said, "Well, that's all, I guess."
"Okay." Lizzy stood and stepped to the door.
"Lizzy?" I said. She turned and looked at me.
"Do you know the Bonita Mar Club?"
"Sure."
"What do you know?"
"I know all the members are going to hell."
"Why's that?"
"The pursuit of money is the root of evil."
"Okay. I need to get in there. Any ideas?"
"Getting into places you don't belong is your specialty, not mine."
I had nothing to say to that.
"What would Lenny have done?" I asked.
"He would have put on his tux."
It was true. Lenny always said there wasn't a place in Palm Beach you couldn't get into if you were wearing a tuxedo.
"During the day," I said.
Lizzy thought for a moment. "It's Nathaniel Donaldson's club, right?"
I nodded.
"Then Lenny would have offered him something too good to resist."
I nodded again.
Lizzy left me and returned to her desk in the outer office. I sat for a moment. She was right. I needed an in. And with a guy like Donaldson, it needed to be something that money couldn't buy.
I jumped up and walked out and told Lizzy I'd see her later. As I reached the door she spoke.
"It's nice to see you in adult clothing."
"You don't like palm trees?"

"Shorts are for school boys."

"Yet they make them in my size."

"I just like this look. It's grown-up."

I shrugged and walked out. Down the stairs and out onto the street and into the lot next door. Spring was in the air and there was a breeze coming in off the Intracoastal. Gulls flew overhead. Palm trees nodded like lazy bartenders. This was the Florida everyone was looking for. Clear skies and cooling breezes. Problem was half the people who came for it ended up trapped between the turnpike and I-95, where the sun baked hot and the breeze never blew. I got in my car and headed into the wind.

It took longer than anticipated. The Flagler Memorial Bridge was open, and a fleet of yachts was passing through, headed for the ocean. I watched them bobble by. I didn't sail. That was Ron's thing. I'd been out a few times, and it was fun all right. But for reasons I couldn't explain I hadn't gone back. I watched a nice-looking cruiser motor below, its tall mast more like a cross to bear without a sail on it. I noted the woman at the helm, and I thought I recognized her. She was short and fit and looked well at ease at the wheel. Then the yacht and woman disappeared under the bridge.

I drove over to Palm Beach and cut down South County Road. The island got thin before I got where I wanted to be. The Bonita Mar Club was an unassuming place, in the way that a lot of massive Palm Beach estates are unassuming because you can't see them from the road. It was a bland terracotta wall, with a coat of arms on it that told me the name of the club. I stopped at the large wrought iron gates. The good news was, I looked the part. As Lizzy had pointed out, I was wearing trousers, which probably helped. I was also in a Porsche. Both the car and I were faking it.

The guy at the gate gave me a good look. I wasn't sure if he had memorized the faces of all the members, but I doubted it. He stepped over to me.

"May I help you, sir?"

"I'm here to see Nathaniel."

I was trying to make it sound like we were old college roommates or something, despite the twenty-year age gap. But the guy wasn't buying.

"Sir?"

"Mr. Donaldson," I repeated.

"Yes, sir. I'm not sure Mr. Donaldson is in residence at this time."

"You're not sure? So your story is that the security people at his club have no idea whether or not he is here. Is that what you're going with?"

"Sir?"

"Get on the phone and tell him Miami Jones is here."

"Miami Jones?"

"Yeah. And tell him I can give him a blow-by-blow of the Coligio wedding fiasco." I waited for the guy to move. He didn't. He just looked at me like I was a trigonometry problem.

"Go on," I said. I hadn't realized before, but it's so much easier to act like an ass if you are sitting in a Porsche.

The security guy moved back and picked a radio handset off his hip and talked into it. He turned around so I couldn't see or hear. It took longer than was necessary. Then he turned back to me.

"Just pull in, sir. The valet will take your car."

He offered me a smile and I nodded and pulled into the estate. It wasn't as big as the Coligio residence, but the place had some history behind it. It had been built by a New York industrialist—which was a title that seemed to cover a lot of territory—who happened to be a buddy of Henry Flagler. Flagler was the brains and the money behind the railroad coming to South Florida. He basically paid for it to extend from St. Augustine down to Miami. As a complete coincidence, every chunk of land that got a train station along the route happened to be owned by Flagler and his industrialist chums. They all built palatial winter homes down the coast, no more so than in Palm Beach. It was true that without Flagler there would be no Palm Beach today. Or maybe it would just be that the beach would be accessible to regular people and not just billionaires. I couldn't say for sure.

The old house had fallen into disrepair when the children of the children of the guy who built it decided they preferred Cannes to Palm Beach, and eventually it was sold for a pretty penny to Nathaniel Donaldson. Never one to miss a trick, he took half the house as his own private residence and opened the other half as an exclusive clubhouse. The initiation fee was reputed to be in the hundreds of thousands of dollars—and members still had to pay if they wanted to stay the night.

I had been to the club once before, for a charity function for wounded members of the sheriff's office. I'd worn a tux that time. So I knew where the valet was, and I pulled up and got out and left the car running, and a young guy dressed like a bull fighter got in and swept the vehicle out of sight. I didn't get a valet ticket. It wasn't that kind of place. A man in a stunning pinstriped suit was waiting by the front entrance, and he extended his hand.

"Mr. Jones," he said, like I was a regular. I didn't even get treatment like that at Longboard Kelly's.

I shook his hand but said nothing.

The guy in the suit ushered me inside. The interior was like an Italian museum. There was a lot of marble and gilded gold, and statues of naked and half-naked ladies. It was grand and opulent, and way above my pay grade. Sally was right—clearly I didn't know art, because half the stuff looked like it had come from a garden supplies store. I looked for a statue of a little boy peeing into a fountain, but I couldn't see one. That didn't mean it wasn't there.

"Mr. Donaldson is currently engaged with a guest, but he has asked me to show you to his private drawing room." We walked down a corridor that was two stories high and arched at the top, like a nave. Then he cut to the right and opened a door. Inside was a room that looked like the Library of Congress. Every wall was floor to ceiling bookshelves, and every book was leather-bound. There wasn't a Tom Clancy to be seen. It was impressive. I liked it a lot. I don't read much, but if I had a room like this one I think that would change.

"May I get you a drink while you wait?"

I fancied a beer, but I went with a Pellegrino. The guy disappeared and left me alone. I sat in a heavy leather reading chair and crossed my legs, and then crossed them the other way, and then uncrossed them. I have big thighs. Crossed legs aren't my thing. The guy reappeared with the flourish of a magician. He swept in and a woman came in behind him carrying a tray. She placed it beside me. There was a small bottle of Italian mineral water and a glass, and a plate of sandwich rounds. She poured the water into the glass, offered me a smile and then retreated. The guy in the suit told me that Mr. Donaldson would be with me momentarily, and he disappeared, closing the door as he went. I thought a cloud of smoke would have been a better effect.

Rich people like to make regular people wait. It's a thing. I'm sure sometimes it is intentional and sometimes it's not, but it always happens. Perhaps that was why they brought sandwiches when you asked for a glass of water. You might be there a while. I hadn't eaten lunch so I nibbled on the sandwiches. I had no idea what I was eating. Bread, of course. But the rest was foreign to me. It might have been turkey, with some kind of chutney. It might have been pig's hoof for all I knew. But it was tasty. I polished off the plate and could have gone for more.

I was standing by the books, looking at what I was fairly certain was a first edition of Sense and Sensibility, when the door opened behind me. Nathaniel Donaldson walked in and closed the door behind him. There were some unusual things about him. He had gone gray as a young man, and his hair hadn't changed in thirty years. Same length, same cut. His skin was an unnatural tan color, somewhere between spray-on and beach bum. He was always a snappy dresser, and even at his beach house he was no different. His suit hung on him better than most people's skin. He moved toward me with a smile that made his eyes close, and extended his hand. I shook it and noted he wore a cologne that made me think of fig trees in Italy, and I wondered how it did that.

"Nate Donaldson," he said.

"Miami Jones."

"Please take a seat." He pointed me back to where my empty plate lay. He took a seat opposite and straightened his cuffs. Then the door opened again and the guy in the pinstripes appeared.

"Get Mr. Jones some more sandwiches, will you?"

"Yes, sir." The guy nodded and retreated, and I looked at Donaldson's cuff to see if he had a secret little call button in there. I saw no such thing.

"So, you used to play ball."

I had to admit, I was taken aback. When you play a professional sport, people know you. It's part of the game. But I played my career, except for twenty-nine days, in the minor leagues. It's a sort of in-between world, where you're famous, but not. People recognize you, but they're often not sure where from. And very few people remember your career after it's done. I wondered if part of the reason I had to wait was that Donaldson was checking up on me. He had a reputation for being that thorough.

"Not many people remember that," I said.

"I'll be honest with you, I don't." He smiled. His eyes closed again. "But a pal of mine knows you."

It was seven degrees of separation. "A pal?"

"BJ Baker. We play golf together."

"How is old BJ?"

"He's still as self-important as ever."

BJ Baker and I were not buddies. Ron and I had worked a case for him, a theft from his house. We found his item, and returned it to his home, but he wasn't the most gracious fellow. He was a former football player, and had a media career. He thought he was the cat's pajamas, and I was a litter box. I don't take kindly to attitudes like that, so I doubted anything BJ had told Donaldson was going to be good. But it seemed that old Nate had summed up BJ pretty well, all on his own.

"Give him my regards," I said.

"I surely will. Now I hear you were at the Coligio wedding?"

"That's right."

Donaldson smiled. "Tell me all about it."

"You want the sanitized version?"

"I want every gruesome detail."

"It's pretty grim."

He sat back in his chair. "Good."

So I told him. I promised I would, and I did. Another plate of sandwiches arrived as I was regaling my host, but the story took my appetite away. Donaldson didn't flinch. He just nodded and grinned, like he'd just won big at the track. When I finished I sipped some water and he steepled his fingers to his mouth.

"Thank you for sharing that," he said.

"Sure."

"You know the history there."

"I know enough."

He nodded. "And now, Mr. Jones. What is it you want?"

"I want?"

"Yes. You didn't come here just to make my day with that story. You want something."

"What makes you say that?"

"Everybody wants something. Anyone who says different is a liar. Are you a liar, Mr. Jones?"

"Not often."

He nodded as if he liked that answer.

"Okay, Mr. Donaldson. What I want is this. I'd like to know if you were behind what happened at the Coligio wedding."

He looked at me, his fingers still to his lips. Like he was summing me up, which I suspect he'd been doing the whole time.

"I like a man who is direct. People who beat around the bush waste my time." He watched me some more. "So I'll answer your question. And the answer is no. I didn't have anything to do with what happened."

Now it was my turn to look at him. I have a pretty good poker face. Not that I play a lot of poker. But I used to like to give batters the I know something you don't know face, just to unsettle them. It's pretty much the same as my poker. So I gave it to Donaldson. He didn't flinch. He'd been in enough boardrooms and done enough deals. He was okay with being checked out because he knew it was part of the process. And he knew he got what he wanted in the end.

Here's the thing, though. I believed him. I believed he had nothing to do with it. He might have been playing me like a buck-toothed man plays a banjo. He was that smooth. But he seemed so at ease. He looked like a man telling the truth. And it meshed with what Sally had told me. That when he took Coligio down, he'd want to do it in a way that left no doubt he was behind it.

I slapped my hands on my thighs. "Well, Nate, I've taken enough of your time. Thanks for the hospitality."

"Any time. Thanks for the story. It made my day."

We both stood and he walked me out.

"This is a beautiful property you have here," I said.

"Thank you, we love it."

"You said you played golf with BJ. Where do you play?"

"I have a course down in Boca. Do you play?"

"Not for a long time."

"You ever want a round, give my office a call."

"I appreciate it. You ever play South Lakes?"

"I only play on my courses. I don't deal in second-best."

"You don't rate the course there?"

"It's a fine plot of land."

We stepped outside and my car was waiting for me. I shook hands with Donaldson, and the valet opened my door and I got in.

Donaldson said, "Has Heath McAllen arrived for the tournament yet?"

I recalled the arrival of the player Ron had said was ranked number one in the world.

"This morning."

"We're old friends. Tell him he should come over for dinner."

"I'll be sure to pass it on."

He stood with his hands behind his back as I pulled away, around the circular driveway and back out through the gates. I headed off the island and toward a fine plot of land.

CHAPTER SEVENTEEN

I took Southern Boulevard back to the mainland, across Bingham Island. I was sitting at the lights at Federal Highway when I glanced to the side and noticed a low brick building with signage on it telling me it was the offices of Yarmouth Realty. Since I was in the area, I thought I'd drop in on old Barry. Perhaps he could tell me more about the financial situation facing the club, and help me figure out who might want to bring them down, if indeed anybody did.

I cut across the lanes of traffic and pulled into the empty lot. The place was in good condition. Fresh asphalt, recently painted lines marking the parking bays. I pushed the door open and found a young guy at the reception counter. He wore a headset and was talking into it. That told me everything I needed to know about him. As I waited I played with the leaflet stands that were on the counter. There was a sheet of current listings in West Palm. I pulled one out and looked at it and noted that although I could look back and see Palm Beach island from the sidewalk outside, none of the listings were there. Everything was on this side of the bridge. The Palm

Beaches are like that. I slipped the sheet back in the stand and looked at the guy. He tapped a button and took another call and offered his palm as an apology. I checked out the next leaflet stand. I wasn't in the market for a home. I had a perfectly good one that I'd gotten for a song during the last property downturn. Sal told me it had probably doubled in value, but I didn't care. I didn't want to sell. I didn't want to live anywhere else. But the sheet I looked at wasn't for local listings. It was for a beach community someplace called Puerto Escondido. It sounded Mexican. It had an artist's rendition of a resort apartment building, looking across a turquoise pool toward the ocean. I wasn't sure why, but in real estate pools are never blue, they're turquoise.

The guy behind the counter finished his call and looked at me like I had just beamed down from the Enterprise. "Help you?"

"Barry Yarmouth," I said. I didn't feel like doing chitchat with this kid.

"Is Mr. Yarmouth, expecting you?"

"Tell him Miami Jones is here."

"Is he expecting you?"

"Just tell him." I gave the kid my look, the one that suggests I'm about to throw a fastball at your head, and he pressed a button. I stepped away from the counter so I didn't lean over and slap some manners into the kid, and sat down. There was a coffee table with magazines. The glossy mags that cities like to commission and local businesses get strong-armed into advertising in. There was a copy of the Palm Beach Post. The headline was talking about the golf tournament. Evidently some people actually gave a damn about it. There was a glossy brochure for another development. Just what Florida needed. I picked it up to see what traffic snarl they were going to create, but the development wasn't in Florida. It was just outside of some place called Dededo. The brochure said it was a western Pacific paradise. I wasn't sure if that meant it was near Fiji or the Philippines. Or somewhere between the two. It was far away, I knew that, but the photos looked like Florida. I really couldn't see the point.

Yarmouth appeared from the depths of the office. He was in another Greg Norman polo and different Nike trousers. I wondered if the golf industry had stolen its uniform from the real estate industry. Barry waved me in and told the kid at the counter to hold his calls. We walked back, past empty desks by large windows. Barry saw me looking at the empty furniture.

"If you're at your desk, you're not selling real estate," he said, waving me into a large private office. Although it was his name on the building, his office was in the middle and had no window. It seemed oddly magnanimous.

"What about you?" I said as I sat.

"Only here for a moment—you're lucky to catch me." He sat, scratching at his arm. He had a small Band-Aid, half covered by his shirtsleeve. "Needles," he said. "Hate 'em."

I couldn't argue with that. I'd had my fair share of painkillers during my playing career, and I wasn't a fan either.

"You not out at the tournament?"

"Actually I'm off there soon. You?"

"I'll be there later. Just came from Bonita Mar."

He frowned. "Bonita Mar Club? Why?"

"Had lunch with Nate Donaldson." It was a bit mean of me, but I figured Barry would give his sore arm to lunch with a famous developer like Donaldson.

"Why?"

"Just shooting the breeze. We have mutual friends."

"You do?"

I nodded. "So Dededo. That's the next hot spot, is it?"

He leaned back in his chair. "That's not for you."

"Why not?"

"You strike me as more a Florida kind of guy. If you're looking to invest, I can get you in on a new community near PGA National. The first phase has just completed. State of the art. Solar power, eco-friendly, the whole nine yards."

"Maybe next week."

"Sure, next week would be better. But they are going fast."

Weren't they always.

"So how can I help you, Miami?"

"I wanted to run something by you. A colleague gave me the idea that someone might want to run the club into the ground in order to buy it for a low price. As treasurer, do you think that's possible?"

"How would they do that, exactly?"

"We'll let's say the tournament got canned, and the club lost that prestige. Your members own the club, right?"

"We're an equity-based country club, that's right."

"So if it all went to pot, they could vote to sell."

"Technically, I suppose. But Keith said we dealt with the health department. It's all good for the tournament."

"Sure, sure. But things happen."

"What things? What are you saying? Do you know of an issue with the tournament?"

"Don't give yourself a wedgie. I'm just spitballing here."

"All right. Okay. But I think the only thing that could stop the tournament now is the weather. And the forecast is good."

"Yeah, I'm talking more like an external thing. Like imagine if there was a bomb threat."

"I don't think that's funny."

"Me either. And I'm not saying it has happened. But now the players are arriving, the cameras are arriving. Now would be the time to try something."

"We have a terrorist threat protocol."

"You do?"

"Of course. Every big event has to have one now. That's why there's extra sheriff's deputies and private security."

"They didn't stop the first green from being damaged."

"No," he said. He looked disappointed, like he was responsible for it, as if it had happened on his watch. "Security is expensive. We had planned on beefing it up from today."

"So someone got their licks in early."

"So it would seem."

"Let me ask you a professional question. As a real estate agent. What's the land worth out there?"

"I don't know. As a tax-exempt club we don't pay property tax, so it doesn't get valued regularly. But I'd say plenty. Depends what someone wanted to do with it."

"Do you know who owns the property around the club?"

"Around it? No. Why?"

"Just wondered. It's mostly residential, right?"

"Yes. And there's an old power substation at the back, along the seventh hole."

"Florida Power and Light?"

"Yes. I'm not sure it's even operational anymore. But it's there, and it's kind of ugly. We planted some Australian pines out there a few years back to hide it. But listen, didn't I hear that the sheriff thinks the green damage was done by a guy at the club? The facilities guy?"

"Ernesto," I said. "He has fallen off the face of the earth."

"Not good timing to do that. With the tournament on. But if he's the guy, it sounds like this is really a disgruntled employee type thing, wouldn't you say?"

"Anything's possible."

"I'm just worried Keith's got everyone on a wild-goose chase."

"Like I say, anything's possible."

Barry stood and I looked up at him. "I think I need to get out there."

"Okay."

"I'm going to meet with the security people, just in case. Make sure we have everything covered."

"Probably a good idea."

"Thanks for stopping in. And do think about that investment opportunity. Perhaps I can give you a call next week to chat about it."

"Call my office. I'm in the book."

Truth was, I'm not in the book. I'm not even sure there was a book anymore. My cell phone isn't listed anywhere that I know of, and the office is listed under Lenny's name, not mine. When he left the business to me I never changed the name. It didn't feel right. It still doesn't.

I walked out with Barry. There was a cool breeze coming in and it was pleasant.

"McAllen arrived at the course a bit earlier," I said.

"He did? Great."

"You're lucky to have him. Number one player in the world. I bet he brings a lot more eyeballs to the event."

"You know, I think you're right. We are lucky."

I shook his hand and got in the Porsche and headed back to the club.

CHAPTER EIGHTEEN

I was lucky to get into the club when I got back. It was like the circus had arrived. There was a procession of vehicles, mostly black. Suburbans, Town Cars, a couple Priuses. The players were arriving. Most of them had caught the morning flights from Dallas-Fort Worth to Palm Beach International, found their hotel rooms or rental homes or whatever golfers stayed in, and now they were descending en masse at the tournament venue. I showed my access pass to a different security guy and he directed me away from the line of players' cars that were taking turns to dock at the front of the clubhouse. I didn't bother with the fancy car section. The tournament was starting to hit full swing, and fancy cars were the norm, so I parked at the back of the lot, away from the hospitality tents, and walked in.
Pro golfers don't travel light. They've got baggage. Figuratively and literally. There were hard-sided cases holding bags of clubs, and sports bags of other gear. There were wheelie suitcases and garment bags. And then there were the people. There were golfers, obviously. But what I didn't figure on was

how much golf was a team sport. There were caddies, and I thought it would end there, but it didn't. There were swing coaches and putting coaches; there were psychologists and visualists; there were managers and agents and wives and kids and a whole range of other hangers-on. I didn't know what half of these people did, but Ron stood with me near the entrance and gave me the rundown. Some players shared coaches, some shared psychologists, some shared agents. One New Zealand player had no one with him and carried his own bag. I thought he might have been a new guy, still making the minimum pay and doing it on a shoestring, but Ron assured me he had several top ten finishes to his name but just preferred it that way. I liked the cut of his jib. Doing it old-school. Ron said the guy would walk the course, take his yardages and then hire a caddy at each event. Ron suggested that could only go on for so long. The guy was sure to run out of steam and quit, or win a major and have a million people tugging at him. Whatever—I'd keep my eye on him.

It was a pretty white crowd. The players, the caddies, the support staff. Mostly white. A few Asian guys here and there, and one black guy. There was no Tiger. Other than color the notable similarity across the guys was how fit they looked. Maybe that was part of the attraction of golf as a spectator sport. The top guys were just as elite as athletes in other major sports like football, baseball or basketball. But unlike those sports, the fans who had left college, gotten jobs, risen up the corporate ladder and become decision makers with corporate expense accounts—and gained ten to a hundred pounds in the process—could still play golf. They could go out on their weekends and hit the same clubs on the same fairways as the pros. You couldn't say the same for the NFL—the torn hamstring quotient would be astronomical.

But the players hadn't gone to pasture. They were lean, and more muscular in the upper body than they looked on television. And they were tall. The average had be somewhere around six foot. Which isn't anything in baseball pitchers these days, or anyone outside of running backs in the NFL, but it's still up there. It didn't escape my attention that the world number one who had arrived hours earlier than everyone else was also one of the shorter guys.

I stayed with Ron until the players began to blur into one. My mind's eye took all the corporate logos that had walked past and mashed them into one logo, and it didn't surprise me that the logo I ended up with looked like the Aqueta logo. I don't know who came up with that garbage, but they were certainly overpaid, and I was willing to bet they attended golf tournaments. I left Ron to the procession of polos and sensible haircuts and wandered up the stairs to the bar. It was midafternoon, and glory be, the bar was open. I scanned the room. There weren't a lot of people there, but there were enough that I wouldn't be the only sad sack drinking. There looked to be a good number of expense accounts at work in the room, and a young guy I didn't know was working the bar. I wandered over to the window and looked out at the practice green. A bunch of the pros were standing around chatting. The shadows were growing longer on the fairway beyond. No one was playing. Today was what we called in baseball a travel day.

"You play?" I heard the question and looked down at a guy sitting alone at a table by the window. It was a typical icebreaker to use at a golf club, but he was anything but typical. For starters, he was older than the rest of the crowd. He had to be pushing eighty. And he was black. I glanced around the bar. He was the only black person in the room. He watched me silently.

"Not regularly," I said.

He nodded the way old guys do, full of confidence that they've seen more stuff go down in their lives than you've had chicken dinners.

"You don't look corporate," he said.

"No? What does corporate look like?"

He nudged his head toward the guys at the bar.

I nodded. The guy definitely knew a thing or two.

"You play?" I asked.

"Only a little, nowadays."

I stepped over to his table and offered my hand. "Miami Jones."

"Jackie Treloar."

"A pleasure, Jackie."

"Mine, I'm sure."

He had a warm smile and was wearing a yellow Pringle sweater.

"You a member here, Jackie?"

"Honorary."

I didn't know what that meant, but I suspected it meant he got the AARP rate.

"Can I buy you a drink, Jackie?"

"That'd be mighty kind of you. Arnold Palmer, thank you, son."

I nodded and went to the bar. The bartender was pouring four Yuenglings and four tequila shots. And it was a Monday. I waited and then ordered two Arnold Palmers. I'd lived in Florida for a long time, and Arnold Palmers were a popular drink around the Palm Beaches. But I had to admit I'd never had one. I'd seen them in cans before, but the guy behind the bar wasn't having any of that. He took the post mix gun and half-filled two pint glasses with ice and lemonade. Then he grabbed a pitcher of iced tea from the fridge and filled the glasses to the top.

"You don't use the cans?" I asked him.

It was like asking a New York bartender if they made cosmopolitans premixed. He frowned and shook his head. "Mr. Palmer would hate that."

"You've met Arnold Palmer?" I hoped it didn't sound like I didn't believe the guy, even though I didn't. But he grinned and nodded to the back of the bar, where I saw a framed photograph of the very bartender with Arnold Palmer himself. Arnold had even signed it. I gave my impressed face and handed the guy some cash. Then I carried the drinks back to the table by the window.

"Thank you, sir," Jackie said as he raised his glass to me.

It was lemonade yellow at the bottom and ice tea brown at the top, and Jackie didn't mix the two. As he tipped his glass the lemonade slipped up the edge from the bottom so that he got a mouthful of both beverages. Genius. I copied his trick, and found the drink to be refreshing, which is a fine quality in a beverage on a Florida afternoon.

"So you used to play more often?" I asked him.

"I used to do everything more often," he said with a smile.

"Ain't that the truth."

"You still a young man."

"Some days less than others."

"What did you play, before, rather than golf?"

"What makes you think I played anything?"

"Like I said, you ain't corporate. And you said you don't play golf regularly. But you got an athlete's body, that's for sure."

I made a note to tell Danielle that I had an athlete's body.

"I used to play baseball."

"Where?"

"All over. New England, California, here in Florida."
"Fine game, baseball."
"Yes, sir, it is. You ever play?"
"Only at school. Golf was my game."
"You any good?"
The old man smiled. "I did okay."
"You play any PGA tournaments?"
"I played a few. When I started the PGA wasn't so welcoming of colored players, you understand? I played mostly non-PGA events back then. I won the Negro National Open. That was a good field."
"I don't doubt it. When did you get your card?"
"PGA? 1964."
"You must have been one of the first black guys."
"One of them. Not the first. That was Charlie Sifford. He got his in '61. That boy could play."
"Still, it must have been hard to break though. Even after Jackie Robinson."
"Yeah, even after Jackie. My pa wanted me to follow Jackie into baseball, but I fell in love with this game." He looked out the window and across the course. Despite the lime and tangerine it was still a handsome course, manicured grass and the ubiquitous palm trees. The sand traps were as white as the finest beach, and the water hazards gleamed like a favored swimming hole.
"I grew up in Mississippi, did you know that?"
I shook my head.
"My uncle, my mother's brother, he caddied at the local club. He brought me along when I was no more than twelve, and I carried bags. There was a doctor who played regular, Doc Mooney. I wanted to go to college to study medicine because a him." Jackie chuckled at the thought. "I figured doctors got

lots a time off to play golf. And old Doc Mooney, he'd get onto the back nine and let me have a hit. Away from the clubhouse, you understand. Not many of the other members shared his open mind."

Jackie sipped his drink. His eyes were distant, a thousand miles and sixty years back in time. I said nothing. I wanted to hear what he had to say.

"You know it was Doc Mooney who paid for me to go to LA?"

"You went to Los Angeles?"

He nodded and a grin swept across his face. "I did. This was after I won the Negro National. And a couple other UGA tournaments."

"UGA?"

"United Golf Association. It was a tour for black players."

"Like the Negro baseball leagues."

"More or less. Did you know that the PGA had a clause in its by-laws that it was for players of the Caucasian race? That was in there. Up until the sixties."

He shook his head. So did I. I wasn't there. I didn't know what folks were thinking, or why they acted the way they acted. But I knew a little about human psychology. I had a master's in criminology that I studied in my final couple years of playing ball. I figured if I was going to join Lenny in his business, I should learn a little about it all. It wasn't the first time that a formal scrap of paper proved to be close to useless. Lenny taught me everything I needed, about investigating and a whole lot more. So I understood that the greatest fear folks have is the fear of the unknown. Things that go bump in the night. That which you cannot see or cannot comprehend. The movie wouldn't be half as scary if you got to see the shark right at the beginning. So I knew that folks feared the unknown, and that was a big reason for the stupidity that ensued. But I couldn't imagine a world where Jackie Robinson didn't get to play at the highest level, or Muhammad Ali or Michael Jordan or Tiger Woods. I think I understood the reasons why it happened, but I couldn't get my brain around the thinking behind them.

"So you went to LA?"

He smiled. It wasn't a Florida smile. It was something deeper, more satisfied. "After Charlie Sifford got his card, Doc Mooney said I had to try get mine. But my wife, she was scared, you understand?"

"Scared?"

"Charlie didn't walk onto the first tee to soft claps and whack his ball down the fairway. There was a lot of resistance, a lot of anger. He got abuse, he got threats. My wife didn't want me to get hurt. Truth be told, me neither. I don't think I could have done what Jackie Robinson did. I wasn't that brave."

"Me either."

He nodded. "But then Pete Brown won the Waco Open. He was the first Negro to win a PGA event. So it was that I got my card, I played a few tournaments, and later Doc Mooney gave me the money to go to California."

I said nothing.

"You ever been to LA?" he asked.

I nodded. I had been. I once played a game in a place called Rancho Cucamonga, in the San Bernardino valley, deep in the mass of humanity that was greater Los Angeles. What I remembered most was the smog. It sat like a brown blanket in the valley. They say the stars shine brighter in Hollywood. That wasn't my experience.

"It was something," Jackie said. "People—and cars—woo, gee. You never seen so many cars. Big old beauties the size of a navy destroyer."

"You played there?"

"Played? Yes, sir. I played." He grinned at me like there was more.

"What aren't you telling me? How did you do?"

"I won." He gave me a nod. It was both self-satisfied and humble. I gave him my impressed face.

"You won a PGA tournament?"

"1966 Los Angeles Open. Yes, sir."

"Wow, that's something."

"Yes, sir."

"A PGA tournament..."

"Yes, sir."

"Good field?"

"You wanna know who was runner-up?"

"Who?"

He held his drink up at me. It took me a second.

"Arnold Palmer?"

"Yes, sir."

"You beat Arnold Palmer?"

"Yes, sir." He beamed like a kid on Christmas morning. He was milking it now. Golf stories are like fishing stories. They get better with the telling. And I was okay with that. I had done some stuff in my life. I'd won a few things, here and there. And I was happy to give the old guy as much road as he wanted, and I was equally happy to go down that road as long he wanted.

"He was a gentleman among men, Mr. Palmer. I tell you that."

"Yeah?" It seemed that I was not only the sole person in the bar who had not tasted an Arnold Palmer, but also the only one not to have met the man.

"You win anything else?"

He shook his head. "No, sir." He wasn't disappointed. It was what it was. I knew that feeling, too. I'd won a few things. But I'd missed a fair few, too.

"I was already thirty when I won that one. My wife and I moved here to Florida, we had two baby girls and a good life. There wasn't the prize money back then like it is now, goodness no. But I paid Doc Mooney back for the money he gave me to go to LA. Every cent. And you know what he did? When he passed on, he left that money to my girls." He shook his head at the workings of humans. I often did the same thing. Fear didn't know color, and prejudice could flow either way. It all depended on who feared the most, and on the character of the person. This Doc Mooney sounded like a stand-up guy.

"I played a little on the Senior Tour later, but never won nothing. But I didn't care. I got paid money to play a game that I had to hide to play in the beginning. You understand?"

I understood. I would have bought my own uniform to play baseball. And although I never made it onto a card in a pack of gum, I had few regrets. I understood very well.

"Is your wife still, you know?" I wasn't sure how to phrase the question.

"She's at home, tending her raised flower beds. I can't drive no more. But the access bus brings me down here, and in the season I can still play the executive course. I'm not long off the tee, but I'm still straight."

"I'd love to play a round with you sometime. Nine holes sounds about my speed."

He looked at me for longer than was necessary, and then he said, "You know, I believe you might actually mean that."

"One hundred percent. I've never played a game of golf with a tournament champion before."

DEEP ROUGH

He looked out again across the lime and tangerine branding, at the championship course. "Perhaps when the circus leaves town," he said.

The bar started to fill and the shadows across the course grew longer. The bartender came out from behind his bar to tell Jackie that the access bus had arrived to pick him up. The guy ignored the protests from the polo shirts at the bar, who were clearly dying of thirst, even though it would probably cost him some tip money. I liked him even more for that. But I told him I'd help Jackie and he nodded his thanks. There wasn't an elevator in the building so Jackie used the railing and my arm to get down the stairs. We found a white minivan at the front door, and he used my arm to push up into his seat.

"Nice talking to you, Jackie."

"And you, Miami," he said. "Be good."

I would try.

CHAPTER NINETEEN

I met Ron back at the bar. He was buying a round and grabbed me a beer. We sat by the window. I was looking out at some guys putting on the practice green below in the failing light.

"You seen Danielle?" I asked.

"Once or twice. Doing the rounds. You learn anything interesting?"

I had spoken with Nathaniel Donaldson, one of the richest men in America. I'd chatted with the club treasurer. I'd shared a drink with the winner of the 1966 Los Angeles Open. I'd learned plenty.

"Not really," I said.

The corporate expense accounts started getting boisterous so Ron and I retreated downstairs. The dining room was full of golfers and caddies and their various other accoutrements. Ron wandered behind the bar there and grabbed two beers and we stood outside. A group of guys in white coveralls were chatting over beers. The course had fallen into darkness and all the bodies had retreated to the clubhouse.

"Who are all these people?" I asked.

Ron nodded. "It's a crowd, all right. Those guys there in the coveralls, they're caddies."

"They look like they work at the Jiffy Lube."

"They wear the coveralls to identify them on the course. And on TV."

"Should they be drinking before a big tournament?"

"They don't have to hit the shots, you know. But you'll find that most of them are on the ball by Wednesday night."

"So the tournament starts Thursday, correct? What do they do until then?"

"Monday is usually a travel day. For a major they'll get here early and maybe practice. But for a regular go-around like this, it's a down day. Some caddies will walk the course. They'll get a course briefing tomorrow morning from the PGA Tour superintendent. Get the yardages and so on. But they'll walk the course themselves anyway. Make notes on where things are. Traps, water. Distances to the greens. And then the players will play a practice round, some will spend time on the range hitting balls, some will putt. All depends on their demons."

"And then?"

"Wednesday is the pro-am. A bunch of corporate sponsors get to play with the pros. We invite some local amateurs, kids on the up, that sort of thing. The guys aren't compelled to play, but most do. It's another walk around the course, and it can also relax them a bit. Then there's the pre-tournament briefing and the dinner, and Thursday we kick off."

"Is the bar going to be that full every night?"

"Afraid so. Even with the hospitality starting up tomorrow, it will be cheek by jowl."

Some of the caddies were horsing around, shooting each other with a hose. It was like a frat party. In the distance of the seventeenth hole I heard the sound of splashing, like someone was getting tossed in the pool.

"You got a pool here?"

Ron shook his head.

I shrugged. I remembered the pressure of professional sports. At this level everyone was a good player. It was usually the mental side that made the difference. But the human mind can't be in the on position all the time. It needed a release. I figured the horseplay and whatever other shenanigans were going on were part of that release.

Then I thought I saw movement on the first fairway. A human body formed from the growing darkness. Then a second body. The first was easier to see because his trousers were white. It was Heath McAllen. He was carrying a short iron, maybe a pitching wedge. He had been the first to arrive, and now he was the last to come in off the course. I suspected that being number one in the world was no accident. He was talking to the other person. The other person was harder to make out. They were blending into the background. They almost reached the far edge of the practice putting green before I noted the curve of the hips and hefty belt and the sidearm.

Danielle smiled as she and the golfer kid approached. A jealous guy might wonder what they had been doing out there in the darkness. There were all kinds of golfing double entendres that fit the moment but not the mood.

"Hey, you," Danielle with a smile. "Haven't seen you all afternoon."

"Been out and about."

"You dashed off pretty quickly."

I thought back to my false positive with the guy who I thought was Ernesto, which sucked the wind out of me. It wasn't so much racial profiling as vehicular profiling, but either way I'd still gotten it wrong.

"I'll give you the rundown."

Danielle said, "Sorry, this is Heath McAllen. Heath, this is Ron Bennett and Miami Jones."

We shook hands. "It's nice to meet you lads," he said, and his accent reminded me that he was Scottish. Or was it Irish?

"How do you like the course?" asked Ron.

"Looks nice. Nasty-looking water out by seventeen."

"We call it the Pacific," said Ron. "You won't want to pull your tee shot on the third, either. The Pacific reaches between three and seventeen, and behind the green on fifteen."

The kid took out a little notepad and wrote that down. "Ta," he said.

"Can we get you a drink?" Ron asked.

"Sure, thanks. A squash."

Ron frowned.

"Lemon soda," said McAllen.

Ron nodded and retreated to the bar.

"You play here before?" I asked.

McAllen nodded. "Once, three years ago." He looked like three years ago he would have been in middle school.

He smiled. "I missed the cut."

Ron returned with a lemonade for McAllen and a club soda for Danielle. I was sure after being in the heat all day she would be keen for something harder, but that would have to wait. She had a thing about not drinking in uniform. She was like that. Me, I'd quit any job that required a uniform if that was the rule.

"You a local?" McAllen asked me.

"More or less. Originally from New England. Local now."

"I thought I heard a little bit of accent. You like it here?"

"I do. It's home."

McAllen nodded and sipped his drink.

"How about you?" I asked. "You got a home? I mean, you guys seem to travel a lot."

"We do that. But no, in the US I don't have a home. I have a place in Edinburgh, and one in London. But I was thinking about getting something in America. Maybe down here." He looked at Danielle. "What do you think, Danielle? Think you could find room for a Scotsman around here?"

"There are plenty of golf courses, that's for sure," she said.

Ron added, "I know a few players have homes around PGA National."

"I'd like to be near the beach."

"Try Jupiter," I said. "Plenty of beaches, plenty of private homes and compounds."

"Jupiter?" he said. "I'd live there just to be able to say I lived on Jupiter." He grinned again. He was an engaging guy. He didn't seem to carry the ego I would have associated with the world's number one player. Not to say he wasn't confident. He was certainly sure of himself. He was young, and he was fit and he wasn't a bad-looking kid. I remembered feeling like that. I don't know where it went. Or when.

I said, "Tiger's got a place there, so I understand."

"That so? I'll have to check it out. Listen, thanks for the drink. I gotta get back to the hotel. Put in a bit of gym time before bed. It was nice meeting you all. Hope we can chat again."

"We're here all week," I said. It didn't even sound funny to me, but the kid nodded and winked, like he had when he had walked by me on arrival earlier that day.

He strode away around the outside of the clubhouse. I figured he knew the inside would take ten times longer to pass through. Such was the burden of celebrity.

"Nice guy," said Danielle.

"He's not what you think he's going to be, is he?" said Ron.

"You guys wandering around in the dark together?" I asked Danielle.

She raised an eyebrow. "Jealous?"

"Only of the swing."

"He was walking the course. I don't even know what that means. But I found him wandering around the first green with a flashlight. I thought he might be some kind of trouble."

"A flashlight?"

"He said he likes to get a feel for the greens. He was actually down on his haunches, literally feeling the grass."

"That's dedicated," said Ron.

I had to agree. You didn't get into any pro sport without talent. But you didn't get to the top without a good old-fashioned work ethic.

I asked Danielle, "You done?"

"I most certainly am. How about a ride home? There's a bottle of sav blanc in the fridge."

"Done deal. Ron?"

"I'll walk out with you. Cassandra will be home, and I've got to be back early tomorrow."

"You get paid to be here?" I asked as we followed McAllen's lead and wandered around the side of the clubhouse.

"No," said Ron. "A lot of members volunteer their time. It doesn't matter. The club's paying you."

I shrugged. All questions of solvency aside, I hoped I would get paid. But first I hoped I'd figure out what exactly was going on.

We wandered around to the parking lot and I told Danielle I had parked at the back. She had been on her feet all day, and I felt bad about it. She didn't seem put out, but Ron said his car was in the one of the reserved spaces at the front and he'd drop us off. We wandered along the sidewalk at the front of the clubhouse to Ron's Camry.

It was an old beat-up model that he'd had for years, and despite living in Palm Beach he seemed to show no inclination to get rid of it. To her credit his lady, Cassandra, had never suggested that he get rid of it either. But right now it wasn't going anywhere. A big lump of a man in white coveralls was sitting on the hood, holding a can of beer. Two similarly dressed guys with beers were on the sidewalk near him. I noted they weren't Jiffy Lube coveralls at all. They had a lot more pockets. They were like full-body utility belts.

"Help you?" I said.

He looked at me through a heavy brow. "What?"

"You're sitting on my friend's car."

He looked down as if that news were a surprise to him. "This piece of crap."

I noted his accent. East end of London was my guess. I waited for him to call me guv'ner.

"Yes," I said. "That piece of crap. You might want to get off so you don't get dumped off when we leave."

"What if I don't want to?"

I was right. It was like a frat party.

"Your call. You can do it now, or you can do it at sixty-five on the freeway. No difference to me."

"You Yanks really think you're something." He slipped off Ron's car and stood before me. He was a big unit. And he sure as hell wasn't a golfer. He was an inch taller than me but a good six inches wider at the shoulders. And I have pitcher's shoulders.

"You got something to say to me, mate?"

I shook my head and Danielle stepped into his line of sight.

"Sir, perhaps you've had enough to drink."

The guy looked Danielle up and down. Then he did it a second time. That wasn't surprising. The first look was to confirm the uniform. The second look was to confirm who was wearing the uniform. It was the third look that annoyed me.

"You get the girls to fight your battles. Typical."

I said nothing. Ron moved to open his car and leave the loudmouth to his business, whatever that was. Drinking apparently. Which I had no conceptual issue with. I don't mind a drink. I don't mind if another guy has one. I don't even mind if he chooses to drink to excess. It's mean drunks that I can't stand. I could tell you some bitter story about my dad being an angry drunk, but that wouldn't be true. He certainly hit the bottle hard after my mother died, but he never hit anyone else. He never so much as raised his voice. He was a quiet drunk, the kind that keeps it to himself, and then gets in a car and drives and kills himself and the person he smashes into. He was that kind of a drunk.

But this guy was just plain unsociable. Danielle decided that discretion was the better part of valor, and stepped off the sidewalk and opened the door. The big Englishman stood looking at me. And I at him. I probably should have followed Danielle's lead. I should probably always follow Danielle's lead. But the guy took a step toward me. He faked a head butt that didn't get within a nine iron of me, so I didn't flinch. He didn't like that much. He turned his beer can upside down and poured the contents all over my shoes. Like I say, unsociable. Then he crushed the can, and threw it at my forehead. Then he stood there with a silly smirk on his face.

So I punched him in the throat.

I don't care how big you are. If you can't breathe, you're done. He doubled over and then dropped to his knees, gasping and making choking noises. I stood there long enough to confirm that he wasn't in fact choking, and when the wheezing breaths starting popping out of him I stepped over to Ron's car and got in the backseat.

Ron drove us to the rear of the lot and dropped us at my car, and then took off for the island. I opened up and slipped down into the driver's seat. Danielle got in next to me. She was quiet. I wondered if I had stepped over a line. Not my line. I was well and truly still within my boundaries. But Danielle was a deputy, and she believed in the process and the rule of law. She liked the fact that there were checks and balances, although she wasn't ignorant of the fact that no system was perfect. I didn't care about that guy. He'd get over it. His buddies would pick him up and dust him off and then they would all go grab another beer and rant about me, and about Americans in general, apparently. What I did care about was disappointing Danielle. I could live with most things, but that was hard to swallow.

So I felt sheepish and I sat for moment in the uncomfortable silence of the car. Then I took my licks and I looked at her.

And she winked at me.

I started the car and I pulled out and set sail for Singer Island, thinking to myself: Miami Jones, you really are the luckiest guy on the face of the whole damn planet.

CHAPTER TWENTY

"Trouble."
It's one hell of a way to wake up. Danielle had flopped on the bed and slapped my side and said that word. Trouble. You can take it to the bank that it wasn't a broken fingernail when it came from the mouth of a deputy. They have a different barometer from the rest of us. It yanked me from my slumber and for a moment I was dizzy. I was that deep under. I was having the sleep of the dead. Danielle's wink in the car the previous night didn't move more than an inch either side of smack center in my mind on the drive home, and I was in one feisty mood when I threw the front door open. But sometimes the heavens are in sync, and she laid a hard, wet kiss on me and the rest was the stuff of legend, but not the kind I'm going to tell. I raised my head from the pillow and saw her naked form bouncing toward the bathroom. I gave more than serious consideration to following her in, but then that word popped in my mind again.
Trouble.
There were several sheriff's vehicles in the lot when we got to the club. I don't know what it is about law enforcement types, but they do love to park haphazardly. Three cars took enough space for a half dozen trucks. I parked at the back of the lot

and we walked in. Danielle's hair was tied back and under a PBSO ball cap. It surprised me when I realized how rarely I saw the deputies wearing headwear in such a sun-drenched part of the world. We went in through the front door and out the back through the dining room and broke left across the seventeenth tee.

Trouble wasn't hard to find. The sheriff's crew had left a trail like army ants. And they had attracted a crowd. Players, caddies, one guy who had arms like a Swedish masseur. The crowd parted for Danielle's uniform and then she held up the yellow police tape and we moved in closer. Closer, but not close.

A ring of deputies stood hands on hips, facing the large water hazard that Ron had called the Pacific. Nearby someone had draped a nylon sheet on the grass, clearly to cover something. We joined the ring and looked at the water. It was flat and peaceful, like its namesake ocean. And like the ocean, that didn't tell the whole story. But I couldn't see what the story was. Nothing was happening. Eventually I got bored.

"So did someone find something, or what?" I asked.

I shrugged at Danielle and she shook her head. Another deputy looked past her at me. I recalled his name was Prosser.

"Greenskeeper saw a hand in the water when he was passing by at dawn. He called it in. We got here and pulled that out." He nodded toward the sheet on the ground.

"That doesn't look like a person," I said. "Not a full-size one, anyway."

"It's not. It's an arm. Shoulder down."

"Grim."

"You don't know the half of it. It's been pulled off like a chicken wing."

"Eew," I said. Danielle frowned at me. Perhaps eew was not a particularly macho response, but Prosser didn't seem to care one way or the other.

"What do you think happened?"

"Oh, I know what happened," he said. "Nearly scared the breakfast burrito out of me."

"What?"

He nodded back to the water. It was a decent expanse of blue-gray and looked from our vantage point across to the third fairway. There were reeds on our side. Not many. Enough to give the scene color. A ring of reddish-brown mulch was laid around the water line. It could have been a postcard. But I didn't see anything scary.

And then I did. You look hard enough you always do. They don't carry scuba flags to warn people. Low in the water, not even a ripple. Two holes—nostrils, and a long snout. And a set of unblinking reptilian eyes.

A gator.

The famous Florida alligator. It was not an unusual occurrence to find a gator in a lake in Florida. There were plenty of gators and even more small lakes. Every housing development plan started by digging a hole in the ground to fill with water and create a "lake" so they could sell water views. And sometimes gators happened into those lakes. Many bodies of fresh water in Florida had signs warning that there could be alligators down below. And it wasn't all that strange that someone got eaten. It happened. Not as regularly as lightning, but more often than presidential elections. Every summer or two some knucklehead would go swimming despite the signs, and they wouldn't come back. But what was odd was that this had happened on a golf course. People don't generally go for a dip in a golf course lake.

"You seen one of these before?" I asked Prosser.

He nodded. "Sure. Had one the year before last. College guy. There was video. His buddies put it on YouTube."

"That's sick."

"Got that right. Worst of it was, the guy is standing right next to the do not swim sign. He slaps the sign, a picture of a gator right there, and he yells screw you gators. Those are his last words. Screw you gators. Then he jumps in. Was like a frog in a blender." Prosser shook his head but broke into a smile. Law enforcement types have pretty warped senses of humor. It's a way to cope with what they see, day in, day out. I raised my eyebrows to Danielle and gave her the furrows.

"You had to ask," she whispered. It was true—I did have to.

"So what now?"

"First we gotta get that damn gator outta there. Then we'll get some divers in and see how many parts we can find."

"Who's going to get the gator out?"

Prosper smiled wide. "Not me, brother."

I decided with that to keep my trap shut, lest I volunteer myself for something.

We waited a half hour, and then a guy from animal control turned up. He looked prepared for a picnic, but far from ready to wrangle a gator. He carried a pole in one hand and a cooler in the other. That was it. I took more equipment on a butterfly hunt. He held a little powwow with Prosser and another deputy, and then stepped toward the water. Prosser came back over to us.

"He thinks it might be challenging."

"Challenging?" I said. "That's what he thinks?"

"He says the gator might be full. He might not take the bait."

"What happens if he doesn't take the bait?"

"They go in after him."

I'd never seen anyone try to catch an alligator before. I recall seeing that crazy crocodile hunter guy on television once, but he mounted them like a jockey. That didn't seem the appropriate tactic. And it wasn't. What I learned was, it is incredibly easy to catch a gator. It's incredibly dangerous too, don't get me wrong. But the animal control guy wandered up to the water's edge and put his cooler down and his pole down and stood for a moment, looking at the gator like he was surveying a fishing hole. Then he opened the cooler and removed a massive chunk of meat. It was like a pot roast for an army battalion. The meat had a thick rope tied around it, and the animal control guy straightened out the rope and coiled it on the ground, and then he wound up like he was tossing a horseshoe and swung the meat around and around and then flung it out into the water.

The gator wasn't in any hurry. But he was like a cat, and curiosity got the better of him. I knew the feeling. The big beast drifted toward the meat that was sinking into the lake. Even in movement the gator made barely a ripple. Then he got serious. He thrashed his tail and leaped forward and snapped down hard on the meat with an audible crunch. Everyone in the crowd winced at the sound, and most of us cast a glance at the sheet on the ground.

Next the animal control guy pulled the rope in. That was it. That was the secret. No hooks or barbs or traps. He pulled the gator to the bank, and with a lot more effort pulled it up onto land. At any point the gator could have just let go. Just opened his mouth and hasta la vista to the whole damned thing. But he didn't. Hundreds of millions of years of evolution gave me the impression that alligators were incredibly intelligent. The dinosaurs, the dodo, even the Tasmanian tiger were extinct, but the alligator remained. But it was all just PR. The fact was the alligator was just lucky. Dumb and lucky. The day the meteor hit and the dinosaurs went bye-bye? The gators must have been underwater that day.

The big reptile was stubborn as all hell. He got pulled out of the water, onto the deep rough that lined the lake by a rope he could have let go of, and he wasn't even hungry. He left an entire arm as evidence of that fact. And it didn't get better for him. The animal control guy dropped his rope and collected his pole and walked around the back of the beast, and, standing just out of reach of the gator's tail, he held the pole forward. It was then I noticed the wire loop on the end of the pole. The gator didn't see it. I don't even know if he was bothering to look. The animal control guy put the loop around the closed jaws of the gator and pulled the loop closed.

The gator couldn't open his mouth. I'd heard somewhere that their downward jaw pressure could break concrete but the muscles used to open their mouths couldn't lift a baby's rattle. Seemed it was so. The animal control guy casually walked up and sat on the gator, just behind its head, and pulled out some black electrical tape. He wound it round and round the snout. When he was done he got up and brushed his hands off, and then removed the pole. The meat was still inside the gator's mouth somewhere.

I was thoroughly disappointed. The gator is a sacred emblem in Florida. Tourists are terrified of them. The mascot versions of them are fearsome. But the reality was anything but, if you knew what you were doing. I made a note to call up every person I knew who had attended the University of Florida and tell them that their mascot was as dumb as a box of rocks.

The animal control guy wandered over. "Just gotta get my truck," he said, as easy as you like. "Can someone sit on him for me?"

I took a second to realize he was suggesting that someone sit on the beast just like he had. I don't care how dumb it was—I wasn't sitting on a gator for anyone. Then the guy looked at me.

"Thanks, pal."

I cocked my head like he was crazy, and then I glanced either side of me and noticed that everyone had moved five paces back, except me. Even Danielle. It must have been something they learned at the academy. I shook my head and damned my luck.

"Just sit tight. He shouldn't go anywhere. But I don't want him scooting back in the water and drowning."

All I heard were the words shouldn't and drowning. I walked a wide berth around the animal. Our eyes connected. It was just him and me. Mano-a-gator. He had to be well north of twelve feet long. I stepped forward slowly. I didn't want to spook him. Then I took a wide step like I was mounting a horse and I straddled the gator. I lowered myself down. It was like sitting on wet rocks. The gator gave a low guttural growl that I felt in my guts. I didn't look up at the gathered crowd. I didn't want them to see the fear in my eyes. And I didn't want to take my eyes off the gator's snout. The slightest hint that those teeth were coming at me and I was out of there. I rescinded my note to call up my University of Florida friends. I wasn't that mean-spirited.

The gator didn't move. I wanted to believe it was a noble beast that knew it was beat, but I was focused on not soiling myself. Then I heard a beep beep beep and saw the tailgate of the animal control guy's truck backing toward me. He got out and dropped the tailgate and then wandered past me. I glanced over my shoulder and watched him take a spray can and paint a long pink line along the animal's back. Then he stood back and took a photo of the gator, including the pink spray and yours truly. Once he was done he stood before me.

"You wanna ride him home?"

I shook my head and jumped off. The guy grabbed the gator at the back of the head and lifted him up.

"You wanna give me a hand here?"

I dropped in on the other side and we lifted the gator from his front legs. He was heavy. It took every bit of effort I had to lift my side. I had deadlifted over two-hundred fifty pounds when I played ball, and my half of the gator felt every bit that heavy. I wondered what he had eaten to make him so hefty, and I regretted the thought immediately.

We pulled him up and got the reptile's head up on the flatbed and then together we pushed him forward like he was a stack of lumber. The guy closed the tailgate and thanked me for the help.

"What's with the pink?" I asked.

"ID. Chain of custody."

"What happens now?"

"We'll need to check what he ate."

"How do you do that?" I asked.

The guy drew his finger across his throat. So it wasn't all beer and skittles for the gator. I hoped he enjoyed his last meal. Then I regretted that thought immediately as well. I really needed to stop thinking.

The animal control guy pulled the pickup forward and off the course, and I walked up onto the fairway and the crowd starting clapping. Not hollering and whooping or anything. This was a golf crowd. It was restrained but it was applause. And it was for me. And it made me feel like an ass.

CHAPTER TWENTY-ONE

A team from the medical examiner's office had arrived while I was mounted on the alligator, and they had waited back with the crowd until the beast had been driven from the course. Then they stepped under the police tape and started setting up. A couple of guys in coveralls erected a canvas tent around the sheet on the ground. A woman directed them and then did the same with a skinny guy in black tights. He looked like the roadie in a college play. The woman trudged over to Prosser and they had words, and then she stepped over to Danielle and me. She smiled from a face that had seen too much sun, not just lately but over the course of her lifetime. She was probably Danielle's age but looked like tanned leather.

"Danielle," she said.

"How are you, Lorraine?"

"I could still be shoveling snow in Chicago," she said. She nodded to me.

"Miami Jones," she said.

"Lorraine Catchitt," I replied. "Like you do with a baseball, not what happens in cat litter."

She smiled. "You got it. You remembered."

"It's a curse," I said. I had crossed paths with Lorraine Catchitt a few years previous, when a girl I knew from a case was murdered and left in an irrigation channel for the alligators to dispose of. The body had been found by a maintenance worker before it was found by the wildlife.

She said, "What is it with you and gators?"

I shrugged.

Catchitt had a morbid sense of humor, even more so than cops. I guess there was a scale to it. Cops saw things other than dead bodies—a forensic investigator with the ME's office rarely did.

"Prosser tells me you two have spoken to just about every person in this place over the past couple of days."

"Most everyone," said Danielle. "Between us."

"Good. If you don't mind I'll need you to try to ID the victim."

"All you've got is an arm?" I said.

"So we'll start with that. But the divers are about to go in. They'll find more. Gators like to take some of their meal and wedge it down at the bottom of the lake for later."

"This isn't a bass lake. I don't think there's a lot to wedge anything under."

"You'd be surprised."

"Can't you get fingerprints?"

"Maybe. Depends on the water damage. And there's dental, but that depends on the condition of the . . ." She looked at me. Last time we'd met at a crime scene, I had thrown up at what I'd seen. ". . . remains."

Danielle said, "Will the ME perform the necropsy?"

"No," said Catchitt. "We only do human autopsies. There's a facility we use for animal necropsies. A veterinarian does that."

The skinny guy in black appeared again. He was still in black, but this time it was the color of his wetsuit. He wore a tank and a mask, and he wandered down to the lake, turned on a flashlight and cast himself out into water.

"What if there's another gator?" I asked.

Catchitt shook her head. "If that big boy had a meal down there, he's not letting anyone else near it. Gators are territorial like that."

The diver disappeared and Catchitt suggested we take a look at what she had. The guys had erected a plastic tent over the lost arm and then started driving stakes into the ground to create a perimeter. It looked like they were going to cordon off the entire lake.

We wandered into the tent and Catchitt put a hand on the sheet. She looked at me again.

"You okay?"

"I don't think this is someone I know personally." It wasn't the body that had shocked me last time I'd seen Catchitt. It was the fact that I had known the body when it was a living, breathing person.

She pulled back the sheet like a magician. What lay on the grass was clearly an arm. It was fully intact. That's not to say it was in great shape. It was more gray than blue and the skin looked like cling wrap. But there were no bite marks or anything to suggest it was related to a gator attack. Except the fact it wasn't attached to a body. The arm extended all the way up to the shoulder. Then there was a ragged nub. I hated the imagery but Prosser was right. It was like a section from a giant chicken wing. The limb had been removed seemingly with care.

"You recognize anything?" Catchitt asked.

It was an arm. That was as far as it went. There were no tattoos, no obvious markings. I shook my head, and Danielle did likewise.

"Worth a shot," said Catchitt. "We'll see what the divers dig up."

"It looks like a clean break. Did a gator really do that?"

She looked hard at the shoulder and nodded. "Probably. They don't sever, not like a shark. They tear, they rip. They clamp down on something and shake and roll. It's probable that this guy bit down at the shoulder joint and ripped the arm clean off. He was probably focused on the biggest piece and that's why this bit floated away. He would have got to it eventually."

I shuddered. I left the tent and noted that a news crew had joined the fray. That's the trouble with a golf tournament—there's always a camera around. I turned my back and watched the ME guys wrapping their crime scene tape around the lake. I thought about Keith, and the tournament. That crime scene tape was going to put a crimp in the tournament preparations.

We waited for about fifteen minutes until the diver started swimming back toward the bank. He had something with him. He got to the water's edge, removed his mask and took stock of the gathered crowd, and then dragged his find around so that he could bring it directly into the tent out of the eye of most of the crowd, and particularly the cameras. Catchitt went into the tent and was in there about a minute. She stuck her head back out and waved us over.

I wasn't keen. But I went. I wasn't playing chicken if Danielle was okay with it. We ducked into the tent. The arm had been covered again. What lay next to it was a mess. It appeared to be another limb. But this one wasn't an arm. My excellent detective skills told me it was a leg. It didn't look like a leg. It looked like a Twizzler you might buy at the cinema snack bar. It was twisted and mauled. But it had a boot on the end of it. That was the giveaway. And it was clothed, sort of. The white fabric had been ripped and slashed, so it was hard to make out.

Catchitt used a gloved hand to turn the part over. It wasn't pretty. It didn't look human. But it was. There was something familiar about it. Not as a limb. I don't have a degree in anatomy. And this thing wasn't even recognizable as a body part.

"You see anything?" Catchitt asked. "You see this footwear before?"

Danielle shook her head. So did I.

Catchitt dropped the limb down and stood. "Oh, well. Worth a try."

I kept looking at it. Catchitt noticed me and went to say something but stopped herself. She knew what I was doing. She had probably done it herself a thousand times during an investigation. Trying to capture a memory that was floating on the air. There was something there, something in the twisted mess of flesh and white fabric.

Then the memory landed.

"The fabric. Right there—that's a pocket." I looked at Catchitt. "A utility pocket. It's coveralls. This belongs to a caddy."

CHAPTER TWENTY-TWO

We reconvened in the clubhouse. The crowd mostly dispersed when we put the word out that every caddy was to present themselves to the briefing room for a prepractice orientation. Caddies began wandering in from the locker rooms, and off the course. They congregated in the room where I had first met the board. The concertina wall was open and the entire space was filled with chairs.

Lorraine Catchitt remained at the crime scene and Danielle and I went to Keith Hamilton's office. It wasn't a big room, but it was private. Keith was waiting. We were joined by Ron, and then Martin Costas and Barry Yarmouth. Dig Maddox was the only board member absent. Another guy came in to make it nice and cozy. He was a lean guy who looked like he might have been a golfer once, although I didn't recognize him. When the door closed Keith spoke.

"Danielle, Miami, this is Kent Andrew. He is the tournament liaison for the PGA Tour."

We nodded and he did likewise.

He said, "You think it was a caddy?"

I shrugged. "It's not positive ID, but it looked like a caddy's coveralls. I don't see anyone else wearing them around here."

"We're getting them all together. We'll take a roll call, do a head count."

"Danielle," said Keith. "What does this mean? For the tournament. Do you have sense of how long the Pacific will be roped off?"

"I think you'll need to get that information from the investigators, Keith. This has gotten beyond my pay grade."

"Best guess?"

"If I had to say, I think the area will be off-limits until well into the weekend, maybe a week or more."

Keith's face flushed. "That's ludicrous. Today is practice."

"I don't know, Keith," she said. She was using her preschool teacher voice, but it wasn't helping. "There might not be any practice. They'll need to sweep the entire lake, and they may want to keep the adjacent areas like the fairway and greens clear. It might have been an accident, but until it's shown one way or the other, they'll consider it a possible crime scene. Plus I don't think the ME's team will want to be in the firing line for errant golf balls."

Keith looked primed for an aneurysm. He looked around at all of us, unable to focus on anyone. "You see, I told you. Someone has it in for us."

Martin Costas spoke. He seemed calmer than the rest. "Kent, what is the tour's position?"

Kent shrugged. "The tour has no position. I've never seen anything like this. A tournament course as a crime scene?" He shook his head. "We need to get a better grip on how long the police need, and whether we are missing a caddy."

"But the show must go on, right?" said Keith.

"I can't say, Keith. I'll need to confer with my people. With the sponsors and broadcasters. I'm not sure how keen they will be to go on. Association with a death like this? It's not the kind of branding the sponsor wants." Kent took in the room and breathed deep. He seemed to be pretty cool in a crisis. "Let's all talk to the folks we need to talk to. I'll postpone practice for this morning. It's not the end of the world. We get rained out of practice now and then. The guys can still use the driving range. That's nowhere near the crime scene. Let's convene at noon and see where we stand. Maybe we can get a practice round in this afternoon. Or tomorrow morning. Before the pro-am."

Keith nodded but said nothing.

"What about the dead guy?" asked Barry.

I don't know why, but everyone looked at me.

"Let's find out if we're missing a caddy."

We were missing a caddy. And that wasn't great news for the tournament, or the club. Or me. As luck would have it the missing caddy was the knucklehead Englishman I had punched the previous night. I would have to fess up to that because Danielle was with me, so I couldn't forget the whole thing or delay telling anyone. That would reflect badly on her.

There were also witnesses. The two other caddies. But oddly they didn't mention our altercation. They said they had enjoyed a few beverages with their colleague and then stumbled out into taxis. They had gotten separate cabs as they were staying in different locations, so they couldn't say whether he had actually left the course. They couldn't actually say for sure whether he had indeed left to get a cab with them, or whether they had left him at the bar. What they could say was whose bag the big guy carried. It turned out he was Heath McAllen's caddy.

As we were leaving the briefing room a guy in a natty suit turned up. He looked like an FBI agent. He was square-jawed and broad-shouldered, and he had a shave that was so close it looked like it had been performed by laser. He introduced himself to Danielle.

"Pete Nixon," he said. "Florida Department of Law Enforcement." He flashed a badge that could have belonged to the sanitation department for all I knew.

Danielle introduced herself.

Nixon said he knew of her. "You did some work with Special-Agent-in-Charge Marcard, of the FBI. He speaks highly of you."

"Thanks. This is Miami Jones."

He shook my hand. He had a good grip. "Nixon," he said.

"Like the president."

"You got it. Only I get subpoenas for my wiretaps."

I nodded. He'd probably heard that line a thousand times, so his answer was well-practiced and rolled off the tongue. But he delivered it like it was the first time, and he was easy with it. He went up a notch in my book. Cops in suits don't start very high up the pole with me. Especially nice suits. But this guy started well.

"What's the FDLE doing on this?" Danielle asked.

"As of now, we're not. This is a county matter. I'm not here to step on toes." Stepping on toes was a big thing with law enforcement. There were city police, and county sheriffs and state investigations, and then the FBI. They were all either very careful not to ruffle each other's feathers, or they did so on purpose. There never seemed to be any middle ground.

"The governor's office got wind of the situation and called the commissioner. So here I am. You know how it goes."
"Why is the governor into this?" I asked.
"A gator attack? On a golf course? During the practice for an internationally televised tournament? I'd be asking what took so long."
"Where are you out of?" asked Danielle.
"Miami field office. I know what you're thinking. How'd I get here so fast. The answer? I was already here."
"Already here?"
"Like I say, this is a high-profile event. We're at all such events. It's a target, right? For terrorists, for whomever. The politicians up in Tallahassee are touchy about any negative press. A blip on the PR radar can cost millions in lost tourist revenue. So we're in the background. In case we're needed."
"Are you needed?" I asked.
"You tell me. What's going on?"
"Let's walk," said Danielle. She shared the short version of what had been happening since we arrived, starting with the wedding and the green damage and ending with the body in the lake.
"So can you add anything?" she asked as we got to the dining room.
"Maybe. Like I say, we're in the background on this one. Let me tell you what I know." He looked at me. "This is delicate."
I got the impression he didn't completely trust me, which didn't hurt as much as it might have.
"I need to tell Catchitt about last night. The caddy," I said to Danielle. I nodded to Nixon and left them to it. I wasn't that concerned about being left out. I was fairly confident Danielle would pass on anything she thought I needed to know.

I wandered back out to the lake. The yellow crime scene tape glistened in the sun like a billboard for everything bad that could happen to a tourist in Florida. It was my feeling that the tournament was going to get canned. It didn't feel like an accident. People did get drunk and go swimming in dumb places, but with all the other strange goings-on at the club, I couldn't even sell that idea to myself. So the sheriff's investigators would want to keep the scene as pure as they could. And the governor would have kittens if he saw shining police tape on the television coverage of the third hole.

Catchitt was taking off gloves as I reached the tape and she waved me under.

"Anything?" I asked.

"Nothing significant. We'll probably get a better idea after the necropsy."

"I feel bad for the gator."

"Let's hope he makes someone a nice pair of boots."

There was that gallows humor again. I didn't laugh and I didn't smile and she didn't seem to care either way. I told her about my altercation with the big caddy the previous night. She listened to the details but took no notes.

"I'll pass it on to the sheriff's investigations team. If they want to talk to you about it, they know how to find you."

A guy stuck his head out of the tent and called Catchitt over. She nodded for me to come. I wasn't keen but I followed. A second guy was standing by the remains of the leg I had seen before. It had been lifted onto a table that looked like a gurney but was stainless steel on top. He had the pocket of the coveralls open with pincers, and had removed something with long tweezers.

"What have we got?" asked Catchitt.

The guy looked at the item through his glasses and I wondered if poor eyesight hampered his work at all. He looked to be holding some kind of paper, but it was wet through and sagged from where he held it.

"Looks like some kind of card. The size is consistent with a business card. But it's pretty damaged." The guy placed the card on the steel tabletop next to the limb and then grabbed a phone and took a photo. He handed the phone to Catchitt. She held it up so we could look at it together.

It was part of a business card. One end of it was mashed and illegible. The other end was torn but bore a small logo in the top corner. It was smudged, but looked like a coat of arms, like a shield. It looked vaguely familiar but I couldn't place it. Under it were the letters O-N-I. And below that three numbers: 561.

"What do you think?" asked Catchitt.

"The numbers. It's a phone area code."

"Right, 561. The Palm Beaches."

"Big area, though. From Jupiter down to Boca, and all the way west to Okeechobee."

"Right. What about these letters? O-N-I?"

I shook my head. "Not sure. The logo looks vaguely familiar, but I can't recall it."

"Never mind. We'll get it to the lab. We'll figure it out."

As I stepped out of the tent another guy in waders and rubber boots approached as fast as one can in waders and rubber boots. He looked hot.

"We found something odd."

We marched around the lake to the section of it that touched against the fifteenth green. It was as far from the clubhouse as one could get and still remain on the course. On the other side of the green was a line of Australian pines, and beyond that I noticed the coils and wires of the electrical substation that the pines were planted to hide.

We stopped by the water. Like the other side, there was a perimeter of red mulch between the long rough and the water. The rough grass wasn't that rough. I'd played courses in New England where Magellan wouldn't have found a lost ball. This stuff was just longer than the fairway, but it looked thick enough for the ball to sit up on it. But two lines of the rough grass had been matted down, like a vehicle had driven over it. The lines led to the edge of the water, but stopped short of the mulch. The red mulch was covered in grass cuttings, as if someone had recently mowed the nearby rough.

"A vehicle has been here," said the guy in waders. I wondered if he was paid extra to state the blindingly obvious.

"What sort of vehicle?" asked Catchitt.

"That'll take some time."

"A maintenance vehicle," I suggested.

Catchitt frowned at me. "You saying it's coincidence?"

"No. I'm saying that it would be hard to drive a Rolls Royce onto a golf course without someone noticing. And there were security people out here all night. The club put extra bodies on for it. Danielle was even out here until pretty late. But no one mentioned seeing a vehicle. But a maintenance vehicle might not raise suspicion."

"Fair argument." Catchitt smiled. She wasn't a handsome woman, and I think she knew that. But she'd either grown easy with it or plain didn't care, because she carried an assurance about her that many attractive women yearned for but few found. Outside the gallows humor I liked her.

She said, "You ever thought about doing this for a living?"

"I'll keep it in mind."

"We need to speak to a course maintenance guy."

"A greenskeeper."

"Yeah, that."

I got on my phone and called Ron, and told him to call Diego the greenskeeper. We waited less than five minutes. Diego arrived in a golf cart that had pretensions of being a flatbed truck. He got out and eyed us with suspicion. I didn't blame him. Someone was going to get the blame, one way or another. He wasn't keen on it being him.

I introduced Diego to Lorraine Catchitt. I just called her Lorraine. I didn't feel comfortable doing the baseball/kitty litter joke. That was hers to do.

"Is there a reason why a maintenance vehicle would be down here?"

He shook his head. "No."

"Maybe trash blew into the water. Would one of your guys come fish it out?"

"Of course."

"But you're saying they didn't?"

"No."

"No, what?"

"No, they didn't."

"It looks like a vehicle was here recently. Like maybe last night?"

"No." I was getting the impression that old Diego was defensive. And while I didn't blame him for that either, it wasn't helping.

"You're saying these tracks are imaginary?"

"No. I'm saying these tracks weren't made by my team."

I stood tall and looked at him. Of course he would say that, but he seemed pretty sure of himself.

"How can you be so sure?"

"You see this cart," he said, pointing at the little vehicle he had arrived in. "The maintenance crew uses vehicles like this. The whole fleet is electric."

"Okay. So?"

"You see these tracks in the grass? You see how far apart they are? These were not made by an electric cart. They are too wide apart. This was a full-size vehicle. Like a pickup truck."

Catchitt nodded. "Possible."

The guy who had found the tracks walked over to the golf cart and used a tape measure to test the width of the tires. Then he put the tape measure against the depression in the grass.

"He's right. It's not a match."

"We'll need an inventory of all the maintenance vehicles used by the club," said Catchitt.

Diego nodded. "Si, okay."

"Diego, could someone get to this point on the course in a vehicle without being seen from the clubhouse?"

He looked around the course, over the fifteenth green and then at the water.

"Si," he said. "If you went straight back here, around the fifteenth and down those pines, you would hit the maintenance path behind the palms over there. That runs around the edge of the course, down around the executive course. There's an access track that goes along where all the hospitality tents are right now. Out to the parking lot."

I thought about the track where I had seen the red Toyota Tacoma appear the previous day, the one that had turned out to not belong to Ernesto the facilities guy.

I was thinking when Diego stepped past me. He had seen something by the water's edge. I hoped it wasn't another alligator. I suspected the sheriff's divers hoped it more than I did.

"What is it?" asked Catchitt.

"Hmm. Nothing."

"Diego," I said. "What do you see?"

"Grass."

It wasn't earth-shattering news. Grass on a golf course.

"What do you mean, grass?"

"Here." He bent down and picked up some grass clippings that lay on the mulch.

"Clippings? You didn't mow recently."

"Of course we mowed. All week. The course has to look perfect." I recalled what he had told me about high-definition televisions picking up the blades.

"So what about it?"

"Look." He held the clippings in his hand. It looked like grass. Long thick blades, like the stuff I had at home. I shrugged like I didn't get his point, because I really didn't.

"This grass," he said, holding up his hand, "is not the same as this grass." He brushed his other hand over the rough.

"Not the same? Are you sure?"

He gave me a look like a doctor when a patient questioned his diagnosis. "I know grass. I told you, we use Bermuda on the fairways and rough, creeping bent on the greens. We overseed the fairways in winter with rye grass." He held up his hand. "But this? This is St. Augustine. See the thicker blades? This grass did not come from this course."

I looked at Diego and then at Catchitt. She looked impressed. I knew for a fact that she would check what he had said was true, but I also knew for a fact that it was. Those Aggies know their grass.

"Where did it come from?"

Diego shrugged. "No idea. Half of the state of Florida is planted with Bermuda grass. The other half is St. Augustine."

"That's it? Two grasses?"

"I don't mean literally. There are lots of different grasses. But they are the big two. St. Augustine is the most popular in residential community developments. It grows and grows. Thick and lush. But it takes a lot of mowing—that's why those communities have to have full-time gardeners. It could take over the state if it wanted to."

I recalled Diego telling me about it before. I also recalled who he said grew most of it. Dig Maddox. And not for the first time that day I wondered where Dig Maddox was.

I left Catchitt to get the lowdown on Diego's maintenance crew. She said she'd call Danielle if she heard anything of interest from the necropsy of the poor old dumb gator. I wandered toward the back of the course, around the fifth green at the back near the power substation. I was following the tire tracks. They arced around the green and then into the pines. Behind the pines was a small track, covered in mulch similar to that which rimmed the perimeter of the lake. Once on the track I lost the tire marks. The track was firm and compacted by years of use. But I followed it along. It was like a secret passage, passing around the edge of the course. I walked a long way around until the trees opened up to a small clearing, still mostly hidden from the view of the golf course. Here I came upon a large shed. It was painted green to camouflage it from the course. I had no doubt if you looked you could see it from the fairway, but you would have to really look.

The shed had a roller door at one end, and the door was rolled up. I looked inside and confirmed it was a maintenance facility. A few more of the electric maintenance carts were parked inside. There were shelves of tools and buckets of who-knew-what. It smelled like wet grass inside.

Beyond the shed the track continued along the perimeter of the executive course, around to the hospitality tent village. I didn't care to go there, so I ducked out of the trees and onto the first fairway. I wanted to find Keith, and I wanted to find Dig. I found Danielle instead. I'd take that every day of the week.

"What's news?" she asked.

"They found some tire tracks down at the lake. And some grass."

"Grass?"

I told her about the grass. "I want to find Dig Maddox. Your buddy from the FBI have much to say?"

"FDLE, not FBI. And funny you should mention Maddox. Nixon did too. He said there were some irregularities with some projects that he had recently done."

"Irregularities?"

"This doesn't go any further."

"Hey, it's me you're talking to."

"And it doesn't go any further."

Ouch. "No further."

"There were some cases where Dig's company laid sod—a lot of sod—in a development project. Only for the sod to die. On two occasions the gardening team was blamed, and their liability insurance had to cover the cost of installing it fresh."

"But it wasn't the gardeners' fault?"

"The suspicion is that it wasn't anyone's fault. They believe the sod never died. You remember Diego said the grass went dormant?"

"They replaced dormant grass?"

"Maybe. Nixon says they may have removed the sod and then replaced it with the exact same sod. Just moved it from one community to the next."

"Like a Ponzi scheme," I said.

"More or less."

"That doesn't seem like the kind of thing the state investigation bureau would be interested in."

"Except that they are concerned about it being the tip of an iceberg."

"Massive sod fraud?"

She grinned at me. "Not sod fraud, you clown. Property fraud."

"By whom?"

"He didn't say. Or wouldn't. There are very powerful people involved. You know who really runs this state."

"Property developers."

Danielle smiled instead of replying. "I need to get going. We have to interview all the caddies and all the players. Find out what happened to the missing caddy."

She touched me on the arm in a way that normally left me feeling giddy, but it barely registered. I was somewhere else. I was thinking about property developers. About powerful people. About the people who really ran the state. I was thinking about that because I remembered something. I remembered where I had seen the smudged logo on the business card Catchitt's guys had found on the leg the gator had left behind. The coat of arms. I had seen it on a set of wrought iron gates. And suddenly the letters made sense. O-N-I. As in the Bonita Mar Club. As in Nathaniel Donaldson's club.

I headed out through the clubhouse toward my car. I suddenly had a hankering for some tasty little sandwiches.

CHAPTER TWENTY—THREE

On my way out to the island I called Lizzy to get an update and give her a new job.

"LCI," she said.

"It's me. Did you get anywhere with the properties?"

"Hello and a good day to you, too."

"Sorry, hello," I said.

Lizzy was an undercover member of the courtesy police. "Good manners take neither a penny nor a pound."

I had no idea what that meant but I suspected keeping my mouth shut was the way to go.

"But since you asked, yes, I got something. The properties around the country club are mostly individually owned homes. There are two properties that stand out. One is a multifamily unit. Sixteen apartments. The owner is listed as an individual in Panama."

"Panama Beach?"

"No, not Panama Beach. If I meant Panama Beach, Miami, I would have used the word beach."

"Okay."

"I mean the country Panama."

"Oh, all right." I slowed as I passed Barry Yarmouth's office again and made my way onto the island.

"The other property is the old power substation."

"Florida Power and Light?"

"No, Mr. Interruption. It used to be owned by FP&L but they sold it about a year ago. It hasn't been in use in a decade. The technology there is old and the replacement cost too high, apparently."

"So who?"

"It was purchased by a consortium based out of Antigua. The local correspondence address is a law firm in Lake Worth. Care of one Keith Hamilton, Esquire."

I nearly drove off the bridge and into the Intracoastal. Keith Hamilton was the point man for the largest single landowner around the club. I considered the possibility that Keith was behind the sabotage of his own club. He had been the one most vocal that it was sabotage. I had to consider the possibility it was a double bluff. No one ever suspected the guy who cried fire.

I thanked Lizzy for the information, and then I asked her to do something new. I wanted to know the details of any development projects she could find that had sod provided by Dig Maddox. She asked how she was supposed to get that sort of information. It wasn't public record. I suggested she start with those projects listed on Dig Maddox's website, and then try a search for projects mentioning Maddox sod. Sod It All was a well-known supplier. Short of that, call the sales offices for every development from Fort Pierce to Lauderdale.

She said she'd get back to me, and I thanked her once again and got an earful of dial tone. Then I reached my destination. The wrought iron gates were closed but the coat of arms on the fence was definitely the one on the card pulled from the lake. Bonita Mar Club.

The guard saw the car and came out to me, and I rolled the window down.

"I'm afraid the club is closed for a private event."

"What event?"

"Members only."

"I just need five minutes of Mr. Donaldson's time."

"Not today."

I waited and looked at the guy. In my experience most people don't like silence. They feel the need to fill it with words. But this guy wasn't most people. He met my silence with silence. Then he spoke.

"I'm going to need you to move your vehicle." He looked behind me, so I glanced in my mirror. There was a big car behind. A nice piece of work. A Bentley, I thought. I'm not a car guy. I don't go to car shows, and I don't sit around Longboard Kelly's talking about them, and I don't have a half-naked girl laying across one on a calendar pinned to my wall. But I could see a large B in reverse on the grill of the tank behind me.

"Sir, now," said the security guy. "Move."

Which probably wasn't the way to go with it. Because it made me turn off my ignition. My Porsche shuddered into silence, and I looked at the guy and gave him the raised eyebrows.

"Sir, you don't want me to call the police."

I disagreed. I was okay with calling the police. "Tell them it's Miami Jones."

The security guy was sweating now. Someone powerful was behind me, someone who needed in through the gates I blocked. But even if I wanted to, I couldn't reverse out now. The Bentley blocked me in. The security guy vacillated and then strode back to the car behind and spoke to the driver. He was there a while, having a chat with whoever was in the back. Then he strode back to the gate. He walked right by me and hit a button somewhere and the gates yawned open.

I started the Porsche and pulled in and stopped forward of the valet station. The Bentley pulled in behind me. I got out and stood by the steps up to the main house and watched the driver get out and run around to open the rear doors. Two guys got out. One I didn't know. The other was instantly recognizable to me. He was big and broad and looked like an ex-football player. That was because he was an ex-football player.

BJ Baker was now a color commentary guy on television and a stalwart of Palm Beach society. I recalled that Nathaniel Donaldson hadn't been too complimentary of BJ, but I suspect everyone's money was the same color green to Donaldson. And media people attracted other rich but not famous people.

BJ took two long strides toward me.

"Still the same minor league pain in the neck I see, Jones."

"It's great to see you, BJ. Really. I didn't know you were a member here. That seals it—I'm definitely in now."

"You're not Bonita Mar material, Jones. We both know that."

"Yeah, you're right. I'm far too honest, aren't I?"

BJ gave me a look like he'd sprayed on cheap cologne, and the other guy wandered around the back of the Bentley to him. I didn't know the other guy. He was tall but didn't wear the physique of an athlete, even a former one.

"What have you boys been up to?" I asked.

"Bit of golf," said the other guy.

"I didn't know Bonita Mar had a course."

BJ took to walking up the stairs and the other guy dropped in beside me. "It doesn't." He leaned in all conspiratorial-like and spoke softly. "You'd think for a hundred grand they'd have a golf course."

"Where'd you play then?"

"They truck you out to PGA National. In a Bentley. Like that softens the blow of wasting a couple hours in traffic. As if I don't have a Bentley at home."

The tall guy grinned and kept walking as I slowed. "See you 'round," he said.

The man in the pinstripe suit I had met on my previous visit approached me. The suit looked the same, the pocket square was a new color.

"I am sorry, Mr. Jones, but Mr. Donaldson is unavailable."

"Sure, Jeeves. Whatever. Just tell him the sheriff's office investigators will be here soon."

"Sheriff's office?"

"Yes. Since Mr. Donaldson's personal details were found on the body."

"The body?"

I nodded with an emphatic eyebrow raise.

The pinstripe told me to wait and dashed off, his heels clicking on the Italian marble. He was gone but a minute.

He said, "This way, please."

I followed him out through the club and across a lawn to a pool area. As we walked I asked him who it was that I had been talking to.

"The guy with BJ Baker," I said.

"He runs Microsoft."

I nodded. So he probably did have a Bentley at home.

The man in the pinstripe deposited me at a large table under an even larger umbrella. Nathaniel Donaldson sat in the shade sipping on an iced tea.

"Get Mr. Jones an iced tea."

I sat, and the pinstripe poured me a cool glass of tea and left us. I had to give it to Donaldson—he was the consummate host and one charming son of a hotelier. But his eyes gave him up. He looked like he wanted me dead.

I sipped the tea. It was cold and strong and good. No sugar, just how I like it.

"To what do I owe this pleasure," he said.

"I thought you'd like to know—your name came up."

"That happens when you are the premier property developer in the world."

Humble, too.

"In regard to a body that was pulled from the water at South Lakes this morning."

"A body?"

I told him the story. Not all of it, but the highlights. I left out the alligator. The more I told, the more his smile grew. Even when I pointed out it was his card that was found on the body, he didn't flinch.

"So why are you telling me this, Mr. Jones?"

"I thought you might have something to say on it, before the sheriff arrives."

"You think I had something to do with it?"

"The thought crossed my mind."

"That's ridiculous."

"That's what they all say."

"Tell you what, Mr. Jones. Why don't we invite the sheriff over to join us for lunch? Maybe you can put your theory to him directly."

"The sheriff is a member here?"

"No, Mr. Jones. But he did get elected on the back of some major contributions from me."

"Of course."

The man in the pinstripe returned. He leaned down and whispered into Donaldson's ear. Donaldson smiled, and then frowned, and then looked at me. Then the pinstripe stood up and marched away again.

"You didn't tell me the full story, Mr. Jones."

"I'm not good with details."

"You left out the alligator."

"I did?"

"You left out the damned alligator." He spat the last words. His face was getting red and not just from the heat. He was working himself into quite a mood. "Damn you, Jones. Why did you have to sit on the damn alligator!"

Now he was fuming. I had no idea how he knew about the alligator, let alone me sitting on it. But either way, he didn't seem to like it. I figured I'd turn the ratchet.

"It's odd that your club doesn't have a golf course. You must be the only club in Florida without one."

His face was building to a perfect crimson.

"I know some guys down in the Lauderhill. They get together to play dominos. They have a little dominos club. Even they have a golf course."

"Damn you, Jones!" He yelled it so loud the entire pool area went silent. I felt like I was getting somewhere. He wasn't as unflappable as he made out to be.

"You've got your eye on South Lakes, haven't you? It's only ten minutes from here. It would be perfect for your members. If only their members agreed to sell it to you."

"You idiot. You think I fed a caddy to an alligator to hurt South Lakes and get them to sell to me? You don't know anything about the deal, Jones. Nothing! Sure, I'd love South Lakes. It's a two-bit dump of a club that I could make world-famous. They're happy with a run-of-the-mill tour event. I would create the fifth major. You get it? And you think I'd feed a guy to an alligator?"

I did think he would feed a guy to an alligator, but I was beginning to feel like at least one of my working theories was wrong. He seemed agitated, but for all the wrong reasons.

"I could have had them, Jones. I would have had them. I know how to put a deal together. I know who to move and where and when. And now this damn gator, and this damn caddy, and you—you idiot—have gotten in my way."

"Gotten in your way?"

"You're wandering around in the dark, aren't you? You don't get it. That club was slowly but surely going down the drain. Nothing surer. Their ratings were poised to be the worst of any tournament for the season. I don't need the club to fail, Jones. I just need the PGA Tour to walk away. And they were going to. Their broadcast partners were ready to walk too. But now . . ." He snatched at his tumbler of iced tea and took a gulp. "Now you've handed them ratings on a platter. A gator attack? A man riding the killer gator? Some bright spark will name the seventeenth hole Gator Alley, you mark my words. Everyone is going to want to watch the killer gator tournament."

White foam formed at the corners of his mouth. He was seriously unhappy. And he wasn't that good an actor. He didn't have anything to do with the gator. I couldn't help explain how his card ended up in the caddy's pocket, but what I knew was he wasn't a direct party to it. He saw the whole episode as a boon to South Lakes. At the same time South Lakes saw the whole thing as a disaster. They were different ways of looking at the same problem, and in a large way it explained why Donaldson was so successful. Sure he knew business, the art of the deal, and he was ruthless to a fault. But he also saw the opportunity in every situation. Suddenly I knew who would be wearing the alligator boots after the necropsy.

"Well, if I can help further, just let me know," I said.

Donaldson looked at me and said, "Pah, pah." He was like a spluttering engine, and I decided to leave before he exploded. I found the valet. He was standing next to my car. He hung the keys out for me. Before dropping them in my hand he spoke.

"I was given a message. The message is, don't come back."

I smiled.

So did the valet. Then he winked, and dropped the keys in my hand.

"Drive safe."

CHAPTER TWENTY-FOUR

I made it back to South Lakes in good time, and I had to admit it really was close enough to Donaldson's club to be a good option for his exclusive members. He had a number of golf properties in South Florida, but the gaping hole in his crown was one nearby to his flagship club. It was an almost unbelievable oversight for an empire that ran some of the most exclusive and expensive courses in the world. And it was obvious that it rankled him to no end. But I had to admit his outburst was genuine. I suspected I'd have to look elsewhere for whoever was behind events. Which made me think back to Keith Hamilton. He was involved in the purchase of the old power substation, and he had conveniently neglected to mention that. It didn't explain the gator. It was possible that the beast had gotten into the lake all by itself. But the tire tracks that didn't match any course maintenance vehicles were suspicious at best. And the cuttings of St. Augustine grass made me think of Dig Maddox. Which made me think of property fraud. Which made me turn full circle back around to

Donaldson. Which gave me a headache, so I stopped thinking about it.

It was like Christmas Day on the battlefields of the Somme when I got back to the club. There were people everywhere but not a shot was fired in hostility. It was as if a truce had been called, and everyone was standing around waiting and thinking and wishing they could stop thinking. I parked and wandered around the far side of the clubhouse. I could see the driving range was in full swing. There were players at every tee box and other players waiting their turn. It was first in, best dressed, I imagined. I saw Heath McAllen smashing little balls way into the distance. I wondered how he would play the tournament without a caddy, and then I wondered if there would even be a tournament. And then I wondered if they would get paid if there was no tournament. I supposed not. Which wasn't so bad for the top guys but not so great for the strugglers in the field.

There was a minimum purse of six million dollars at every PGA Tour tournament, and the winner usually took home north of a cool million. A top player could earn three million in a year and not win a single tournament. A few wins in tournaments you and I have never heard of could see that hit six to eight million. Plus endorsements. But the guys who made up the bulk of the field were not so lucky. The tour midpoint on the money list was closer to six hundred thousand. Which sounds pretty sweet, but that figure was the mean, not the median, and it dropped off pretty quickly from there. The tour low from the previous year, I learned, had been only six thousand dollars. And because the players were for all intents and purposes independent contractors, they had to cover from that their travel, accommodation, food and caddy payments. And then there was the secondary tour, like the minor leagues of golf, where the players struggled week to week in pursuit of that treasured PGA Tour card. The midpoint of the secondary tour was sixteen thousand for the year. That's below the poverty line. I wondered how those players did it, let alone the caddies. I supposed the caddies didn't pay for their expenses—that was taken care of by their employer golf pro. But down there, near the bottom of the jar, a guy could make more teaching golf. And it made sense why the caddies waited to do their drinking at an open bar. Which made me think of the English guy who had been munched by the gator. Which made me think of the run-in I had had with him. Which made me think of the caddies drinking out back, and what I had seen and heard.

Which made me break into a sprint.

I ran down the seventeenth fairway for the tent. I got there and found some of the county investigators, but no Catchitt. So I turned and ran back to the clubhouse, which I realized was a false flat. It was actually uphill. I was sweating by the time I got back to the clubhouse. I found Ron there.

"You seen Danielle?"

"Not lately. You coming?"

"Coming?"

"To the meeting. We're reconvening in the boardroom. To decide if we're calling the whole thing off."

I went with Ron. We got to the briefing room with the concertina walls. Only now it seemed we were referring to it as the boardroom, since the board was coming in rather than caddies. It was like Air Force One.

Keith was waiting. I whispered to him that we needed a word, and then moved into the room. Martin Costas and Barry Yarmouth came in with the PGA Tour liaison guy, Kent Andrew. Another guy came in. He was dressed preppy, blazer and slacks, and he wore a CBS logo on his breast pocket. He had excellent hair. Thick and full and lush, like a golf course, but black. He leaned against the wall. The final person to wander in was Dig Maddox. I hadn't seen him in too long.

Keith coughed to bring attention to himself, but it was habit rather than necessity since we were all looking at him already. He seemed to be searching for the words.

"I don't really know where to begin," he said, which was a beginning in itself. "We have lost a caddy. A well-known and well-liked member of the tour community."

I wasn't too sure about the well-liked bit, but I figured maybe the big cockney caddy was a swell guy when he was off the booze. He wouldn't have been the first.

The door opened and another guy came in. Him I knew. He wore a sportscoat in a herringbone pattern and fancy boat shoes. He had no hair. Not on his head, not where most of us have eyebrows. His face looked like a baby's. Keith frowned at the interruption.

"Can I help you?" Keith asked.

"I seriously doubt it," the guy said. He leaned against the wall next to the CBS guy.

"This is a private meeting," said Keith.

"I know. Continue."

"I don't think you understand."

"No, Hamilton. You don't understand. You are about to cost our great state of Florida millions of dollars, and the governor of said state up to ten approval points. That isn't going to happen. So continue. I'll tell you when to stop."

Keith's mouth had fallen open and he seemed to have the opposite problem of an alligator—he didn't know how to shut it.

I said, "Keith, this is Max Beck. The governor's chief cook and bottle washer."

"Chief of staff, thanks, Jones."

"That's what I said."

Keith looked at the hairless man. "You're from the governor's office?"

"You catch on quick, but no. I am the governor's office. Now let's move on."

Keith brushed himself off as if he had gotten dirty from the exchange with Beck, and he continued.

"The Palm Beach County Sheriff has declared the Pacific a potential crime scene. They do not anticipate being done before Thursday, when play begins. I have investigated with Kent the possibility of rerouting the course onto part of the executive course, but with the corporate hospitality tents already in place the PGA Tour has deemed it impractical."

Excellent deflection of blame, Keith. Spoken like a true lawyer.

"Our sponsors also have grave reservations about their brand being associated with the incident." He looked at the guy in the CBS jacket. "Paul? What is the network's position?"

"Our advertisers are uneasy, Keith. I'll admit that. But mostly they're uneasy about the tournament being pulled. That is going to cost them, and in turn cost the network. We will lose a million viewers nationwide, minimum. That will hurt us, and I have to be honest, it will hurt you too."

"Us?"

"If those losses come about due to the negligence of the hosting club, well . . ."

"Negligence? There's no negligence."

"A caddy got eaten by an alligator, Keith. On your course. You owe a duty of care as a minimum. But allowing killer alligators?" Paul the CBS guy looked around the room. He stopped on Martin Costas. Martin nodded.

"He's right, Keith. This does not bode well. I think we need to start looking at indemnification."

"Martin, that's preposterous."

"It's not, and you know it."

"What do you mean, indemnification?" asked Barry.

Martin said, "I mean, Barry, covering our backsides. The sponsors, the players, the caddies, the family of the lost caddy, the tour, the networks, the advertisers. They all lose if we kill the tournament. And if the area around the Pacific is off limits due to a police investigation, I see no other option."

"The governor will not be happy about that," said Beck. "You're talking millions of eyeballs in the Midwest and Northeast—where they have just had a late-season snowfall—lost to the charms of our great state. That's a lot of tourist money down the sinkhole. The governor will not be happy at all. Not with the club, not with you clowns as custodians of the club. I'd say you can kiss your club goodbye."

I seriously thought Keith would explode. I've never seen someone literally have a stroke, but I imagine the seconds before a stroke look just like Keith Hamilton right then. He lost all color, his skin turned a shade of gray, and his eyes fluttered like a starlet.

I decided it was time to jump in, if for no other reason than I didn't want to have to perform CPR on Keith. "Can I say something?"

Every eye turned to me.

"There may be another way to look at this. First, I don't think the gator ate a caddy."

"What?" said Barry. "They found him. Well, parts of him."

"Parts, yes. But I recalled that last night when some of the caddies were drinking after walking the course, I and some others heard a splash. I was out the back of the clubhouse. I asked Ron if you had a pool."

Ron nodded. "You did. We don't. But I remembering hearing it, too."

"I think it was whoever got eaten entering the water. But it wasn't the missing caddy, because I ran into him after that. In the parking lot."

"You're sure it was him?" asked Martin Costas, ever the litigator.

"I am. We had a memorable encounter."

"So what?" exclaimed Barry. "Who cares who it was? Someone got eaten by a gator, right? It's still a crime scene."

"Yes, someone did. So maybe it's a crime scene. Maybe it was a drunken accident. Either way the sheriff's office will keep it off-limits until they know one way or the other. But it was pointed out to me that this is not all bad news."

"Not bad news?" said Keith. "How on earth is this not bad news?"

I looked at Paul, the guy from the network. "What do your sponsors want?"

"Market share. Eyeballs."

"Right. And what is your most profitable programming?"

"Sport."

"Aside from that?"

"Unscripted drama," he said.

"In other words, reality television."

"Right. Your point?"

"People love drama. And let's face it, golf tends to be light on drama. Outside the majors, audiences are waning. Am I right?"

"The corporate market is strong, but yes, total audience share isn't what it was. I still don't see your point."

"Let's put it this way. Which tournament would get more viewers? The Aqueta Open at South Lakes, or the Aqueta Open at the course with the man-eating gator?"

The CBS guy leaned back and thought. He was really churning it through. Then he started nodding. Then he smiled.

"The gator open. You might have something."

Kent, the PGA Tour guy looked at Paul. "What's that worth?"

Paul thought on it again. "Could be a ratings point, could be two. But it could mean more in the 18–35 demo. That audience loves reality drama, and the advertisers love that audience." He looked at me. "This could work."

"Okay, are we forgetting something?" asked Barry. "There's still a crime scene in the middle of the course."

The group fell silent. I looked at Dig Maddox. He looked unhappy, and I couldn't quite pin down why.

"I think I've got an idea for that, too," I said. "We can't play through the area because until further notice it remains a crime scene. But the lake is out of play anyway, right. It's a marked water hazard. A player hits a ball in there, he has to take a penalty drop. So why not change the current crime scene tape into out-of-bounds tape. It removes the visual connection between the crime scene and the sponsors, but still preserves the potential crime scene."

"You're asking the sheriff to mess with an investigation into a death," said Barry. "I don't think he'll do it."

"I do," I said, looking at Beck smoldering in the corner. "If he got a call from the governor."

Beck smiled, which resembled an eel and made me shiver involuntarily.

"And the governor isn't asking him to pervert the course of justice," I said. "No crime has actually been proven yet. It's just an active investigation. But this way, the integrity of the scene remains. No gallery can go through the out-of-bounds area, and Keith can get some members to marshal the area so any investigators who are there don't get hit by a foul ball." I was fairly sure foul ball wasn't a golf term, but I didn't care. My point was made, and it had landed well.

Keith said, "Paul?"

The network man was still nodding and thinking. I wondered if he was dreaming up on-screen graphics and stats for the commentators, like other famous golf accidents, or the top ten most dangerous courses.

"I think we can work with this."

"Kent?"

"If the police tape can be removed, then yes, I think we can change the course rules to make the area surrounding the lake out-of-bounds rather than a water hazard. A player can take a shot from inside a water hazard, if he thinks he can. But out-of-bounds the player is penalized stroke and distance, so he has to take the shot again. It might make the course a bit tougher, but I think the sponsors will be okay with that, and I know they'll be excited about any additional potential audience. It might even boost ticket sales."

"Mr. Beck?" asked Keith.

Beck nodded but didn't say anything. He had already dialed a number, and his cell phone was to his ear. He pushed away from the wall and stepped out of the room.

Keith said, "All right, in that case, I put it to the board. All in favor of Mr. Jones's plan?"

Keith put his hand up, as did Martin and Ron. Barry shook his head but followed suit. Dig Maddox frowned. He didn't look keen for reasons I couldn't fathom. But he succumbed to the peer pressure and waved his hand halfheartedly.

"Unanimous. Thank you, gentlemen. We all have work to do."

The meeting broke up. I wanted to talk to Keith, and I wanted to talk to Dig. But there was someone I wanted to talk to more. I needed to find Danielle. I wanted to tell her my plan, so she could pass it on to the sheriff. I didn't want him getting blindsided by the governor calling to tell him to do something quite irregular. News of whose idea it was would inevitably filter through to the sheriff, and I didn't want him holding my actions against Danielle. I figured if she warned him of the plan he would be thankful. He would be ready when the governor called. Hell, he could even position it as his own plan. The sheriff was an elected position, so he may have been a law enforcement officer but he was also a politician. I figured making it look like Danielle helped him get an IOU from the governor would do both him and Danielle good in the long run.

I found Danielle and told her my plan. She wasn't as impressed as I had hoped, but she came around. She understood how the power was wielded in the sunshine state, like everywhere else. She got on her phone and called the sheriff's office to tell him the plan. She was still on the phone when the missing caddy came wandering into the clubhouse, holding his head like he had the mother of all hangovers.

CHAPTER TWENTY—FIVE

The big Englishman looked like he'd been on a bender. He was pale and thirsty and sucked on a water bottle as he walked. The plus for the guy was that he wasn't gator food. The minus was that he had to be out of job. I couldn't imagine missing a practice round and leaving your pro high and dry was the done thing. The other caddies just nodded as one, as if it were par for the course. Danielle finished her call to the sheriff and was primed to rip the big guy a new one. But he hadn't actually broken any laws. It wasn't illegal to turn up for work late.

The caddy found Heath McAllen and I watched from a distance as they had words. The big guy didn't seem too remorseful and I wondered if he was going with the best form of defense is attack approach. I couldn't see that working, but then McAllen put his hand on the caddy's shoulder and together they walked over to the clubhouse and into the players' locker rooms. McAllen came out alone shortly thereafter. He saw me and wandered over.

"Looks like he's not gator bait, after all," I said.

"Thank goodness."

The kid looked calm and easy about the whole thing. I wondered if he was suffering through an abusive relationship and was in denial.

"You can't be okay with that?" I asked.

"With what?"

"The guy missed practice and was suspected of being dead, all because he was in a booze coma."

"It happens."

"Yeah, it happens. But I gotta tell you, you seem like one of the most professional guys out here. You were first to arrive on Monday, you walked the course yourself, and you were first at the range when the practice round was delayed. I don't see how having an unprofessional caddy fits your plan."

"Can I tell you something, Miami? In confidence?" His open face grew serious.

"Sure. Of course."

"Alfie's had a tough year."

I raised my eyebrows.

"I know, I know," he said. "But this has been really tough on him. We spend a lot of time on the road, you know? And things have not been good at home. His wife is divorcing him."

I had to say, I was on the wife's side in this one.

"And she has custody of his bairns—his kids. He hardly sees them. Now I'm not saying it's an excuse to drown yourself in a bottle, but what kind of a friend would I be if I deserted him now?"

"I hope you don't mind me saying, but you're his employer, not his friend."

"No, I'm both. And I'll be honest. I wouldn't be where I am without him. When I need him on the course, he's there."

"Because he knows that you need the seven iron?"

"No, not for that. He calms me. When I'm struggling with my game, he knows what to say, and when. He knows when to keep his trap shut, and when I need a good talking-to. A good caddy doesn't just carry clubs, Miami. A good caddy is your partner. He doesn't hit any shots, but he makes the shots I hit better. And despite what you might think, we are friends. And I wasn't brought up to walk away from a friend in need."

I said nothing. I just looked at the kid, and pondered his Scottish upbringing. I wondered for a moment how proud his mother must be of him. He was a damn good golfer, but that was insignificant next to the fact that he was a damn good human being. My mother had died when I was in high school, but I hoped she was half as proud of me. I wondered whether that would be the case. Danielle had once said she wanted to make an honest man of me. She said it one time and never mentioned it again. I thought about it a lot. I wondered how it was and wasn't the case. I wondered if she smiled at the kid when she spoke with him because she saw things in him that she saw in me, or if she saw things in him that she wished she saw in me.

It was too heavy a train of thought for a golf course, so I patted McAllen on the shoulder and I wandered off to find Danielle. I suddenly needed a hug. I found her standing by the practice putting green. I didn't get my hug. She waved me over and put her phone on speaker.

She said, "Lorraine, I have Miami here. Can you say that again?"

"Hi, Miami. We just finished the necropsy of the gator. We found the remains of a man in his belly. The remains had a wallet. With a driver's license."

"Who was it?"

"The license says Ernesto Cabala. That mean anything to you guys?"

I looked at Danielle and nodded.

"He was the facilities guy here at the club," said Danielle. "The one we wanted to speak with in relation to the viral outbreak at the wedding."

"Well, someone didn't want him talking," said Catchitt.

"You think it was murder?" I asked.

"The guy was dead before he hit the water. You get pulled in by a gator you fight, at least a bit. You get water in your lungs. His chest cavity isn't in the greatest shape, but there's no water in the lungs. He was already dead. Someone put him in the lake."

"Which suggests that someone knew the gator was there," I mused.

"Most likely," said Catchitt. "If I were a betting woman, and I am, I'd say they didn't just know the gator was there. I'd say they put it there."

Danielle thanked Lorraine for the call and hung up. We stood looking down in the general direction of the Pacific, although we couldn't see the water hazard from where we stood.

Our attention was taken by the sudden busyness about the place. Caddies were rushing here and there, and most of the pros were headed for the locker rooms. Ron wandered out with a canister on his back and a spray wand in his hand.

"What's going on?" I asked.

"Sheriff just called. He has allowed the crime scene to be nominated as out-of-bounds so the tournament can continue alongside the investigation."

"The governor call?" I asked.

Ron shook his head. "Beck says not yet. Seems the sheriff came up with the idea all on his own. Beck says the governor will be calling him to thank him for understanding on the matter, and to offer the state's help with the investigation. Anyway, I need to go pull down that police tape and spray paint out-of-bounds lines. We're about to open up the course for a practice round." He held up the wand like a gunslinger and gave Danielle a wink. Danielle gave me a sheepish grin. It wasn't a hug, but it would do for now.

"So I think it's safe to say old Ernesto was not working alone." She nodded. "We need to walk through the whole thing again. We've missed something."

"Just what I was thinking."

"Do you mind if I help with that?" said the deep voice behind us. We spun in place as one to see the FDLE guy, Nixon, standing behind us.

"Special Agent Nixon," said Danielle.

"Deputy."

"You guys are called special agents?" I asked. "Like the FBI?"

He nodded. "We are the FBI, for the state of Florida."

"But they have federal jurisdiction. That trumps you."

"It does, Mr. Jones. But then they have to spend time in the rain in Virginia. We get to stay in sunny Florida."

I had to admit it seemed like a fair trade.

"The governor send you?" I asked.

"Of course he did."

"So he can take credit for a county investigation?"

"He'll take credit for it regardless. That's the beauty of being governor. But my boss has given me the okay to share with you whatever I feel is relevant to share. So maybe we break this thing open before the television cameras get turned on?"

I shrugged. I was okay with it. I was getting paid one way or the other, and I figured appropriating Nathaniel Donaldson's plan for the gator golf tournament and presenting it to the board had guaranteed that the club was going to be happy to pay. So I left it with Danielle.

"I think we could use all the help we can get," she said.

We wandered over toward the hospitality tent where the wedding rehearsal dinner had happened, and where they had all picked up the bug. We thought about sitting in there to work, but despite the tent having being cleaned to the standard required by the health department, I just didn't fancy it. We turned tail and took a table in the corner of the dining room.

"So what do you know?" said Nixon.

"It starts with the wedding," said Danielle.

"Or before, if you believe Keith."

"Right, but we don't know that and we have no intelligence on it."

"Fair enough. The wedding."

Danielle continued. "The health department says the wedding party got sick as a group because the virus was put in the chairs at the rehearsal dinner. Connie Persil said the chair backs were covered in it in a way that suggested it was no accident."

"But only the wedding party got sick," said Nixon. "You were at the wedding, right? You didn't get sick."

"No, but we weren't at the rehearsal dinner."

"Okay, but you were sitting on the chairs, weren't you? At the ceremony."

I pondered that. It was a good point and had been nagging at me for some time. Connie Persil's finding never quite made sense to me. As I was thinking it through a waitress came over and asked if we wanted anything. We ordered iced teas.

"Maybe the contaminated chairs were put at the front, where the wedding party sat again," I said.

"Who moved the chairs from the dinner site to the ceremony site?" asked Danielle. "We didn't ask that. We should have."

"It's never too late," I said. The waitress brought our drinks over and I asked her if she could ask Natalie Morris to join us for a moment.

We sipped our drinks as we waited.

"But do we know that the dinner was the source?" asked Nixon.

Danielle nodded. "Connie Persil confirmed it. The incubation period of the norovirus is 12–48 hours. This was about twenty hours, so right in the middle. And her environmental tests said that the chairs were the only contaminated surface."

"Okay, so someone definitely did it," said Nixon. "And you think it was this Ernesto guy."

"It was our suspicion," said Danielle. "And now he's dead."

Danielle looked across the room and I turned to see Natalie Morris walking toward us. She was still dressed in all black, and she cast her eyes around the dining room for anything amiss as she passed through.

"Deputy, Miami. How can I help?"

I asked Natalie to sit and then said, "This is Special Agent Nixon. We're just trying to piece together events at the wedding."

Natalie nodded with a grimace.

"I know, I don't want to think about it either, but here we are. And there's one thing we don't get. How come the people at the rehearsal dinner got sick but the rest of us didn't. The health department says the virus was on the chairs, and we all sat on the chairs."

"No, you didn't."

"Well not us specifically. You're right, Danielle and I were standing at the back. But the rest of the congregation."

"No, I mean they didn't either," said Natalie. "The chairs for the dinner weren't the same chairs used at the ceremony."

Danielle sat forward. "They weren't?"

"No, Deputy. Because of the tournament. We had set the hospitality tent up already for use as a private VIP dining area. We used dining chairs that we took from storage. The rest of the chairs, the ceremony ones, were basic fold-up chairs that we hired for the tournament, so we put them to use."

I leaned back in my seat and looked at Danielle. She looked disappointed, like she'd missed a trick, and she'd done it in front of an FDLE agent.

"We should have asked that before."

"No reason," said Nixon. "Sounds like the health department should have been a little more specific. And it wasn't like you could walk into the contaminated tent to figure it out."

I wasn't sure why Nixon was backing Danielle up, but she relaxed when he did. Maybe he was playing her. Maybe he liked her. He certainly didn't appear to know we were an item. Or maybe he'd taken the long route on his own fair share of cases and had beaten himself up over it just like Danielle was.

Danielle picked it up. "So, Natalie. Can you confirm that Ernesto put the dining chairs out?"

"Yes, he did. He got them from storage, on his dolly. He set them out, and he cleaned them."

"With bleach, is what you said before?"

"Yes, with bleach. We have a stock of it in the storeroom."

"And he set up the chairs for the ceremony."

"Yes. The same way. The rental people delivered them, and Ernesto and the delivery guy brought them around to the back."

"You saw him do this?"

"Yes, I saw him. The delivery guy left them in a few piles, and Ernesto unfolded them and put them out and sprayed them with bleach."

"Why spray them with bleach if they had just been delivered?" I asked. "Aren't they cleaned?"
"You'd hope so, but Mr. Yarmouth wouldn't like us to assume it."
"Mr. Yarmouth? You mean Barry, the club treasurer?"
"Yes."
"What has it got to do with him? Is he a germaphobe?"
"No, I don't think so. But you saw what happens if things don't get cleaned properly."
I sat back. I did see what happened. It would stick with me to the end of my days.
"What has Mr. Yarmouth got to do with facilities?" asked Danielle.
"He sort of oversees it. The club isn't that big, you know. And most of the facilities stuff has to do with hiring tents and chairs and stuff, which is all money the club pays out. And Mr. Yarmouth oversees all that as treasurer. So Ernesto has—had—to deal with that. So I guess it was more he had a lot to do with Mr. Yarmouth, rather than Mr. Yarmouth was his boss."
"Who do you report to, Natalie?" I asked.
"Mr. Hamilton," she said with a nod.
Danielle said, "So is there anything you can tell us about the day you prepared the rehearsal dinner? Anything unusual?"
Natalie thought and shook her head.
"And this bleach. Where is that kept?"
"In the storeroom."
"Who has access to it?"
"Anyone with a key. Me, Ernesto. Chef Lex. And some of the board members, I guess."
"Can you show us where it's kept?"
"Sure." She stood and led the three of us out of the dining room into the hallway between the dining room and the

kitchen. We turned away from the entrance of the club and down a corridor. Natalie stopped by a door and unclipped a keyring and fumbled for a key, and then used it to open the door. She flicked the light on and walked in.

It was a utility cupboard. Not massive but big enough for the four of us to fit in. Rows of shelving lined both long walls, stacked with rolls of paper towels and fake candles and flashlights and washcloths. There were a couple of dry buckets at the end, with mops sitting in them. The room smelled like Pinesol. Natalie bent down to the lowest shelf. She had a good shape about her.

"Huh," she said, and stood up. She looked at some other shelves and moved some rolls of paper towels out of the way. "That's odd."

"What's odd," asked Danielle.

"It's not here."

"The bleach?"

"No. I mean, yes, the bleach. It was there, on the bottom. It's not there now."

"Could someone else be using it?"

"Sure, they could be using it. But not eleven bottles of it."

"Eleven bottles?"

"Yes. We order it from a big box store. It comes in a pack of twelve spray bottles. We got a full new pack delivered last week because of the tournament. A lot of people mean a lot of mess. Ernesto broke the pack open on Friday. I remember him doing it. He took the first bottle."

"And the rest are gone?"

She looked around the storeroom once more. "Yes. Eleven bottles are missing."

CHAPTER TWENTY—SIX

"**Okay, Natalie, let's** take a step back," said Danielle as we moved out of the storeroom. "I want you to walk us through what you saw and where. And I mean actually walk us there physically. It might jog your memory."

"Sure, Deputy. So, I was in the kitchen when the deliveries came. There was stuff from the big box store, and stuff from the uniform place that does the caddies' uniforms. I remember it because we got some new plastic containers. Chef Lex keeps herbs in them. I came out here and then I waited while Ernesto checked and signed for the delivery. He carried everything into the storeroom, and he handed me the package of containers. We were talking about something—I think he was unhappy about something. Yes, that was right—he wasn't happy about not getting paid extra for the overtime he was working for the tournament."

"He wasn't being paid?"

"Oh, he was being paid, but I think he wanted double time or something. He doesn't get tips like the servers and kitchen staff, and I asked if he had taken it up with Mr. Yarmouth. He said he had, and Mr. Yarmouth told him there was no money, that the club might even take a loss on the tournament."

"That's a good treasurer," I said. "Tighter than a drum."
"So what happened then?" asked Danielle.
"Nothing. I mean I went back to the kitchen."
"When did you see Ernesto again?"
"Outside. I went out to check on the hospitality tent."
"Show us."

Natalie led us out to the tent. It had been arranged into ten tables with a bar at one end, for the corporate VIPs.

"So I came out here. It wasn't set up like this. It was one long table. And not these chairs. I don't know where the other ones went."

"The health department took them away to be decontaminated," said Danielle. "So Ernesto was here?"

"Yes. He set it all up. And then went back to get the bleach."

"Wait, you said he opened the package of bleach bottles when you were talking at the storeroom. Why did he need to go get it?"

Natalie looked confused. I could see she was trying to remember. I hoped she didn't try too hard. The human mind was a wonderful thing, and it was more clever than it let us know. Our own brains kept things from us, told us little lies. Eyewitness testimony had been the benchmark of the legal system since the Magna Carta, and probably before. But it was faulty. People's memories didn't work the way they assumed they did. I covered it when I studied criminology. Research showed time and time again that our memories were prone to error, and worse still, were prone to simply making things up to fill in the gaps. Or to please cops when put under pressure in questioning.

"Yes, that's right," said Natalie. "I was here, making sure all the flower arrangements for the table were right, and Ernesto did a loop of the room. Looking around as if he had lost something.

He looked confused. Then he walked out. I was coming out myself when he returned. He held the bottle up to me, as if it meant something. I didn't think about it. But now we're here, I think maybe he had forgotten it somewhere and he went back to get it, and he was showing me he had it."
"So you left then? Where did you go?"
Natalie searched her memory. "I went upstairs. We were arranging the drinks for the dinner. I went to make sure the bar had everything ready."
"You were serving drinks from upstairs?"
"No. We arranged to have wine and soda on ice here in the tent, and a beer keg." Her eyes flashed open. "Yes, a beer keg."
"What about the beer keg?"
"There was a problem with it. A line burst or something."
"What did you do?" asked Danielle.
"Chip, he's the bar guy, he said he needed help. He asked me to get Ernesto. So I ran back down here."
"Where exactly?"
Natalie strode over to the door to the clubhouse, near where Danielle and I had stood for the wedding ceremony. "I was here. Ernesto was coming out of the tent."
"Coming out? Why?" asked Danielle.
"I think he was done. He had the bleach and his cloth in his hands. He looked done, I guess."
"Okay, and . . ."
"And I called to him. Said we need help."
"And?"
"And we ran upstairs. To the bar."
"Let's do it," said Danielle. Natalie led her inside and up the stairs to the bar. Nixon and I followed. The bar was almost empty. Most of the corporate guys had migrated to the hospitality village over on the executive course, and the caddies

and players were getting themselves together for a delayed practice round.

"So what happened here?" Danielle prompted.

"We came up and Ernesto went over there to the bar. Chip was holding a keg closed, I think, to stop it bursting and flooding the bar with foam. He told Ernesto to close the line, which he did."

"And then?"

Natalie shook her head. "Nothing. I mean they tapped the line, and Chip used a dolly to take the keg down to the hospitality tent."

"What did Ernesto do?"

"He went downstairs with Chip. Yes, he carried some ice down. And then he connected the party lights in the tent. After that I'm pretty sure he left."

"He left?"

"He was done. He doesn't work service, so he left. He gave me a nod and said goodnight as I was coming through the dining room."

We stood in silence for a moment, looking around the bar, and looking out the window at the top of the hospitality tent.

"If there's nothing more, I need to get back to it," Natalie said.

"Sure," said Danielle. "Thanks for your help."

"Not a problem. If you need me, I'll be around."

She turned to leave.

"Natalie," I said. "Sorry, one more question. This bleach you use. It's industrial-strength stuff?"

"You don't want to drink it, if that's what you mean."

"No, it's not. What I mean is, did Ernesto wear gloves when he was using it?"

Natalie nodded. "I don't know how I forgot that. Yes, he did. Yellow ones. Regular rubber gloves. The ones you use in your kitchen."

Not in my kitchen. "Was he wearing them when he cleaned the tent?"

"Yes, I think he was."

"What about when he helped carry the ice? Can't be easy to carry ice in rubber gloves."

"I can't say for sure, but no, I don't think he was."

"Okay, thanks, Natalie."

"Sure. Happy to help." She gave me the Florida smile again and I started to wonder if it was reserved just for me.

"So what happened to the gloves?" Nixon asked.

"Forget the gloves, think about the bleach. He came up with it in a hurry, and then he helped stop a beer flood. Then he wandered downstairs. Where's the bottle?"

Nixon looked around the bar, canvasing each nook and cranny. I nodded Danielle toward the bar. She frowned, and then looked. And then she got it.

Danielle strode over to the bar. The bartender, Chip, looked at her uniform and smiled.

"Cleaning supplies?"

Chip nodded at a cupboard at the end of the bar. He leaned over and pulled the cupboard open.

"What do you need?" he said.

"I need you to stand back."

Nixon and I looked over her shoulder. Danielle took a drink stirrer and used it to push a bottle of Windex out of the way. Behind the Windex sat a bottle of bleach, with a pair of yellow rubber kitchen gloves casually tossed over the top of it.

"Not bad," said Nixon.

Danielle used a pair of food service gloves to put the bottle into a white trash bag. She dropped the gloves in as well, and then used the bag to remove the food service gloves, letting them fall inside.

"I need to call Connie Persil."

Danielle took the bag and went downstairs to make her call. Nixon and I watched her go.

"She's pretty good," Nixon said.

"You don't know the half of it."

He turned to me. "She have a boyfriend?"

"She does."

"Is it serious?"

"Pretty serious."

Nixon and I stood in silence for moment. Then I left. Small talk is not my strong point.

CHAPTER TWENTY—SEVEN

The practice round went off without incident, which was some kind of relief to everyone, but mostly to Keith. I felt bad about bursting his happy bubble, but I had things I needed to know. He was standing near the clubhouse in his club blazer, a picture of golfing fashion. He was watching Heath McAllen putting on the final green under the eye of his trusty English bagman.

"How's it going, Keith?"

"You might have saved us, Miami. That alligator idea. Genius."

"Actually I stole it from Nate Donaldson."

Keith scrunched up his face. "You know Nathaniel Donaldson?"

"Sure, we're like old college roommates."

"But he's got to be thirty years older than you."

"Well, perhaps not that close. But I'm glad to help. I do have a question, though."

"What is it?"

The small gallery watching McAllen's practice round clapped softly as he sunk his par putt. I didn't know how his round had gone, but he was smiling.

I said, "We've been checking up property ownership around the course."

"Why?"

"It's a working theory. If a developer is trying to hurt the club, he would probably buy up the surrounding property to force a deal."

"That's your theory?"

"It's a working theory. And guess what we found? The single largest landowner around the perimeter of the course? It's you."

He frowned deeper. "Me? You really need to check your sources, Mr. Jones."

"No, I don't think so. The old power substation out the back of the course. FP&L sold it recently to a consortium based in Antigua. With a local address at your law firm, care of you."

Keith looked at me. He wasn't giving much away. "What is it you think you know, Mr. Jones?"

"Mr. Jones was my dad, Keith. And what I know is that you withheld information about a landholding adjacent to the course. A holding that gives you motive for closing your own club."

Now his poker face gave way. But the face that replaced it wasn't angry or petulant or even guilty. It was sad.

"You think me capable of that, Miami? My own club?"

"I think anyone capable of anything, under the right circumstances."

"I'd rather open a vein than hurt this club."

"In which case there must be an easy explanation."

He shook his head and cast his eye at the next group walking onto the eighteenth green.

"Nothing is easy, Miami. You should know that. Even in law, life is not black and white."

"I agree. But you're stalling."

"I own just a share of the substation property, Miami. I don't have the kind of money needed to buy it all. If I did, I assure you I would have. But not for the reasons you think."

"I don't think anything. Yet."

Keith sighed. "I got wind of the imminent sale by FP&L. They haven't used the site in years. And with the economy recovering, the time was right. But I found out that a property developer with designs on our club did indeed want it. So I did all I could. I put a consortium together to buy it from under the developer. To stop them linking it to a closure of our club."

"Who was the developer? Nate Donaldson, right?"

He shook his head as the gallery clapped another putt. "No, Miami. The developer was Antonio Coligio."

"Coligio wanted to develop this club?"

"Why not? That's what he does."

"That doesn't make sense. I spoke with him. I don't buy the idea that he poisoned his own wife at the wedding."

"You're assuming those two events are connected. But I don't think you know Mr. Coligio the way you think you do."

That was true. I didn't know him at all. But I know people. I used to be able to stare down a batter and know whether he was sweating on a hit to save his career or if he was on a hot streak. There are tells. And I had seen Mr. Coligio's reaction to his wife getting sick at the wedding. His first instinct was shock. Granted, it could have been because he hadn't expected her to get ill even when everyone else did. Maybe her chair wasn't supposed to get contaminated. But the next reaction—and it was instantaneous in my mind—was to go to the aid of his wife. I can forgive a second of hesitation when confronted with a loved one vomiting. It isn't a pleasant thing. In the end you help, but it isn't pleasant. But Coligio didn't hesitate. He went straight to her aid. I couldn't see a guy who reacted like that even considering putting his wife in harm's way. It didn't figure.

"So who is in your consortium, Keith?"

"I did it the way I did it so that the major player couldn't control things, couldn't take it over."

"Okay, but who?"

"Martin Costas and Barry Yarmouth are in it. To keep the club safe, you understand?"

"But they aren't the money, Keith. Who's the money?"

He hesitated. He didn't want to share. But I was going to make him.

"This would be a great story in the Palm Beach Post. I know a reporter there."

"You wouldn't. This is in confidence. This is a privileged conversation."

"That's your concern, counselor. Not mine. And all bets are off if you're lying to me."

His jaw clenched. It was like getting blood from a stone, but I was getting it or I wasn't leaving the damned golf course.

"The money is Nathaniel Donaldson."

I blew air, a long slow exhalation. "You're in bed with Nate Donaldson?"

"No, we are not in bed with Mr. Donaldson. Listen, Miami. Sometimes the enemy of my enemy is my friend."

"And sometimes your enemy acts like your friend and then turns around and shanks you in the guts."

"You have a very evocative turn of phrase, Miami. But you don't see. We needed his money, but we hold the cards. He can't build a damn thing on that property without our say-so, and if he tries to get his hands on this club he won't get any such thing. Once the tournament is done and we have solidified our position with the PGA Tour, then we might consider a project. But it will just be residential housing. It will have nothing to do with the club. No on-course properties. Just apartments that happen to be nearby."

We looked at each other and then turned to watch the putting on the green. It was only practice, but everyone seemed to take it pretty seriously. I wasn't sure what to make of Keith Hamilton. He talked a good game. But I reminded myself he was a lawyer. They were paid to manipulate language to their advantage. They were about as trustworthy as novelists.

I felt my phone ring in my pocket and Keith gave me a dirty look that I nearly shoved back down his throat. I skipped away from the green and answered the call. I always answer calls from Lizzy. The wrath of God is too great not to.

"Lizzy, how are things in the real world?"

"Underpaid. You asked me to do some digging about your friends at the golf club."

"Country club," I said for no other reason than to be a smarty.

"Which country?" she replied. I had nothing to say to that.

"What did you find?"

"First is Martin Costas. He's into a lot of stuff. Has a lot of clients in Palm Beach, but he doesn't live there. He's been a member of the chamber of commerce there for years, and according to Cassandra has been courted by plenty of nice clubs. But he has declined every offer. He attends a lot of stuff, but has kept all his club affiliations in West Palm."

That all married up with what he had more or less told me.

"He handles some of the legal affairs for Dig Maddox. Mr. Maddox also has in-house counsel."

"So the board shares a bit of work around. Figures."

"You asked about Dig Maddox's projects. He lays more grass than I can believe the world needs. I made so many calls my ear hurts."

"You should get an ice pack for that."

"Thank you for your concern. He grows most of his grass out past Wellington, and some out west of Port St. Lucie. When the economy tanked he let everything in PSL die, and then claimed the insurance. The insurance company wouldn't pay so he sued. They settled out of court."

"For how much?"

"They don't talk about that stuff, Miami. Anyway I found one project where Sod It All was the supplier to a project linked to your club."

"Do tell."

"It's a new development west of Palm Beach Gardens. Capricorn Lakes. Does anyone believe that lakes stuff? They're like bathtubs. Anyway, it's one of those eco-friendly communities. Solar power, reclaimed water for gardens, charging ports for electric cars, that sort of thing."

"What's the link?"

"The sales agent for the community is Barry Yarmouth, and the escrow for the first sales was facilitated by Martin Costas."

"Okay, so more of the board doing each other favors. Anything suspect about it?"

"Not really. It looks like it's only ten percent built. Sounds like they can't get enough builders."

"That's Florida. Sell the dream, 'cause the reality's a swamp."

"And you love it."

"Yes, ma'am. I do. Thanks for the info. Let me know if you hear anything more."

I watched the sun falling below the distant Australian pines, and the last of the golfers were finishing their practice and heading for the locker rooms. I was fairly sure I could make out the silhouette of Heath McAllen out on the driving range. The kid worked hard. And so did I. Granted, neither of us worked in a coal mine. It wasn't that kind of hard. But I was tired and the sun was low. I knew Ron would hang at the club and I could avail myself of free beers, but I needed to recharge the batteries and come at things with fresh eyes in the morning. I needed a comfortable stool and a cool beer, and a place where everybody knew my name and didn't speak ill of it.

I called Danielle as I wandered around the clubhouse. I saw another old red Tacoma pickup and it felt like a ghost.

"Hey you," she said.

"What happened to you?"

"I got a ride over to the diagnostic lab. They're testing the bleach bottle."

"Gotta think that bleach would kill the virus, wouldn't you?"

"I would, but leave no stone unturned. What are you doing?"

"I feel Longboard's calling."

"I'm at Gun Club Road. Come get me?"

"It would be my honor."

I was in the lot when I saw Special Agent Nixon. He was headed for his bland Crown Victoria.

"Headed back to Miami?" I asked.

"No. I'm here for the duration. You know a hotel around here?"

"It's Florida, pal."

"With a golf tournament on. I might end up driving all way home after all."

It was only a couple hours to Miami, maybe three if he lived south and hit traffic. I don't know why, but I took pity on the wannabe G-man.

"I'm headed for a drink—you wanna join us?"

"As long as it isn't at a golf club."

"Doesn't get more un-golf club."

"Maybe one then. If I gotta drive home."

"I got a sofa. You're welcome to it."

He nodded. "We'll see how we go. Appreciate it."

I told him I was going to the Justice Center on Gun Club Road first, which got a frown, but he knew it and followed me there. I didn't see his face as Danielle came down in a white T-shirt and jeans and threw her uniform bag on the poor excuse for a backseat of my Porsche. I figured he'd hate me forever, but I could live with it.

But he didn't. We got to Longboard's and sat under the colored glow of the fairy lights and drank beers and ate smoked fish dip that the owner, Mick, made from scratch. Our agreement was that there would be no work talk, and Nixon was good to his word.

When we got home to Singer Island I threw some sheets and a pillow at him and he thanked me.

"Mi casa, su casa," I said, as I turned to follow Danielle to the bedroom.

"You're a lucky man," he said.

"I know."

"She's pretty lucky, too," he said.

I wasn't sure what he meant by that, but I took it as some kind of compliment, so I gave him a nod and headed off to find the sandman.

CHAPTER TWENTY—EIGHT

Nixon was an excellent houseguest. He was awake and on calls when I dragged my carcass out of bed, and he had folded the sheets and left them on top of the pillow. Based on that I found him a towel and offered him the shower. Then he exceeded all expectations and took us all out for breakfast.

Danielle had a veggie omelet with feta cheese and Nixon ordered corned beef hash. I grew up in New England so I knew a thing or two about hash. Boston was the only place in the world I ordered it anymore. It had been a few years. Nixon's looked passable but not Boston wicked. I took an egg and bacon bagel. I usually don't go for bagels outside New York, but the owner of our diner was an ex-pat Brooklyn Jew, so I was in excellent bagel hands.

"We're back on the clock, right?" Nixon said with a smile. He had a very clean shave, and it made me wish I'd bothered.

"We are," I said.

"Good," he said. "Let me fill you in on a few things I've learned. Nathaniel Donaldson is a major donor to the governor—I'm sure this comes as no surprise. But they are also golfing buddies. I know some guys on the governor's protection detail. Word is Donaldson's majorly miffed about not having a world-class course north of Boca. He's been petitioning the governor—on the quiet of course—to help him fix the situation. Now, the governor can't be seen to be doing anything to hurt a private club. Especially one that also has a membership roster full of donors. The feeling is he was positioning Donaldson as some kind of white knight in case one club or another fell on hard times."

Danielle pointed her fork at Nixon. "You said he was positioning Donaldson."

Nixon smiled and nodded. "Right. I heard last night there was call between the governor and Donaldson. There were raised voices. At least on the governor's end. He wasn't happy. He seems to be of the mind that this whole alligator thing could have gone bad for Florida tourism. He's still not convinced it will work."

Nixon ate some corned beef hash and chewed his food before he spoke again, but he was clearly going to, so we stayed quiet. I sipped my iced tea.

Then Nixon said, "Ask me why he's not convinced."

I played. "Why is he not convinced, Nixon?"

"I'm glad you asked, Miami. It's because word is in Tallahassee that the whole box and dice was the idea of one Miami Jones."

I sat back in my chair. Danielle smiled wide, shook her head and stabbed her omelet.

"That wouldn't make the governor happy."

"You have history?" asked Nixon.

"We do."

"Well, my buddies say the governor went wild-eyed when Nate Donaldson tried to claim the alligator tournament idea as his own. The governor was heard to call him a self-aggrandizing f

—." He stopped and looked at Danielle. "Sorry. You know what I mean."

The guy had excellent manners. My office manager Lizzy would love him. She's big on things like that.

"Sad thing is, it was Donaldson's idea," I said.

Nixon beamed. "Really?"

I nodded. "I basically accused him of feeding a caddy to a gator he had put there. He went ballistic. Not because I had more or less called him a murderer—that's water off a duck's back—but because I didn't see the damage I had caused him. He figured the publicity would save the tournament, and the club."

"The man knows publicity," said Danielle.

"Got that right."

"And now you're getting credit for it?" Nixon looked as happy as a clam. "That's got to get in his craw."

"But here's the thing," I said. "I didn't think he was faking it. I think the whole gator thing was a surprise to him."

"So you don't think he's involved?"

"I think he's as bent as a mountain road, but I don't think he had anything to do with gatorgate."

Nixon laughed. "Gatorgate. Where do you come up with this stuff?"

"That one's all me. I'm here all week."

"So if not Donaldson . . ." Danielle left the thought on the air.

I sipped some tea.

Nixon said, "There's the Keith Hamilton angle you told us about yesterday."

"Yeah, and I'll be honest, I can't read Keith. He seems genuinely upset by the whole affair, and he does seem to love the club as it is. So he might be telling the truth. He might have put the consortium together to save the club. I just don't know. I never play poker with lawyers."

"You never play poker," said Danielle.

"Conceptually."

Danielle continued. "There's also the Donaldson link to that deal. If he isn't involved in all this stuff as you think, then that suggests the deal is as Keith says. To save the club."

"All right," said Nixon. "Moving on."

I raised an eyebrow and watched him. I didn't know who made him chairman of the board, but I figured someone had to keep my thoughts on track, so I went with it.

"What about the sod deals. Maddox?"

Nixon shook his head. "I spoke to some folks. Just between us, there's a case building, but the feeling from those guys is that this is just typical Florida stuff. An insurance hustle. There's no real angle for Maddox to make money at the club. But . . ." He chomped into a forkful of hash and we waited as he chewed. Then he took some coffee just to completely milk the moment. "The same cannot be said for some of the folks he deals with. First, there's Martin Costas."

"What's his story?" asked Danielle.

"I did some checking and he is actually under observation by our federal friends."

"The FBI is interested in Martin?" I asked.

Nixon nodded. "Observation. It's what they say when they don't have enough to mount a full investigation. But I went to college with one of the liaisons for territorial field offices. She's getting intel from Guam."

"Guam?"

"Yes, Guam. It's a US territory. The FBI has an office there. Actually I think it might just be one guy working out of his spare room, but regardless. My college friend says there is interest in Martin Costas because of irregularities in a property deal there. She didn't know too much, but she said there might be some sort of property scam going on. Using down payments on apartments there to cover losses on a development here called Capricorn Lakes."

That name rang a bell. It was one more layer peeling from the onion.

"And who would be more expert at pulling a property scam than a Florida lawyer?"

"Right," said Nixon.

"So you think Martin might want to cash in his chips with a big payday at South Lakes in order to cover his losses?" asked Danielle.

"The thought had occurred."

We ate and drank and let that thought percolate. We finished up and Nixon took care of the check and I liked him more and more. When we got out to the lot the day was in full swing. The sun was high and hot, but not as hot as the previous day. The forecast for the tournament was Florida postcard stuff. A white cloud might arrive to add depth to the sky, but that was about all. It was the kind of stuff Florida boosters dreamed of, and they don't have to dream that hard.

"What's on today at the club?" asked Nixon.

"Pro-am," I said.

"What is that, exactly?" asked Danielle.

"It's where the professional golfers play a round with the amateurs. Usually the amateurs are corporate guys who have bid on the right to play with a certain golfer, and the money they bid goes to the tournament charity."

"All ten percent of it," she said.

"Better than a poke in the eye with a putter. And for the pros, it's one more chance to play the course before things get serious on Thursday."

Nixon said, "What does your gut say? Is there likely to be another attempt to disrupt the tournament?"

I shrugged. "Vandalism, viral poisoning, murder. My gut wonders why you would go that far and then give up?"

"Unless you thought you might get caught?" Danielle mused. "There's a lot of extra security now. And the PBSO will have a full complement from today."

"Which reminds me. Do you need to be at the course?"

"I do. But first I want to speak to Connie Persil. Find out about that bleach container."

Danielle stepped away to make a call. Nixon eyed me.

"I need to warn you," he said.

I frowned.

"About Danielle."

I frowned more. It was like an aerial photograph of the Sahara desert.

"I want her."

I took a deep breath in through the nose, out through the mouth. It calmed me. The other option was breaking Nixon's pretty little nose.

"You want her?"

He nodded. "Special Agent Marcard speaks very highly of her."

"You mentioned."

"He also said that she rejected the idea of joining the FBI because she didn't want to leave Florida."

"He said that, did he?"

"He did. But the FDLE, we're like the FBI for Florida. It could be the best of both worlds for her."

"So why are you having this conversation with me?" I asked. "You asking me for her hand in marriage? Because I don't know if you've noticed, but folks don't do that stuff anymore."
"Call it courtesy. I know you've got a thing. I can see what she means to you, and vice versa."
"It's really her call."
"I know. I wasn't asking your permission. I guess I wanted your opinion, as biased as it might be."
"You asked Marcard. He's not biased."
"No, he's not. He's a good guy. His words were I'd recruit her in a second."
"There you go."
"You'd be okay with that."
"I'm okay with whatever Danielle wants to do. I'll tell you straight, I think she's wasted as a deputy. But she seems to love it. So like I say, it's her call."
"Yes, it is."
We fell silent as Danielle wandered back with her phone in her hand.
"Connie says she wants to meet at the lab." She looked at Nixon. "You want in?"
"If you want me there."
"Three heads are better than two." She looked at me. "Right?"
"In everything but lovemaking and chess."

CHAPTER TWENTY-NINE

The laboratory was a nondescript place at the south end of Palm Beach Gardens. Like everything in Palm Beach Gardens it could have been an office block or a shopping mall. There were signs for the laboratory and a travel clinic, and posters talking about such lovely things as West Nile virus and yellow fever and malaria and E. coli bacteria. The halls were sanitary in the fashion of a hospital but I fought the compulsion to hold my breath.

Connie Persil was sitting in a waiting area like a patient. On one side was the clinic, and a stand-up banner told me that I needed to get inoculated if I wanted to go to South America or Asia or Africa or parts of Europe. It was like a travel poster for staying home. Connie stood and Danielle introduced Nixon, and then Connie led us the other way, into the lab.

"This is the top infectious disease laboratory in the state, outside of Miami," Connie said. I wondered why we couldn't have this chat in a bar.

"I want to show you something," she said. She led us into a room that looked like a laboratory. It was white. The floors, the ceiling, the cupboards. Connie led us to a microscope. At least that's what I thought it was. It was bigger than the ones I remembered from school, and it too was white. But we didn't look into the microscope. She offered us hard plastic chairs and we sat in a row against the wall like kids outside the principal's office. Connie hit a button and a black monitor screen came to life. The picture took a moment to materialize. And when it did, I had no idea what I was looking at. It looked like a ragged cauliflower, only green. The cauliflower was suspended in midpicture, with other similar cauliflowers floating around and behind it.

"You know what this is?" she asked with a touch of the dramatic that I didn't think she possessed.

"An alien life form?" I said.

"Norovirus," said Danielle.

"Right, Deputy," said Connie. "Norovirus. But not just any norovirus. As I mentioned at your bar the other night, the assays that this lab runs can tell us not only what genogroup a virus is, but what genotype. That's like a subcategory, and it can help track where a particular strain might have originated from. The genogroup most harmful to humans is genogroup II. That's what this is. It's no wonder the people at the wedding got sick, or that the incubation period was so brief. This is one nasty little bug."

"What do you know about it?" asked Danielle.

"Well, we know that it was on the chairs in the hospitality tent, in quantities that almost ensured contact would result in contamination and illness. And thanks to you, we know that it came from the bleach bottle you found. Good protocol by the way, Deputy. You could have easily gotten contaminated."

"Hang on, doesn't bleach kill the virus?" I asked.

"It does. It's most effective."

"So why didn't it die in the bottle?"

"Excellent question. And the answer is because the bottle had been cleaned out. There would have been only trace elements of the bleach left. Not enough to counteract the virus. And that bottle was one heck of a viral solution."

Danielle sat forward and gestured at the blob on the screen. "How can you be sure that the virus in the bottle is the same one that infected the people? I mean it looks likely, but in a courtroom the presence of a gun at a shooting is proof of nothing. We have to match the ballistics. How can we do that here?"

"That, Deputy, is also an excellent question. And in a fashion we can do the equivalent of a ballistics match. That's where the genotype comes in. These viruses mutate, which is why it's so hard to stay on top of them. The most common genotype doing the rounds in the US these days is a variant known as GII.4. That is what we most commonly see."

"You mentioned before this was different?" Danielle asked.

"Yes, it's a new genotype."

"It's new? How?"

"It mutated, somewhere, and someone brought it here, that's how. People pick these things up from contact with contagious people or contaminated surfaces. Then they get on airplanes. We can thank modern aviation for the spread of viruses around the world."

"So you can link the bottle to the sick people from the wedding."

"We can. Same genotype. Never before seen in the US, and now in your bottle and in the patients." Connie leaned back against the counter with a satisfied grin.

"Do you know where the virus originated?" Nixon asked.

"That's what's taken some time. When we found the new strain in the patients we had to run tests again. Once confirmed, we put the news on the wire to see if there had been other cases. There had. It seemed the virus originates from the Cordoba region of Colombia."

"So someone went to Colombia and brought the virus back?" asked Danielle.

"Yes."

I asked, "Did Ernesto go to Colombia? Or was he from Colombia?"

Danielle shook her head. "He was US-born and raised. From Mexican parents. And we found no record of a passport."

"It wasn't Ernesto," said Connie. "We got a sample from the necropsy. He didn't have the virus."

I said, "But he sprayed it. I think we can agree on that. So how did it get in the bottle? I mean, sure, someone put it there. But how?" I pointed at the alien cauliflower on the screen. "How do you get that thing into a spray bottle."

"That part isn't very pleasant."

"I'm a big boy. I can take it." The words came out of my mouth but I wasn't sure they were true. I could live a long and happy life not knowing the secret to how the virus got in the bottle.

"Feces," Connie said.

It was Danielle's turn to frown. "Excuse me?"

"The bottle contains a water-based solution. In the solution we found contaminated human feces."

Some days it doesn't pay to take a case. Some cases weren't worth any amount of money. I know, it's a human bodily function. We all create waste and we all need to get rid of it. But this one was going to hang around in the recesses of my mind longer than most. Of that I was certain.

"How?" asked Danielle before I could tie a gag around her mouth to stop her asking questions to which I didn't want the answers.

"Someone put it there."

"But I mean, where would you get it? It's not like there's a market for that sort of thing."

The picture formed in my mind before I could stop it. A market—a Middle Eastern-type place with heavy-bearded traders and spices and fresh dates. And a stall doing a brisk trade in human waste. If I woke up in hot sweats dreaming about that later, I was waking Danielle up for sure.

"No, I can't imagine there is," said Connie. "I think the logical explanation is that it belonged to the person who put it there."

Nixon said, "You mean they harvested their own—"

"Yes, Special Agent. It would appear that way."

Danielle nodded. "So chances are, they were sick?"

"Yes."

"So we've narrowed it down to people who showed symptoms."

"At some point," said Connie.

"Meaning?"

"Meaning the virus could survive in that water-based environment for months."

Danielle sat back like she'd almost caught a break but then lost it. But I wasn't so sure. I felt like we were getting somewhere. Investigations are like baseball games. Momentum is everything. When you can't catch a break, you don't. And then when things swing your way, you have to make hay. You have to ride the momentum.

"So our perp has been to Colombia. And they've been sick. But not months ago. You don't hold onto something like this and wait for your opportunity. This is not a pistol sitting in your bedside table. The opportunity and means came together. So our perp got sick recently. Not days, but not months either. And they either disappeared off the map for a time, or they came into contact with the people. People who themselves may have gotten sick."

"No. No one else outside the wedding has contracted this strain of the virus."

"No, Connie. No one else has reported it. Not the same thing. Not the same thing at all." The cogs were spinning now. Momentum was ours. Truth was we knew some stuff that didn't link together very well, but that was irrelevant. A batter didn't go from hitting .200 to hitting .400 inside a week because he suddenly got good. What he got was confident. His mind clicked into the right place for the world to slow down so he could see the curveball coming his way like it was being thrown by a child. My world was slowing. My mind was clicking. I had to get the hell out of stomach bug central.

I stood and thanked Connie for her time. I wasn't sure if Danielle or Nixon had more questions, and I didn't care. I had places to go and people to see. Danielle and Nixon followed me into the parking lot.

"Eew," said Danielle.

Nixon was wiping his hands on his trousers, but I wasn't sure if he knew he was doing it.

"What now?" he asked.

"You need to get to the course?" I asked Danielle. She nodded. I looked to Nixon. "Can you give her a ride?"

"Sure. What are you doing?"

"As an old friend would say, I need to see a man about a dog."

CHAPTER THIRTY

Nixon had mentioned the Capricorn Lakes development over breakfast when talking about Martin Costas. It wasn't the first time it had come up in conversation, so I decided since I was in the neighborhood I'd visit. I preferred to drop in without a uniformed deputy with me. Sometimes the uniform helped, sometimes not. I suspected this would be a not.

It looked like every other master-planned community in Florida. There was a gatehouse that stood empty until the developer reached a quorum of homeowners to pay for a guard. There were fresh white sidewalks and swathes of green grass that to my until recently untrained eye looked like St. Augustine. There was a small row of houses—single-family homes with pastel stucco and small yards that looked over a manmade lake that really ranked as more of a dam. The first release of houses in a long cul-de-sac. Probably four model homes and twelve more sales. The St. Augustine grass looked long and healthy, and ran around the finished homes and along the main road, which led to where the clubhouse and community pool were. Everything else was graded flat. Stakes marked the plot lines. There was no grass there, just sandy-looking dirt.

I drove around the clubhouse. Every community had one, a place with barbecues and a pool table and sofas for guests to lounge in, which in reality hardly got used because people preferred to use their own grills and lounge on their own sofas. This one looked dark and vacant. A pool that seemed disproportionately tiny compared to the size of the estate sparkled in the sunlight, inviting me in. Water sold real estate in Florida, even forty-five minutes from the ocean. Fake lakes and community pools, that's where the gold lay.

I returned back down the smooth blacktop and turned into the completed street. I was right. There were signs in front of the first two homes on either side, telling me the model name and the square footage. None of them looked particularly open. They weren't as big as they first seemed, but perhaps to the eco-friendly crowd that was a selling point. But from what I saw, the eco-friendly crowd wasn't that big of a market. I passed the models, drove to the end and then did a slow loop around the cul-de-sac and headed back.

I stopped outside a house and parked behind an old red Toyota Tacoma. I was starting to think that I was the only person in Florida who didn't own one. There were a couple guys in green uniforms. One was trimming the hedges that hid the air-conditioning units from view. The other was spraying something onto the hedges with a wand connected to a canister he wore on his back. I got out and heard the buzz of a lawn mower, and then saw the ride-on unit between the houses as it zoomed back and forth across the rear lawns that led down to the thimble-sized lake.

One of the gardeners saw me approach and gave me a nod.

"How's it going?" I asked.

"S'okay."

He watched me through wary eyes. I didn't think anything of it. A lot of gardeners, like a lot of manual workers in Florida, didn't always have the right paperwork. And not having paperwork meant there was always someone out there looking for you, to send you back where you came from. I didn't care they were here. I didn't want to mow my own lawn, and I wasn't getting my door banged down by offers from the neighbors' kids to take the job on.

"I'm thinking about buying a place here."

"It's nice."

I nodded. "Not too many houses."

"No yet."

"Yeah. Say, you know what's out there?" I pointed out in a general westerly direction. Out where there were no graded plots.

"Nature," he said.

Nature, all right. It was the damn Everglades. What every eco-friendly buyer wants. A view of the eco.

"You ever see any animals here?"

"Animals?"

"Yeah, you know. You ever see any gators in the lakes?"

The guy looked at his buddy, who had stopped working on the hedge under the front window of the house.

"Que?"

His buddy ambled over. I nodded hi to him. "You know, alligators."

"No," said the buddy. "No alligators."

"No? This close to the nature."

"No alligators."

I nodded. "You guys here full-time?"

"Si."

I smiled at the first guy. "Doesn't look like a full-time job yet."
"Soon. When you buy."
"Right on. How many guys you got?"
"Cuatro."
"Three," said the buddy. "They hire more guy. Later. See?"
"Sure, sure. Anyone home here? You mind if I take a look at the lake?"
"No, is okay."
"Cheers."
I left them to their hedges and wandered between two houses. The small rear yards of both places were covered by mesh cages to keep out the bugs. One can get too eco-friendly. Beyond the cages was more lush grass, which ran down to the water. The lake was ringed by what might have been marketed as a beach, except it was at a forty-five degree angle to the water, and was only about six inches wide all around. A sign was planted just below the water line. It warned there might be alligators down below. That sort of sign was mandatory on any freshwater lake in Florida. The marketers would have moaned but the lawyers would have insisted.
The guy zoomed by on the mower and offered a nod, which I returned. It was pleasantly warm in the sun, and this far from the coast we were practically on the gulf side of the state, so there was no breeze. The guy on the mower was sweating hard, and I didn't blame him. It was tough work, and the plants grew 365 days a year. Even in summer these guys had to work to keep the eco at bay. I watched the guy stop the mower but not switch it off. He wiped his face with a cloth. He must have been losing pounds per day, and I wondered what he ate to keep going.
I left him to it and wandered along the water's edge, past the rear of the houses. I got to the last house and stopped. Beyond

me on one side lay graded plots, on the other side was scrubby swamp. I'd seen wild ground like it before. It housed all manner of beasties, from snakes to wild pigs. I heard a door slide open and turned to see a woman step out of her home into her caged backyard. She looked like an aviary exhibit at the zoo.

"Hi," she said, stepping to the screen.

"How are you?" I asked, moving up from the lake. "Beautiful day."

"Another one. You buying?"

"Giving it some thought. You like it here?"

She shrugged. It wasn't a ringing endorsement. "It's fine. It'll be better when there are more people. They'll get around to putting in the resort pool and the gym."

"How long you been here?"

"Almost a year."

"Seems quiet."

"It is. Except for bugs. And the gators."

"You hear gators?"

"Yeah. Did you know they bark? It's quite a noise. I think it's a mating thing. Or maybe territory. I don't know."

"You see any?"

She shook her head. "No, not really. In a year I've seen one. Do you have pets?"

"No."

"Kids?"

"No."

"Then you'll be fine."

"You see a big one?"

"They're all big aren't they?"

"True enough. Where'd you see him?"

"In there." She nodded at the lake. "The guys just came and got him out."

"Where'd they take it?"

"No idea. Out to the 'Glades, wouldn't you think?"

"I would."

"I hope I didn't put you off. Like I say, it's the only one I've seen."

"Not a problem. It's Florida, am I right?"

She nodded.

"It's nice meeting you," I said.

"You too. Hope to see you around."

I waved and walked back down the lake and out to my car. The gardeners seemed to have stopped for a break. I didn't blame them. They had retreated to the shade of a couple palm trees that stood outside the nearest of the model homes. Two of them were sitting on the grass quietly munching on something that resembled coconut. The third guy lay out on the thick grass, a towel covering his face. I was familiar with the position. Hangovers and Florida sun don't always mix well. I passed them and noted the garage door was open on the model. It looked like the gardeners were using it as temporary storage, since their entire reason for being was in that solitary street.

I drove out and stopped near the gatehouse. I pulled over but was still partially blocking the road out of the community, but traffic was so close to zero that I was it. In most gated communities the security person would have dashed out of the gatehouse to give me the move on. But there was no guard, so I sat for a while with the top up and the air-conditioning on and brought up the internet on my phone. My fingers were too big for the screen and it was laborious work, but I learned a thing about geography. I kept at it until I heard the familiar buzzing of the lawn mower.

I wandered back on foot. I had another itch to scratch. I walked down the only populated street. The third of the gardeners was still lying on the grass in the shade of the palm, towel over face. I wondered if he had fallen asleep. One of the other guys had taken charge of the mower. Clearly there wasn't yet enough work to keep three guys busy. I edged past the prone figure and slipped into the garage. It was a two-car job, and was filled with a combination of real estate stuff and gardening gear. There was a high pile of mini bottles of water from a big box store, and flats of cola and lemonade. Realtors offered cool drinks at open houses as a point of necessity. There were boxes of snacks—chips and little cookies and pretzels. On the other side there were weed whackers and jerry cans of two-stroke gasoline. A set of golf clubs stood in the corner. There was a steel locker that had a hefty padlock on it. The garage smelled of wet grass and Oreos. I care for neither, so I slipped back out. The guy on the grass didn't stir. I walked back to my car and was getting in when my phone rang. It was Danielle.

"Where are you?"

"Palm Beach Gardens. Why?"

"It's Heath McAllen."

"What about him?"

"He just received a death threat."

CHAPTER THIRTY-ONE

Heath McAllen looked like he'd just opened his birthday presents. I know sportsmen are supposed to be cool under pressure, but I had been a professional sportsman, of a fashion, and I knew that it was all a lie. I could take some breaths and hold my cool on the mound as well as the next guy, but that didn't mean I enjoyed it when the moron in front of me on the freeway cut in front without bothering himself with a turn signal.

But Heath McAllen might have been different. He was smiling and relaxed, sipping a can of something mixed with green tea. His hand was covering what the something was, and my mind could not come up with any ideas that made sense. He gave me a nod as I walked into the conference room cum briefing room cum boardroom. The concertina walls were all open. Heath was kicked back with Danielle and Nixon. Keith was there, but he didn't do kicked back. There was another man I didn't know. He was big guy, like he'd been one of those professional wrestlers back in his heyday.

"You all right, kid?" I asked.

Heath nodded to me. "Cannae complain."

Danielle handed me a piece of paper. "Heath found this in his locker after his practice this morning."

I took it and looked at it. It was a standard letter-size piece of paper with a message printed on an inkjet printer. There was a smudged line down the length of the page about a third of the way from the left edge. The message was to the point.

McAllen - You play, you die.

I looked up. "Hardly the work of a master wordsmith, is it?"

"Is this guy for real?" It was the wrestler.

"He's for real," said Danielle. "MJ, this is Brad Shift, Heath's American agent."

"Soon to be global agent, am I right, Heath?" The guy gave Heath a grin that showed off his too-white-to-be-true teeth.

Heath shrugged. "What do you think, Miami?"

"What do you think?" I asked him back.

"What does he think?" Brad Shift shook his head like it was joined to his vast neck by a Slinky. He made eye contact with everyone in the room, and then ended with me. "What does he think? What are we paying you for?"

"You're not paying me, so shut the hell up. If I want a peanut, I'll go to the concession stand."

The guy stood up. "You want something from me?"

"Silence."

Danielle stood. "Mr. Shift, relax, please." She glanced at me and gave me a frown.

"Heath?" I asked again.

"I don't know what I think."

"Who has access to the locker room?"

Danielle said, "All the players, the caddies. Some of the staff, some members. It's quite a list."

"Any way of tracking down the printer?"

"Only if we have a suspect. We'd need to know where to look. We're checking here obviously, but otherwise it's a needle in a haystack."

Nixon said, "The real question is, how seriously do you want to take it?"

"What's your professional opinion?" I asked Nixon.

"Doesn't feel credible. But I'd say discretion is the better part of valor."

"If he pulls out, he could fall down the money list," said Shift. "That's a million bucks just for topping the list. He can't pull out."

"What does he get if he dies during a round?" I asked.

Shift thought about it. "There's insurance."

I shook my head. I wanted to ask him if he knew what a rhetorical question was, but I didn't feel like having to then explain what rhetorical meant. Heath shrugged and offered me his infectious smile.

"It's your call," I said to him. "Danielle and the other sheriffs can keep an eye out, and there's lots of course-side security. But ultimately, it's your call."

"You didn't answer my question," he said. "What do you think? What would you do?"

"I'd play. But I don't take well to being told what to do."

"Me either. I want to play."

"All right! Yeah!" yelled Shift. He sounded like that one idiot in every golf gallery who feels the need to yell It's in the hole! after every tee shot. He probably was that idiot.

"Can I make a suggestion?" said Keith. "We can add some extra roving security to Heath's playing group, of course. But I'd feel better if we had someone closer."

"How do you mean, closer?" asked Danielle.

"I was thinking carrying his bag."

"His caddy?" I said. "Good luck convincing the big guy to step down."

"He doesn't need to step down," said Keith. "He isn't given the option. Heath, what do you think?"

"Miami's right. Alfie's not going to like it. But I got to admit, I wouldn't mind having an eye on me."

"But who's going to do it? A cop?" asked Nixon.

"I was thinking Miami," said Keith.

"Me?"

"I think that's a great idea," said Heath.

"I can't caddy a PGA tournament."

"Why?" asked Heath.

"I don't know how."

"You play golf?"

"Occasionally."

"You know your numbers one through nine?"

"Yes."

"And you're certainly capable of lifting the bag."

"Think about this, Heath."

"Relax, Miami. Just think, if I win, you're in for ten percent."

"I don't want the money, Heath."

I looked at Danielle for help. I didn't get it.

"It's settled then," she said. "Miami will substitute as Heath's caddy."

"Who's going to tell your caddy?" I pleaded.

"I'll do it," Heath said.

He was a stand-up guy. I didn't envy him, but I sure as hell didn't want to take his place. He stood up and wandered out with his big agent.

"Get a good sleep," he said as he went. "We've got an early morning tee time."

I stayed where I was. I gave Danielle the eye, and not the eye that invites one to cross a room. She beamed like the cat that got the cream. She was having way too much fun.

Then a deputy I didn't know rapped her knuckle on the door frame. She was young and blond and had her hair tied back like Danielle.

"Ma'am, the threat letter," she said to Danielle.

"Yes?"

"We found the printer."

"You're kidding."

"No, ma'am. It's from one of the offices just here."

"Which office?" asked Keith.

The young deputy looked at a small notepad in her hand. "The office belongs to the vice president. No name."

We all looked at Keith.

"Martin?" he said.

"Thank you, Deputy," Danielle said.

"Yes, ma'am." The young deputy stepped away and we focused back on Keith.

"Martin?" Keith repeated, to himself this time.

"Does anyone else have access to that office?" I asked.

"I don't. I guess someone does. We had the keys redone last year, as part of a security audit. Barry thought the locks had been around for fifty years, and he might have been right. But now? Just Martin, as far as I know."

"What do you think?" Danielle asked Nixon.

"It's pretty dumb if he used his printer here," he said.

"And he's not dumb."

"But how do we solve most crimes?"

"Someone does something dumb."

I wasn't sure I needed to be there for the conversation, so I made to leave.

"Where are you going?" Danielle asked.

"Apparently I need to get my beauty sleep."

"You going to say anything to Martin?"

"No, that's your job."

She nodded. "I say we keep it quiet for now. We don't want to tip Martin or anyone else off."

"Right on."

"I'll catch up with you later?"

"I most certainly hope so."

I wandered out to the reception area, where I saw Natalie Morris. She shot me the Florida smile and I shot it right back at her. It never ceases to amaze me how a great smile can readjust your mood. It was only midafternoon, so I wasn't really ready for sleep, but I figured I'd head home and mentally prepare myself for my first PGA Tour performance.

My Porsche was sitting in the sunshine, so I dropped the roof first thing. That cooled things off, but I knew that it would only be a matter of weeks before I would be keeping the lid up and turning the air-conditioning on. When that happened the little car would feel like a sardine can with bucket seats. But today I flicked on my shades and revved the engine.

The impact hit the driver's side window hard. The entire car wobbled, and I don't know how it didn't shatter. I almost left my own body from shock, but I collected myself quickly. I tend to do that. And when I did I looked through the window and saw the massive frame of Heath McAllen's caddy, Alfie.

He looked like a bear in coveralls. His arms were raised like King Kong and he bellowed an unholy sound that came from another dimension and hit me in the chest like a shock wave. Clearly Heath had told him about the caddying arrangements, and clearly he wasn't happy about it. He came in for a second impact, his hands joining together in one huge fist, more an anvil than a human appendage, and drove it into the window again. The window flexed in a way that I never thought a window should, but again it resisted the impact. Score one, whatever company supplied Porsche with their windows. I punched the car into gear. I was done.

But Alfie wasn't done. The failure of the windows to cooperate enraged him further. He moved forward and then drove his fists down onto the hood. For reasons I cannot even begin to fathom, the hood crumpled into a large dent under the same impact withstood by the window. It made me wonder why they don't make cars out of autoglass.

"Hey, easy," I yelled. I dropped the transmission back into neutral and got out. I wasn't going to fight this beast. He was scarier than the gator. But I slammed the door and he turned to me. We really had to talk. And I really needed to be ready to run.

"Just cool it," I said in my soft voice. It isn't like Danielle's soft preschool teacher voice. Hers would soothe a raging tiger. Mine just sort of comes out condescending, like I think the listener is an idiot. Which to be fair, is often the case. I don't know how Alfie took it, but I do know it didn't improve his mood.

"Aaaargh!" was all he had to say. He grabbed me, one paw on the shirt and one at the belt line, and he lifted me up. I was like a bag of flour to him. But I don't weigh what a bag of flour weighs. I'm six foot one, and a touch over two hundred pounds on a good day. That's a lot of dead weight. Alfie lifted me like he was flipping pizza dough. He must surely sometimes forget that he is even carrying a bag full of golf clubs.

I yelled, "Alfliiie!"

"You steal my job, you scumbag. I'm gonna tear you a new one!"

He screamed as he spun me around like we were a new and exciting event at the Olympics. They could call it pitcher pitching. Grab a professional baseball pitcher, pick him up and toss him as far as you can. Extra points if he played in the major league, and double extra points for CC Sabathia. That dude is massive.

Alfie rotated at the hips the way you should when you are holding another human above your head, and he drove from the knees and thrust me away. I flew. Not with grace. I'm not a swan. But I was definitely airborne. The Wright brothers would have called it a successful test. For me, not so much. I flew out into the plantings around the clubhouse, and then descended fast and certain, into the outer reaches of an agave plant.

I hit hard on my back. It knocked the wind out of me. But like I say, I recover pretty quick. When I played quarterback at high school, I got hit a lot. But the other teams got more frustrated about it than I did, because I always bounced up and gave them a cheeky grin, in the way only a sixteen-year-old boy can mock a two hundred fifty-pound defensive lineman. I felt indestructible. I didn't feel that now. I felt sore. But I sucked in a couple of deep breaths and sat up. I was facing the agave plant, and I was thankful I hadn't landed in the middle of it. They might still be collecting barbs from inside me.

The sound of my car pulling out of the space attracted my attention. I wanted to yell, to tell the crazy English giant to stop, but I couldn't form the appropriate sentence, so I got up instead. The Porsche looked like a toy with Alfie at the wheel. In his white coveralls he looked like an overbred mechanic taking a car to the shop. But he punched the gears and sped away across the parking lot.

I ran. I'm not a great runner. Used to be that we'd say that big guys like me weren't built to go fast. But then Usain Bolt is six-five, so that theory went out the window. But I ran often, with Danielle along the beach at Singer Island. So I hold my own. I put the big ones in. I don't really know what I was doing. I wasn't going to catch a Porsche Boxster. That only happens in the movies.

The strange thing was, I didn't feel angry. The red mist hadn't descended on me. More than anything, I wanted to talk to the guy. I'm not always so forgiving, but I think a little version of Heath McAllen was sitting on my shoulder, pleading to my better angels. Heath was a kid by many standards. Most guys in their midtwenties think they know it all, but the truth is they don't even know what they don't know yet. But Heath saw the good in this giant moron. And part of me wanted to be as good a man as him.

Alfie didn't head for the exit. He sped down the lane toward the hospitality tent village set up on the executive course. I had visions of him racing through there, collecting wasted businessmen as he went. But at the last second he yanked on the wheel and the Porsche responded the way fast cars do, and he launched off the pavement and onto the grass. I wondered where the hell he was going, but I suspected he hadn't thought it through. Then I reassessed that thought. I was only halfway across the lot but I could see what lay ahead. He was screaming across the deep rough between the first tees of each course layout, headed for one place and one place only.

South Lakes wasn't a misnomer. It was so far south in the United States that it was actually further south than the part of the country referred to as the Deep South. And it had lakes. Lots of them. Not all as big as the one called the Pacific, but they were there, ready to collect balls from wayward golfers. The lake Alfie was headed for was bigger than the so-called lake at the Capricorn Lakes development, although it was by no means large. But it was certainly large enough.

Alfie hit the water at speed. The Porsche skimmed across the surface of the lake like a skipping stone, and for a brief second I thought the thing might actually race across the water and drive up the other side. But it didn't. The laws of gravity and viscosity and moron-ness took hold and the Porsche came to a stop about ten feet in, and then sunk. It wasn't a deep lake. Golf course lakes aren't designed for bass fishing. They're designed so the club can easily fish out the balls and then sell them back to the errant golfers who put them in the drink in the first place. So the Porsche settled with the water line just above the door frame, and the reclaimed water gently filled the interior until all that was visible was the top half of the windshield.

The big Englishman slipped out over the top of the door and waded his way to the bank. I made it to the water's edge at the same time. I was breathing heavily and I really didn't want to have another fight, if you could call it that. That word implied some kind of an even match, and we had established that our weight classes were at opposite ends of the spectrum. I put my hands on my knees and sucked in some big warm gulps. A good crowd spilled out of the corporate hospitality tents to see my car sink. There was a quiet murmur across the watching faces, like a final hole gallery waiting to see if the player chokes on his putt or wins the day.

Alfie stepped up to the long grass and looked at me. He didn't approach me. He just stood there with a satisfied look on his face. I shook my head.

I said, "I don't want your damned job."

"Didn't stop you from taking it, innit."

"I don't want the money, I mean."

"Sure. Tell me another one."

"I was going to give any prize money to you. I don't want it."

His face contorted in confusion. He wanted what I said to be true, but he wasn't buying it. Because if he bought it, if he believed that I didn't want the cash, then he had just done a very stupid thing.

I stood up. I was sweating and I wiped my brow with my arm, which didn't do much. "I wanted your help."

"No, you didn't." He said the words without conviction. "Did you?"

I nodded. "I'm not a caddy. I'm just trying to keep the kid safe. And for reasons that totally escape me, he seems to care about you."

The big guy shifted in his wet boots. He glanced back at my sunken car.

"Oops." It wasn't exactly poetic, but I got the meaning.

"I still need your help."

He frowned. "Okay."

He stepped to me and offered his hand as if a schoolteacher had made the bully shake hands with his victim. Because that always solved the problem. But I took his hand.

"You don't want the money?"

I shook my head. "But you are paying for that." I looked at my sad car.

His face dropped. "A Porsche, huh?"

"Yeah. But don't worry. It was an old one."

CHAPTER THIRTY-TWO

Being a caddy was easy. In the same way running a front office at a baseball organization was easy. In the front office you just put on a suit, sat on your butt for ten hours a day, and went to a lot of meetings where you ate donuts and drank coffee. But the success of a front office isn't in what you did—it's how you did it. Caddying was the same. Any schmo can carry a bag. Within reason anyway. They are heavy. A player is allowed a maximum of fourteen clubs in their bag, and most carry the maximum. Why wouldn't you, when you aren't actually carrying the damn things yourself? Half of them would have their caddy carry more, but there was actually a penalty in the rules for having more than fourteen clubs.
In the 2013 PGA Championship a player named Woody Austin discovered he had accidentally started his round with fifteen clubs in his bag. He was assessed a four-stroke penalty for the error, even though he never used the extra club. And here's the kicker. He reported himself to officials. He might have been able to sneak around and hope no one noticed. But he didn't. He turned himself in and took his licks. For all the pomp and

environmental degradation and corporate largesse that I could blame on the game of golf, I had to admire how often players acted with that kind of honor. If I ever have kids, I'd be okay with them taking up golf. They could do worse than learning that kind of personal responsibility.

Of course the reality was that it was Woody's responsibility but his caddy's fault. Alfie made that clear to me as he walked me around the course after he drove my car into the water. When he wasn't drinking or had a full head of steam he was actually an okay guy. Personally I thought he needed to sort those shortcomings out before I would actually declare him decent. Decency isn't a part-time gig. Despite that he did take his job seriously. The bag and everything in it were the caddy's domain. If the player liked lip balm, carry it. If he liked to eat a banana at the turn, make sure one was waiting as you came off the ninth green. He knew exactly how far Heath hit each club, and he made notes about the distances to the green based on features that I didn't even see, like sprinkler heads and knots in trees. Not approximations, but measured to the nearest yard. He explained when I should talk to Heath and when I should not. He told me to watch for the whites of Heath's knuckles when he putted, because that meant he was getting stressed and was gripping the club too tight. He told me a couple of very raunchy jokes that I could use to put Heath at ease, and advised me to make sure no television cameras were close by when I told them.

When we took the first tee the next morning, everything was different. The course looked the same—the lime and tangerine branding was everywhere—but the crowds were bigger and the air seemed heavier, like a storm was brewing. But the skies were clear and Heath's first tee shot made a stunning sound and flew straight down the middle of the fairway to gentle but appreciative applause.

I kept my eyes open. Searching the gallery, and the trees and fairways for anything suspicious. I saw nothing. I handed Heath clubs and talked about yardages. I didn't see the white knuckles. He seemed well at ease, despite the death threat. He was in his office, doing his thing. I had a million questions to ask him, but I didn't want to put him off his game so I kept them to myself. We both passed the water hazard known as the Pacific without a word. I noted the white out-of-bounds line painted on the rough grass. I didn't see Lorraine Catchitt or anyone else in there.

Heath shot a decent three under par, sixty-nine shots for his round. He was the clubhouse leader when we got in about lunchtime, which meant he was in first place of all the players who had completed their first round so far. He wanted to work on a couple of things, so he gave an interview with the television guys, and then went to the driving range. I went with him. Alfie had told me he would be hanging around but he wouldn't make an appearance. The story doing the rounds was that Alfie had the flu, and I was carrying the bag until he got better.

"You were top-notch today," Heath said as he swung through a chip shot that looked perfect to me.

"You didn't do too bad, either."

"There's a lot of hazards just short of the greens. This thing could come down to short play."

I nodded. I knew short play meant hitting shorter shots, which were usually done using the higher-numbered irons, which had a greater angle on their heads to create loft. Heath's short game looked as good as a short game could get, but he hit two hundred chip shots on the range anyway.

Afterward he asked me to clean the clubs and lock up the gear. He left to do another interview, and then he was escorted by a unit of deputies over to the corporate hospitality tents to make an appearance on behalf of one of his sponsors. I wasn't sure where he got the energy. I was beat. Granted, I had carried the bags, but he had hit the shots, and using up mental energy sapped you as much as using physical energy. I knew something about expending mental energy. The physical and the mental were connected. If an athlete got physically tired, their mental acuity dropped off. Gym time wasn't just about hitting the ball farther—it was about keeping as mentally sharp at the end as they were at the beginning.

After locking up his clubs I did what caddies seemed to do, and I headed up to the bar. Folks were seated along the windows, watching the afternoon rounds go by. I sat at the bar. Ron wandered in.

"How's the new career?" he asked, taking a seat.

"A good walk ruined."

"Your man did well."

"He did. He's a good kid."

Ron smiled and ordered a beer.

"Thanks for helping out," he said.

"They're paying me."

"You know what I mean."

We touched glasses. "Any time. How's the rest going?"

"All good. The gate receipts are up. The alligator thing has brought a lot of folks in."

I shook my head.

"I'd say the weekend will be a sellout. We'll be turning them away."

"Good result. For the club, I mean."

"Stellar."

We sipped our beers and I watched the bartender, Chip, doing his thing. It was a good spot and I could see what Ron liked about it. There was something familial about it. Some folks went to church, some folks played golf. Both groups often spoke to deities, just in different terms. And they both got a good dose of community from the experience. I used to have that, in the locker room. Sports are like that. It doesn't matter if it's professional or collegiate or just a bunch of friends running around on the weekends. Sports bring people together. And then we get older. Professional sports careers like mine end. A lot of guys struggle with that. It's not just the fact that they suddenly have to go and get real jobs. They miss the camaraderie, the brotherhood. Or sisterhood, for that matter. I knew plenty of female athletes who suffered the same malaise when the family that had built up around them was suddenly no longer there. People graduated college and got jobs and had families and found all manner of reasons to stop being active and let those relationships drift away. I knew more than a few guys who had been the life of the party in college but hit their forties and found they had no true friends left. We're social beasts. Solitary confinement is a punishment for a reason. I was glad Ron had this place. I was glad Jackie Treloar had this place. I was glad it and all the other clubs and churches and communities existed. I didn't always agree with their view of the cosmos, but I knew the world was a better place for the people coming together like that.

I was almost done with my beer and considering whether it would be to my and Heath's detriment if I had another, when Special Agent Nixon came striding up the stairs. He nodded when he saw me and he came over.

"Nice round," he said.

"He did well."

"Can we talk?" he said it in a way that suggested it wasn't something he cared to share with Ron or anyone else.

"I was just about to leave," Ron said, which was a lie because he was only halfway through his beer, and Ron would rather lose a limb than leave a beverage unfinished.

"No, you finish your drink." I got down from my stool. "Let's take a walk," I said to Nixon.

We wandered out the front of the club toward the corporate hospitality tents.

"Where's your car?" asked Nixon.

I shrugged. "Shop. They fished it out early this morning."

"Shame. It was a nice car."

"It was too small. What was it you wanted to say?"

"I followed up with my old college friend at the FBI. About Martin Costas."

"And?"

"Nothing."

"You wanted a private chat to tell me you learned nothing? In the future let's just agree to assume that unless notified otherwise."

"No, I didn't learn nothing."

"Then what did she say?"

"Nothing."

I stopped walking and looked at him like he was a bad dog.

He said, "You're not getting it."

"Or maybe you're not saying it."

"She told me nothing, in a way that told me plenty. You understand?"

"Go on."

"I asked her if she had spoken to her colleague in Guam, and she said there was nothing doing. I asked what she meant by that, and she said forget Guam, there is no guy in Guam."

"Okay, that's weird."

"It gets weirder. I asked about Martin Costas, if she had learned anything more. She said Martin Costas was not a person of interest to the FBI."

"He was the other day."

"It's a new dawn. Today's he's clean."

"What does that mean?"

"I don't know. I'm going to try to hit up some other avenues, but I don't think they'll go anywhere. This was a friend of mine. She wasn't just telling me in a professional capacity that there was no interest. She was telling me to stay away from Martin Costas. Maybe for my own good."

A guy in golf attire wandered by and slapped me on the back and said good round, and I realized I was still wearing my caddy's coveralls, complete with Heath McAllen's name on the back. I wondered how many shots the guy thought I made. I turned back to Nixon.

"Why would your friend warn you off? Is it political?"

"Everything is political. But it's also a red rag to a bull. I want to know now, even more than I did before."

"Did this woman know you well at college?"

"Are you asking if I slept with her?"

"No, I'm asking if she really knew you. Would she know that telling you to back off would have the opposite effect?"

He nodded. "I see what you mean. Sure, she probably knew me well enough to think that."

"So, either she really wants you clear because it could hurt you, or she wants you looking."

"Because she can't?"

"Maybe. It's a theory."

"He's connected to some powerful people in Palm Beach, right?"

"That's the word," I said.

"Someone in the FBI is covering up. Maybe they're covering up for someone powerful."

"Maybe."

"Someone like Nathaniel Donaldson."

"The guy has clout, that's for sure."

Nixon looked around the course and then back to me.

"What are you doing now?"

"A shower, and a massage if I can find one."

"Do that later. I need your help."

"To do what?"

"To do something I can't do."

CHAPTER THIRTY-THREE

Nixon and I headed for the VIP hospitality tent. It had been ground zero as far as the norovirus was concerned, and I was tempted to hold my breath as I entered. I thought Nixon was a bit of a chicken for staying outside, but I heard his idea and saw his point. I showed my access pass to the big unit sweating in his suit by the entrance, and then felt the cool of the fans as I took a look over the space. It was still arranged in a series of round tables that each held ten very important mouths. Waitstaff shuttled between the bar at the end and the tables. Food was on a number of tables, a late lunch that must have been brought across from the clubhouse kitchen, but most of the VIPs seemed to prefer wine or beer. The patrons were well dressed even for a golf club, and I was glad I had chosen to delay Nixon's plan and grab a shower and ditch my caddy coveralls. As it was, a polo and khakis still felt underdone.
I saw Martin Costas toward the rear of the room. He was suited up but still had an open collar. Formal casual, or casual formal. I wasn't sure. But I weaved my way between the tables to the vice president of the club. He had a vacant seat on one

side and a blond woman on the other. The woman was older than her outfit or lack thereof suggested, and Martin was paying it all due attention. I moved around the table toward the vacant seat, and Martin lifted his eyes for the merest second and saw me.

"Mr. Jones," he said. "Good round today."

I still wasn't sure why people kept congratulating me for Heath McAllen's work, but I let it slide.

"Martin," I replied with a knowing smile. I stood by the vacant chair until Martin offered me a seat. I took the seat and smiled at the blond woman.

"Mr. Jones, this is Miss Tiffany."

Miss Tiffany was stretching the definition of the word miss, but I gave her a nod and she offered me a smile that wasn't quite as cute as she thought it was.

"Did you enjoy the round?" Martin asked.

"It was a good walk."

"A good walk spoiled, I think was Twain's quote."

"It would have been spoiled if I was hitting the shots."

"Point made. Heath's one heck of a golfer."

"He is that."

"I thought you might be at practice. Isn't that what the pros do after their round?"

"They do. But I was pretty happy with my performance."

Miss Tiffany had developed a look of confusion, which manifested itself as a vacant stare. If I had to guess, I'd have said her face had been rendered incapable of a frown.

"You're a golfer?" she asked.

"Today I'm a caddy," I said.

She nodded and gave a breathy oh, as if she couldn't fathom why the help would be sitting down in the VIP tent. It all became too much for her, and she asked Martin to excuse her while she powdered her nose, which was a phrase I hadn't heard in a while, and suspected in her case it was literal rather than a euphemism. She stood gingerly and made her way to the exit in footwear not designed for the terrain. We watched her go and then Martin turned to me.

"Would you care for a drink?"

"Perhaps a water."

"Taking your new role seriously?"

"I think the kid deserves it."

He nodded and waved to the server, who brought a pitcher of ice water and poured me a glass.

"How is your other job?" Martin asked.

"I think the two are one. I'm certainly not carrying Heath's bags because I know the course inside out."

"Quite."

"But I am learning a thing or two, on both fronts."

"Good to hear."

He didn't ask what I had learned, which most people did. I stayed quiet waiting for him to continue. Folks generally liked to fill the silence, lawyers more than most. Talking was their game. But Martin Costas wasn't one of those. He was a listener. I got the impression that was exactly what he had been doing with Miss Tiffany, and I wondered if that was the reason he did so well in Palm Beach. He was a five-hundred-buck-an-hour listener. Attorney-client privilege was better than the psychologist-patient version.

I sipped my water and took another tack. "So, my guy's got a real shot at winning this thing."

"He certainly does."

"Big payday. For him and for me."

Martin raised an eyebrow.

"Apparently the caddy gets ten percent," I said. Although I wasn't planning on keeping the dough, Martin didn't know that.

"Even the step-in caddy?"

"Whoever carries the bags, according to the tour."

Martin nodded. "Well, good for you."

"It is. So I was thinking, if I do get this little payday, I don't want to squander it."

"No."

"So, I heard about an investment opportunity."

"Always smart to invest."

"Someone mentioned something about a new development. Capricorn Lakes."

He didn't flinch. He dressed like a used European car salesman, spoke like a librarian and had the facial expressions of a Russian politician. He wasn't giving anything away.

"Your name came up. Is there anything you can tell me?"

Martin sipped his wine. "Who was it that referred you?"

"I don't recall. It wasn't a referral as such—it was just a conversation I heard."

"A conversation you heard."

"Yeah. Since I already knew you I figured I didn't need to arrange a referral. I'd rather keep my investments to myself."

"Yes, of course."

"So, Capricorn Lakes. It's the latest thing, I hear. Eco-this-and-that."

"Mr. Jones—"

"Miami."

"Miami. I really don't think Capricorn Lakes is for you."

"Really?"

"Really."

He wasn't going to bother to explain why unless pushed, so I was going to have to push. I wasn't expecting that. He wasn't a developer or a realtor, but I had no doubt those guys offered bounties to lawyers like Martin for referring sales. And no one involved in property in Florida gave up a sale. It wasn't done. Maybe elsewhere, but not in Florida. In Florida people lived to shift real estate.

"You holding out on me, Martin?"

"Not at all."

"It sounds like you're onto something good and you don't want to share."

"I'm not a real estate salesman, Miami. I just handle transactions. Usually for developers or high-end purchases."

"And Capricorn Lakes is not that?"

"Mr. Jones, have you visited the community in question?"

It felt like a trick question, like a hand grenade Danielle would throw at me, a question with no correct answer. I wondered if he knew I had been there. I wondered if the gardeners had told him I was there. I wondered how the gardeners would even know who I was. I didn't give anyone there my name. And I hadn't been wearing my usual palm tree print shirt and khaki shorts, so I didn't think I was particularly memorable.

I said, "I haven't had the opportunity. It's been a busy week."

"It has. My counsel would be for you to finish your business here, and once that is done, go visit the development."

"Why?"

"To see what you're getting into. If you still think it a wise investment, come back and talk to me. If not, I do know a couple of very good investment managers who would be more than happy to assist you."

I sat back and sipped my water. He was a clever guy. Smarter than me for sure. What worried me was how streetwise he was.

I had thought I had his measure on that score, but now I wasn't so sure.

I noticed Miss Tiffany stepping back into the tent, her heels on the grass making it look as if she were walking barefoot on broken glass. I stood and thanked Martin for his time.

"Of course. Good luck for tomorrow."

I nodded and offered a smile to Miss Tiffany as I wandered out and got a blank stare in return. I found Nixon standing by a food truck, eating a Cuban sandwich. He was a lean guy, fit without being overdone. He didn't get that way eating piles of fatty meats and cheese. He saw me coming and wiped his mouth with a paper napkin.

"What's news?" he asked.

I made my perplexed face. "I don't know. I brought up the investment idea, like you said. And I brought up Capricorn Lakes."

"And?"

"He begged me off. Told me it wasn't for me."

"Wasn't for you? What's his angle?"

"I don't know." I was suddenly hungry, so I ordered a Cuban sandwich as well. I collected my dripping sandwich from the guy in the truck and Nixon and I walked away toward the clubhouse.

"I can't figure the guy," I said. "It felt like maybe he knew I was trying to set him up, and he wanted me well away from the deal."

"That tells us something."

"Only if it's accurate. Because it might be something else."

Nixon waited until he swallowed a mouthful. "What else could it be?"

"He might have been warning me off a deal he thought was a bad deal."

"Honesty?" Nixon frowned. "How often do you run into that?"

"Not often enough," I said.

As we stood in the afternoon sun I caught a glimpse of a familiar gait, and we watched Danielle wander over from the corporate hospitality village. She was chatting with a fellow deputy. When they got close she noticed us and broke our way.

"You guys look worried," she said with a smile that would dissolve most of my worries. Most of them.

"Thoughtful," I said.

"Intriguing."

"That's what I'm going for."

I realized that neither Danielle nor Nixon knew I had already visited Capricorn Lakes. It was the sort of thing I would ordinarily share with Danielle, but for reasons I couldn't pin down I decided to keep to myself. I wasn't sure if it was because of the guys tending the gardens, or because of Martin Costas, or because there was something important I'd put into my mental filing cabinet that I thought I'd lose to the ether if I spoke about it.

Danielle said she had thirty minutes to grab something to eat before she went back to work. Nixon and I wore the shiny grins of freshly devoured Cuban sandwiches, so she begged off and went to eat with her colleague. I told her I was going to find Heath McAllen and see if he needed anything. We both left Nixon standing there like a flagpole in the wind.

CHAPTER THIRTY-FOUR

I didn't find Heath McAllen. A PGA Tour official at the driving range told me he had been and gone, and that he had a sponsor's dinner that evening. I took that as my cue to exit stage left. I was tired and confused. I resolved to go home, grab a beer and think things through. I got to the parking lot before I realized my problem. I didn't have a car. I had no way to get home. I cursed the big English caddy. A taxi was going to be as difficult to find as a Florida accent, and I was giving serious consideration to walking the fifteen miles when Heath McAllen wandered out of the clubhouse. He was freshly showered but otherwise looked the same. He wore trousers and a polo. His ball cap was the only thing he had left behind, and his full head of wavy brown hair rustled in the breeze.

"There's my caddy."

"Sorry I missed practice, boss."

"Don't do it again." He smiled and I found it to be infectious. A large black SUV pulled up to the entrance.

"Sponsor's dinner?" I asked.

He nodded, sheepishly. "Not my idea of a good time, but I cannae complain about the pay. What about you?"

"Thinking about how to get home." I looked across the parking lot like it was a meadow in the Wild West and I had a week-long ride ahead. Heath watched me briefly before the penny clicked home.

"Oh, right. No car." He looked embarrassed, as if it were he who had driven my car into a lake. "Can I give you a lift?"

"Not necessary. But thanks."

"No hassle. They'll drop me off and then wait for me. They might as well take you home while they're waiting."

I looked at the car. The driver had the rear door open. "It would be my pleasure, sir," the driver said to me.

Heath got in and I followed and the driver took us to Palm Beach.

"Where's your dinner?" I asked.

"Some place called The Breakers. You know it?"

I nodded. I knew it well. It was one of Ron and Cassandra's haunts. It was, in fact, where they had met. Ron and I were there on a case, and Cassandra was at a fund-raiser for the governor. We were in tuxedos so we looked the part, and Cassandra had taken a shine to a dapper-looking Ron, which had not worn off.

We cruised out past Bonita Mar and up the palm-lined driveway to the grand old building that was as much a part of the island as the ubiquitous trees. I told Heath I'd see him on the morrow, and he shot me the wink and got out into a throng of fans. I noticed that a lot of them were young women.

When I had been a kid my dad had taken me one time to a minor league game. The New Haven Ravens played at Yale Field, not far from our home. I was in junior high and doing well with baseball, and I liked to think that my dad took me because of that. He wasn't a big baseball fan, and we'd never gone to a game before. But we had recently lost my mother to cancer, and I think it was my dad's attempt at trying to save us. To bond, as fathers and sons do over a hotdog and America's pastime. The field was nothing special. The Yale college team played there too, and I guess that was how my dad got tickets. He worked at the university as a janitor, and they took care of their people. I remembered the smell of the field, grass and popcorn, as we approached the gate. We arrived early for batting practice, and afterward the home team players signed autographs. I'll never forget how big those guys seemed. Arms like lumber and chests like bank vaults. One of the players signed a ball, dirty with infield clay, and handed it to me. I thought I'd gone to heaven.

But now kids don't ask for autographs, they take selfies. If you don't get a photo with the famous person then it never happened. Stories aren't enough anymore. Now we all need evidential proof.

The driver closed the door and pulled away, leaving Heath to his fans, that trademark grin to be plastered across social media websites alongside complete strangers.

The driver took me home to Singer Island. The sun was low and thinking about clocking out. I thanked the guy for the ride, and he said it was his pleasure and he seemed to mean it. I pulled out my wallet to offer him a tip but he waved it off.

The house was quiet. My house usually is. I don't have kids and I don't have a television, so that keeps the noise level down. But the silence was unnerving, as if it were underscoring the point that I was alone. I didn't like the feeling at all. I'm normally quite fine in my own company. I enjoy solitude. Perhaps like a lot of people I enjoy it on my own terms, not when it is thrust upon me. I slid my phone into the dock connected to a speaker on the kitchen counter, and I turned on some Tim McGraw. I took a beer from the fridge and found Tim singing about living as if I were dying just didn't suit my mood, so left him to it and wandered out onto the back patio.

I lay back on my lounger and chose not to look at the empty one beside me. The sun was falling over Riviera Beach, and water on the Intracoastal was pastel. I took a sip and took a deep breath. I was having trouble getting a handle on things. There were too many moving pieces. The wedding party and the fathers of the bride and groom—who didn't seem overly fond of each other. Nathaniel Donaldson, whom no one seemed particularly fond of. Keith Hamilton, who appeared to be prepared to open a vein for the club, but who had purchased adjacent land prime for development. And he had done that in cahoots with Martin Costas and Barry Yarmouth. Or at least with their full knowledge that the cash came from Donaldson's pocket. And there was Dig Maddox, who seemed happy to sell the same grass over and over again.

I decided to go back to the beginning. Right to the beginning. To the primordial part of the whole thing. The virus. It was fast and it was nasty. Connie Persil had said it was a new strain, never seen before in the United States. But it was here. There was no doubt about that. Connie would be trying to track it back to its source, but the trail went dry one step back from the wedding party. Connie would check all the sick family members, but I had a hunch she would come up with nothing. The answer was in the bottle of bleach. The virus was there, lurking and waiting. Or more specifically someone was holding it and waiting to use it. The virus wasn't malicious. It didn't plan on hurting anyone. There was no malice aforethought. It was like a gun. It got fired, or it didn't. But like a gun, someone had brought it to the party when they shouldn't have. And that someone was the link to the source point.

I resolved to call Lizzy in the morning and get her hunting for the source. I resolved to confirm what Connie Persil knew. I resolved to get some good sleep and be at the course early so I could give a young golfer the support and protection he deserved.

I sucked back the rest of my beer and looked at the lights begin their nightly twinkling across the water. I considered another beer. I thought about how I had done something Nixon couldn't do, and how he could now do something I couldn't do. I looked at the empty lounger beside me.

And I resolved to not let it stay that way.

CHAPTER THIRTY-FIVE

The morning bloomed the way spring mornings should. The sky azure, the breeze light. Danielle had come home late and tired and was still sleeping fast when I got up and found Ron waiting outside my house in his Camry. The car rattled like a stagecoach but never broke down. I couldn't say the same for my cars.

"Thanks for the ride," I said, getting in to find him offering a travel mug of coffee.

"Anytime. If I didn't say so before, sorry about the Porsche."

"I'm not. It wasn't me."

"I didn't want to say anything."

"Yes, you did. You said plenty." I looked at him. "And as usual you were right."

He punched the old car into gear and pulled away.

"Danielle was there late last night," he said.

"I know. She's working hard."

"She always works hard. This is above and beyond."

I sensed there was something more he had to say on the subject, but he didn't say it. Ron liked to travel with the window down, like a Labrador, and it didn't make for great conversation when he picked up speed.

The course was coming to life when we arrived. There were catering trucks delivering food and waste management trucks taking it away. The corporate hospitality tents were silent like a boardwalk in winter. Ron parked and we walked up to the clubhouse. He went right and I went left and found my way to the locker rooms.

Some clubs had separate rooms for the players and caddies, and other clubs didn't even let the caddies into the clubhouse. South Lakes was a little more relaxed. Players had one side of the rooms, caddies the other. The players' side was nicer to be sure, but the caddies' side wasn't the worst. I unlocked the locker and removed the coveralls and put them on over my shorts and polo. I hung a pair of trousers in the locker in case Keith Hamilton and the fashion police happened by after the round. Once dressed I removed Heath's bag. I counted all the clubs and came up with fourteen, which was where I wanted to get to. It was then I noticed a number of the other caddies were looking at me. Not a welcoming committee exactly. They shared knowing glances like they knew something I didn't know. Which was a state of affairs I took as read. They did this for a living. They knew plenty. But I knew some stuff as well. I'd spent years in locker rooms. Real locker rooms, not this fancy kind with leather-topped benches and lockers where you didn't have to supply your own padlock. I'd lived through ballpark locker rooms where the dominant scent was a mix of sweaty jock straps and tiger balm, and hijinks involved low-grade explosives.

I checked that I had everything that Alfie said I should have. I knew I was getting plenty of smirks from the other guys, being the newbie who checked everything twice over. But I didn't care. They didn't know that it was exactly how I had prepared when I played ball. Once I was in the locker room my focus got locked in and preparation was everything. And I knew a second thing. It was clearly how Heath McAllen prepared. He was focused and fastidious to a fault.

And I knew a third thing. I didn't give a damn what these guys thought. I got everything together and hefted the bag up onto my shoulder.

"You got the new pin placements, right?" asked one of the caddies. He wore a grin like he'd thrown me a curve ball. I knew that the hole locations were changed for each round. I had no reason to know what those new placements might be yet.

"I live here," I said. "The pin placements will be where I say they'll be."

I didn't wait to see the guy's reaction. That's the problem with posing a zinger and then making a dramatic exit. You can't have your cake and eat it too. If you hang around to see the reaction, you lose the drama of the exit. If you go with the drama, you lose the opportunity to see the dumb look on his face.

I could live with my decision. I wandered out to the putting green and waited in the shadow of the clubhouse. I looked over the large scoreboard. Heath McAllen's name was third down the list, having been overtaken by players with afternoon rounds. Heath wandered out about five minutes later. He stopped by me.

"You're here early," he said.

"Early round, right?"

"It is. Those guys give you a hard time in there?"

"Nothing I can't handle."

He nodded and looked across the course. "Shall we go and hit some balls?"

I carried the bag over to the driving range and Heath did some stretches and then asked for the sixty-degree wedge. I pulled the loft club out, wiped it down with a towel despite having cleaned it and gave it to him. He took a couple of air swings, and then pulled a ball toward himself with the club. Then he fired the ball high into the sky. He repeated the process ten times, and landed ten balls within the space of a dinner plate about a hundred yards out. He handed me the club and asked for the next one. I wiped the used club with the towel and put it away as Heath went through the process again. He did it over and over, from the shortest distance wedge all the way through to his long driver. The driver sounded like two Italian cars hitting each other and went farther than I could see. He used thirteen of the clubs in his bag before he handed me back the driver.

"Nice drive," I said.

"Ta," said Heath. He watched me wiping down the large head of the driver.

"You look like you played a bit of sport, in your time."

"In my time?"

He smiled. "You know what I mean. Most sports careers are done by midthirties. Golf is different."

"Golf and quarterbacks. How old are you?"

"Twenty-four. You?"

"Older than that."

"But you didn't play anything before?"

"Baseball."

"At university?"

"Yes. And then professionally."

"You look like a baseballer. What'd you play?"

"Pitcher."

"Nice. You guys play much golf?"

"A bit. Some guys played a lot."

"Why don't you take a swing?"

I frowned at him.

"Go on," he said. "I'd like to see you take a swing."

"I don't think caddies are supposed to hit. I think it's a rule."

"It's not a rule. I'm sure they frown upon it, but I don't care if you don't."

He shot me the smile. It was all teeth and pretty darn cocky. It reminded me of someone, a few years previous. I held up the big driver and looked at it. And I shrugged.

"What the hell."

I stepped up to the box like a batter and teed up a ball. I didn't stretch and I didn't take a practice swing. Golf is like baseball. It's a rhythm thing. You can overthink it. Most people do. I dropped the massive club head behind the ball, dug my feet in like Babe Ruth, wiggled my backside because it felt like the thing to do, and pulled the club back.

I swung it up high around my shoulder, propped for a moment and then drove my momentum down. I wasn't planning on hitting the cover off the thing. I just wanted to make clean contact. But I drove my hands down and popped my hips and the club head hit the ball with a solid thwack.

I stayed in position with the club wound right back around my shoulders and then I lifted my head to see. The ball was a missile and it was getting smaller and smaller as it flew into the distance. Heath let out a low whistle.

"Nice," he said. "That's got to be close on three hundred yards."

I moved back to the bag and wiped the club clean, and then I returned it to the bag.

"You should be out here, with us," he said.

I shook my head. "I can't putt."

I picked up the bag and wandered over to the practice green. I handed Heath his putter, and he took a bucket of balls and hit his way around the green as I watched. He was relaxed and easy. He was doing what he believed he was put on earth to do. Maybe he was. Maybe he'd learn later that there was more to it than that. Or not. He chatted with some of the other players, and as he did a tall guy sidled up to me. I glanced at him. He was in a pressed blazer and trousers with a crease up the leg that could have cut diamond. He was groomed better than any of the greens on the course and wore the scent of the best-ever leather club chair. He looked at me and offered his hand.

"Jim Nantz," he said.

"Yeah," I replied poetically. I knew Nantz. Everyone knew Nantz. He'd been hosting golf coverage on CBS since Adam took up the game. "Miami Jones," I managed to say.

"Caddying for McAllen?" It wasn't really a question.

"I am."

"How's that going?"

"Going well. He's a good kid."

"He is that. Isn't it strange that Alfie isn't carrying the bag this week?"

"He's working through some stuff."

"Divorce. That's hard."

I shrugged. I didn't know. It wasn't something I had lived through.

"I get the feeling there's more to it," he said.

He sounded like a journalist trying to get a story. And then it struck me that maybe he was. I'd never thought of golf commentators like that. Nantz was a honey-voiced guy who spoke in whispers and never raised the hackles of the golf clubs that hosted him. I couldn't imagine him digging dirt like those shows that follow the every move of reality television stars. But I decided to play my cards close.

"Not that I know of."

"Anything to do with the alligator who ate the guy?"

"I don't think so. That idea getting a lot of airtime? The alligator?"

"We can't quite figure out how to frame it, you know?"

I nodded. "We could rename the seventeenth hole Alligator Alley." I smiled.

Nantz turned and looked at me.

"Alligator Alley." He smiled. "Faldo is going to love that."

He slapped my shoulder and wished us a good round and wandered off. I decided not to talk to anyone else. Ever. I waited and watched Heath and then fifteen minutes before our tee time I called him over, as Alfie had instructed me to do.

Heath wiped himself down, and then took a slug of Gatorade. Then we made our way slowly toward the first tee. We were playing with the same two players as the previous day. Both of them had shot over par, and were well off the pace, but they all shook hands and showed each other the ball that they were playing so everyone knew which ball belonged to whom. Then the course steward announced Heath to the gallery. The patrons offered a polite clap and Heath took his fairway wood and stepped up and after the same couple of practice swings, he whacked the ball way down the fairway, straight and true.

I glanced around the gallery and saw nothing of note but the smiling face of Deputy Danielle Castle.

Heath started well, two birdies in three holes, to move to co-leader. We played the third with a glance toward the water. I kept the Alligator Alley thing to myself. I wondered if the television guys would use it. I wondered if the governor would care. Heath shot even par for the next six holes, and then hit his iron into the trees on the par three tenth. We studied the shot out and he decided to pitch for the green. The only risk was a sand trap at the back if he went long. He went long and landed on the beach. He hit a good recovery wedge out of the bunker and onto the green, and putted smartly but dropped a shot.

It was on the following hole that I noticed the white knuckles when he putted. He hit an eight-foot putt four feet past the hole, and dropped another shot. It was time to pull out one of Alfie's bawdy jokes. Problem was I couldn't remember them. He didn't write them down and I wouldn't have carried them in my pocket if he did. So I figure I would go my own way. I knew from my own experience that when a pitcher started to lose his rhythm, the pitching coach would often be sent out to chat. It wasn't that the coach had some sage piece of wisdom to offer. The objective was much simpler. To get the pitcher's mind off whatever the hell he was thinking that was making him so hinky. The fact was that by the time a guy got to play professional baseball, even in the minors, he knew the mechanics of pitching. Sure he could get better or learn a new trick, but he was well versed on how to actually pitch. The idea of the on-mound chat was to get him to stop thinking about it and just do it. Golf seemed pretty much the same deal.

"Can I ask you something?" I began as I slipped the putter in the bag, walking off the green.

"Sure."

"Why did you play?"

"What do you mean?"

"After the death threat? Why did you play? You weren't concerned?"

"You seemed pretty capable."

"But you were going to play before I stepped in to caddy."

"You don't miss much, do you?"

"I don't miss anything. It's figuring out what's important that's the trick. So?"

"I just put a deposit down on a new car."

"A car?"

"Yeah. A Lamborghini."

"So?"

"So if I win this week, that'll pay for it."

"That's all? You blow off a death threat for a car."

"It's a hell of a car."

"I'm sure."

We reached the next tee and I looked at the notes and handed Heath his driver. Heath took it with a smile.

"Besides, I'm from Scotland. You've seen Braveheart. We donnae back down from a fight."

He gave me the wink and stepped up to the tee. Some people might think it crazy to try getting a sportsman focused by referring him back to a death threat. But there was method in my madness. Whatever he'd been thinking about—what was making his knuckles white—that was gone. Now he was thinking about his heritage, and how they wouldn't stand to take crap from anybody.

And then he smoked his drive down the middle of the fairway.

CHAPTER THIRTY-SIX

Heath found his mojo on the back nine and slotted home two birdies and an eagle on seventeen to come in as clubhouse leader again. I kept my eyes open, and Danielle followed our group the entire rounds, but there was no sign of trouble. Heath wanted to work some more on his putting, and he said he'd see me later. But I told him I was there for the duration, so I handed him his putter and stood by the practice green as he worked on things. He hit most of the balls into the holes, so I couldn't quite see the problem.
After that we went back to the range and he worked on his short game.
"I'm telling you," he said, "this thing's gonna come down to short play."
He could have hit a soup can nine times out of ten with his wedge, but I supposed it was the tenth one he was worried about. We worked for another hour or so, him hitting balls, me watching him do it. I was beat when he decided to call it a day.
"What's on your agenda today? More sponsors dinners?"

"Nah, quiet one. Probably just go to the hotel. Need to get away from all this," he said, waving his hands around the course. I could understand his point. He lived in a bubble, and it could feel claustrophobic in there. Don't get me wrong—it was a nice bubble. On the big tour no one was worrying about how they were going to pay to keep the heat on, or having to feed their kids cereal for dinner because it was the only thing in the house. It was a damn comfortable bubble. It was chauffeured cars and private planes and endorsements from companies that made a lot of money doing things that no one understood.

"You wanna go somewhere?" I asked.

"What? You mean you and me?"

"Sure. Somewhere local. Somewhere they won't care who you are."

He smiled. "Sure, that sounds brilliant."

It was brilliant. Longboard Kelly's was always brilliant. It had no view, which kept the riffraff in and the tourists away, but it was like a breezy blanket, cool and comforting. The black SUV stopped in the lot and Heath gave a broad grin at the sight of the place. It sure wasn't The Breakers, but it was just as Florida. I told Heath's driver to come in, but he wouldn't. He said he would wait with the car.

"This is Longboard Kelly's. People don't wait in the parking lot at Longboard Kelly's."

He shrugged but wouldn't be moved. At least not by me. Heath and I took seats at the outdoor bar under the palapa and I told the bartender, Muriel, about the guy waiting out in the lot. She charged out there, breasts pulsing against the tight tank top that was like her second skin, and she dragged his sorry backside into the courtyard.

"You can drink soda, if you must," I offered as a consolation.

Muriel didn't know who Heath was, but she took a shine to his boyish smile and his fancy accent. I think Mick recognized him, but playing a good round of golf doesn't get you far in Mick's book. Mick served up some fish dip and some conch chowder. The kid was in heaven.

I left him in the care of Muriel and wandered to the back of the courtyard, near where the surfboard with the shark's bite taken out of it was mounted. The cell phone reception always seemed best there, and I called the office.

"Lizzy," I said. "How's the fort?"

"Quiet."

"Why don't you come out to the golf course tomorrow?"

"How many reasons do you want?"

"As you will. Can you do something for me? I need you to call a hospital, about the norovirus."

"The one where the wedding party is? I think they've all been discharged now. Except maybe the bride."

"No, this is a different hospital."

I told her what I wanted and I heard her scribbling notes on her pad. I thanked her and hung up, if that's what one does when one hits the little red telephone picture on their phone. Then I made another call.

"Hey, where are you?" asked Danielle.

"Longboard's."

"This is me making a sad face."

"I wish you were here, too. I brought Heath. He seemed like he needed a bit of reality."

"Most of the country comes to Florida to escape reality, you realize that?"

"My reality."

"Okay, then. That's nice of you. I'm really pleased you're taking this so seriously."

"You don't think I take things seriously?"

"I don't mean that. It's just that Heath looked like he needed someone to take him under their wing for a while. He could do a lot worse than you."

"I do my best."

"I know. So to what do I owe the pleasure of this call?"

"I can't just call to hear your voice?"

"You can, but you didn't."

"Okay. I want you to get Nixon to do something."

"He doesn't report to me, but I can ask him."

"Yeah, okay. Ask him to check with Homeland Security. Ask him about people entering the country from Colombia."

"Entering where? Miami? Orlando?"

"No. Not Florida. Somewhere close though. Maybe DFW, or ATL."

"Okay. Who are we looking for?"

"Anyone we know."

"That could be quite a list."

"Narrow it down to flights between two and three weeks ago."

"Where are you going with this?"

"I'm not sure yet. I haven't got a handle on it, but it's out there somewhere."

"Okay. I gotta go. Don't let Heath drink too much."

"I'm all over it."

"Love you."

"And I you."

I looked to the bar and saw Mick regaling Heath and his driver with some kind of tall tale, so I took the chance to make one last call. Connie Persil picked up on the second ring.

"Have you seen any more cases of the virus?"
"No. It's like it was isolated."
"Did you look outside Florida?"
"Why outside Florida? None of the victims had been outside Florida in the week previous. The families were all local."
"What about the source?"
"There's no evidence as yet."
"Is there anyone you can try?"
"Sure, I can make a call to the CDC. We've already sent them a report, but they would have flagged any large-scale outbreak."
"Why don't you give them a call?"
"I'll do it right now."
I stayed in the back of the courtyard, watching Heath at the bar. He looked relaxed, which was exactly how I wanted him to be. Those guys can get pretty intense on the course. And off it. I knew what Longboard's did to recharge my batteries, and it had more to do with the people than the beverages.
My phone rang as I stood there. It was Connie Persil.
"The CDC says they have another couple cases. In Atlanta, Georgia. They haven't yet been able to trace them back yet."
"Atlanta. That helps, thanks."
"Keep me in the loop if you learn something, okay?"
"You bet. And right back at ya."
"Of course."
I was about to make another call and thought the better of it. I didn't know what Danielle was up to but she had sounded busy, so I decided to send her a text message to suggest Nixon concentrate his inquiries with Homeland Security on flights into Atlanta.
I ambled back to the bar. The late afternoon sun was pleasant and the beers were cold. I could have settled in for the duration, but I was conscious of Danielle's words, and I didn't

want to let her or Heath down by letting him go wild. I asked Muriel to switch him to lemonade, but she said she had a better idea, and she showed me the label on a bottle of non-alcoholic beer.

"How did that even get in here?"

She shrugged. "Mick doesn't know. I got it for emergencies."

"You are a fine piece of work," I said.

"And you, Miami Jones, are all talk."

She opened the bottle and poured it into a glass and gave to Heath. He kept on drinking without missing a beat, engrossed in a story Mick was telling which sounded suspiciously like a reworking of Moby Dick.

By the time I poured Heath into the back of his courtesy SUV he was more sober than when he had arrived.

CHAPTER THIRTY-SEVEN

After getting Heath McAllen into his SUV and making sure the security was in place at his hotel, I stayed for one more beer at Longboard's before I decided what was good for the goose was good for the gander and I headed back to Singer Island. I didn't have a car so I got a cab, which was easier from Longboard's than it was from the tournament site, and not nearly as far. It was still only early evening so I had the driver drop me at City Beach and I went for a walk, watching the gulls swoop and dive for supper.
I had eaten enough at Longboard's so I made some iced tea at home and stood at the edge of my property near the water. A retaining wall dropped into the Intracoastal, and Friday evening boaters were enjoying the spring sunshine. I stood for a good time, waving at the passing boats and getting lots of waves in return. I wondered why we treated each other like that on boats and hikes, but rarely anywhere else. But that was all I thought. The saline air cleared my head of theories about what was happening at South Lakes. I took lots of deep breaths and felt a calm descend. By the time I came in it was dark and I was

bushed, so I grabbed a battered old copy of The Deep Blue Good-By and took it to bed.

When I woke Danielle was beside me. It was still dark out. Heath McAllen had finished in equal second place after the second round, and we weren't due to tee off until the second-to-last group, after lunch. So I shifted my weight across and wrapped my arm around her and got a face full of her hair. It smelled faintly of jasmine. Danielle let out a soft moan but didn't wake. I didn't sleep. I lay there, arms wrapped around her like we were tandem skydiving, breathing in her hair. My whole body was relaxed. I stayed that way for a couple hours.

Danielle woke with the sun and gave the soft moan again, and then slowly rolled over to face me. She smiled and traced her fingers across my face. We didn't speak for the longest time, just looking over every line in each other's face. There was a lot more for her to look at, and she took her time. Then the day invaded my peace.

"I asked Nixon to check with DHS."

"Okay."

"He thought it was a good idea."

"Okay."

"I think he thought it was my idea."

"Okay."

"You planned it that way."

"Okay."

She smiled and her eyes grew shrewd. "You know what else he said?"

"Nope."

"He said he wanted me to apply to the FDLE."

"That so."

"Yeah. I could become an investigator."

"That would be cool."

"They don't normally take applicants who don't have extensive local investigations experience."
I said nothing.
"But he said the commissioner was on a drive to recruit more women. And he said I had gotten a good reference from the FBI field office in Miami."
"Nice timing."
"I don't like getting something I didn't earn."
"It's always better to be lucky than smart."
"Still."
"You ever think you've had to work harder than a man to get where you are now?"
"Every day."
"So you paid your dues in a different way."
"You think I should do this?"
"You should do what you want to do."
"I could stay in Florida."
"Good."
"But I might end up anywhere. Tallahassee for a while, then maybe Miami."
I said nothing. Danielle looked at me and the little crease between her eyes appeared. For a moment I feared she was going to ask me what I wanted her to do, but she didn't.
"What would you do?" she asked.
I took an unnecessary pause. I knew what I would do. No question, no debate.
"I wouldn't do it."
She pushed back from me a little so she could actually focus on my face. "Really?"
"Really."
"Why? It could be a great job."
"It is a great job."

"So?"

"So it isn't here. Everything and everyone I love is here. Longboard's is here. Ron's here, Sal's here. You're here. Miami's a hoot, don't get me wrong. But I don't want to be two hours from the life that I love. I want to be right in the middle of it."

She nodded and rolled onto her back and looked at the ceiling. There was a lot going on in there. I hoped I hadn't said too much. The fact was, it was a great move for Danielle. She had been courted by the FBI field office in Miami before, but she didn't want to go to Virginia and then be posted who-knew-where in the country. But the FDLE was a state law enforcement body. She would stay in Florida. The farthest she would be posted would probably be the capital, Tallahassee, which was six hours away. After the academy, chances were she would be posted to the biggest office, in Miami, only one and a half hours away with light traffic. It wasn't far. I had driven it many times before, and would do it many times in the future, one way or the other.

I got up and showered and dressed, ready for a day's golf. Danielle followed me into the bathroom and I made smoothies while she did her thing. I used the last of the pineapple. I looked at the crown, all spikes like a dinosaur plant. I had heard you could plant the heads and they would grow into pineapple plants. I resolved to try it sometime. But not today.

Danielle drove her patrol car into the club. She asked if I had thought about a new car and I said I hadn't. I asked what sort of car she thought I should get and she threw the question right back at me and asked what I wanted to get. I told her not a Porsche. She nodded.

I left her to meet up with her colleagues and wandered into the clubhouse. I texted Heath McAllen, to make sure he was awake. He texted back to say he was in the gym, and would be on course a couple hours before tee off. Since I had nothing to do I went out the back toward the eighteenth green. Diego the greenskeeper was finishing up relocating the hole position. Each day he used a tool like a large apple corer to dig out a new hole where the course steward told him, and then he removed the cup from the old hole and put the grass and soil from the fresh hole into the old hole. It was more or less the same process he had used to repair the vandalized first green. He waved and then drove away in his little electric truck. I turned and looked up at the leader board. Heath's name was up there in big letters, still third from the top. Equal second. The other guy on second was the Kiwi who carried his own bags into town. He didn't do that in PGA Tour events because the rules required the use of a caddy. The leader at the halfway point was an Australian dude with a killer swing and a similar temper. I had heard he had once finished a round with only eight clubs, having destroyed the other six in tantrums on the course.

"Hope your guy doesn't win."

I looked down from the board to see Dig Maddox approaching. He wore a jacket and trousers and looked strange in them. He looked like I felt in similar attire. We were both shorts and shirts guys. That was about all we had in common.

"Appreciate the sentiment," I said.

"I got some cash on that Aussie. If he holds it together."

"Isn't betting against the rules?"

"I'm not playing in the damn thing. 'Sides, a little cash makes it interesting."

That wasn't my experience. I played ball with guys who liked to bet. Most stuck to the ponies, but a few bet on the major leagues. A handful bet on their own games. They all claimed to only bet on their own team winning. Apparently Shoeless Joe

Jackson and Pete Rose meant nothing to some guys. I also found that if a sport was interesting already it didn't get more so with a wager, and if it wasn't of interest to begin with then nothing could save it.

"Good-looking grass," I said in a swift and artful segue.

Dig shook his head. "Overseeded. I got a new strain of Bermuda in the works that won't go dormant. You won't need all this damn ryegrass in the winter."

"I thought St. Augustine was your thing."

"You know a lot about grass all of a sudden."

"It's been an educational week."

"Yeah? Sure, I do a lot of St. Augustine. For residential and commercial applications. It thatches too much for golf. Like hitting off rattan."

"You do Capricorn Lakes?"

I watched to see his reaction. He wasn't such a good poker player.

"Who the hell told you that?"

"It's on their website."

He shook his head. "Freakin' internet. Damn spies in the sky looking down on everything we do and plastering it on the freakin' internet."

I recalled my visit to Capricorn Lakes. I had spent some time while there looking on my phone at the very satellite maps Dig resented.

"Not a lot of grass there," I said.

"Course not."

"You don't get paid to lay sod?"

"Yeah, I do. And when I don't get paid, I don't lay sod. You got it?"

It seemed I was annoying him, and that made me smile.

"What you grinning at?" he spat.

"Just another beautiful Florida day."

"Could use some rain." Only a grass guy would say that.

"What do you make of what's going on? The gator, the threats?"

"That knucklehead got eaten by a gator because he was a moron. I told Barry as much. The idiot couldn't stack chairs properly. I mean, how hard is that? You know he once accused me of cheating on the course? Moron. Accused me of kicking my ball out of the rough. Tried to get him to give him a fifty to keep quiet."

"But you didn't."

"Of course I didn't. Moron. He had no proof. His word against mine."

What I noted was that Dig had not protested his innocence. He hadn't claimed he didn't use his foot. There was a warped sense of honor in that. Besides, he wasn't the only one. When I had played more golf, back in my baseball days, it was referred to as the fifteenth club, or the Adidas nine iron. Got a bad lie? Wait until your playing partner wasn't looking and give the ball a good kick. Some guys subtly lifted their ball up in the rough grass to get a better lie, and other guys went all the way and just kicked a foul ball back into the middle of the fairway. It was cheating to be sure, but Dig wasn't the only one who was guilty of it.

I said, "Ernesto didn't make a threat against a player. He was dead."

"Drama. Probably cooked up by the tour."

"The tour? You don't think it might harm the club?"

"Don't see how."

"Bad PR might drive the tournament away."

"Nah. You were right about that, a rogue gator's gonna bring the galleries in, not turn 'em away." He shrugged and took a step like the conversation was done. "I don't care one way or the other. Damn tournament eats into my golfing time. We can't use the course for three weeks before. But do I get a rebate on my membership dues? 'Course not."

He stomped off without another word.

CHAPTER THIRTY-EIGHT

Heath teed off the first with tendrils of cloud reaching across the sky to add depth to the scene. He was in good spirits and I was taking all the credit for that, despite the fact that I had never seen him in any other mood. His playing partner was a guy from South Carolina who chewed gum like it was tobacco and spoke in a drawl so relaxed it took minutes to say hello.

After two rounds, or thirty-six holes, the field was chopped in half. Those who failed to make the cut were once known as trunk-slammers. They'd take their clubs and put them in the trunk of their car and drive away. Now they just slinked off to their jets and cursed their wicked luck. A smaller field and groups of two players rather than three meant it was easier for the television network people to focus on the players of interest, and Heath was one of those. A cameraman and a sound guy and a whispering commentator followed our every move. I was reminded of Alfie's advice to not tell bawdy jokes near a camera, but I found their presence reassuring. It would be a bold individual who tried to harm a golfer under the gaze of a national television audience. I discounted all the nut jobs who would love the free airtime. This was not the work of someone who wanted to publicly claim responsibility.

Both golfers went head-to-head on the first nine. Seven pars and two birdies, leaving Heath locked in second place and his partner one shot behind. The Aussie in the lead teed off in the group behind us, and stayed one shot up most of the afternoon.

Ask anyone who has ever played the game at any level and they will tell you that golf is a cruel mistress. One shot, one bad bounce off a sprinkler head or a plugged lie in a sand trap could be the difference between winning and not. Or even making the cut and playing for the cash or going home without a check. For some guys it was the difference between making the tour the next year or being relegated to becoming the friendly neighborhood pro at their local muni course.

All the guys had played a stretch where nothing went right, even when just prior they had been hitting the ball perfectly. There was no rhyme or reason to it. It could happen at any time and to anyone, and it had happened at one time or another to every guy in the field. They called it throwing up on themselves, which was a horribly prescient image given the events that had unfolded at the club. But whatever it was, it happened that afternoon.

We heard the roar from the green. The group behind was on the tee of the same hole and had hit their first shots. Only one of the balls had sailed wide and ugly and taken a dip in the water. The gallery following the final group was silent. It was the scream of the hotheaded Aussie we heard. He cursed his ball's flight before it even hit the small water hazard. The penalty shot for hitting into a water hazard was one shot, so the Aussie took a drop and hit his third from behind the water hazard, and when he shanked his shot and that too went in the water the language got positively blue.

Heath sunk his putt for par, and smiled at me as he picked his ball from the hole.

"He's gonna cop a fine for that."

"You think?"

"You don't get to say bad words on television. That's rule number two."

"What's rule number one?"

"If you win you better remember to thank your mother."

We walked to the next tee and I looked back to see the gallery rushing down the outside edges of the fairway. The Aussie had hit his fifth shot into a sand trap just short of the green. Patrons were letting us walk away and were staying put around the green. Word of a meltdown traveled fast, and the only thing fans loved to see more than great golf was horrific golf.

"I don't know how you do it," I said, wiping Heath's putter down.

"Do it?"

"Live in the fishbowl. You've always got eyes on you. Every move you make. You're a young guy. Young guys make mistakes. I made plenty. But yours end up on the sports pages of the newspaper."

"They still have newspapers?"

I had nothing to say to that. "Or on television."

"You get used to it."

"I don't think I could."

"And you're probably right. Lots of guys play good golf. But tour golf is different. It's more of a mental challenge. If you can block it all out, the TV, the galleries, all of it, you can win. If you can't, well you can't."

"I still don't know how you do it."

"Yes, you do. You played baseball."

"It wasn't the microscope that this is."

"But there were crowds, distractions. How did you focus?"

I thought for a second. "I took a deep breath and closed my eyes and when I opened them I could see nothing but the batter and the catcher. Some nights I couldn't even see the home plate umpire, right behind them."

"There you go."

"So you just focus on the ball and nothing else."

"For me, it's a little different. I like the crowd. I like the noise. I don't pretend that they're not there. I pretend I'm not there."

"You're not there?"

"Yeah. Like I'm invisible. So all these people are around, the cameras and everything. But they can't see me. I'm invisible. If I hit a bad shot they won't see it, so it takes the pressure off. If I hit a great shot, I reappear and soak it in. You'd be amazed at what you can do when you're invisible to the world around you."

I nodded. There were a lot of psychologists hanging around the tour. A lot of guys were fragile that way. I could see why. But Heath was something else. He was number one, and he was only twenty-four. But he seemed to have lived another life already and brought that wisdom forward with him. I envied him. And then I thought about his life on tour, and how if he didn't have a sponsor's dinner he went back to his hotel room alone, and I reassessed my position on it.

By the time we walked off the eighteenth green the die was cast. Heath had shot three under on the back nine, and the South Carolinian had shot two under. But the group behind had been a mixed bag. It was a Down Under pairing and the Kiwi who preferred to carry his own bags had kept pace with Heath to be co-leader as they came up the eighteenth fairway. The Aussie had shot two more bogies on thirteen and fifteen to drop a couple more shots back, and then hit the now famous Alligator Alley on seventeen and plonked his ball into the out-of-bounds crime scene. He shot a nine on that hole, and killed any chance he had of winning, while also committing assault and battery on his four hybrid and his seven iron. He putted the eighteenth green with a fairway wood after smashing his putter against a palm tree near the seventeenth green.

Despite playing well and being co-leader after fifty-four holes, Heath still wanted to work on his short game some more so we hit the practice range. After a half hour the shadows were growing long, and I told Heath I needed to do something. I was watching him hit but I couldn't get something he said off my mind. Something about being invisible. I got a security guy to come stand nearby and watch for anything, but I was growing increasingly certain that he was in no danger.

I wandered back to the clubhouse and up to the bar. It was busy with players and VIPs. I didn't see any caddies. Perhaps they drank elsewhere. I was still in my coveralls but I didn't stop to be assessed for correct clubhouse attire. I made for the window. I found the person I was looking for in the corner, taking in the scene.

Jackie Treloar had an empty glass in front of him. My arrival pulled him from the scene and he smiled at me and offered me a seat. I asked him if I could get him another drink and he deferred, saying the access bus would be by any time to take him home.

"Your boy is doing well," he said.

"He is. He's a good player. He's a good kid."

"He sure hits it long. Those clubs now, and the gym time, I'm sure."

"Yeah, he's pretty fit. And dedicated."

"If you're gonna do something, do it right."

I nodded to that.

"Can I asked you something, Jackie?"

"Sure, son."

"How often do you come here? To the club?"

He nodded gently. "Most days. In the week. Not so much on the weekend. Sometimes the kids come over on the weekend."

"But most days during the week?"

"Yes, most days. I think my wife likes the alone time, you know?"

I nodded. I knew.

"Do you play much?"

"Like I think I told you, not so much. I get in a round once a week maybe, but just on the executive course, you understand. My old bones don't make it round eighteen anymore."

"You play last week?"

He shook his head. "No, son. The course was closed for tournament preparation."

Which was exactly what Dig Maddox had told me.

"So what did you do?"

"I did what I always do. I sit here for a couple hours and watch the world go by. Sometimes I talk with Chip up at the bar. If it ain't busy he comes over to visit with me for a while. Most other folks don't pay me no mind."

"You're invisible."

Jackie frowned. "When I was young I was a black man playing a white man's game. I wished I could have been invisible. Now I'm just an old man. None of these guys pay me no mind. Don't get me wrong, I don't blame them. They're wound up in their own lives. Just like I was. Just like you were. So I don't mind being invisible most the time."

It was his invisibility that had meant I, along with everyone else, had failed to talk to him about events before. And it was his invisibility that I was counting on now.

"Were you here last Friday? Before the wedding?"

He thought back a week, and I wondered if it was a bridge too far for him, but I should have been ashamed of myself for the thought. He was as sharp as a tack.

"Yeah, I was here. That was the day the keg exploded. Am I right?"

"That's right."

"Yeah, I remember the Mexican kid was setting up all the chairs and such in the tent over there. And then the keg exploded and there was beer foam going everywhere, and he came running up to help Chip."

"Right. Did you see anyone else that day? Did you see anything, interesting or not?"

He did. And what he saw was interesting. Very interesting. He talked until Chip came from behind the busy bar to let him know that the access bus had arrived, and again he offered to help the old man down the stairs. I told Chip I'd take care of it so he could get back to his work.

I walked down the stairs with Jackie and helped him out to the minivan.

"It was nice talking to you, son."

"Always."

He bent down and the driver helped him get in and sit down. The driver left the sliding door open so I stepped forward.

"Don't forget, we've got a date to play a round," I said.

Jackie smiled. "That's mighty kind of you, but you don't need to play no round with an old man like me."

"I'm not a member," I said. "I need a member to play."

He nodded. "Remember, I only play the executive."

"Nine holes is all the focus I have."

"Then it's a date."

The driver must have hit a button because the door started beeping and then it slid closed under its own steam. I stepped back and watched the bus pull away. As I watched my phone rang.

"Lizzy," I said. "What do you know?"

"I know everything," she said. It wasn't my place to doubt her. I left that to her maker. But she told me what she knew and I had to agree, she pretty much did know everything.

"You do good work."

"I know. I am underpaid for my value."

"I'm inclined to agree."

There was static on the line, then, "Really?"

"Yes. Let's talk about that when I'm next in the office. Remind me in case I forget."

"I won't let you forget."

I knew that to be true. I was turning back to the clubhouse when a black sedan pulled up and Special Agent Marcard, FBI agent in charge of the Miami field office, got out of the back.

"I might have known you would be here," he said.

"Special Agent, what a surprise."

"Can it, Miami. Where's your better half? On the course?"

"I doubt it. Play's finished. Why?"

"Is she with Nixon?"

"Usually," I said with a little more venom than I intended.

"Then let's find them."

We walked into the clubhouse and I found Natalie Morris, and she used her walkie-talkie to put the word out. Special Agent Marcard and I wandered out to the practice putting green. Heath was working on his putts and we gave each other a nod.

"You a golf fan, Marcard?"

"I play tennis."

It didn't really answer the question, but it put me off further small talk. We waited until we saw Danielle and Nixon walking over from the corporate hospitality tents and Marcard took off to meet them halfway. I figured I should follow.

Marcard was still walking when he said, "Why is the FDLE making inquiries to the Department of Homeland Security about incoming flights from Colombia?"

Nixon frowned. "It's an investigation. What is the FBI's interest?"

"The FBI's interest is not your concern at this time."

I smiled at Danielle. "I love a good pissing contest."

All three of them looked at me. Not in a good way.

"We have an investigation," said Marcard. "Ongoing. I don't want it fouled up by the FDLE."

"That wasn't our intention, sir," said Nixon. He was a clever egg. The sir went a long way to placating the FBI man. Nixon knew how to play the game. He would go far. Just not with me. In my book he was a little too good-looking to be trusted.

"Why don't you tell me what you've got, and we'll see what we can do." Marcard was throwing Nixon half a bone, and I wondered if he'd take it. He did. He told Marcard what Danielle had told him, and he told the FBI man everything else that he knew. Then Marcard nodded.

"Right. So the grass insurance scam, that's one hundred percent yours. The vomit thing, that sounds like Palm Beach County. I really don't want any part of that." He wasn't alone there. "And the property thing, that's ours. There are things going on you don't know about."

Nixon wasn't jumping for joy, but he nodded. Danielle said nothing. Marcard turned to me.

"And as usual, Jones, you've been annoying powerful people up and down the coast. Mr. Coligio and Mr. Donaldson for starters. What do you know?"

He asked, so I told him. I told him I knew about the grass scam and how it was going down. I told him that a hospital in Colombia had treated an American for a severe case of gastroenteritis, which subsequent tests had shown was caused by a new strain of norovirus. I told him that the American had given a false name and fled the hospital and subsequently the country, following my own golden rule of never letting authorities in masks know if you are sick. I explained how that person had flown from Cartagena to Atlanta, and then driven from Atlanta to Palm Beach, in what was sure to have been a very unpleasant trip, punctuated by plenty of stops. I explained how it was that person who was responsible for the illness that had befouled the wedding, and that they were behind the damage to the course and the ugly demise of Ernesto the facilities guy, and it was they who had threatened Heath McAllen. Then I outlined the basics of the property scam because I didn't yet know the specifics. But I explained who was behind it all and how that linked to everything that had happened on the course. And I laid out a plan to get the whole thing sewn up—lock, stock and barrel.

Marcard stood stone-faced and then said, "Every time we meet you seem to be laying out field operations for the FBI—have you noticed that?"

"I never take credit for them—have you noticed that?"

"I have," he said.

CHAPTER THIRTY-NINE

The final round of a PGA Tour tournament is the money round. People remember the winners of tournaments. The only reasons they remember the leader after fifty-four holes is because they either go on to win or blow a big lead and crash and burn.

I didn't sleep a wink the night before. I was nervous on multiple levels. I had intermittent doubts that I had summed things up correctly, but the more I played it through, the more I convinced myself I was right. But those mental battles took most of the night. The rest was taken by doubts that my plan would work, or that it would work but not prove anything, or that someone might be hurt. And then as the sun broke through and I felt drowsy I started thinking about Heath McAllen's chances.

I got to the course early. Danielle woke when I did and she drove. We didn't speak about my lack of transport. I went to the locker room to make sure Heath's clubs hadn't been stolen overnight. I was confirming their presence and then counting them in a very OCD fashion when I heard the guttural bark.

It was a sound that I had never planned to become familiar with, but one that had become second nature since I set foot on this infernal golf course. It was the sound of a human being barfing. I didn't want to hang around for it, but my better angels made me stick my head into the lavatory area and see that the person was all right. A man was on his knees in a cubicle, face down to the toilet bowl. Although he certainly didn't sound well, the man didn't sound in any danger. I figured it was the kind of intimate act that a guy didn't want another guy hanging around for, so I made to leave when the noise stopped and I heard a groan and the man whispered Oh Losh! I knew the accent and voice.

"You okay, Heath?" I asked. I was suddenly very worried. I'd seen the effects, and anyone who picked up this particular strain of norovirus wasn't standing unaided, let alone playing a winning round of championship golf.

There was nothing in reply, perhaps the wiping of a chin, and then, "Never better."

He hefted himself up and turned to the basin and washed his face. I waited by the door until he had gathered himself. He looked pale, and he wasn't a tanned guy to begin with. But he gave me a half a smile, and although it wasn't his usual stunner, he was trying.

"Final round jitters," he said.

"You're sure? That's all?"

"Happens every time."

"And here I was thinking you were an ice man."

"We get on the course, I'll be fine."

"You do know you don't tee off until one o'clock."

He nodded. "Couldn't sleep." Then reality kicked in. "Why are you here?"

"Same."

I decided not to tell him about the reasons I couldn't sleep. It didn't feel relevant, and I didn't see the need to fill his head with irrelevant stuff. Since there were still hours until the first group teed off, let alone our group, I told Heath I'd take him off course for a coffee. His courtesy car was on call and I directed the driver to a small Cuban-run place that I knew near the airport.

It was nothing to look at: cinderblock and peeling paint, and a sign painted by someone with no aptitude for graphic design. But the Cuban coffee would put hairs on a baby's chest and start a stone heart, and it settled Heath's stomach and got his cylinders running. The woman who ran the cafe made the most wonderful pastries filled with cheese and ground beef. The space was bare and the lighting industrial but the room sang with the rattle of Spanish, and Heath took it all in like he'd driven for twenty minutes and landed in another country. I didn't have a queasy stomach so I went for a second round of pastries and Heath ate a banana.

We returned to the course in plenty of time for warm-ups. Heath had a number of preround commitments. He signed a bunch of shirts and a sheaf of posters, and then spoke to Jim Nantz in their temporary studio as if it were just another day at the office. In my experience most days in the office rarely began with a session face down in the porcelain bowl. But Heath seemed to have gotten that out of his system and was now in his element.

I polished every club and by the time I was done I was the only person in the locker room. It was uncomfortably calm, given the crowds that I knew to be outside on the course. Heath joined me on the range and he worked his way up the clubs, hitting each one ten times. Then he practiced with ten balls on the putting green, a crowd of onlookers watching as intently as if he were playing the final hole of the tournament. With fifteen minutes before tee time I called him over and he toweled off and did some stretches.

"I'll be right back," I said.

"You need to go, now? Too much coffee, man."

I nodded and dashed away into the clubhouse. I got more than a few strange looks as I made my way past the dining room and down the hallway to where the administrative offices were. I got to Keith Hamilton's office and stopped. The door was closed and the hallway was quiet. I turned the knob and found the door unlocked, as I expected it to be. I moved inside and closed the door and went straight to the desk. I picked up the desk phone and punched in the number I had been given. It took longer than was necessary, but the call was answered.

"I know what you did," I said without letting the other end speak.

"Who is this?"

"I know what you did," I repeated. "Now it's pay-up time. Maintenance shed, four thirty. Don't be late."

I didn't wait for a response. And I knew they wouldn't call back, because I knew the call would show up as Keith Hamilton's office at the club. So now someone would show, or they would not.

I ran back out to the tee. Everyone assumed I needed a nature break, and I could live with that. The Kiwi who liked to carry his own bags actually did that and brought his own stuff to the tee, where he handed it off to his caddy for the weekend. Heath had done likewise and brought his own bag. He gave me a grin and head shake. I wondered for a moment whether I should tell him. I decided no news was good news.

We all shook hands, and each of the players wished each other the best of luck. Both guys seemed to mean it, but I suspected otherwise. Golf was very much a battle against yourself, but ultimately if another guy shot one stroke lower than you then you lost, regardless of whether you won the internal war.

Both drove the first fairway right down the middle, and I got the feeling that this thing was going to go down to the wire. They were young, fit guys and they walked with purpose, striding down the fairway to the applause of the crowd, knowing they still had four hours of work ahead, but living the moment anyway.

The bag felt heavier than before. I had checked it thrice over and no one had punked me and filled it with bricks, but it still weighed on me. I handed Heath his club and he landed the ball on the green, about ten feet from the hole. The Kiwi landed eight feet out. Heath smiled and held up his hand at waist height to the crowd around the first green. It was a demure form of thanks for the applause, as if he were embarrassed by it. He marked his ball and threw it to me and I cleaned it with a towel and handed it back to him. He put it back on the ground and took up his marker, and then proceeded to sink his birdie putt. The crowd cheered. I wasn't sure who they were rooting for exactly. One player was from New Zealand, the other Scotland. The closest local was the South Carolinian in the group ahead, who had parred the first and was therefore still another shot back. No doubt some bright on-course commentator would earn their chips by proclaiming that golf was the real winner here.

The players traded shots across the front nine holes. The Kiwi picked one up on three, and then Heath got it back on six. They were still even as we turned for home and started the back nine. Heath took some Gatorade as we waited on the tenth tee. He was smiling and easy. It looked like a Friday afternoon with his buddies, not championship Sunday. I waited and looked at my watch.

The timing was both critical and unfortunate. I didn't want to leave Heath McAllen holding the bag as it were, but I needed all eyes on the backside of the course. Almost all eyes, anyway. The good news was that we were waiting. The group in front were still on the green, and our group couldn't tee off until the group ahead had putted and cleared the way. They were taking their sweet time. It was common on Sunday, when the pressure was high and big bucks and livelihoods were at stake. Guys took that little bit longer over each decision, over each shot. It was like freeway traffic. Each small additional sliver of time was magnified by the number of times each guy took that time and the number of guys in the field, and the net result was a traffic jam.

Slow play frustrated most players, even though it was caused by the players themselves. But it was worse at the pointy end of the tournament, where the winner would be decided. Then they played just as slow and took just as long to make their decisions, but when they got near the end and their shot decision was made, they wanted to play it. They didn't want to stand around thinking about it. Too much thinking was a sportsman's mortal enemy. Men and women who made their living in an athletic pursuit had done their thing so many times —whether it was a golf shot, or tennis stroke or a shot from the free-throw line in basketball—it was second nature. Their muscles knew the moves and their bodies knew the rhythms. The only thing that got in the way was the mind. Overthinking it. And the major reason for overthinking was time. Or too much of it.

But the time was on my side. It meant when it got to 4:10, we were still only on the fifteenth hole. That was when I leaned over to Heath and said, "Dude, I need to go do something."

He looked at me and then looked down the fairway and then looked at me again. "Now?"

I nodded. I was going to make up some story about using the bathroom or something, but I had decided to keep that one for the media. Heath deserved the truth. But he didn't need it.

"It's the guy," he said. "You're gonna get the guy."

"Right. But I'll be back."

"Do. I don't want to walk up eighteen without you." Then his face dropped. "What about my bag?"

He wasn't just lazy. The PGA Tour and most country club rules didn't allow a player to carry his own clubs. But I had anticipated this, and I turned to the gallery and nodded. Ron stepped forward. He looked euphoric, like he'd just won the Masters rather than being asked to carry another man's gear. But like me, it was as close as Ron was ever going to get to playing in a PGA Tour event.

I stepped over to the rules official who was walking the course with our group. He was a member of the club, an older guy in a Panama hat, and I told him I was ill and needed to use the facilities. I said I'd be back ASAP. It wasn't against the rules to change a caddy midround. The rules even allowed for a member of the public to step forward and carry the bag if it came to that. The only issue the custodians of the rules—the United States Golf Association, and the Royal and Ancient Golf Club in Scotland—had with changing caddies was that it could not be for the purpose of coaching or offering additional advice. The rules official of course knew Ron, and he was pretty comfortable with the idea that Ron wasn't going to tell the world's number one player anything he didn't already know.

"Get back before eighteen," the rules guy said. "The network will cover that from tee to green."

I nodded to him, and then to Ron, and then to Heath. I got three nods in return. Then Heath grabbed a club from his bag and stepped over to me. He handed me the club.

"Just in case."

There was an old saying, never bring a knife to a gunfight. I wasn't sure how a golf club fitted into that scenario. But I didn't have a knife or a gun, so I took the club.

"You might need it," I said.

"Nah, it's a fairway wood. I never hit it. I've been thinking about changing to a hybrid anyway."

I nodded thanks, and then I took off club in hand, for the rear of the course, away from the nearest bathroom.

It took me ten minutes to run back to the rear of the course, and then five more to make it to the copse of Australian pines that divided the main championship course from the executive course. As I reached the pines I peeled my coveralls off like a snake discarding a skin. White coveralls were no one's idea of covert. I edged along the perimeter of the club grounds, along a tall hurricane wire fence, until I could see the maintenance shed.

It was a basic structure, four walls and an iron roof. Not hurricane-proof, but then nobody lived there, and it was sheltered from any weather by the trees. The walls were painted green to camouflage the structure from the adjacent golf courses, but up close it was a cruddy-looking building. I supposed it was like looking behind the curtain and seeing how the magic was performed. It didn't match the pristine look of the rest of the club. But it was designed to hold maintenance vehicles and grass seeds and pesticides and whatever else the greenskeepers used to keep a completely unnatural tract of land looking as natural as it did.

The front roller door was open about a quarter of the way, so that a man would have to bend down to pass under it. I waited until a few minutes before four thirty, when I watched a man wander through the trees, looking around as if he was fearful of being seen. He stopped by the roller door. Then he looked around one last time, but saw no one. Almost everyone else was on the other side of the course, watching the final holes of the tournament, so the man ducked under the door and into the shed.

The man, as expected, was Martin Costas.

CHAPTER FORTY

I stayed hidden in the trees, watching. I knew I wasn't the only one. I saw no more movement so I slipped along the fence line to the rear of the shed, where I had noticed a door the day Ernesto had been found in what was formerly known as the Pacific but was now known as Gator Alley. I broke out of my hiding spot and made for that door and stopped by it, looked around and then turned the knob. It was open, and I slipped inside.

The interior of the shed was dark despite the sunny day. The heavy trees shielded the structure from sunlight like the floor of a rainforest. The remaining light bounced off windows so grimy they appeared to have last been cleaned when Arnold Palmer was a boy. The light that there was burst in from under the roller door like a bank of LEDs. From the dark end of the shed I stepped around one of the electric maintenance carts. I held Heath McAllen's fairway wood like a hiking stick.

I saw the figure dip under the roller door, into the strip of light, and then stand there, so I could see only the silhouette of his legs. He took a couple of steps to the side and I heard the flick of a light switch. But nothing happened. The lights inside the shed didn't come on. It was as if someone had tripped the breaker. I smiled. The switch was flicked back and forth a few times in that way people do, as if impatience alone were capable of summoning electrons to come and do their thing. But the figure got the point, and stepped back toward the middle of the shed.

"Cute," he said.

I said nothing. Martin Costas said, "I know what you did." His voice came from near where I stood, behind an electric maintenance cart.

The figure stood in place and I took two steps forward. I knew the silhouette could make out my shape, but not my identity.

"You went too far," said Martin.

The figure rustled his feet. "Don't be stupid, Martin. We can work this out," said Barry Yarmouth.

"I don't see how. You're running a Ponzi scheme, Barry. The project in Guam is sinking you. The territorial legislature has put so many roadblocks in front of you that you've gone broke. Your project site is right on the endangered habitat for the Hawksbill turtle. But you know that."

"It's one project, Martin. You know the business."

"But you've sold homes that don't exist on lots that are on protected land."

"Technicalities."

"Are technicalities why you've sold almost half of the sites at Capricorn Lakes but only built ten percent of the homes?"

"Building delays."

"You've built nothing in a year."

"The money's coming, Martin. It's all under control."

"You mean selling South Lakes?"

Barry Yarmouth stood silently. I watched his legs in the light coming from under the roller door. Then I noticed something by his leg. He was holding a golf club.

Martin continued. "That's your plan, isn't it? Selling off South Lakes Country Club. And the power substation land was the first step."

"That was Keith's idea."

"I thought that, too. But it was you who brought it to him. Because Nathaniel Donaldson brought it to you."

"Is that what you think?"

"I know Keith wants to be the savior of his beloved club. That's why he made out like it was his plan. But it became his plan, Barry. Didn't it? You wanted it to look like Keith's plan. You wanted him to process the paperwork and look like he was lead on the deal. And you and Donaldson would be the silent parties. And then when you had run South Lakes into the ground, you and Donaldson would have a two-thirds majority to develop the substation property as golf course housing. Except Keith blew your plan. He brought in a fourth person. He brought me in. So now you only control fifty percent, and you can't do anything."

"I don't know why he trusts you so much."

"He trusts me because over twenty years I've given him reason to. Trust is earned, Barry."

Barry took a couple of steps toward me. He thought the body he could see was Martin Costas. But Martin was safely behind a maintenance cart. It was Martin's voice, but it was me he stepped toward. And I had eyes on the shape of the golf club he held by his side.

"Mr. Donaldson would have made you rich, Martin. You're too stupid to see that."

"I'm as wealthy as I want to be, Barry. You're too greedy to see that."

"Whatever, Martin. You're out."

"You think it's that easy?"

"Yep, I do."

"What are you going to do, Barry? Kill me?"

"You'll never play ball, Martin. You're some kind of boy scout."

"My share doesn't go away if I'm dead, Barry. You do understand that? I have heirs."

"Who will take the money and run, Martin. Heirs always do."

I was considering the logic of that argument when the silhouette burst into action. I saw the figure dash toward me and I heard the swoosh of a golf club traveling through its arc. Only this one wasn't headed down toward a ball. It was coming from up high, down toward my head. The problem was it was in darkness and I couldn't see it.

I pulled Heath's fairway wood up by either end and held it above my head. Barry's club connected with all the force of a fairway drive. Heath's club took most of the impact but at a cost. Barry's swing cracked the shaft like a twig, and then continued through. It still had a fair bit of momentum when it hit my shoulder, but not enough to break anything. I was thankful that the club head, which I figured to be some kind of iron, missed my right ear, and I felt it thump into the rear of my shoulder as Barry drew the club back for another swing.

I now had two halves of a golf club, one in each hand. I could have done some kind of martial arts nunchuku move with them, if only I knew any martial arts. What I wasn't going to do was wear another blow from Barry's club. That was really going to hurt. So I did the only thing I could do. I went at him.

I took two long fast strides and jabbed the fat club head into the darkness like it was a pool cue. The club was called a fairway wood, but the head was actually made of metal these days, and the hefty metal thumped into Barry's chest as his club swung by me with another swoosh and connected with thin air. It was an unfortunate miss. The top half of his body launched backward from the impact of my parry, and his own club continued around on its arc until the iron head cracked into his own shin.

Barry crumpled to the ground with a high-pitched yelp. "Damn it, Martin," he screamed. "You're gonna pay for that."

"I don't think so," I said, standing over him. I was aware that he might have been down and in pain, but he still had a golf club in his hand.

"Lights," I said. It took a couple of seconds, but the breaker was thrown and the lights flickered on in the shed. Barry was on the dirty concrete, holding his shin. There was no compound break in his leg, but I couldn't say any more than that. What I could say was he had dropped the club, so I kicked it away. Barry frowned as his vision cleared and his brain processed what he saw. Then his face turned into a Doberman scowl.

"You," he said.

"Me." I smiled. They say never kick a man when he's down. They don't know what they're talking about. Barry made to sit up and I put my foot firmly into his chest and pushed him back down.

"You don't know anything," he spat. "You don't know anything!"

"That is often true," I said. "But not today. Today I know that you attempted to kill me, thinking I was Martin."

Martin stepped from behind the maintenance cart. He didn't look as jubilant as I did. If I had to say I would have used the word sorrowful.

"Self-defense," said Barry.

"No dice, Barry," I said. "And I also know you killed Ernesto Cabala."

"Try proving that, smart guy."

"I have, and I did. See, I figured out that Ernesto knew something about someone that he tried to use to his advantage. He tried blackmail. He had a record of doing it. He had tried to blackmail Dig Maddox about cheating on the course. But he chose poorly, because everyone knows Dig Maddox cheats on the course, and Dig doesn't care what most people think of him. He told Ernesto to stick it. But Ernesto learned something new, and he tried it again. On you."

"You keep talking, Jones. But you have nothing. That guy went swimming with a gator."

"He did, you're right. But there's a problem. The gator didn't kill him. He was already dead when he went into the lake. You killed him. I don't know if it was premeditated or just fury, but you did it."

"You're delusional, Jones," Barry said from the floor.

"As I say, often, but not today. I went to your development, Capricorn Lakes. I thought Martin might have been up to something out there. Sorry, Martin."

"That's all right, Miami. It was an assumption."

"It was. But out there I learned a few things. I learned that you have done very little building in a year. The handful of residents who bought the first allotments have been waiting a long time for their resort pool, and some neighbors. And I learned that there had been a gator in your lake out there."

"It's Florida—there are gators everywhere."

"That's true, for sure. But there was something unusual about your gator. He traveled twenty miles. From your lake to the lake here on course known as the Pacific."

"You can't be serious," said Barry.

"I can, when I try. See, I know this because Lorraine Catchitt, the forensic investigator on the case, discovered that the gator had ingested not only parts of Ernesto, but a large amount of a flowering grass that doesn't grow here on the course. It's an Everglades grass called muhly grass, and it covers a large part of the land adjacent to your development."

"That proves nothing, Jones."

"No, it proves that the gator moved a little farther than gators usually do. They aren't migratory animals, as a rule. But it made me curious. How would a gator move so far? With help, is the obvious answer. And then I recalled the tire tracks by the lake here. And the St. Augustine grass clippings. Again, not from here. I've learned more about grass this week than I ever wanted to know. And I learned that this course is Bermuda grass overseeded with ryegrass. No St. Augustine. But there is St. Augustine around the houses you actually built at Capricorn Lakes."

"St. Augustine covers half the state," Barry said.

"Again, true. But there's the muhly grass, the St. Augustine and then the sand that was left by the lake. Again that doesn't occur naturally here, but it does match the soil you dug out to make that poor excuse of a lake you created on your development."

Barry edged away from me a little and sat up. "I'm leaving, Jones. You have nothing. It's all circumstantial, and not very good."

"Until we marry up all these facts. Two grasses and sand from your community. A gator that traveled farther than your average gator tends to go, even on vacation. So I wondered who moved him. And I remembered. You have gardeners out at Capricorn Lakes. I chatted with them. I got the distinct impression that at least some of them might not have had the right kind of immigration papers. Those kinds of people are often exploited, which you've got to admit, sounds awfully like you."

Barry snarled but said nothing.

"So I thought, Miami, is it possible that someone at Capricorn Lakes blackmailed these undocumented workers to transport a gator from there to here? At the time I thought it might have been Martin. Again, apologies, Martin."

"Again, accepted."

"But it wasn't Martin. It was you, Barry."

"How many times can I say no proof, Jones?"

"As many as you want. And you might have been right, until we got an eyewitness."

Barry's face went blank, but he pulled himself together quickly, if unconvincingly. "Did not."

"Did too, right, Special Agent Marcard?"

Marcard stepped from the rear of the shed. "Indeed. We just spoke with a Mr. Iglesias, your gardening foreman. He told us that you forced him and his colleagues to relocate the alligator."

Barry shook his head. "A truck with an alligator just drove onto a course full of security people?"

"I couldn't figure that, either," I said. "Until I recalled that you told me you were in charge of getting more security on the course. You did, but first you sent Mr. Iglesias in under cover of dark."

"He's an illegal—he has no credibility."

"You should check with the kid who runs your real estate office," I said. "He's an annoying little guy, but he isn't stupid.

He knows that you can't hire a team of people who don't have paperwork. One of them has to be a resident, because you have to file at least one legitimate work authorization. Mr. Iglesias is a US permanent resident."

"He's allowing illegals to work here. He's a criminal," said Barry.

"Is that so, Special Agent Marcard?" I asked.

"There's no evidence of that. We haven't been able to locate all his workers, but that's not really an FBI job. The witness is a resident, that's all I know."

"He's lying," said Barry, his voice breaking as he said it.

"That so? Interesting," I said. "Did Mr. Iglesias have anything else to say?"

"He did," said Marcard. "What was that, Deputy Castle?"

Danielle stepped into the light from behind Marcard. I wondered for a second how many of them were hiding back there. I knew Marcard would be there. Danielle was a surprise.

Danielle said, "He told us he had seen you drive away from the development in a red Toyota Tacoma, which he remembered because that is the same truck that he uses with his gardening business. He thought you had taken his truck. But he checked, and his truck was still there."

"But who else owned a red Tacoma, Deputy?" I asked, smugly. It happens to the best of us.

"Ernesto did. And I've just spoken to a resident of Capricorn Lakes, a Mrs. Lassiter, who told me she had seen a red truck return late on the night before Ernesto's body was discovered. She thought it was the gardeners."

"So maybe it was," said Barry.

"Except she thought it odd that the truck drove into the marshland beyond the development. We've just had a look. We found the truck out there, hidden in the long grass."

"And what else did you find?" I asked. I was starting to enjoy myself.

"We found blood in the bed of the truck. Blood we believe will match that of Ernesto. And about thirty yards from the truck we found a golf club."

"A golf club?" I asked in mock surprise.

"Yes. The club head had blood on it as well. And fingerprints."

"Whose fingerprints do you think they'll be, Barry?" I asked.

"Not mine."

"Really?"

"I don't know. Maybe. My golf clubs were stolen."

"That old chestnut? There's a set of clubs in the garage at your development. I saw them. There were only thirteen in the bag. Which isn't against the rules, but it is unusual. For a guy who plays as much as you."

"I don't play that much."

"You're a member of a club that costs five figures a year in dues, and you wear nothing but golf attire. Sorry, Barry, not buying that. Except that you haven't been playing lately, have you?"

"The course was closed for tournament prep, genius."

"It was. But you're the treasurer and prior to the biggest financial week of the year for the club, you've been MIA. Natalie Morris told me you hadn't been around to help, but I thought at the time she meant as in that day. But she didn't. She meant she hadn't seen you in weeks. Right, Deputy?"

Danielle said, "Correct. Seems no one recalls seeing you before the Friday of the wedding dinner."

"So what?" Barry snarled.

"So I had my office manager, Lizzy, make some calls," I said. "She found out that an American citizen had been hospitalized in a place called Puerto Escondido. The patient had severe gastrointestinal upset."

Barry scrunched his face. "What has this got to do with anything?"

"The patient did not provide ID, but only spoke English. No Spanish. Which was important, because Puerto Escondido is in Colombia. And the patient discharged himself without signing out. Lizzy got very curious about that behavior so she paid five hundred bucks to a PI in Cartagena to drive down to the hospital with a picture of you, Barry. It's not a big place—they remembered you."

Barry looked at me but said nothing.

"And I remembered the place, when Lizzy told me. I recalled that you had brochures for a development in a place called Puerto Escondido. Coincidence? There seems to be a lot of that happening, Barry. Lizzy spoke to a local official in Puerto Escondido. He said that the project was on hold because the correct paperwork hadn't been filed. I took that to mean you had failed to come up with the cash to pay off the people you needed to pay off, am I right? You're a little cash-strapped right now, it seems."

"You think you're so clever, Jones."

"Barry, let me tell you something. The smartest thing a person can ever do is to surround themselves with folks who are smarter than they are. That's what I do. That means I have people like Lizzy tracking down a sick American in a region that has been pinpointed by the CDC as ground zero for a new strain of norovirus. A new strain that incredibly seems to have found its way to a wedding ceremony in Lake Worth. How did that happen, Agent Marcard?"

"According to the Department of Homeland Security, a US citizen by the name of Barry Yarmouth left the United States three weeks ago from Fort Lauderdale to Cartagena, and returned to the US into Atlanta, six days later."

"Why Atlanta?" I asked, with a grin.

"Glad you asked, Miami," said Marcard. "It seems to have been an attempt to not be traced back to Palm Beach."

"But it was traced back, wasn't it?"

"It was. A car was rented in the same name at ATL and returned to a Hertz location in West Palm Beach."

"Did you speak to the Hertz office?"

"We did. This morning. The desk agent remembered the return, which is a pretty good memory for the time passed. But she told us that the customer was memorable because he looked, and I quote, like he had the plague. She thought the customer looked so sick that she ordered the car to undergo extra cleaning, which was a smart move on her part. Might have saved a lot of other people getting sick."

"But some did get sick," I added. "Connie Persil told me that the CDC have found cases in Atlanta of people who had visited the hospital with symptoms similar to that of norovirus. The symptoms weren't severe, so they hadn't had cause to track it further, until now. Now it seems one of them works at the car rental center at ATL."

I looked at Barry. He said nothing. His goose was cooked. But the worst was yet to come.

"Ernesto wasn't a bad guy. He wasn't a good guy, either. He was poorly paid and tried to supplement his income with bribery. That's no excuse for murder. But what gets in my craw? Not Ernesto, as much as it should. It's what you did to that poor bride."

Barry looked at me and I stared him down. I'm good at it. I had a lot of practice looking at batters from the pitching mound. But Barry was easy, because his world was crashing in around him. He dropped his eyes from me, but I didn't reciprocate.

"You got the idea when you learned that one of the members was taking advantage of the tournament prep and using a hospitality tent and the temporary deck for a wedding. You found out that the other side of the wedding was a connected Palm Beach family. And you had learned that the virus you picked up while you were in Colombia trying to piece together your failed deal was easily transmitted. As treasurer, you are responsible for signing off on the ordering. Natalie Morris handles the food, and Chip the bartender does the beverage, and Ernesto did the facilities, but it all came through you. But when I spoke to you at your office, you called him the facilities guy, like you didn't know his name. Even though he reported to you. But you knew him. You knew that he had ordered a fresh batch of bleach in preparation for the tournament. The order passed over your desk. And you knew his process. You knew he would bring the dining chairs out and then clean them. Natalie told me that was always the process."

I stopped for moment, still focused on Barry. The words didn't come easily, and I had to fight myself to not smack him around with the busted club still in my hand.

"You went to the storeroom. You have a key. Ernesto had opened the flat of bleach bottles and taken one to the hospitality tent. He left it on the deck while he carried the chairs into the tent. You took it. Then you—and I can't believe I'm saying this—you switched it out for your own bottle. But your bottle was different. You threw out the bleach, washed it out with water and then put fresh water back in it, with a sample of your own—"

I looked at Danielle for the word I didn't want to use.

"Poop," she suggested.

"Right. Norovirus-contaminated poop. You were sick and kept some. I'm sure you learned on the internet that the virus can live for ages in a water solution. And you put your bottle back in the storeroom, where Ernesto was sure to see it and use it. And he did use it. He sprayed it all over the chairs, and then everyone came to enjoy a dinner between two families coming together as one. And you made them very, very sick." I thought again about the bride, stopped in the middle of the aisle, the look of horror on her face.

"You make me sick, too," I said. "But you messed up. Ernesto was supposed to put the bottle back in the store room and then you were going to take it away and put the uncontaminated bottle back. But he didn't. He got called up to the bar, and while he was there he forgot it. But Ernesto figured it out later. When he discovered he was suspect number one, you went and asked him where the bottle had gone, didn't you? And he figured out that the spray was the answer. That's what he confronted you about. But you had already panicked. You didn't know which bottle was yours, so you decided to take all the bottles."

I shook my head at him. "You thought you could move around the club like a ghost. Like you were invisible. But you weren't invisible. Someone saw you. Someone who was invisible to you. Jackie Treloar. He sits at the club barroom every day, watching the world go by. He's invisible to almost everyone except Chip. Jackie saw you take the bottle from the deck. Then as he was being helped into his access bus later he saw you carry the flat of bleach bottles to your car. Eleven full bottles. But not the right one. That one is with the authorities, and a DNA test will show it belongs to you. And I'll bet Heath McAllen's prize money today that the other eleven bottles are in the locked storage locker in your model home at Capricorn Lakes."

I felt my grip tighten around the half club in my hand. I wanted to use it, and not to play a round. Danielle sensed it, as she always does. She stepped forward and put her hand on my shoulder.

"We'll take it from here," she said. "Haven't you got a tournament to finish?"

CHAPTER FORTY-ONE

I didn't take the stealthy route back. I cut straight across the course, running the breadth of the first fairway like it was the main street of a ghost town. I was carrying the two halves of the broken club in one hand and my caddy's coveralls in the other. The scoreboard near the clubhouse told me the last group had just finished the sixteenth hole. I hit a roadblock before I hit the seventeenth. The gallery that had been spread across the entire golf course had now focused its mass on the final two holes, and it was like a Westfield mall on Christmas Eve. Having all eyes focused on those holes had worked in my favor when I wanted Barry Yarmouth to feel invisible enough to follow Martin Costas to the maintenance shed, but now it was against me.

That was until I was noticed by a guy who was so far back in the gallery that he couldn't see the actual golf being played if he were ten feet tall. He was watching the event on his cell phone, and I wondered if he wouldn't be more comfortable at home. But the television network had covered my unlikely exit, so the guy at the back knew more than the folks at the front.

He glanced at me, and then did the old double take. On the third try he grinned.

"You're him," he said.

I nodded.

He smiled. "Get your suit on, man."

I dropped to the grass and slid my feet in and then pulled the coveralls up. Then the guy in the gallery let out the kind of bellow you rarely hear at golf. In a game where camera clicks brought the ire of all but the most tolerant or deaf of players and caddies, shouting was generally not considered good form. But this guy must have been in the navy, because he yelled make a hole, like he were a Klaxon. Everyone turned to the noise, some amazed and some just annoyed, but they did as the man said and he acted as my point man and drove a wedge into the crowd. He kept repeating the command like he was making his way the length of a submarine, until we finally burst out the other side of the gallery, onto the fairway on the clubhouse side of Gator Alley.

A volunteer who had made a beeline to shut down the noise saw me. I nodded thanks to the guy with the megaphone voice and he nodded back, happy to have assumed a prime viewing location. The volunteer put his hand firmly in my back and ushered me away back toward the tee.

Heath and the Kiwi had both hit their tee shots on the seventeenth. Heath was ambling along the lake side, deep in thought. Ron was a step behind, his face the color of pickled beets. I walked toward them until the volunteer with me stopped suddenly. He nodded at the ground, and I noticed a ball laying on the grass. It was well off the fairway, closer to the water than not, sitting up in the deep rough. I stepped over to it and waited for Heath to arrive. He saw me and nodded. I could hear Ron puffing from twenty yards away.

"You made it," said Heath.
"More or less," I said.
"You get him?"
"We did."
"Brilliant."
"So what's happening?"
Ron arrived and dropped the bag down. "Here," he puffed. "This is a young man's game."
I wasn't sure if he meant playing or caddying, but I take a comment about being a young man wherever I can get them these days. I watched Ron walk back to the gallery, and then glanced at Heath.
"I dropped one on fifteen, and he got one on sixteen," he said, nodding in the direction of the Kiwi. So a one-shot lead had become a one-shot deficit. The Kiwi hadn't hit his drive as far as Heath, so he had farther to hole and would hit his second shot before Heath. We turned our attention to Heath's ball. It was then I noticed the white line. It had been painted on the grass with some kind of spray paint. I looked along it back toward the tee and saw the white wooden stake bisecting the line. It was then I realized what the line was.
We were next to the lake formerly known as the Pacific, now known as Alligator Alley. The scene of the crime. The spot I had argued should be turned into an out-of-bounds area so as to ensure the tournament could go ahead with a crime scene in the middle of the course. Now we looked at the out-of-bounds line that Ron had painted on the ground. And Heath's ball.
"What does this mean?" I asked, although I was pretty sure I knew.
"Out-of-bounds is stroke plus distance," he said. "I run back to the tee and play my third shot from there."
"That's not great," I said, helpfully.

"No, not great. Except . . ." He bent over and looked at the ball. Then he stood up. "We need a ruling." He repeated the request to a volunteer, who repeated the request to another guy. The guy in the Panama hat. He was standing just on the fairway side of the rope that was keeping the gallery in place. I noticed the Kiwi wandering over to see what all the fuss was about. The Kiwi and the Panama hat arrived at the same time. The Panama hat asked what the issue was. The Kiwi guy said nothing.

"I need a ruling," said Heath again. He looked at both his playing partner and the rules guy. Everyone looked at the ball. It was a white ball sitting for all intents on a white line that itself was painted on the long grass. I knew the line marked the out-of-bounds of the course. Outside that line was like a foul line in baseball. The ball was no longer in play and had to be hit again, back from the place where it had last been hit, plus a penalty of one stroke.

"What's does on the line mean?" asked Heath.

The rules official looked at the ball and sighed. "Sorry, Heath. The line is out-of-bounds. So a ball on the line is also out-of-bounds."

Heath looked at me. "As they say back home, bugger."

I nodded. He was taking it well. Playing his third shot from the tee essentially put him out of the tournament unless the Kiwi had a major and unlikely meltdown.

"Hang on, mate," said the Kiwi. He got down on his haunches and was careful to not disturb the ball, but he pointed in close. "Correct me if I'm wrong, but the out-of-bounds mark goes straight up from the inside edge of the line."

"Correct," said the rules guy.

"Well, from where I'm standing, the edge of the ball is inside the line, and therefore on the playing surface. And again, correct me if I'm wrong, but the entire ball must be out-of-bounds. If any part of the ball is in play, then the ball is good." He looked up at us standing around him, his face a blank, like the smart kid in class who had just explained string theory as if it were the two-times tables.

The rules official stepped around me and straddled the white line, one foot out-of-bounds, the other on the course. He put his hands on his knees and looked hard. He took longer than was necessary to evaluate the situation. Then he stood up and nodded.

"Matt's right," he said. "Part of this ball is in play. And part is enough. This ball is good."

Heath let out a long slow hiss of air, and the Kiwi I now knew as Matt stood, nodded and walked away to his own ball.

"What about Heath?" I asked the rules guy. "He'll have to stand out-of-bounds to play the shot. Can he do that?"

The rules guy shrugged. "He can stand where ever he wants. It's the ball that counts."

I nodded definitively and the rules official stepped back out of the way. Heath and I gathered around his bag. We looked down the fairway. It was a par five hole but the flag looked a long, long way away. Like different zip code away. I fumbled for my notebook that Alfie the caddy had given me.

"From here, 282 yards to the green. Pin is ten yards on and tucked in behind a sand trap in front of the green on the right side." I looked at him. "What do you think?"

"Fairway wood," he said.

That didn't make me feel like a million dollars. His fairway wood was in my hand. In two pieces. I held it up.

Heath smiled. "Not the fairway wood then. I can't reach the green with a hybrid. I could lay up, and maybe still make birdie." Heath looked over at Matt the Kiwi. "But so can he. So

I go to the eighteenth one down. Best I can do is equal him with a birdie on eighteen and get a play-off, assuming he only makes par."

"That's not the worst result."

"But I haven't made birdie on eighteen this week."

"There's that."

We looked over at Matt as he hit his fairway shot. It went long and straight and landed on the left side of the fairway, still about twenty yards from the green but well away from the sand on the right. It was a smart shot for a guy one shot in the lead.

"Maybe he doesn't have a short game," I said.

"He has a short game," said Heath.

"So?"

Heath looked at his bag and pulled out the driver. It was a long, unwieldy club with a massive head on the end that made it nigh on impossible to control off the tee. But on a tee there was a margin of error. Players didn't generally hit the driver off the grass. The face didn't have enough loft to get it high up off the ground, and the lack of precision made it more likely to fly wide and ugly rather than straight and handsome.

"You sure?" I asked.

Heath shrugged.

"Can you hit it off the grass?"

"I can. Sometimes it even goes straight."

I nodded.

"What would you do?" he asked.

It was the same question Danielle had asked me, although not on the same topic. I tossed it around. There was time. There was no group behind us, and the network was going to stay with this tournament until the end. It was the Gator tournament after all. I took some time because again I wanted to give Heath an answer worthy of the both of us. But the rub was this. I've never had a million-dollar shot. I made it to the big leagues, the majors, The Show. But during twenty-nine days in major league baseball I never got to pitch in a game. I wasn't bitter about it, but it did leave its marks. Perhaps I took risks in my life now because I had failed to take risks then. I didn't think so. I just liked to leave it all out on the field. I had shaken off my share of catchers and pitched a fastball to a fastball hitter. Sometimes I won, sometimes I lost. I won a college world series and I won minor league pennants. But I never did it with a million bucks on the line.

"I'd take the shot," I said.

"Why?"

"How badly do you want the money?"

Heath grinned. "Pretty bad. It's a nice car."

"If you come second, and come second again next week, can you buy it a week later?"

"Sure."

"So, the question is, how important is the win?"

He frowned for the first time I could recall.

"How important is the win to you?" he asked.

Now I grinned. "The win is the only thing. Money comes and goes. Bruises fade."

Heath nodded. "Heroes last forever."

"Something like that."

"Let's do it."

"You sure?"

"You can make a lot of money on tour getting nothing better than top twenty results. But your last win might be your last win. I never take that for granted."

"Okay," I said. "Talk me through it."

We moved behind the ball and looked at the shot ahead. It was still a long way. We stood in the deep rough on the left side of the fairway. The pin was on the right side of the green behind a sand trap.

"It's gonnae look ugly. I have to aim my feet and body like I'm gonnae shoot way out left over the gallery. You might wannae warn them, 'cause they're gonnae think I'm crazy. But the ball is gonna fade. Even if I hit it clean, it's gonnae fade plenty."

I wanted to ask what happened if he didn't hit it clean, but that didn't feel helpful so I held onto it.

"All right," I said. "Hit the damn thing."

I jogged forward and told the gallery to stay alert. It was pointless. It would take half an hour to get them all to move back out of harm's way, and if the ball went into them it was going to be like a rifle shot. You can't prepare for a rifle shot.

Heath took his stance and dug his feet into the heavy Bermuda grass and aimed left. I heard the gallery stir like an unsettled herd of cattle. The ball was back in Heath's stance nearer his rear foot. He took a moment and I think he held his breath. I certainly did. Then he swung the long, luxurious swing.

Grass flew and the sonorous tink echoed off the club. We all shot our heads left and watched the ball sail high and wide over the gallery as if it wanted to leave the course. Then it seemed to change its mind midway, and it veered right. The ball banked further right and back over the seventeenth fairway and descended. It hit the fairway and loped forward, still spinning to the right.

If I could have held my breath while already holding my breath I would have done it. The ball pitched forward and rolled toward the edge of the sand trap. That wouldn't be a disaster but it would most likely mean second place. The ball missed the lip of the sand trap by what I would learn later on the television was about two inches, and it ran on across the green, following its fade to the right, until it came to a stop.

Six feet from the hole.

I heard some roars playing baseball. Even in the minors crowds got rowdy. And I sat in the bullpen for some major league games where the atmosphere was electric. But the sound on the golf course at that moment was something else. The demure opera clapping was pushed to the wayside by a wave of cheers that I felt in my chest. It was as if the course itself were applauding being beaten.

I picked up Heath's bag and it felt as light as a pillow. Heath passed me his driver and strode up the fairway, waving gently from the hip in that casual way that golfers do. Lapping up the applause but not losing his cool, knowing he still had a putt to make and another hole to play.

Matt the Kiwi took his third shot from in front of the sand trap and landed his ball four yards from the hole, but it stopped and spun backward another couple yards. Heath walked up onto the green and marked his ball and threw it to me to clean. The gallery was no longer a gallery. It was a crowd, and it didn't want to stop cheering what they knew was a miracle shot.

Matt took his time and hit his putt but missed, and then tapped in for his par five. Then Heath replaced his ball, took a long look at the putt from behind and then stepped up and tapped it firmly into the hole, as if the entire thing were a fait accompli. He had taken three shots to get in the hole, two under par, or an eagle as it was known in golf parlance. He had turned a one-shot deficit into a one-shot lead in one hole. A hole where he was a quarter inch from being out-of-bounds. Such was life.

Usually in the sport the known result was a bore. A game four in the World Series with the leading team up three-nil never held the drama of a game seven with the two ball clubs tied at three-all. But somehow golf was different. Golf fans loved drama as much as anybody. There were a plethora of examples of two guys dueling it out down the final hole, or even in a sudden-death play-off. My father used to go on about Watson and Nicklaus at Turnberry in '77, and Larry Mize's chip-in to win the '87 Masters.

But there was, strangely, something poetic about the player who walked down the eighteenth fairway knowing he had won. The gallery cheered and the commentators crowed and the player in question waved and offered his thanks to the golfing gods and tried to hold it together. Not that Heath McAllen had won the tournament. Any slip-up could let Matt the Kiwi back in via a playoff. A horror hole could lose it.

But that didn't happen. His tee shot was up the middle and long, and his fairway shot landed in the heart of the green, twenty feet from the hole. Matt was in a similar position with equally good shots, but on this day that wasn't enough. He took his two putts to finish with a par, and stood back as Heath took the same two putts to make the same par and win the tournament by one shot.

In the roar of the crowd I offered Heath a handshake and took a bearhug, like I was part of the celebration. But I wasn't. I felt good, no doubt. But mostly I felt good that I hadn't messed up the kid's chances. The work was all his own. Even though he hadn't walked a single hole with Heath that week, his regular caddy, Alfie, was owed more credit for the result than I was. Alfie had told me what to do and when, because he knew his charge and he knew him well.

I watched from the edge of the green as Heath accepted the winner's trophy, an ugly crystal thing that would make roses look bad, and a giant check that seemed unnecessarily large given the number written on it. There were interviews and more interviews. Heath spoke with the local broadcasters, and with Japanese and Australian television, and then with a guy in a trilby hat from BBC Glasgow.

I went back to the locker room and accepted the congratulations of the other caddies, both given and accepted without enthusiasm. Then I cleaned Heath's clubs. I considered slipping in a hundred to replace the broken fairway wood, but I figured he probably got his clubs free from the manufacturer as part of an endorsement deal.

Matt the Kiwi was the second-to-last guy to leave the locker room. His caddy for the weekend had cleaned his clubs, but Matt picked them up himself and hoisted them onto his back in a harness that reminded me of an old-school backpack. He wandered by me and gave me a smile.

"You caddy here regularly?" he asked. Obviously he didn't catch much of the coverage during the tournament.

"Not much," I said. "It was more a favor."

He nodded. "Well, if you want to do me a favor next year, I'll be swinging through about the same time."

"Give me a call."

"I'll do that. Just ask for the Miami Jones, right?" He readjusted the weight across his shoulders. "Have a good one, mate," he said, and he walked out, looking for the next tournament, leaving me in the quiet of the locker room. After all the hubbub during the week, it suddenly felt dark and lonely, and I with it.

Telling the Kiwi to give me a call felt like a throwaway line, but the more I thought about it, the more I realized it wasn't. He seemed like a nice young man. Carrying his own clubs was a bit cheap for a guy who just won three quarters of a million bucks for coming second, but each to his own. I liked him. And what he had done with the almost out-of-bounds ball was damned classy. He was the one who had noticed the ball was technically in play. Without him Heath would have picked the ball up and run back to the tee to hit again, and that would have cost him any chance at a win. Matt knew that. All he had to do was keep his mouth shut. But he didn't. He spoke up, knowing that it might cost him a win. It did cost him a win. But he didn't seem put out by it. And he hadn't sought or been given any credit for what he did. It hadn't been seen on the golf coverage. Jim Nantz had interviewed him as runner-up but never asked about it. I knew, Heath knew and the rules guy knew. Maybe some gallery patrons with bionic hearing knew. In a world where good deeds seemed to require applause, Matt just did the right thing because it was the right thing, and I liked him a lot for it.

Heath came in for a shower a good two hours after me. He looked happy but exhausted, and I wondered how anyone did this week in, week out. Baseball was famous for being a long campaign, not a single battle, and it was true also of golf. He thanked me and asked where he should send the check for my share of the winnings.

"I told you, that belongs to Alfie. He just needs to replace my damned car."

"If you're sure."

"I am. What will you do now? Is there a celebration dinner?"

"There is. Every sponsor has a party, so I can do the rounds."

I nodded. He deserved it. He was a good kid who worked hard. We could all learn a lesson. Me as much as anyone.

"What about you?" he asked. "What are you up to? There's a few media guys who would love to know the story behind your midround disappearance." He grinned.

"Club repair, right?" I winked. "Nah, I'm off to Longboard's. I need a change of scene."

He nodded and I did likewise and we shook hands. I moved to leave him to his shower.

"Miami," he said.

I turned to him.

"I didn't half mind that fish dip. You wouldn't have room for an extra at Longboard's?"

I smiled. "You're driving."

CHAPTER FORTY-TWO

I made it home tired but refreshed. An hour at Longboard Kelly's was therapy that couldn't be beat. Real people who lived real lives always did that to me. A poet would call them salt of the earth, but what the hell do poets know? They haven't worked a day in their life. Don't get me wrong, a poet laureate is a fine thing for a nation to have, but those guys are hardly Dr. Seuss. Mick and Muriel and the usual crowd helped me emerge from the insular bubble I had lived in all week. Pro golf is fun, but it ain't real life. The good news is, it seemed like most of those guys knew that. They were tapped in to the fact that they were living the dream. Flying your own jet around the world, hitting a little white ball for a million bucks wasn't any kind of reality, but it was some kind of a life. Even for the guys down at the bottom of the money list, the ones who struggled and got sent back to Q school to qualify for the tour again, they knew it was a dream. Forget win—they were trying to make the weekend cut so they got paid. They lived in cheap hotels and drove their cars from event to event. And they were living the dream. It beat the hell out of digging ditches.

Danielle didn't make it to Longboard's. She texted to say she was finishing up at the corporate hospitality tents, where all the expense account drinkers were getting booted off course to fill up the local hotel bars and become the problem of the Lake Worth Police Department. Then she was getting a ride home. After a couple of beers with Heath I decided I also wanted to be at home. The new millionaire bought a round of drinks for the bar, which wasn't necessary but was much appreciated by all. He looked tired. I wasn't sure how he was going to pick himself up for the following week. But he didn't want to leave. I knew the look. I'd been the same, once upon a time, BD. Before Danielle. I hated when Mick turned the lights off and closed the bar, although there were plenty of times he and Ron and I stayed at the bar in the dark after the crowd had gone. Now Longboard's was a refuge, not a home. I had a home. And as I looked at Heath, struggling to stay awake but not wanting to return to a celebrity-designed bland hotel room, I realized that my home wasn't in Singer Island. It wasn't in New Haven, Connecticut, or Modesto, California, or any other place I had lived. My home was where Danielle was. My home was Danielle. I enjoyed my house in Singer Island. I really enjoyed the view. But I loved the view when I watched it with her sitting beside me.

"Where's your next tournament?" I asked Heath.

"The Players."

"TPC Sawgrass? Not too far. Will you drive?"

He shook his head. "I'll take the jet tomorrow morning."

That was the ticket. Those morning commutes in Jacksonville could be murder.

"When will you get home next?"

He smiled, but he looked older doing it. "The Open is at Troon this year. July."

I nodded. Almost three more months. An hour feels like a long time when you're melancholy. Three months seemed unbearable. But he was a young man, energy to burn, dreams to chase. I hoped he enjoyed the ride. There was plenty of time for other things later. If he was able to get off the carousel long enough to find those things. The life could be addicting. Golfers could play on tour and compete well into their forties, and then there was a senior tour for the over-fifties. A lot of guys stayed on the ride, all the way to the end. Searching for something that they didn't realize they would never find on a golf course. Some of them got the message. Some of them found balance. Many didn't.

I walked Heath out to his courtesy SUV and his driver opened the door. Heath got in and put the window down.

"It's been an adventure," he said.

"Life should be. What's the point otherwise?"

He smiled the smile. It was young and genuine and sold a lot of golf merchandise—I was sure of that.

"Maybe I'll see you next year," he said.

"I'll be here."

"Or I might get a place down here."

"I know some property going cheap."

He nodded and I watched him as the SUV pulled away, and the last I saw was him flopping back into his seat. He didn't bother putting the window up. Ron would approve.

Muriel was coming off shift and offered to give me a ride home despite living in the opposite direction. I tried begging off but she wasn't having it. She drove down the long street that runs from the A1A toward the Intracoastal. Her headlights lit up my dark house, and the thing in the street in front of it. She stopped in the middle of the road and we both leaned forward to look at the vehicle parked across my driveway.

"What is that?" I asked.

"It's a Cadillac," she said.

"That's no Cadillac. It's an SUV."

"It's a crossover. A big car or a small SUV, take your pick. But it's a Cadillac, I guarantee you."

The thing looked like a giant sleeping panther.

"Why is it parked across my drive?"

"Why does it have a red bow on top?"

Many questions. We both got out. Muriel left the headlights on and we wandered over to the SUV. The badge said it was called a Cadillac all right, but it looked like a soccer mom had gotten drunk and abandoned her vehicle in my street. Muriel wandered around the front and then stopped by the huge red bow that sat on top of the roof, like the SUV was some kind of gift.

"There's a card," she said, pulling an envelope from the bow and handing it to me.

I opened it and read it.

"Sorry about your other car. Ron says this is right up your alley. Cheers, Alfie."

"Alfie?" asked Muriel.

"He trashed my Boxster."

"And replaced it with a Caddy?"

"This is no Caddy. This is Ron."

Muriel laughed and kissed me on the cheek and told me to be good, and she got in her car and drove away, leaving me in the dark, staring at a soccer mom's car. It was locked, so I tried the mail box and found the key. Inside the car smelled new, and it was cleaner than Lex the chef's kitchen. It had a few miles on the clock so it wasn't brand-new, but that didn't bother me. It was the SUV bit that bothered. I liked to think I was a convertible kind of guy.

I was standing in the dark, looking at the thing when I got lit up by headlights again. They stopped before me and a door opened and Danielle appeared from the light. The car was a patrol car, and the young female deputy who I had seen at the golf course earlier in the week waved as she drove away. Danielle stopped beside me.

"Nice car," she said.

"It's a Cadillac," I said.

She said nothing. She just smiled.

We left the SUV where it was and went inside. We grabbed a bottle of wine and went out to the patio. I sat back on my lounger overlooking the twinkling lights of Riviera Beach. The Intracoastal was quiet and sleepy, a Sunday night after another spectacular Florida spring day. The town was snuggling down for slumber, Monday only hours away. I sipped my drink and looked at Danielle. She was looking at me.

"What?"

"You did good," she said.

"You too. How's your friend Nixon?"

"Back in Miami. He had nothing more to do."

"There's a fair mess to clean up."

"Most of it's either federal or county, in the end. Marcard says they have all sorts of evidence against Barry now, on the property scam. He was propping up his mini-empire by selling bridges to nowhere."

"A Florida specialty."

"But here's something I don't get. Ernesto Cabala was in caddy's coveralls and had Nathaniel Donaldson's business card on him," she said. "Do you think Donaldson was involved?"

"I've been thinking about that. And I do think Donaldson was involved. But not to the point where it can be proven. The groom from the wedding—Nicholas Coligio—remember he told us how Donaldson bought Bonita Mar to spite Coligio senior? Well, Sally told me there was history. A big deal that

Donaldson put together in Rhode Island. Sal says Donaldson did all kinds of unsavory things to make it happen. You can imagine, right? But when the time came, Dom Coligio swooped in and made the deal without Donaldson. Screwed him over. I figure maybe Donaldson learned something there. He got Barry to do all the dirty work because Barry was desperate. Like the power substation deal. I think Donaldson pulled the strings, but Barry was the puppet. And it wouldn't surprise me if Donaldson planned to screw Barry just the way Coligio had done to him. As for the coveralls and Donaldson's business card? I think Ernesto nabbed a set of the coveralls. They were delivered the Friday before the wedding, that's what Natalie said. I think he used them to go incognito around the club. And I suspect he either got the card from Barry, or maybe he tried to shake down Donaldson too."

"You think Donaldson was involved in the murder?"

"No idea. I suspect not. I think Barry was freestyling by then. Either way, I don't think there's any evidence that will stand up in a barroom, let alone a courtroom. We were lucky to find what we did."

She nodded. "It was Martin Costas who turned the FBI onto the whole thing. How did you figure that out?"

"Nixon told me, in not so many words. His FBI contact was all talk about Guam, and then she went really silent. We thought she might be protecting Nixon from something, but then I realized that she had been told to keep away from it."

I sipped my drink. "It was confirmed when Marcard turned up. I suspected he was protecting an asset, not an investigation. And when Jackie Treloar told me he had seen Barry taking the bleach bottles away, I knew Barry was the bad guy and Martin was helping the FBI. Martin was totally up for a sting. He's more game than he looks. And he's also more ethical."

"He is. He did some legal work for buyers at Capricorn Lakes, but then nothing happened, nothing more got built. He smelled a rat."

"You play in the sandpit long enough, you see it all."

Danielle sipped her wine. "But he went to the FBI because he turned up the Colombia property connection."

"But the FBI seemed focused on the Guam angle. Why?" I asked.

"Guam is a US territory, Colombia is not. It was easier to put a case together."

"So Barry's going to go down for fraud?" I asked. "Feels a bit like Capone going down for taxes."

"You'd think. But Special Agent Marcard says they're stepping back. He thinks Barry might get five to ten for the fraud, but for murdering Ernesto? That's life. So he's giving Barry to the county to prosecute."

"I never realized the FBI was so magnanimous."

"Marcard's a lawman. He just wants the guy put away."

I made my impressed face and sipped my wine. I felt my eyelids growing heavy.

"So what about Nixon?" I asked.

"He's okay. He didn't get the Ponzi property thing and he didn't get the murder thing, but he will get the thing with Dig Maddox replanting the same grass."

I smiled. "It explains why Dig was in such a grumpy mood all week. He saw the writing on the wall."

"And apparently Martin Costas knows something about that too, and since he isn't going to be busy with the FBI . . ."

"Martin's not going to be popular around the country club."

"Only with the crooks."

I gave her a face. That word covered a lot of territory.

She said, "Nixon was there for the governor anyway, and the tournament was a huge success. Biggest ratings for a non-major in years, he said. The governor's happy so he's happy."
"And you?"
"What about me?" she asked.
"FDLE?"
"Nixon says the governor himself will write me a reference."
I made my impressed face again. "You best play that card before he gets out of office. Those things have serious use-by dates."
"What do you think?"
I knew it was only a matter of time. She had asked me before what I would do, but that wasn't the same question. And it was easier to answer. But telling her what I thought she should do didn't sit easy with me. I was conflicted. There were pros and cons, as always. And I just didn't feel good about influencing her decision. I wanted her to be happy, and just like the golfers that roamed the country, her professional life was important. It was part of who she was.
"It's a good opportunity," I said. Sometimes I am just a big chicken.
"Yes, we covered that. I want to know what you think. And don't go saying that you don't want to influence my decision. I want you to influence my decision."
"You do?"
"Of course, you idiot. I'm not sitting on the lounger next to you because it happened to be spare the first time I came over."
"It was spare when you first came over."
"I know. But that's not why I stayed, is it? We're not two people watching the world go by in close proximity, are we? Aren't we something more than that?"

"Yes, we are."

"Right. Then you have a say. You don't get to make the decision. We all make our own decisions in the end, but you most certainly get a say. If you don't influence my decision then that means your thoughts don't matter. And they do. They matter a lot."

I nodded but I said nothing.

"So?" Danielle asked.

"So I want you to be happy. And personally I want you closer rather than further away. But this isn't just a job we're talking about it. It's who you are. You're an officer of the law. That isn't a job, it's a calling. And I can't get in the way of your calling."

We both sipped our wine and looked at the lights on the water. I had no idea what Danielle was thinking, but my mind was a blur of data. There was too much going on in there to make sense of it, but one thing kept at me, like an oven timer that beeped and beeped and beeped until it was dealt with. It was the signal through the noise. And the signal made my guts churn. Because despite everything, the signal was telling me this was the end of something.

Danielle finished her drink and stood and walked inside. She came back out with the bottle and poured two more and then sat down again.

"I'm going to go for it," she said.

I knew she would. I knew she had to. You can't mess with your calling. Time overcomes the heartbreak of a lost love, but the kind of heartbreak that comes from denying your calling follows you to your grave.

I nodded. I felt thirsty, but not for wine.

Danielle put her glass down and sat up and spun in place so she was facing me.

"I just need you to tell me something before I go."
I looked at her. It was dark out but she was radiant. Even when the world at large couldn't see it, it was the truest thing I knew.
"Anything," I said.
"I need you to tell me you'll marry me."

GET YOUR NEXT BOOK FREE

Hearing from you, my readers, is one of the best things about being a writer. If you want to join my Readers' Crew, we'll not only be able to keep in touch, but you can also get an exclusive Miami Jones ebook novel, as well as occasional pre-release reads, and other goodies that are only available to my Readers' Crew friends.

Join Now:
http://www.ajstewartbooks.com/reader

ACKNOWLEDGEMENTS

Thanks to Constance Renfrew and Marianne Fox for the editorial support and proofing.

To the betas, especially Andrew and Heather.
Whilst Jackie Treloar is a fictional character and not representative of any particular golfer, his trials on the early days of the Tour were based on fact.

The 1966 Los Angeles Open was in fact won by Arnold Palmer.

As well as being the first to get his PGA tour card, Charlie Sifford was the first African American winner of the LA Open in 1969.

As always, any and all errors and omissions are mine, especially but not limited to golf cart jousting on the fairways. That's poor form, right there.

ABOUT THE AUTHOR

A.J. Stewart wrote marketing copy for Fortune 500 companies and tech start-ups for 20 years, until his head nearly exploded from all the stories bursting to get out. Stiff Arm Steal was his fifth novel, but the first to make it into print.

He has lived and worked in Australia, Japan, UK, Norway, and South Africa, as well as San Francisco, Connecticut and of course Florida. He currently resides in Los Angeles with his two favorite people, his wife and son.

AJ is working on a screenplay that he never plans to produce, but it gives him something to talk about at parties in LA.

You can find AJ online at www.ajstewartbooks.com, connect on Twitter @The_AJStewart or Facebook facebook.com/TheAJStewart.

Made in the USA
Lexington, KY
14 October 2016